# BY ANY OTHER NAME

## Erin Cotter

SIMON & SCHUSTER BFYR

NEW YORK | LONDON | TORONTO | SYDNEY | NEW DELHI

SIMON & SCHUSTER BFYR

An imprint of Simon & Schuster Children's Publishing Division
1230 Avenue of the Americas, New York, New York 10020

SIMON & SCHUSTER BOOKS FOR YOUNG READERS
and related marks are trademarks of Simon & Schuster, Inc.
For information about special discounts for bulk purchases, please contact
Simon & Schuster Special Sales at 1-866-506-1949 or business@simonandschuster.com.
The Simon & Schuster Speakers Bureau can bring authors to your live event. For more
information or to book an event, contact the Simon & Schuster Speakers Bureau at
1-866-248-3049 or visit our website at www.simonspeakers.com.
Interior design by Hilary Zarycky
The text for this book was set in Sabon.
Manufactured in the United States of America
First Edition
2  4  6  8  10  9  7  5  3  1
Library of Congress Cataloging-in-Publication Data
Names: Cotter, Erin, author.
Title: By any other name / Erin Cotter.
Description: First edition. | New York : Simon & Schuster Books for Young Readers, 2023. |
Audience: Ages 14 up | Summary: In London, 1593, sixteen-year-old Will Hughes makes
his living on Shakespeare's stage, but after the famous playwright Christopher Marlowe is
murdered, he teams up with young Lord James Bloomsbury, and together the two hunt the
elusive assassin as their forbidden feelings for each other ignite.
Identifiers: LCCN 2022061601 (print) | LCCN 2022061602 (ebook) |
ISBN 9781665940719 (hardcover) | ISBN 9781665940733 (ebook)
Subjects: CYAC: Mystery and detective stories. | London (England)—History—16th century—
Fiction. | Spies—Fiction. | Murder—Fiction. | Courts and courtiers—Fiction. | Gay people—
Fiction. | LCGFT: Historical fiction. | Detective and mystery fiction. | Gay fiction. | Novels.
Classification: LCC PZ7.1.C674766 By 2023 (print) | LCC PZ7.1.C674766 (ebook) |
DDC [Fic]—dc23
LC record available at https://lccn.loc.gov/2022061601
LC ebook record available at https://lccn.loc.gov/2022061602

*To my parents, who never told me to stop reading—*
*even at the kitchen table.*
*And to Loren, who believed in this story first.*

# April 1593
## London

*I have heard*
*That guilty creatures, sitting at a play,*
*Have by the very cunning of the scene*
*Been struck so to the soul that presently*
*They have proclaimed their malefactions;*
*For murder, though it have no tongue, will*
*    speak. . . .*

—WILLIAM SHAKESPEARE,
from *Hamlet*

# CHAPTER ONE

JUST SOUTH OF the river Thames is a theater called the Rose.
The name is misleading, for a persistent fog of London's foulest stenches perfumes the stage. Should a man find himself there alone, he's like to be relieved of his purse at best or have a knife slipped betwixt his ribs at worst. 'Tis a question of when, and not if, a carelessly lit pipe *poofs* the building into a pile of ashes. Then the good people of London would cheer to see it dashed from the earth because the Rose Theatre is beyond a doubt one of the most disreputable places in all of Queen Elizabeth's England.

But I love the piss-sodden place because it pays me to do the thing I do best: pretending to be someone I'm not.

The Rose is where I am, on an April afternoon, a crowd thickening before the stage like milk before it spoils. Today we are performing *The Tragedy of Dido, Queen of Carthage*. We've reached the part where Queen Dido laments the loss of her lover, and it's supposed to be very tragic. Usually I can muster up a few tears from the crowd for this bit. But today the tears shall not come—no, instead the audience is *laughing* at me.

"I'll frame me wings of wax like Icarus, / And o'er his ships will soar unto the Sun, / That they may melt and I fall in his arms . . ." My voice cracks, and titters ring out in the first rows of the audience. A drop of sweat—heavy with the white lead paint plastered on my brow—rolls into my eye and stings something fierce.

"Aye, she's got the stones for the part all right!" someone crows.

The laughter swells like an ugly pimple. A sprinkle of roasted hazelnuts bounces off my skirts. I swallow and tug down the bodice of the dress, revealing a tuft of the itchy hay that serves as my tits. A woman in the front row points and whispers to her friend, both laughing.

I turn away from them. *Good God, keep it together, man!* One wrong step on the rain-slick boards and I'll be on my arse and truly give the crowd something to roar about. As a boy actor, I play all the women's parts in the plays. While the audience doesn't really believe that I am a woman, I must do my best to keep up the charade. Otherwise the crowd turns mean, and Henslowe, the theater manager, threatens to dock my pay.

I stumble through the next lines, my voice cracking on every other word. Zounds, was this dress always so sweltering? I try to furtively wipe away the sweat, but even this elicits another hail of hazelnuts and laughter. The crowd eagerly presses forward in the balconies overhead, faces rapt. Even the rooks nesting upon the thatched roof have stopped screaming, allowing the wide gray sky overhead to swallow my shaking voice. I spot the other players of the Admiral's Men hidden in the theater's wings, here to witness my embarrassing failure—including my delicious Thomas, his perfect face pale as a corpse. Fantastic.

This tragic play has become a comedy, and 'tis all my fault.

After a long, hideous lifetime we reach the play's finale, where I'm supposed to cast myself into a pyre, and then I can stay offstage where no one can laugh at me.

The torch-bearing boys surround me. I sweep across the stage, one hand over my brow, my face drawn into a mask of utter despair. "Live false Aeneas, truest Dido dies . . ."

I move to throw myself through a secret panel in the stage's center, except, right at the last second, my boots slip on hazelnuts. I cant sideways and crash into one of the torch-wielding boys. He yelps and falls with me, dropping his torch.

Right on the train of my dress.

The crowd's laughter turns to shocked gasps and screams as the fabric bursts into flames. I tear off my wig and beat the blaze as a great wave of ale and mud and God knows what else surges over me from the crowd. The fire sputters out, and the screaming fades to a puzzled murmuring.

I scrub the slop from my face and stare. The ragged tail of my gown smokes whilst the scent of roasted hazelnuts fills the air like a Twelfth Night celebration. Several awestruck faces stare back at me from the front rows as if they can't decide if they've witnessed the very greatest or the most terrible play of their lives. One pale girl, so small it's got to be her first time at the Rose, breaks into a delighted gap-toothed smile and starts clapping. One by one, the rest of the crowd joins in until the entire theater is filled with thunderous applause and whistling.

I gather up what's left of both my skirts and my dignity and take a single curtsy before Henslowe, the theater manager, seizes me beneath both armpits and drags me offstage.

"*Bloody hell, Will*, you nearly murdered us all!"

I wriggle free from his grip and hold up a finger. "I did no such thing!"

Henslowe paces, his white face red. The swan plume on his hat tickles the sagging ceiling overhead. The front of the Rose Theatre may be all soaring balconies and wide-open skies, but backstage is dim and cramped as a dungeon. "You certainly know how to go out with a great fuss!"

"Wait and see how I'll top it tomorrow," I say with a wink.

Henslowe doffs his fancy hat and runs a hand through his thinning hair. "We all heard you, lad. You've been an unwomanly height for a while, but between that and the man's voice . . . well, you're not fooling anyone now."

I tug the stays on my bodice. Out tumble my tits to lie in a great heap upon Henslowe's polished boots. "Oh, you don't think so?"

He cocks an eyebrow at me.

I raise mine right back at him, wishing I could raise only one eyebrow, instead of both, for it would doubtlessly be far more powerful than me standing here shirtless with my brows near in my hair, unable and unwilling to process that my tenure as a boy actor in the Lord Admiral's Men is over. I'll never again play the virtuous lady or the swooning maid when the villain is led to justice. I'll only be myself, Will Hughes, another jobless, penniless, and soon to be homeless boy roving about the streets of London digging for crusts in the gutters.

Henslowe tugs at my singed skirts and lets out a small

scream. "And how am I supposed to find another costume?"

I punch the wall and whirl to face him. "D'you think I asked for this to happen?" My voice cracks again. "There's a way to fix this!"

Henslowe blinks like he's never heard a more ridiculous statement in his entire life, his red-blond mustache quivering. "How, Will? *How?*"

"If I may, my lord," an oily voice simpers.

We turn toward the door.

Some . . . *boy* stands there. His doublet is at least two sizes too big, and he's barely scrubbed the dirt from his face. He seems about twelve. Naturally someone's bloody here for my job already, like a scavenger waiting on living flesh to become carrion. Everyone wants to work at the Rose Theatre. 'Tis far from the worst way to earn your keep in London, and sometimes Henslowe lets us eat the hazelnuts from the stage floor.

Henslowe eyes the boy up and down. "Well. What've you got, then?"

The lad strikes a pose. "Wretched Zenocrate! that liv'st to see / Damascus' walls dy'd with Egyptians' blood, / Thy father's subjects and thy countrymen; / The streets strow'd with dissever'd joints of men, / And wounded bodies gasping yet for life . . ."

'Tis Zenocrate's speech from *Tamburlaine the Great*. Except he's gone and mucked it up with all these flailing arm gestures and eyes rolling so hard he's surely got an excellent view of his brains. Utter rubbish. Even still, he's a pretty thing. Exactly the sort of lad the Rose crowds would go wild for.

"Have you ever acted before?" Henslowe asks when the boy finishes.

"Yes, sir. I've been in *The Brief and Tedious Comedy of Gammer Gurton's Needle* at the Curtain Theatre."

I snort. The Curtain Theatre is run by a bunch of fops and mummers. Young fresh-faced lords right out of Cambridge writing the most horrible swill you could imagine. Such as the aforementioned *The Brief and Tedious Comedy of Gammer Gurton's Needle.*

My friend Kit Marlowe says the Cambridge boys—third and fourth and fifth sons of lords, who've not a chance of inheriting even a vegetable patch from their fathers—can't write plays because they're too stuffed up their arseholes to see the world as God intended. I think he's right. All the Cambridge boys are trying to be the next Marlowe anyway. He's the reason the Rose is the most lucrative theater in all of London. Rumor has it even Queen Elizabeth herself enjoys Marlowe's plays. But whenever I ask Kit about it, he smiles and changes the subject.

Henslowe sighs. "Well, lad, you're not good, but you're not bad, either. We'll try you tomorrow and see what you've got."

The boy breaks out in a face-splitting grin revealing a small black spot on one of his front teeth. He's not going to stay pretty for long, this one.

I face the stage manager with an indignant harrumph and hook a thumb against my chest. My skirts puddle to the dirt floor, leaving me standing in naught but my ragged smallclothes. "What about me? You can't give my role away like that!"

"Will," says Henslowe, keeping his eyes firmly upon the timbered ceiling and ignoring my person. "It's not over yet. You can start playing men's parts."

"Oh, so who am I to be tomorrow? All the parts in *Dido* are already taken!"

"You know I can't force a player from his part halfway through. I've made promises, and they've all got bills to pay."

"Yes, just as I have bills to pay!" I stab a finger into my chest. "Henslowe, you've really left me high and dry with this turn."

Henslowe throws up his hands and storms off. "Come back in a fortnight, Will! That's all I can promise right now."

I get dressed fast, every movement stiff and jerky. One by one the other players come in and return their costumes and scrub the face-paint from their skin. Thomas, still costumed in Aeneas's armor, catches my hand with his. "Are you all right?"

There's a pink burn on my calf from the fire, but I know that's not what he means. "I'm fine."

His eyes remain huge with concern. "Would you . . . would you like to come back with me?"

And even though Thomas and his lips and his hands are my second, third, and fourth favorite things in all of London after the Rose Theatre itself, I'm shaking my head. "Not tonight, but sometime soon, yeah?"

I clap his shoulder and head out into the streets, trying and failing to outpace the panic nipping at my heels because this morning I woke up with a full belly and a roof over my head and a job, and somehow, in the span of a single bloody afternoon, I'm on the verge of having nothing at all.

# CHAPTER TWO

ECAUSE GOD LOVES to spite a man when he's down, on my walk home it starts to rain. A miserable drizzle that feels more like winter than spring. I pull my cap lower on my head and do my best not to feel sorry for myself, though I've quite a bit to be sorry about.

London becomes a cesspool in the rain. The streets overflow with chamber-pot filth, offal, and rotten vegetable peels, whilst carriages and horses roll through the dark puddles with no regard for those of us who've got to walk. I only narrowly avoid being splashed by a navy-clad gentleman atop a bright chestnut stallion as I pass beneath the shadow of St. Paul's broken spire in the shiny central districts. The muck worsens when I reach the poorer districts beyond, where tenements and brothels list into each other like rotting teeth along the crooked streets.

I'm utterly soaked when I reach the alehouse whose attic I call home. Inside the building fires burn so fiercely that the casements are thrown open, and out leaks the oily stink of burnt onions and howling laughter. There's a new notice plastered beside the door: a crude drawing of a cloaked figure, the two smallest fingers missing from the right hand.

BEWARE THIS MAN: REWARD FOR THE HALF HAND! the paper reads in smudged ink.

I tear the parchment away when no one's looking.

I nip down the alley along the pub's flank. There, a narrow rickety staircase leads to a door squashed beneath the pub's thatched roof.

Home sweet home.

Currently there's a bloke balancing himself on the railing as he retches beside the stairs. I scowl. Christ, the sun hasn't even set yet. There are benefits to living above a pub, but peace and quiet and cleanliness aren't among them. I won't be missing this part of London when I finally get out of here. I pinch my nose as I pass the man.

"Better mind yourself, mate. Stay here long enough and we'll be charging you rent."

The man lifts his red-splotched head, wiping his mouth across his sleeve. Oh no—'tis Thatcher, our landlord and the alehouse's owner. I wish I could report that it's an anomaly to see him foxed from his socks this early, but, well, 'tis certainly not the first time.

"My apologies, dear landlord. I didn't recognize you with your head betwixt your knees."

He frowns slowly, like he's not exactly following what I'm saying. "What's that in your hand?"

I resist the urge to hide the wanted poster behind me. "This? We're out of privy paper again since *someone* doesn't find it worth his time to make sure his patrons can wipe their arseholes."

Thatcher's eyes slit dangerously. "Yer no patron; you're a tenant. And the rent's due tomorrow."

My insides clench, knuckles white where they clutch the sodden paper. God no, this won't do at all, not with me freshly jobless. "Why, that hardly seems fair. 'Tis always due at the end of the month!"

Thatcher stands, and I wince into the wall. Even though I'm on the third step, he's as tall as me and twice as strong. Thatcher's built like a bearbaiting dog and meaner than one when he wants to be. He'd throttle me before I skipped out without paying him.

"I changed my mind. I want that money tomorrow." Thatcher leans his face so close to mine, I can count the broken blood vessels in his pink nose. "Don't ferget."

I nod furiously and barrel up the rickety staircase to a splintering door, slamming it tight behind me.

The scent of fresh bread and stewed meat bewitches me at once: a heavenly aroma that does wonders to chase away the dampness and cold that festers in this cupboard we call home. My stomach clenches again, an unwelcome reminder that it's been quite a spell since I've eaten.

"What's all this?"

Inigo, my chamber-fellow, glances up from the cooking pot, black curls cascading over his brown forehead. "Oh, there's plenty to share. 'Tis your favorite, Will! Rabbit and dried plums."

I bite my lip as another coin flicks onto the debt I already owe Inigo, a debt I'd truly rather not have. He already saved me from the streets last summer when the plague shut down the theaters and nearly cost me everything. "That lad's given you a home when all I could give you is a scrap of blanket and a spot on the floor," Marlowe always says whenever I make not so subtle suggestions about my moving back in with him instead. Like scrabbling tooth and claw for the privilege to sleep in the moldy attic is a prize worth struggling for. Still, there is something about Inigo that reminds me of home, even though we swore when I moved in with him that this was a temporary arrangement. A bit of business, nothing more. Maybe it's in the warmth of his smile, or how he's always making my favorite meals when I do not ask him to do so, but whatever he does, Inigo makes it mighty hard to resist liking him.

"No thanks, I've already eaten," I lie.

"Oh, quit bellyaching and let the bloke feel Christian." Maggie—our other chamber-fellow—doesn't even look up from digging out God knows what from beneath her toenails on our only mattress. I'd say she's more man than woman, but that would be an unjust insult to women and men alike. She's more a feral cat than anything else, and Inigo took her in like she was an abandoned kitten and not the mean-eyed stray she truly is. She's perfectly content to let Inigo do all the work whilst she sits and waits to lap up the cream of his labors. I don't like her, but as another soul who's squatting with Inigo, the only person here who actually claims this address as his home, there's nothing I can say or do about her. Worst of all, Inigo *likes* Maggie for some godforsaken reason.

I dangle the crumpled wanted poster before her nose. "I

thought you said you'd quit thieving after you were spotted last time?"

Maggie snatches the paper from me, eyes like iron. She's hacked her dark hair to her chin, and it frames her white face like a set of hideous curtains. "Who are you, my wet nurse?"

Inigo slams the cooking pot between us. "Oh, stop it, you two! Let's eat it quick before Thatcher notices I'm missing downstairs."

God, it smells so good. I can almost taste the dried plums gone soft with spice and butter. "I told you, I'm not hungry." My stomach gives an uneasy flip at what I've got to say next. "And I ran into Thatcher. He wants our rent tomorrow."

"Why'd he change the date? Did you piss him off again, Hughes?" Maggie brandishes her spoon at me like a knife. "Because it certainly seems like you did!"

"I've done no such thing!" I protest, heat crawling up my neck.

Maggie sighs and rolls her eyes like she doesn't believe me at all. "Might as well get this over with, then. Pay up, lads!" She pulls several crusty shillings from the folds of her skirt and tosses them on the floor. Inigo lifts a small leather satchel from a peg and counts out several more silver coins, placing them in a careful stack.

I stare at the growing pile, fresh panic spreading over me like the puddle seeping under the door, soaking and ruining all our things.

Maggie elbows my side. "Where's your share?"

I swallow and hold up a finger. "First of all, 'tis not my fault."

Inigo's shoulders droop. "Oh not again—"

"However!" I say, raising my voice over his. "I've lost my job, but I'm working on it, all right?"

"Rules are rules." Maggie jerks a thumb at the door, grinning. "You're out, then. You ought to know, since you made the rules."

Maggie is not wrong; however, I *did* create these rules in the hopes of restoring Inigo and me to our happy household of two. This has mischanced tremendously, and I hate the smirk Maggie is giving me now.

"Let's not be hasty; I can spot him this week. 'Tis no trouble at all!" Inigo empties his purse. Three pennies more tinkle to the floor. One rolls into the toe of my boot and falls face-side up. Queen Elizabeth's stern profile glares at me.

"Oh." A blush burnishes Inigo's cheek. "I . . . must've spent the last of it on supper."

This is a familiar dance, one we do nearly every month. Inigo's always spotting someone's share of the rent. He's soft as the sweet loaves he pulls from the hearth downstairs each morning.

I think of my fat leather coin satchel buried beneath the stairs and bite my lip.

Inigo and Maggie are not my friends. "Friend" is merely another word for the bloke who will leave you behind once he's got enough coin for a nicer chamber and good, dry ale. The only way to survive in London is to look out for yourself and keep your head down. But if this is the case, why does my gut twist horribly every time Inigo forks more food onto my plate?

I should let it go. I *am* letting it go. I never asked him to do these things for me.

Maggie heaves an unladylike sigh. "Well, if we can't pay, then we'll all get the boot." She strides to where she's left her things in a pile. She drops her skirts and stuffs her legs into breeches, cursing me under her breath all the while. Then she pulls black leather gloves over her hands. The fourth and fifth fingers of the right hand lie limp.

I stare at the glove. "This is madness. The wanted notices are still up for you. There was one right outside our door!"

She shrugs into her cloak. "Let's hope the rain's taken them down, then."

"I'll talk to Marlowe!" I say quickly. "He'll have something for me."

Maggie scoffs. "You follow that playwright about like a lovesick whore, when he's a lying wagtail up to no good."

My jaw tightens. "You've met him once, Mags. For all of five minutes."

"Aye, and I've a woman's intuition, and I know a bad man when I spot him."

I very much doubt Maggie has got a woman's anything, but now is not the time to argue with her. Not when she's hellbent on thieving and bringing the bloody City Guard to our door. If our landlord discovers he's harboring a known thief with a reward on her head, then we'll be calling the gallows home next.

Christopher Marlowe, my first and oldest friend in London, can bail me out of this mess. He took me in when I was a boy—homeless on the gray streets, shaking with thirst, and hungry for a smile—and put me onstage. He knows my deepest secrets, and I know his. Maggie doesn't know a damn thing about Kit.

"Marlowe will have something for me, I swear. He always does."

Maggie eyes me long and hard, one hand on the door. Finally she drops it. "Fine. Do something about this tonight."

Sighing mightily, I turn around and head out into the rain I've just left, the only thought propelling my legs this: *One day soon I'll be far, far away from cruel, cold London, and I'll never have to live like this again.*

# CHAPTER THREE

T IS EASY TO find a playwright in London.

Simply go wherever the ale is cheap and plentiful and you'll like as not find a whole crowd of wordsmiths sharpening their quills before the fire.

A group in our usual corner of the Seven Stars alehouse is already well on their way to drunk. The decent quality and handsome cut of their coats give them away as Cambridge boys, even if their full tankards and sad attempts at playwriting had not already. I try to squeeze past them, but they all sit there blocking my way like great stuffed-up toads, ignoring me completely.

I see myself as they must, white skin grimy with dirt and clothes much the same, silver-blond hair neither short enough nor long enough to be fashionable. A nobody with nothing, not worth moving for.

A figure sits hunched at the farthest end of the table, oblivious to the hurly-burly. A plate of untouched beef sits before him. His quill twitches madly across a square of parchment blotted with grease. A smile lifts my lips.

I must confess, this is my favorite version of Kit Marlowe. The one so lost in thought, he's like to need a compass and map to find his way back.

"Hello, Kit. Been a while."

Marlowe glances up. "Will. What are you doing here?" The softness in his eyes sharpens as he examines the room behind me. "I've told you a dozen times, 'tis better if you call on me at my home."

"I know, but I need to ask you about something." I give him a searching look, my stomach tightening. "What's wrong with meeting here, anyway? We used to drink here all the time."

"I wanted to be alone to think. But of course . . ." He gestures toward the Cambridge boys. One lord is kneeling while his mates pour a tankard of ale down his throat. All pretenses of attempting to create fine literature have been abandoned.

"'Tis always like this. It's an alehouse," I say. "No one comes here to think. They come here to drink."

Marlowe flaps a hand at me. "Yes, but a writer still must eat. And I've the most delicious idea for a play."

The sour feeling in my soul lifts for the first time since my disaster at the Rose Theatre. If Marlowe's got a new play, it'll mean I have a new part before Maggie can pitch all my belongings into the street. "Tell me more!"

Marlowe loosens; his smile blossoms into a grin. "There's this scholar, and he's interested in necromancy, right? So he summons the devil and swaps his own life for magic. I shall call him Doctor Faustus!" He slaps the table for emphasis, and I wince.

"Hush now. Summoning the devil and magic? That's heresy!"

Marlowe shrugs. "Well, the clergy won't be in favor, of course. There'll be a nice moral bit at the end about how magic is bad and we shouldn't make pacts with the devil."

'Tis a miracle Marlowe hasn't been arrested by the queen's authorities already. His wagging tongue has flirted with treason as long as I've known him. I don't know how he gets away with it.

"Why the sudden interest in my work?" Marlowe asks. "Don't tell me you've got an itch to take up the quill."

I roll my eyes. We both know I can't write. "I'm in need of a new role, and soon."

His eyes dance. "Who do you think you are? Blustering up to the best playwright in London and demanding he write a part only for you?"

I bat my eyes at him. "And wouldn't the best playwright want the best player to do his words justice?"

"Sorry, lad. There's not a good boy's part in my next one."

I swallow, suddenly nervous. "I need a man's role this time."

I've seen the way the Rose Theatre watches my delicious Thomas play the hero. He matters to them, in a way I don't, and I want to be noticed too. Zounds, I can imagine it already! The crowd shouting my name and the smile I'd flash them in return, dashing but not too dashing, lest anyone think I remain unaware of my talents. And let's not forget the fat, snug purse that comes with snagging the play's titular role. My fingers drift to my belt, touching where it would hang.

Yes. The part of the hero shall look quite nice on me.

"It's about time you've shed your skirts, but your timing is rubbish. The plague's about the city, and rumor says the Master of Revels will close the theaters until it passes," Marlowe says.

I moan and thunk my forehead on the table. "Christ Almighty, not *again*!"

"At least you've got a home with the baker lad this time," Marlowe reminds me, as if I'm about to forget where I curl up on a musty blanket at night.

Home. The word makes my breath catch, sliding under my skin, into the blue veins of my arms, twisting paths disappearing into all my secret parts. Places I cannot visit and cannot see.

I don't know what "home" means anymore.

Once it meant a cottage with a yellow thatched roof perched on a golden hill overlooking the sea. My sister's and brother's little red heads bobbing as they tore down the beach. My mother's rough hands cupping my cheeks, promising me they were sending me off with the roving men for a better life, one with enough food to eat and book-learning. Promising me that she'd wait for me to return, however long it took.

My hand goes to the cross against my heart. I've kept it on my person ever since my mother pressed it into my hand as I was taken from her. Marlowe doesn't know what it's like to be sent away from family in the arms of strange men because they're too poor to feed you. He doesn't know what it was like when those strangers who promised me safety and education sold me into indentured servitude like I was nothing more than a beast.

I straighten my spine and shove away the last dregs of the past. I don't get paid to dream of other places; I get paid to make others dream. That's why I've got to keep playing at the Rose Theatre. I was taken from my family as a burden; I shall return to them a blessing, richer than anyone they've ever known, and we shall not be parted from each other ever again.

Marlowe touches my arm, startling me from my dark thoughts. His eyes are so full of kindness, I have to look away. "You could ask me for money. I'd give it to you."

I jerk away. "No. I've got to do this on my own." Never mind that I was already thinking of money—I swear, the man's got an uncanny sense for what I'm thinking—Marlowe's already yanked me from the streets and put me onstage. I can't accept more from him.

"Oh God, I knew this would happen." Marlowe flings himself back with a great sigh. "Do you know what your problem is, Will?"

"I've no job to pay the bills?"

"No. You won't accept help, even if it kills you. You've always acted like you've got a score to settle with the entire world."

"I just asked for a part in your play, didn't I?"

Marlowe sighs again. "You asked for a *job*, not for help. I cannot simply give this part to you. The other players will accuse me of playing favorites."

"I wouldn't ask if I didn't really need it." And it's true, though it nettles me to admit it. Pride's a luxury an out-of-work player can't afford. "You won't regret it, I swear."

His lips twitch, fighting a smile. "I've heard that one before."

Well. What did he expect? It's not easy being an in-work player either.

"Hey, you! Yeah, that's right!" a voice roars from the end of the table. 'Tis one of the Cambridge boys. If I'm not mistaken, it's the one who let his friends pour ale down his throat. But there's also a fair chance I *am* mistaken, as they all look alike. "Isn't that the player who played the girl who sounded like a boy today?"

"Oh, Aeneas, my love, save me!" another mimics in a screechy falsetto.

The group bursts out laughing. My face grows hot. I know not why Marlowe associates with these spoilt lapdogs. They're a bunch of fools playing at being artists while their lord fathers' money pours into their pockets. Slumming with players and playwrights is all a lark to these rich nobles, a game to whittle away the time until real life begins. But for me? This is my life and livelihood, and 'tis not a game at all.

Marlowe nudges my side. "Sure you don't want to take up the quill? That was near poetry."

Had I spoken aloud? I suppose so—but why shouldn't I say what we all know is true? I'm on the chair's edge, fists balled. "The lot of them and their fathers and bloody Queen Elizabeth herself can all be hanged for what I care!"

The mirth eases from Marlowe's features. "You can't mean that."

I expected Marlowe's laugh, or a smile, at the least, not his furrowed brows and twisted mouth. Seems awfully rich for a man who flirts with blasphemy and heresy with every scratch of his quill. My anger deepens.

"I do mean it. If the queen died tomorrow, the whole

kingdom—nay, the whole world—would be the better for it. Mark my words."

He's already shaking his head. "You truly think if the queen died it would make things better for you? For your family?"

I cross my arms. "They're leagues and leagues from London, aren't they?"

Marlowe lifts a single finger. "Ah, but the queen has no heir. And no husband, either. All her siblings are conveniently dead as well. Who would inherit the realm?"

"'Tis the whole point! There wouldn't be any queen. We could all do as we please."

"You think *you* could do as you please?" He laughs like I've told a great jest. "Do you think these Cambridge boys and their fathers would stand for that? The nobles are the ones who have the most to gain from their queen's death, and they know it. Do you think these noblemen would not take up arms and press all the other men they could, on pain of death, into their services? Have you ever seen a man die, Will? The stink of his shit is in your nose for days. Imagine a score of men dying. Their blood would turn the fields fallow for a decade. Imagine—"

I shove away from Marlowe, chair squealing. "Zounds, you've made your point! If the queen dies, the entire realm is plunged into chaos. Got it."

His smile is back, thin as a knife blade. "Now you see."

Marlowe's words unsettle me—but not as much as his attitude. I run a hand through my hair and blow out a shaky breath. "Why do you do that?"

"Do what?"

"You take a perfectly normal evening and turn it strange for no reason. Why do you quarrel with me when there's nothing to quarrel about?" My words are hard, but inside, my heart still riots.

The candles around us flicker in a blast of damp air. A group of men has blustered into the alehouse, already loosening their cloaks, even though there's not a single chair left to sit in. There's a glint at their throats through the smoke, and I squint closer, certain I'm wrong, but no. Their cloak clasps are gold. A far cry from the frayed leather cord on my tattered cloak. There's Cambridge boys and their fathers' money—then there's the men with the real money.

Men with real money don't come to places like this.

One of the men catches my look and stares like he already sees my secrets. A shiver inches down my spine.

"Kit, those nobles are staring at us."

"Nonsense, you're imagining it," he scoffs. But I noticed how his attention snapped away from the newcomers as soon as I spoke of them, how there's a new tightness to his face.

A wrong feeling grows in me. "Let's go somewhere quieter and you can tell me more about your play. This place is getting too crowded for my tastes."

The playwright gestures to his parchment and quill with a rueful smile. "I've unfinished business here still. But since you're leaving, take this. If you won't take my coin, you'll at least let me buy you a meal." Marlowe shoves his untouched dinner into my hands—knife and all.

I stare at the meal, the back of my neck prickling. *Don't come here.* Isn't this what he's been trying to tell me all night? I want to ask him what's going on, but I'm suddenly scared of the answer. "Well . . . g'night then."

Marlowe grabs my hand as I pass. "When this play's done, you'll be my Doctor Faustus, all right?"

I summon up a smile, but it's limp as a dishrag. I thank him and leave, only to slink to the window outside and watch.

Marlowe lingers at our table. One of the mysterious men laughs with the barkeep and slips something across the counter. The barkeep gives a subtle nod. The rest of the men stomp upstairs to the private rooms for hire.

After a long pause, Marlowe gets up and follows them.

I stare at Kit's empty seat, my knuckles going white on the plate he's given me.

Galls me to admit it, but Maggie was right: Marlowe's up to something, and he's not nearly as good a liar as he thinks he is.

# CHAPTER FOUR

WRETCHEDLY EARLY THE next morning, Maggie and I lurk in the nicer part of town, our breath eddying out in gusty clouds. The sun barely gilds the white plaster walls far overhead, its warmth well out of reach. Last night when I returned with the promise of a job but no coin, Maggie pinned me beneath a sharp stare and said, "Tomorrow we're thieving." Then she curled up on her cloak like a stray cat and ignored me the rest of the night.

Maggie knows I'm rubbish at thieving. For one, I would like very much to keep both my hands attached to my person, and for two, though I'm great for theatrics, once very real blades are involved, I'm useless. 'Tis a sight unmanly, aye, but I was made to play the hero on the stage, not on the streets.

"So why are we waiting here, exactly?" I ask.

Maggie draws her cloak more tightly around herself. "We're waiting for the square to get busy enough so that no one will notice us. And then you're going to make a distraction with your pretty face while I pick some pockets, because *someone* failed to get his share of the rent before it was due." She glares at me. "Told you Marlowe would be useless."

I bristle. "He gave me a job, didn't he?" But even though I

got exactly what I wanted, I can't silence the voice that whispers it was all a scheme. Did Marlowe really mean to give me the job, or did he just need me gone before he could follow those strange men?

"Mags . . . before you joined up with me and Inigo, did you know other thieves in London?" I swallow. "Noble thieves, perhaps?"

Maggie snorts. "Every bloody noble is a thief. You already knew that." She gives me a searching look. "Why're you asking?"

I hesitate. Even though Inigo dragged Maggie into the flat six months prior, I still know near nothing about her. Not that I blame her. I'll never forget Inigo bringing her upstairs, a heap so bloody I thought she was already gone. The splintered bone poking from tatters of sinew and skin. There's no merry story behind being maimed and left for dead on the streets of London; I know it better than most.

But . . . what if she knows something that would help Marlowe? Or help me understand what he's doing? Maggie's not my friend, but she's not my enemy, either. She wouldn't be out here filching our rent money if she didn't care something for me or Inigo.

I tell her about Marlowe and our conversation. Rather than tell me to shove off or shut up, she listens intently, her head cocked ever so slightly.

"Is Marlowe in trouble?" I finish. "I don't want to meddle, but—"

"Never mind bloody Marlowe! You brought up *killing the*

*queen in a public place?* Have you a death wish? That's one way out of the month's rent."

Zounds, I hadn't thought of that. The strange noblemen could've overheard me. *Anyone* could've overheard me. Sure, 'twas the ale talking, but men have been drawn and quartered for less. "Forget it, all right? I didn't mean what I said."

*Except you did,* a traitorous voice whispers. *Every word.*

'Tis hard to harbor love for the queen who allows her men to take sweet-voiced boys from their families and force them to entertain in cities. Some crooked men, like my kidnappers, realized there was more money in selling boys than giving them to the church choirs like they were supposed to.

I was one of the lucky ones.

I realized what was happening and slipped away when we reached London, tiptoeing over the other slumbering boys and armed men to shimmy out an open window. I still think of the other boys sometimes. Wonder if they figured out what was happening before being sold into indentured servitude like mules.

Wonder if I should've said something on my way out instead of leaving them behind.

The name everyone knows me by—Will Hughes—is no more real than the lies my kidnappers fed my parents about giving me a better life. I've got enough problems without worrying if they're still out there, still looking for me.

Maggie laughs unexpectedly. "Everyone wants to kill the queen, Hughes. 'Tis our realm's most beloved pastime."

A burst of annoyance goes through me. "Well, do *you* want to kill the queen, then?"

I'm answered with silence. Maggie flexes her scarred hand. "What would you do if someone paid you to kill the queen of England?"

Maggie's always doing things like this—asking me outlandish nonsense to pass the time. This one's far less inspired than her question last week: Would I rather be farted upon by His Holiness the pope or the king of France?

"I'd tell them they're mad. No one's killing the queen without losing his head himself." I strike a ridiculous pose for her. "We both know my face is my best feature."

But Maggie doesn't even crack a smile. "What if you couldn't get caught? People like us know the world is better off without kings and queens. If I had the chance, I'd kill her. And I wouldn't stop there. I'd kill every other king and queen and liar in the world till none were left and it was just people doing what they wanted with no unfair taxes or tithes or aught else lording over them!"

We're somehow facing each other. Maggie, her mouth a grim slash, her stare daring me to contradict her, and me, shaken through and through, as though someone has looked into my soul and given voice to its most secret truths.

"You shouldn't say things like that outside. Some people think the queen is made queen by God!" I whisper.

"And who told us she was chosen by God?" Maggie asks.

"Why, the clergy."

"And who is head of the clergy, Will?"

"It's . . . the queen of England. She's head of the church," I answer slowly, suddenly understanding what Maggie is getting at.

"That's right. The queen does whatever she must to make sure people like us stay quiet and powerless."

If Marlowe's and my conversation flirted with treason yesterday, this one has taken treason to the altar, married her, and is expecting a child nine months hence. I do not know what has happened to Maggie before, but I understand more clearly the cauldron of anger boiling in her heart which scalds all who dare draw too close.

"What do you mean, 'people like us'?" I haven't told her about my family's past troubles with the Crown, and the suspicion she somehow figured me out makes my hackles rise.

Maggie slaps my shoulder, suddenly grinning. "Why, the downtrodden and poor. English subjects too ugly for dear old Elizabeth's love."

I make a disagreeable noise. "People pay good coin to see this face."

"All right. You're just downtrodden and poor, then." Maggie slaps me again and juts her chin toward the sunny market square beyond the alley's maw. "Let's steal something."

Cheapside Market is quite the sight. Grand buildings line the cobblestone street, their doors thrown open to beckon shoppers within. Servants for well-off merchants scurry about with purpose, and well-heeled-ladies' maids swoon over fine fabrics. Tents selling firkins of fruit and bolles of honey and bolts of haircloth crowd the streets. Closest to us, there's a tent with glazed cakes glistening in the sun. My stomach rumbles at the sweet scent. Zounds, it would be so easy to reach out and grab one.

"Don't get us caught before we're even started!" Maggie

shoves me into the market square before I can snatch one. "Leave the hard work to me. 'Tis time for you to do some entertaining." She unfastens her cloak and tears it off in a fabulous swirl worthy of a player. Beneath it she's wearing a brilliant indigo gown trimmed in russet. Only the scuffed boots peeping beneath her hem betray her true rank.

My eyes widen. "How'd you manage all that?"

Maggie steps into the crowd with a wink. "I won't be sharing all my secrets. Meet me back here in a quarter hour." She tosses her cloak at me and vanishes.

Maggie isn't daft enough to do her light-fingered work in the center of the square, so that's where I go. With a bravado I'm certainly not feeling, I spread Mags's cloak out on the ground, strike a pose, and begin to sing.

> *The fiddler's wife was fine and neat,*
> *And decently attired,*
> *And she full well could do the feat*
> *The barber oft desired*

At first people bustle past me, but when the words settle into their ears, they stop with grins on their faces and laughter on their lips.

> *While he did please his ladies fair*
> *And trimmed them both so neatly*
> *That she did wish to have a shave*
> *He did it so completely*

I'm singing loud as I can as though volume alone can drown out whatever Maggie is up to. Of course, my cursed voice is cracking again, but this seems to add to my audience's merriment. A few even toss a penny on Maggie's muddy cloak.

I get through "The Crafty Barber of Deptford" twice before someone shouts, "By the alderman's decree, there is to be no bawdy poetry in the streets!"

Through a break in the crowd I spot them: puckered Puritans, enemies of all the merriment and fun which makes life bearable in London. Much as I'd love to stand my ground and have a laugh at their expense, I doubt my arrest is the sort of distraction Maggie is looking for, so I do what any man with a lick of sense would do.

I grab my money and run.

I weave through the crowd, ignoring the outraged gasps, and disappear into a vegetable stand. The girl freezes, mouth open, when she spots me. A single onion falls from her hand. I snatch it from the air with a roguish grin, hand it back, and disappear into the crowd in time to see the Puritans rush past like hounds on the trail of a fox. A slow grin takes over my face. Zounds, there's no feeling like getting away with ruffling a Puritan's black feathers!

To live in London is to teeter on a knife's edge. Fall and you bleed, but balance for long enough and sometimes you might snatch a victory from the very people who would rejoice to see you stumble.

The victories, few as they are, make me feel as though my time in London just might be worth it if they take me where I want to go.

I skip back to our rendezvous spot and wait, bursting with impatience to regale Maggie with the story of my great success. The church bells chime out the quarter hour.

And yet, well after the bells fade, I'm still the only one in the alley.

*But of course you are. It hasn't even been ten seconds yet,* the sensible part of me reasons.

But as the minutes drag past, worry gnaws my gut. Is this the third or fourth time Maggie's thieving has saved us from homelessness? It pains me to confess that I've lost track of how much I owe her at this point. I balk at taking Inigo's coin but think little of spending Maggie's stolen spoils. Does this make me a criminal as well?

A bunch of shouting breaks out in the marketplace. My chest squeezes tight. I'm about to step back into the square when something smashes into me and knocks out my breath.

Maggie.

Swiftly she undoes the cloak around my shoulders and sweeps it around her own. She flips the hood up as the Puritans go tearing past our hiding place.

"You're—late—" I wheeze, a hand on my chest.

"Oh, stop acting like a nursemaid." Maggie draws out a heavy leather purse. Its drawstrings are cut, and the fabric swells with clinking coins.

I throw an arm around her. "Oh, Mags, you brilliant knave!"

She shrugs off my arm. "Stop it. You'll crush your gift." She pulls out three of the heavenly glazed loaves I was admiring.

I'm fairly certain I say "thank you" before I'm gnashing on a huge mouthful of cake, but I also might've forgotten.

Maggie punches my arm as we make our way back toward the disreputable part of London. "You better save some for Inigo."

'Tis still truth that Maggie unnerves me, and I still would rather she didn't pick the grime from her toenails on our only mattress, but right now she's my favorite person in the whole entire world.

# CHAPTER FIVE

WHEN WE RETURN home, we find Inigo sleeping in the filth outside our staircase. The sight is so unexpected and strange, I gawk for several moments before Maggie's shocked gasp sends me scrambling to his side.

"Inigo!"

He groans and opens his eyes. They widen at the sight of us. "You've got to go! Now! They know who you are!" Up close, his eye sockets are bruised, the whites of his eyes red. Fear spikes through me.

"His leg is broken," Maggie says tersely. "Badly."

With a burst of horror, I realize I'm kneeling in a pool of blood. Something juts up horribly beneath Inigo's cloak.

He clutches at Maggie desperately. "I swear, I didn't mean to say anything—"

A shadow suddenly cuts over us. "Well, well. What a touching scene this is!" A leering man swaggers out from the alley. A red scar bisects his cheek, and a bludgeon hangs from his leather belt.

I swallow with an audible gulp.

Only nobles and the City Guard are allowed to bear weapons in the city of London.

And the City Guard is a bunch of hired bullies.

Someone's figured out who we are. But who? I think back on the strange men I saw with Marlowe last night. Did they overhear my treasonous words about the queen and follow me home?

Maggie gives a jaunty grin that makes her appear even more ghastly than usual. "There's nothing to see here, sir. My brothers and I have had an accident befall us."

I fight the urge to groan and cover my face. Indeed, with Inigo's brown skin, and my pale blond hair to Maggie's black, any fool can see there's not a shared drop of blood between us.

The guard grins lopsidedly. "Brothers, eh?"

"Brothers in Christ, she means!" I amend quickly, trying to draw his attention to me from Maggie. "There's only simple Christ-loving, loyal English subjects over here, good sir."

The guard snatches Maggie by the neck, pressing her cheek to his scarred face. "Yer far too pretty to be kin to this lot, girl."

Maggie hisses and sinks her teeth into his flesh. With a howl, the guard flings her away, clutching at the wound already beading with red.

She lands in a crouch, red-stained teeth bared. "Touch me again and I'll bite your—"

A bludgeon smashes between her shoulder blades from behind.

Maggie goes down with a gasp. Another City Guard stands behind her, this one tall and thin as a rapier. The second guard yanks Maggie's arms behind her and sticks his knee in her back, pinning her to the ground. Maggie bucks and hisses like an alley cat, but she cannot stop the first guard from grabbing her wrist and peeling off her glove.

He squeezes her hand with the missing fingers so tightly, the skin goes white.

"Oh, this is the Half Hand all right!" The scarred guard cackles, his eyes shining with the prospect of a fat reward.

Our traitorous landlord, Thatcher, ambles out from his pub. "Told ye I let a room to the thief. Did you really have to torture my best cook to figure it out?"

Inigo whimpers, and Maggie spits at Thatcher's feet.

The landlord hooks a thumb to his chest. "Oh, so that's what you think of me! Well, I'll have you know not everyone in London would take in an unnatural lady thief and her disreputable co-conspirators!"

Zounds, we sound like the punch line in a Cambridge boy's play.

I stare from Inigo's crumpled form to Maggie's bucking body, desperation racing through my veins. I should have left London ages ago. Didn't I tell Maggie some bloke would recognize her sooner or later? That Inigo was a fool for sheltering her? My life savings is there, buried behind Thatcher's boots. It's not as much as I wanted, but 'tis a start. Enough to bring me home to my family far away from foul London and its stone-eyed queen.

I can almost see the fields and fleece-gray skies, smell the tang of salt air, and hear the noisy specks of gulls gathered thick on the beach. I close my eyes, will the vision into sharper focus, but blast it—the scene dissolves, and all I can see are Maggie and Inigo.

Inigo, inviting me in after he found me sleeping on the

stairs leading to his attic for the third night in a row. Maggie, who despite her prickliness, never complained when the winter cold was my closest bedfellow and I would press my back against hers, stealing her warmth.

Goddamn it. I've been trying not to let these two become my friends, but they became my friends anyway.

I step forward, willing my voice steady. "How much?"

Everyone's head snaps toward me.

"How much for what?" Thatcher growls.

I nod toward Maggie. "How much is her reward?"

"A pound!" the scarred guard crows. His comrade elbows him sharply, cursing.

I duck beneath the stairs and start digging. My leather coin satchel was the first thing I bought with my first wages from the Rose Theatre. It had felt like a promise then—like every coin I put in it was bringing me closer to the life I wanted. But now, beneath Maggie's and Inigo's stares, unearthing the bag fills me with squirming guilt.

Thatcher's sour breath wheezes into my ear. "What the hell are you doing?"

I rise, holding the satchel stained by water and discolored by soil. I untie the neck of the bag, revealing the glimmering coins. My entire life savings. Looking at it makes my breath catch.

"Look at Will, being gallant, dipping into his secret stash for us! Careful, or I'll start to swoon!" Maggie's eyes are twin daggers. "Tell us, did you bury all your earnings here before you let Inigo spot your rent or afterward? Before or after I stole to keep us from starving?"

Inigo says nothing at all, which feels a hundred times worse.

I swallow hard and look to the guards, holding out the purse. "'Tis yours if you let us go in peace. Please."

Thatcher glances at the guards. The thinner one nods. "All right. But I'm not releasing her until you pay us," the thin guard says.

Maggie screams and struggles, but the guard shoves a rag in her mouth and holds her still.

I tip the sum that was supposed to bring me to my lost family into Thatcher's hands, and it feels like I'm pouring out my life's blood.

Though it makes me feel dizzy to see all my coin in another's clutches, a great sense of peace sweeps over me and dulls the ache of the coin's absence. I've done the right thing. There's no question of that. *You've earned coin before, and you'll earn more again—eventually.* I cling to this thought with the tenacity of a drowning man clasping a splintered oar on the sea.

Thatcher grins. His smile is an awful expression and shows far more of his blackened gums and missing molars than I'd like. "Ooh, well isn't this just the icing on the cake!"

I nod toward Maggie. "Let her go now!"

Thatcher pockets the money and shakes his head. "Yer pretty, but yer stupid, lad."

Before I can process the words, something smashes into my head. For a breath 'tis nothing but white spots and waves of pain, and then, blessedly, I'm carried off into merciful darkness.

# CHAPTER SIX

WHEN I COME to, the light is at a different angle in the sky, and my head throbs something fierce.

"Will?"

We're still in the alley. I suppose I ought to be glad the City Guard didn't drag us into prison along with Maggie, but it doesn't feel like a boon with the way Inigo shakes beside me, his curls limp and greasy as eels. He's trembling so hard, his teeth clatter. I can't believe he's talking to me—if I were him, I'd want naught to do with me whatsoever. Shame pours through me, the heady wash of it making the pain in my skull spike.

"Aren't you angry with me?"

Inigo says nothing at all.

I slowly sit up. Every movement sends a painful stab through my temple. "Well, I'd be angry, if I were you."

"'Tis for the best I'm not you, isn't it?" he snaps like someone who is very much angry with me.

A panic fizzles at the edge of my nerves, threatening to overwhelm everything else. We've lost our home. Maggie is arrested; Inigo is injured. Every penny I possessed now lines the pockets of thieves and liars.

"You lied to us," Inigo says quietly. "You always had the money to pay your way."

My jaw tightens. "I didn't lie. I just didn't tell you about it."

"That's the same bloody thing!" Inigo shouts. "Maggie said you were up to something suspicious, but I told her to leave it alone because I knew you wouldn't do something like that, but you did!"

More shame—hot and bitter—fills me like black bile. I've disappointed *Inigo* of all people. The bloke who won't even kill the spiders in our attic. I move to speak, but he stops me with an angry gesture. "I know you've got your real family out there somewhere, and you'll call me daft, but I thought"—his breath hitches—"I thought we had something, you, me, and Mags. Something worth saving." He spins his back to me and paws at his eyes.

An awful pressure builds in my chest. If God could find a way to smite me off the earth at this very moment, that would be great. He's right. I was going to abandon whatever fragile, strange life we've staked out without a single hesitation. Like it meant nothing at all. Like he and Maggie meant nothing at all.

I seize Inigo's hands. "I'll make it up to you."

He jerks away. "There's nothing you can do. They'll kill Maggie. And we both know I'm fated to be worm's meat with this leg."

I spring to my feet. "Not if I can help it." Perhaps Maggie is right, and there is a streak of gallantness in my soul. And even if I can't help, it would be a crime if I deprived her of the opportunity to say *I told you so* one last time. "I'll be back. I'm going to fix this."

Inigo curls away. "You won't be."

My hands fist; a dozen retorts burn hot on my tongue: *I can, I will, believe me!* But as I stare at Inigo's back, the words fizzle away. Nothing I say will make any difference at all. I'll have to prove I'm a man of my word before he believes me.

Fine.

I can do this.

I *have* to do this.

I zigzag to Marlowe's through the seedy streets. The alleys are a blur. Flashes of billowing laundry, startled chickens scattering. Outside the playwright's home I stop, ragged lungs keeping pace with my pounding heart, fist raised over his familiar door.

And hesitate.

Kit's home has always been my sanctuary, and I've run here on instinct. But will he actually help me like he said he would? Our last encounter—where he hustled me away with lies—sits uneasy on me. A pressure builds in my ears, drowning out the noise of the streets. *Your friends are in trouble, and it's your fault.* I don't know if I ought to be here, but there's nowhere else to go. Marlowe's my last hope, whether he likes it or not.

I release a shaky breath and knock on his door.

No one comes.

I pound with both fists.

Still nothing.

I glance over my shoulder before reaching into a deep groove of the house's masonwork. The pin is still there, left over from winter, when it rained so much, the door swelled shut and would barely open. I ease it now between the door and the frame until I feel the door bolt and nudge it aside.

Inside 'tis all hotchpotch as usual—splintered oak burls, leaves of paper spilling from every surface, dust motes catching the late afternoon light. My shoulders ease down from my ears at the sight. Of course Marlowe can help. He always has the answers. Soon it shall be as though this nightmarish day never happened at all. Another dashing tale we can tell other players over a round of drinks.

Low voices reach me from behind the closed door of the bedchamber.

"Do you think I don't know why you're asking me to do this?" Marlowe demands.

"I—I don't know what you're talking about," an unfamiliar male voice stammers.

Marlowe laughs softly. "Oh, I reckon you do. And I think it best if you leave now."

There are footsteps, and the door suddenly swings open.

"By God, Will?" Marlowe is framed in the doorway, hair billowing wild about his shoulders. "What the bloody hell are you doing here?"

There's no time to be subtle. "Please. You've got to help! Inigo's hurt and Maggie's been arrested and the City Guard is after me next!"

His expression tightens. "Now's not a good time—"

I seize his wrists, dragging him closer. "You told me once I never ask for help. This is me begging you!"

The silence roars. Marlowe's face remains unmoved. A hideous feeling blooms in my chest and spreads through my limbs. Kit's always been there for me. Why would he do nothing now, when I need him more than ever?

A throat clears.

I spin around so fast, I take the oak burls off Marlowe's desk.

There's a bloke standing in the bedchamber doorway. The fineness of his cloak's wool explains everything I need to know. A bloody Cambridge boy. Why on God's green earth would Marlowe be entertaining one of them in his bedchamber? He's certainly not Marlowe's usual sort. The boy summons a peculiar half smile to his face, as though he's terribly sorry to be interrupting but he's going to do it anyway.

"Perhaps I could be of assistance, sirs?" Chestnut hair falls to his shoulders and frames his overly bright eyes. There's a dewy freshness on his face, an *earnestness* I've never seen on anyone. He is like a church spire cleanly scrubbed and sparkling in the sun. I dislike him at once.

I snort and cross my arms. "I very much doubt that."

The lad lifts a finger. "You're looking for a doctor for one friend and a pardon from the City Guard for the other? I can do that."

"Oh yeah?" I give him my meanest squint and relish how he looks away. "What's in it for you?"

"I've need for a discreet man to run a playhouse for me."

Well now, that's easy enough. I haven't done it before, but I've seen Henslowe gnawing his nails and yelling enough to get the idea. Helping a Cambridge boy with one of his silly vanity plays is very much the opposite of keeping my head down and looking out for myself. But desperate times and all that. "Tell me more."

Marlowe steps betwixt us. "You won't be doing this, Will. 'Tis treason to go against the queen's orders."

A burst of irritation goes through me. Who does Marlowe imagine he is to forbid me from doing anything when he lies to me about whatever he's up to? "The lord's asking for someone to run a playhouse, Kit. He's not plotting to murder the queen."

"It's an *illegal* playhouse," Marlowe snaps. "Henslowe stopped by this morning. He was supposed to bring me an advance for *Doctor Faustus*, but instead he said that the Master of Revels has closed all the playhouses because of the plague." He laughs bitterly. "We both know you would hang if the wrong people found out about this theater. You can't trust this lord."

*The theaters are closed?* A heavy dread pools in my throat and sinks right down to the pit of my stomach. My job starring in Marlowe's next play is gone now. Which means that Marlowe's out of a job and pay too. We're all sunk together.

"I've got nothing to give." Marlowe turns to me, hands outstretched, an awful expression on his face. "I can't help you this time."

The despairing silence grows bigger and bigger until it feels I'm in the jaws of a huge beast, soon to be swallowed whole.

The Cambridge boy clears his throat. "Well then . . . if you change your mind about my offer, I'll be outside." He leaves, only to pop his head back in at once. "I'm not trying to kill anyone either, I'll have you know!"

Somehow the silence goes from awkward to excruciating after the lord leaves. I stare at Kit. Though my friend is but an arm's length away, it feels like a huge distance. Nothing I can say will stop him from staring with pity. I'm not asking for help; I'm asking for the impossible. I've run smack into a wall, and there was never an escape at the end of this alley.

Except . . .

I did not know the word "impossible" lay within his vocabulary. Here is the man whose words have charmed queens and made men question the word of God. Impossible? No, nothing is impossible for Marlowe.

"What about your other business? Would you pay me to help with that?" I say.

Marlowe gives me an odd look. "What are you talking about?"

"Don't be daft. You're not only writing plays. You're up to something else, too."

Marlowe's face clouds over quicker than a storm across a summer sky. "Stop spouting nonsense," he says coolly. "You're seeing things that aren't there."

He's lying to me, and it's so obvious, I know not to be offended or frightened.

"Enough lies!" I shout. "I know you're up to something, and I know you've been keeping it from me."

Marlowe starts to protest, but I cut him off. "I've *seen* the men who follow you! And how you speak to them when you think no one's watching. I've been watching you, and you can't fool me any longer. I don't care what unlawfulness you're tangled up in as long as you bring me in with you. Give me a chance. You *owe* me that."

Marlowe give a surprised laugh. "You've got keener eyes than half the ones I work with, I'll give you that." He circles me appraisingly. "And I already know you could play the part well. You could be just the man I'm looking for." He stops and smiles sadly. "But I can't involve you in what I'm doing—not anymore."

Frustration knots in my chest, hot and hard. "Involve me in what?"

He chuckles again. "Obstinate as a rock, aren't you?"

His laughter sends a rush through me. "Christopher Marlowe," I hiss. "Tell me the truth of what you've been doing, or I swear, I'll tell the City Guard you're up to something. Let me in, or I'll rat you out!"

The playwright goes very still. His raven-quick eyes study me as though he's finally seeing me clearly for the first time. A chill sweeps through me that has naught to do with the temperature. "That would be very daft. Because I'd have to do something about it, and I doubt you'd like it very much."

His words sink in slow as a poison. "Are you . . . threatening me?"

His lips twist ruefully. "I'm afraid so, Elias Wilde."

My true, given name—the one that connects me to traitors—claps louder than thunder. Only two people in all of

London know it, and I thought I could trust each of them with my life.

Marlowe continues. "I know one band of child catchers who'd be glad to get word of the boy who gave them the slip. 'Tis hard to lose an indentured servant boy. The pretty ones don't come cheap." His voice goes quieter. "And imagine what they'd do if they knew you were the son of the man who rebelled against Her Majesty."

"You—you'd send me back to those men? Tell everyone who I am?"

The Wilde rebellion. When my father and uncles raised their sickles and shovels against the queen who came to steal the land they had lived on for centuries. Their humble tools were no match for the soldiers' weapons, nor their fires. My family was forced from their land by English lords and their endless hunger for more, including the common lands which once belonged to all men, the vast green fields where my father's family raised their flocks for generations. Among the only survivors, my parents used the last of their coin to escape the smoldering ruins of their livelihoods and lives to create a new life without friends or family in the middle of nowhere.

Marlowe takes up his quill-sharpening knife, my gift to him last Twelfth Night, and turns it idly. "I'd rather see you locked up than dead. I'm keeping secrets for your own good." He seizes my elbow, the knife pressing into the meat of my forearm. "Don't say a word to anyone about this. I'll know."

I make a soft sound and nod once. Marlowe smiles warmly and cups my cheek. "That's a good lad."

# CHAPTER SEVEN

SLAMMING KIT'S DOOR behind me, I plunge into the street and straight into the Cambridge boy. In the daylight he's far younger than I thought. He cannot be more than a year or two older than me. I thumb away the fierce stinging in my eyes and move to speak, but he beats me to it.

"Forgive me for asking, but are you quite all right?" His keen eyes are the bright brown of a newly shucked chestnut. "You seem . . . troubled."

His observation and concerned look stop me, and I hold back the hysterical laughter clawing up my throat because, by God, what hasn't troubled me at this point? Did he *not* hear me explain everything in Marlowe's? Zounds, isn't Cambridge a place where lords go to grow smarter?

"I'll run your bloody playhouse," I growl, ignoring his question. "But I've got conditions."

The lord raises a single eyebrow, as if he's got reservations about my wits. "What are these conditions of yours?"

"Save my friends now and I'll work for you. Then you'll pay me ten pounds when your play's done."

Ten pounds is an unfathomable sum of money. More than enough to return to my family. If the only person in all of bloody London who can help me is some doe-eyed lord, I'll be damned sure to make it worth the risk I'm taking.

"And you mustn't tell anyone my whereabouts," I add quickly. "Or the deal's off." I don't know if Kit might change his mind about trusting my silence. My chest squeezes at the thought. I don't know Kit at all anymore.

He gives me a pensive, searching look. It goes on for so long, I nearly ask if his ears work before he finally says, "Very well then. The job is yours."

I duck my head so he can't see my grimace. This boy-lord doesn't know how it absolutely galls me to say yes to his bargain. I can never let on how I despise him and all that he represents—not while he's got me in his pocket. *This is all Kit's fault*, I think bitterly. *His lies and falseness brought me to this.*

"In addition to running the rehearsals, I'll need someone to find the players as well," he says.

"Fine. And the plays? Do you need someone to find those too?" I ask bitterly.

His neck flushes scarlet. "There's no need for that. You see . . . the plays are mine." He delivers this line with a forced bashfulness that nearly makes me gag.

"Let me guess. You're also writing under a pseudonym, and your father has no idea."

He tilts his head to the side, a barely-there smile on his lips. "How did you know?"

*I've been rubbing elbows with Cambridge boys like you since I first came to this foul city!* Instead of shouting this to my new patron, I swallow back my resentment and stick out my hand. "Do we have a bargain, my lord?"

The noble stares at my hand as though it is riddled with plague boils. Then he takes it gingerly, and I am surprised to feel rough calluses on his skin.

"You never gave me a name," I say.

He frowns as though it hadn't occurred to him I couldn't possibly be aware of who he was.

"Well?" I say sharply. "Deal's off if you can't be honest with me."

He sighs, as though bracing himself for a great pain. "James Edmund Bauffremont of Bloomsbury."

Christ, what a mouthful! With a fancy name like that I'm growing horribly more certain I'm dealing with a level of nobility I've never seen before. The queen could be his godmother for all I know. I squeeze the lord's hand back, very aware that I've either saved all our sorry hides or damned us entirely.

"It's a pleasure to meet you, my lord," I grumble, not sounding like I mean it at all.

His barely-there smile returns. "Oh no. I can assure you, the pleasure is all mine."

We find Inigo in an unconscious pile outside Thatcher's pub, left like a rotting carcass. Bloomsbury and his manservant, Cooper, help me tie Inigo to a horse and take us to an unremarkable building squeezed betwixt two taverns stinking of ale and piss. One of the bottom windows is nailed shut. A thrill of unease goes through me.

"What's going on here? This is not a place for a lord. If you've fool-taken us to murder us and sell our bodies—"

Bloomsbury grasps my forearm, his voice infuriatingly level. "Mr. Hughes, you asked me for secrecy, did you not? This house is my laboratory."

I tug myself free. "You've brought us to your lavatory?" Why would a noble reserve an entire building solely for the purposes of washing? Are we such street rats that we must be blasted with lye and perfumed water before Bloomsbury will have anything to do with us?

Bloomsbury sighs. "No, a *laboratory*. It's . . . a place for my work. Do not be alarmed by it. I can assure you staying here will suit both of us better than you staying in my family's ancestral London house."

I've seen the nobility's town houses. Huge, hulking things that require a small army of servants to run them, all of them in the shadow of Queen Elizabeth's palace. I shudder at the thought of being that close to the queen. But it only takes one step inside Bloomsbury's secret laboratory to make me wonder if I truly am better off here.

The timbered ceiling is hung with herbs: faded bunches of lavender, broad-leafed comfrey, boughs of goldenrod, and fragrant dill. 'Tis a scene from a witch's hovel or a gathering of goblins or some other unholy hellscape. My stomach lurches. Oh God, what have I dragged us into? Maggie's going to be furious.

The lord points to a shut door. "You have free rein of the entire house save this room." And then he *smiles* at me as though this is all perfectly normal and pleasant and he certainly has no designs on skinning us alive and pickling our innards. "Now, could you please help me move your friend upstairs? I've already asked my manservant to summon a doctor to attend to his injury."

Inigo's slipped into a delirious fever, and the sight of his bloodless face frightens me. I pace just outside the door while the doctor works, my boots stamping muddy prints all over the floors. 'Tis well past dark when the doctor leaves and allows me inside.

Inigo is still and small on an enormous mattress, his leg in a lumpy splint. I drag the empty washbasin over, turn it upside down, and sit. I touch the cross in my pocket, offering a prayer. *Please don't let him die.*

This entire bloody mess is my fault. If I had just paid my share of the rent instead of hoarding coin, Maggie wouldn't have had to steal. If I hadn't been so selfish and secretive, Thatcher would have left Inigo alone. If I had just minded my own damn business, I would have remained blissfully unburdened from knowing Kit Marlowe is as false as the plays he pens.

Kit *threatened me*. It didn't seem like he much wanted to, but he did threaten me all the same. While I should want naught to do with him after this, his betrayal still leaves a hollow ache in my chest that feels suspiciously like sadness. I know not what to make of it.

Ever since I became a player at the Rose Theatre, life in London has been tedious, but tolerable. Now, between this Bloomsbury bloke and Marlowe's mysterious threats, I feel like I'm being swept up in something far bigger than myself, and I don't like it one bit. Keeping your head down means keeping it on your shoulders. What's happening now feels an awful lot like courting danger, and I know what happens to lads like me who do that.

Inigo's eyes snap open, and a terrified gasp tears from his chapped lips.

I brush a damp curl from his forehead. "Hey, you're all right now."

His fevered eyes latch on to mine. "And Maggie?"

"She'll be here soon." Or that's what Bloomsbury says at least.

Inigo's eyes flutter shut as if that one effort stole all the spirit he had. I'm about to go, but he speaks again. "You came back."

I release a long, unsteady breath. "Of course. You didn't really think I'd leave you, did you?"

His brow furrows. "I—I didn't know what you'd do."

His words are more painful than a knife to the ribs. I've spent so long thinking Marlowe was the only person I could trust, I didn't see the person he was becoming—or see that Inigo has been twice the friend that Marlowe ever was. Shame fills me, a scalding guilt. Inigo deserves far better company than me.

I seize his clammy hand. *I'll never let you down again* is what I want to say, but the words snag in my throat, the promise all at once too enormous to make. "It was the least I could do, after all you've done for me."

He smiles dreamily and nestles deeper into the blankets. "You play the hero's part quite well. Always knew you would, Elias."

I whip my head toward the door, relieved to find it shut. Normally, I'd tell Inigo to mind himself with my true name, the fewer people who know it the better, but this time my true name on his lips is the sweetest sound in the entire world. I squeeze his hand and dearly hope I haven't heard him mutter it for the last time.

When I wake the next morning, I'm half-sprawled across the foot of Inigo's bed. At some point in the night I managed to wrest one boot from my foot, but the other clings doggedly on. I drag myself upright and slap a hand to my neck as a sharp pain splinters through it. A sour smell wafts from my clothes. I cannot remember the last time I bathed, and yesterday's drama did little to improve the situation.

The doctor is already in the room. When I stand, he wrinkles his nose and makes a *shooing* motion toward the door.

Bloomsbury's manservant, Cooper, waits for me in the hallway. "My lord has already departed to free your friend from the bailiff's prison. Would you care for breakfast while you wait, sir?"

I'm standing there shod in a single boot and stinking to high heaven. I'm about as far from a "sir" as they come. "Perhaps I could bathe first?"

The servant bows. "Certainly."

He takes me to a chamber with a filled wooden washbasin. Fragrant steam curls from the water's surface. I peel off all my clothes and step into the tub at once.

And zounds, it feels *wonderful*.

The heat unknots the snarls in my muscles and warms me to the marrow. I sigh and lean back fully even though I'm fairly certain this vessel was not made for sitting. The suds slosh dangerously close to the basin's rim. Someone's left a window open, and the trill of birdsong eddies past. There must be a garden nearby. I close my eyes and breathe in the perfumed air.

"Is everything quite all right?"

I startle awake in a basin of tepid water and wilted bubbles. A splash of filthy water surges out and slaps the floor as I scramble out.

Bloomsbury stands at the open door wearing a plush emerald doublet and a shocked expression.

I snatch a now-soaked cloth and hold it against my important bits. "Nothing's amiss here! No need to worry!"

The lord shields his eyes, throat bobbing. "I can see that now! Thank you!"

The blush on his neck makes me grin. For someone so even-tempered he's easy to embarrass. I slip the fact away for later. Heckling him will be good fun for me!

I towel myself off and hop into one leg of new breeches, nearly braining myself on the bed frame. "Have you gotten Maggie yet, my lord?"

A feral, female scream rends the air from somewhere deeper in the house, followed by a streak of curses that would make a sailor whistle approvingly.

"Miss . . . Maggie is being fitted for proper attire." He looks heavenward and closes his eyes. "She has been . . . resistant."

"You may want to scrub her, as well," I advise. "She wouldn't know her own arse if you put her before a mirror. That's how long it's been since I've seen her bathe."

It pleases me to see the crimson deepen on his neck, though the more rational part of me wonders what sort of wealth or power he must possess to free a known thief so easily. *A lot.* My pleasure at nettling him vanishes at once. The bath was nice, yes, but Bloomsbury is not my friend, and I am no guest of his.

"Let's get on with it then," I say gruffly, stepping past Bloomsbury. He reaches out and grazes a spot on my head.

"What's this?"

I wince and pull away. I don't like the way he talks to me by demanding answers instead of making conversation. "'Tis nothing."

He frowns again, aging a decade at once, all embarrassment gone. "You should've let the doctor take a look."

Zounds, this is how it starts. First he'll say he can help me, and next I'll wake up half-dead on a bloodstained table surrounded by knives. 'Tis bad enough I already fell asleep in the bath. "No. I enjoy bleeding. 'Tis good for the constitution. Rich folks pay to be bled, y'know."

"Mr. Hughes," Bloomsbury says sternly, brow furrowed so deeply, he's going to look like an old man before he hits five and twenty. "You're being ridiculous. Come with me."

Against my will, the lord leads me downstairs through the damned apothecary which serves as his house, dodging a myriad of plants along the way. He commands me to sit in a chair while he bids Cooper to fetch his *things* from the laboratory.

I scowl with a bravado I don't feel. If this lord wanted a ruffian, well, I can play that role as well as any other. "What *things* are we talking about? I won't let you touch me with none of them leeches."

There's that barely-there smile again. The sight of it sends a curious spark through me. I'm beginning to suspect I'm on the outside of some private joke he's got with himself, and I'm hungry to know what's going on behind his careful words and measured looks. "No leeches. You have my word."

Cooper returns with a leather case not unlike the one the doctor possesses. Bloomsbury swipes a cloth through a bowl of warm water and tends to me. His touch is gentle, but I still wince. The City Guard truly laid a good one on me.

"You seem to have training in the medicinal arts," I observe.

"I am familiar with them." He smears a cool tincture across my skin that smells like the air after a summer rain.

"Seems a tad odd for a playwright to know about wounds, doesn't it?"

The lord continues dabbing at my head. "I am a man of many talents, Mr. Hughes." His expression doesn't change a bit. It frustrates me to no end that I cannot tell if he's lying or not. I've never been to a school, so I've no idea if it's strange he knows medicine and letters both. Usually I'd ask Marlowe questions like this, but I'd sooner peel off my own fingernails than talk to him again. Christopher bleeding Marlowe will be the reason why my insides end up in a jar tucked on a shelf in the lord's secret laboratory.

Bloomsbury finally sits back. "Now don't touch that for at least a day."

My fingers probe the throbbing ache anyway and come away sticky. I've no doubt whatever he's given me would cost an entire week's wages. I grit my teeth. It's all too much—Inigo's care, Maggie being here, the clothes, the bath. There's a catch somewhere, and by God, I'll sniff it out. "Why are you doing this?"

Bloomsbury frowns as if I had asked a distasteful question, moving a breakfast tray to the table. "Whatever do you mean?"

"Sheltering us. Feeding us. We're supposed to be the ones working for you."

He gives me an incredulous look, like he can't quite believe what he's heard. "How are you supposed to help me with my play if you're homeless and starving? Do you think your friend will recover in a squalid boardinghouse crawling with rats?"

My face goes hot, and I shove a bit of bread into my mouth, chewing furiously. What a world apart Bloomsbury must live in that he can hold our lives and livelihoods in his pocket as if it were nothing for him. As if we were adorable street puppies he's decided to collar and perfume and pretend are lapdogs! "What if we don't want to stay with you?" I say.

Bloomsbury sighs and drags a hand over his face, a crack in his calm. "You can't really mean that. Forgive me for asking, but what has happened in your life that causes you to distrust Christian charity with such fire?"

I inhale sharply. His words draw dangerously close to

everything I don't want him to know. I draw myself up even taller and scowl. "Nothing in life is given freely. Particularly the things which bear the illusion of freedom."

Before he can reply, Cooper reappears. "My lord, Mr. Hughes, may I present Miss Maggie—"

Maggie barrels past him, not waiting on her introduction. "Just Maggie, I said! That's it." She is wholly unfamiliar in a plain dress which has neither holes nor filth nor any other imperfection upon it. There's no chance the clothing will remain unsullied for long.

Bloomsbury smiles and stands as though Maggie were a charming lady and not a wild animal he has unwisely let into his home. "Please take my seat. I imagine you and Mr. Hughes have quite a bit of catching up to do."

"Damn right we do!" Maggie launches across the table and seizes my chemise by the throat, her bodice dragging through the jam and staining her front purple. "Will Hughes, you bastard," she hisses. "What on earth have you dragged us into this time?"

# CHAPTER EIGHT

I
T IS SOON obvious Lord James Edmund Bauffremont of
Bloomsbury is hiding something. While I'm used to playwrights locking themselves in a room all day, it is very odd
that ghastly odors waft from under Bloomsbury's door. And
when the lord does leave his room, there's no ink splotches on
his hands—like he hasn't written a single thing all day.

If Bloomsbury is not writing, what else is he doing?

"Please don't ever save me again," Maggie says for the
hundredth time over breakfast. "Not if this is how you're going
to do it." She trusts Bloomsbury less than I do. We'd flee, but
Inigo's bedridden, and while Maggie and I butt heads about
everything else, we agree we shall not leave Inigo alone in this
strange house to save our skins.

"Apologies for saving you from further dismemberment or
death," I say. "Do tell, how would you prefer I bail you from
prison the next time you're arrested?"

"He's a bloody Cambridge boy!" Maggie says like I'm the
thickest person she's ever met. "Why couldn't Marlowe be useful this time?"

"I told you already. I asked Kit for help. He couldn't do it,
all right?" I snap, pushing my food away.

She pillows her chin in her hand. "I've been thinking about what you said about Marlowe being caught up in something unlawful," she says. "I reckon you're right about it."

I swallow back burgeoning nerves. More than once, I've tried to talk about Marlowe with Maggie, but every time I open my mouth, Marlowe's final words stop me. *Don't say a word to anyone about this. I'll know.* His threat follows me like a hideous shadow.

Would Marlowe really hurt me? Do I want to find out? I know the answer to my last question is an emphatic *certainly not*, so I say nothing at all and keep my worries to myself.

"Marlowe's slippery—too slippery to be an ordinary thief or coney-catcher," Maggie says. "But there's more than one kind of unsavory sort in London."

"What do you mean?" I say, unable to stop myself from asking, even though I'm better off not knowing.

Maggie crooks her finger, and I lean closer. "There's whispers that the queen has spies all over London," Maggie says. "And I reckon Marlowe is among them. I know it seems madness at first, but think of it. The rumor the queen enjoys his plays. That he hobnobs with nobodies such as ourselves and gentlemen alike."

My breakfast churns. There's a horrible sense to what Maggie's saying, and I wish she'd stop staring at me like she's expecting answers. *One word from Marlowe, and the queen of England could know who I am.*

"Is there anything else you can tell me about him? Anything he did or said that would cast suspicion on him?" Maggie's eyes are wide and dark as a winter river.

I look to my clenched hands on the table. "No, he hasn't said or done anything suspicious."

Maggie sits back with a sigh. "That's a pity, then. Be nice to have a reason for why Marlowe's gone and stuck us with this bloody lying Cambridge boy!" She pins me beneath a glare. "You need to discover what this Bloomsbury bloke is up to, and soon, otherwise I'll turn us in to the City Guard myself to escape him!"

But managing Lord Bloomsbury's play only leads to more questions.

His illegal theater is an abandoned brothel just beyond Southwark. Only a thicket of tangled trees hides it from the road. If the building could talk, it would scream, spit upon my boots, and then laugh in my face. I am half-worried the rotted thing will collapse and kill us all before the play's over.

"Who's the bloke running this show?" William Shakespeare, the most obnoxious player and playwright in all of London, demands after rehearsal one day. His ink-stained arms are crossed over his chest, his hair a wild snarl like usual.

"I'm not telling you," I say crossly.

Shakespeare brandishes Bloomsbury's play at me: *The Most Lamentable Tragedy of Abelard and Heloise*. "He must be rich if he's been able to give each player his own script."

I ignore him. I'm certainly not going to gamble with our safety and the promise of a plump purse to satisfy Shakespeare's curiosity. The man roots about for gossip like a greedy hog for truffles, his quill just waiting to add it all into his latest play. Lord only knows how he found me in the first place. I purposely did not inform him of the player auditions so I would not be forced to endure his company, and yet, here he is.

"Don't get caught up with the nobles, lad, 'tis not worth it. Marlowe doesn't think so either," Shakespeare says.

I snatch Shakespeare's wrist. He startles, his script falling and fanning all across the floor.

"Don't you dare tell Marlowe I'm here, all right?"

Shakespeare's bushy eyebrows rise. He's got a hundred questions on his face, but, for once, he keeps them to himself. "I won't. But I can't promise none of the other players will. Especially for the right price." The man puzzles over me like a line in one of his plays. His scrutiny makes me squirm. It pains me to say he's got a keen eye on the world—as keen as Marlowe's—and I don't like what he might be seeing in me now. At best, he'll flap his great gob and tell everyone what I'm up to, and at worst, he'll write about me in another one of his blasted sonnets that make Inigo and Maggie scream with laughter.

"Please just don't say a word," I say quietly.

Shakespeare makes a great show of sighing. "If you insist, Hughes."

By the time Shakespeare leaves, I've spooked myself worrying, and my fingers are clumsy with unease. I drop the key twice trying to lock up. The second time I stoop to snatch it, something shoves me betwixt the shoulders.

Christ! 'Tis a giant red stallion, his eyes rolling and white and his nostrils flaring crimson. I scream and fall against the door.

"Ares! Mind your manners!"

High in the saddle is Bloomsbury, trying to rein in his beast. He's dressed in a curious getup of baggy breeches, an undyed chemise, and a shapeless cap pulled low over his brow. My fear vanishes, annoyance taking its place.

"Are you . . . in disguise?" I say.

Bloomsbury dismounts and scoffs. "Of course."

The effort is entirely unconvincing; he is dressed like a prince pretending to be a beggar who is clearly a prince all the same. The Rose Theatre crowd would lap this up like fresh cream. "Forgive me for saying so, but you may want to try harder next time, my lord. Unless you wish to drag all your noble titles through the mud when the players discover who you really are."

He draws even closer, foiling my efforts to lock the door. "Try harder? What part of this is unconvincing?"

Zounds, he's hopeless.

"The fancy horse, for one."

"Lots of people ride horses."

The stallion stamps his hoof and tosses his head, as if to say *I am not like other horses*. A fact which is obvious to all, except his master.

I resist the overwhelming urge to roll my eyes. "What brings you here, my lord? 'Tis dangerous to linger." The sun is slanting lower through the leaves overhead. I've no doubt this scraggly forest hosts murderers and highwaymen and other unsavory sorts once the sun's down, and I've no desire to still be here when they come prowling. The players have already found the remains of two bodies during rehearsal.

"I want to see how the theater's coming along," Bloomsbury demands, his eyes rapt on the door.

"I live in your house." I lock the door with a satisfying
snick. "You could've asked me there."

"Yes, but I want to *see* it." He gestures toward the iron key
clasped in my hand. "Would you mind?"

I bite back a sigh and unlock the door once again.

Inside, the theater is the same as ever: cramped, dim, and
dusty. There's a hole in the ceiling, and a single shaft of sunlight
beams down on broken crates. A rat scuttles past and disappears.

Bloomsbury regards the room like it's the kingdom of
heaven and he's been welcomed there by Jesus Christ himself.
He walks the perimeter, spellbound, one finger trailing along
the rotting wall. "It's no Rose Theatre, but it shall do quite
nicely." Abruptly he turns to me. "However, I am not sure
about some of Heloise's lines."

"My lord, you *wrote* her lines."

"I am aware of this. I meant the way in which she is acted."

My mouth falls open. "Have you been spying on us?"

"Only today." He pauses. "And the day before that."

I drop my face into my hands. "My lord"—Bloomsbury
clears his throat, and I grit my teeth—"James, then," I growl.
"If you continue to lurk here, someone is going to notice."
God, if we're discovered, there goes my money and everything
else I've got going for me.

He hops onto the raised dais that serves as our stage, then
pivots toward me. "It's *my* play. And Heloise's player pleases
me not."

I resist the urge to roll my eyes once again. "I hired the best player who auditioned. The options were not impressive. Most boy players did not heed my call for auditions. Believe me. If I could, I'd act the part myself, and the entire play would be better for it."

Bloomsbury quirks an eyebrow. "Is that so?"

I waggle both my eyebrows right back at him. "Surely you've seen me act."

Ah, there it is! His furrowed brow. I bite back a smirk at the sight, pleased at having gotten to him once more.

He taps his chin thoughtfully. "You were good in Thomas Kyd's *The Spanish Tragedy* last summer, to be sure. But there were times when I thought you could be . . . better."

I ball my fists, good humor gone in an instant. "Oh, like *you* could do so much better!"

He shrugs, smiling in that coy way I'm starting to resent more than anything else. "Perhaps I could."

My blood simmers. Bloomsbury may be my patron, but I tire of his insufferable confidence, his infuriating calm. The way he sits with me and Maggie most mornings like it's completely normal to invite strange London riffraff into his home and then refuse to answer any of our questions about what he's doing in that stinking laboratory of his all day.

And yet.

*He saw me last summer and remembers.* The realization whispers under my skin, filling me with a helpless sort of wonder and a burning desire to ask him more about what he saw. I'm not the sort of person one remembers. Out of my skirts,

out on the streets, I'm nothing remarkable. I imagine Bloomsbury on the Rose Theatre balconies overhead, hair bronzed
by the summer sun. Perhaps he eagerly leaned forward on his
elbows for a better look as I played the vengeance-minded
maid, Bel-imperia. Perhaps those dark eyes went wide with
shock when my character was betrayed and murdered, his gaze
following me as I slipped offstage.

Perhaps the sight of me moved him, lingered in some secret
place.

The idea of him seeing me before I saw him burns like a
freshly lit candle, thrilling and new. I don't know why I keep
thinking of it. I shake my head to banish these odd thoughts.

In the present moment, Bloomsbury's damned curious gaze
still watches me. "Have I said something to upset you? Please
forgive me."

"You didn't upset me!" I protest. "It's—it's simply rude to
tell a man you could do his work better than him. Which I
assumed you'd know already, as a man of the theater yourself.
I'm not offering to write your bloody plays after all, am I?"

His infuriating smile is back, and I realize, beyond a doubt,
he's only said all this to upset me and succeeded. "I suppose
I've still got more to learn, then."

I bite back a scathing reply, cheeks flushing. Whatever lack
of experience Bloomsbury claims he has, his inspired performance as the most vexing person I've ever met is certainly coming from somewhere. How far must I go to learn his secrets?
Why would a man be so willing to court treason for the lark of
a play? The theaters will be open once the plague diminishes.

Then he can toss Henslowe a fat purse to stage his vanity project at the Rose. All he must do is wait several months at the most. There is no need for urgency.

"My lord, forgive me for asking, but aren't you worried about attracting the queen's attention with this play?"

"Not particularly."

A knot of frustrations tightens in my chest. "But she is the *queen*."

Bloomsbury's brow furrows. "Yes, and you seem awfully worried about her. Is there a reason why?"

I keep my outward appearance perfectly neutral, whilst within I curse myself ten different kinds of daft. Bloomsbury is a lord. Likely as not the queen is his third cousin or something, and every anniversary of her coronation Bloomsbury and his odious lord father must lick her toes or however nobles pay their respects to royal kin. 'Tis best not to mention the queen at all. My very life and livelihood depend on how well I can keep my mouth shut.

"I am to be married several months hence. This is my last moment for boyish capers." Bloomsbury nearly drags a hand through his hair and thinks better of it.

Now, this is painfully untrue. Bloomsbury is a man—a rich one at that—and I know how men treat women. Even bloody Will Shakespeare has a wife and a child he's all but abandoned somewhere in the countryside.

"Why did you ask Marlowe if he'd be willing to stage your play?" He has to have asked Marlowe for a reason, and Maggie's words about Marlowe and spies are rattling around in me like the final penny in a purse. Is Bloomsbury caught up in whatever has Kit in its claws?

"I'm familiar with his work, so I thought he would do a good job with my work as well," Bloomsbury says confidently.

My brow furrows. "But . . . Marlowe doesn't stage any of his own plays. That's the theater manager's job. All the playwright does is write the words."

His neck flushes, and he loosens the collar of his chemise. "Well, of course! I had rather hoped Mr. Marlowe would make an exception for me."

He's lying. I nudge a stone with my boot, stung by an unexpected hurt. Of course Bloomsbury's got something he's keeping from me—why bother with the illegal playhouse and such if he has nothing to hide?—but his answers have only created more questions. How would a playwright, even a talentless Cambridge-going fool of one, not know how putting on a play works? It's like he's never seen a play before, even though he claims he has.

Before I can press Bloomsbury further, outside a voice bursts into a bawdy tavern tune.

We turn to each other with wide eyes. "Someone's here!" I cry.

Bloomsbury seizes my arm. He yanks me behind the dais, to the floor, out of sight from the open doorway.

"Why don't you shout a little louder, so he can find us?" he whispers crossly.

He doesn't release me. His nails press divots into my bare skin. His fingers are long and graceful, the lean muscle of his arm disappearing up the cuffed sleeves of his ridiculous costume. The borrowed rough-spun chemise that gaps at the collar, a freckled shoulder all but slipping free. His skin bears a tapestry of crisscrossing white scars like thorns, and I want to ask him when he lost his valiant battle with a briar rose. Even despite the ill-fitting disguise, I can tell he's all elegant lines beneath it. He's . . . well, he's handsome, which is rather irritating. I groan, wishing I could unlearn this new fact. A man's got to live by his standards, and one of mine is to never look twice at a member of the peerage. No good ever came of making eyes at noblemen.

"Don't fret. Perhaps it's just one man," Bloomsbury says, mistaking my pained noise for fear.

We're so close in the narrow space, my face is shoved into the crook of his neck. A sweet, woodsy scent overwhelms my nose. I close my eyes and breathe deeply. Lavender. Aye, he smells of flowers, because of course he does. Christ.

Bloomsbury finally releases me, brow furrowed. "Did you just . . . sniff me?"

My face goes hot. "Don't be ridiculous. I've done no such thing!"

He shushes me again with an impatient flap of his hand. Outside, the lonely voice reaches the chorus, and another three join, the song punctuated by jolly laughter and shouting.

I swallow back a curse. It could be an entire pack of highwaymen, bristling with cutlasses and knives and God knows what else. Zounds, I said lingering here was foolish, but does he listen to me?

Bloomsbury motions for quiet, as if I'm too thick to figure it out on my own, and we rise to tiptoe across the floor and creep outside. Behind us, the old brothel's door slams shut, and Bloomsbury turns to me with a glare.

The singing stops.

"It might only be travelers." Bloomsbury unties his horse quickly. "No need to fear yet."

Four armed men crash through the trees. One holds a bow with an arrow notched and ready.

Bloomsbury's face pales. He gropes at his waist for an absent sword hilt. Not finding it, he swings himself up in the saddle in one smooth gesture and thrusts a hand toward me. "Come on!"

I just gape at it.

I am a city lad through and through. I've ridden a horse all of once before and hated every second of it.

An arrow thunks into the soil beside me, the fletching vibrating. Another arrow buries its point beside the first. I scream.

"Quit dallying!" Bloomsbury shouts.

I press my cross against my chest and seize his hand. I barely get on before we're off at a gallop, another arrow whizzing past. Black tree limbs twist overhead, eager to dash us from the saddle. I close my eyes and hold the lord's waist as tightly as I can.

"Hughes, not so tight!"

"Not on your life!"

Ares tears from the trees into the road. Bloomsbury gives

the stallion his head. The horse gains speed until my cheeks sting in the wind and I hardly know when his hooves touch the ground and when they do not.

Soon the clamor of the highwaymen fades. Somehow I've managed to find my seat behind Bloomsbury, and that means I'm pressed, groin to neck, to his well-muscled back. My cheeks warm. God Almighty, I've rarely been this intimate, even with lads I've kissed before. There's a pinch behind my ribs at the reminder of my delicious Thomas. I have not thought of him for days. He did not heed my call for auditions. A better lover would reach out, find him, and ask how he's doing with the theaters being shut down by the plague. A better person would act instead of doing nothing but wrestle with his own guilt.

Ares slows to a bouncing trot when we reach the edges of Southwark, and then a walk as the road swells with more people. London is all bronzed rooftops and curls of gray smoke across the water. From a distance, the city looks like a treasure chest, full of hidden promise and riches.

Bloomsbury tosses his head back and begins to laugh.

It's unsettling. But then he keeps at it for so long, something warm kindles within me. He turns with a wild grin, his cheeks ruddy as a boy's on May Day. "Being a playwright is so much more exciting than I had imagined!"

It's the first time I've seen him smile. Not the barely-there one he gets whenever he's making sport of me, but a real one that turns his furrows into laugh lines and lights him up from within. My own smile takes off, a slow expression that needs a moment to find its wings, like a moorhen bursting into flight.

Should I really be so suspicious of this man—boy, really—who has shown me and my friends nothing but kindness? He appears far more likely to fall victim to a villain than play one himself. Perhaps he truly is merely rich and foolish and eager to witness his words brought to life on the stage before marrying someone as boring and dull as he is.

These thoughts roost in my head as we join the carts, horses, people, and pigs all plodding across London Bridge at a snail's pace. The bridge's stench hits us first, the ripeness of rotting flesh, and then the shadows cut over us. Severed heads are spiked atop the great stone gate, in various stages of decay. A hush quiets the crowd as they pass beneath the traitors and cowards whose skulls Queen Elizabeth has demanded be displayed for all to witness. *Look what happens to those who displease their queen,* they say.

Bloomsbury draws a hand over his nose and mouth. "It is particularly ripe today."

"'Tis always worse in the sun, my lord."

Bloomsbury glances over his shoulder, sobering at once. "You mustn't call me lord among so many when I'm dressed like such."

"Still in disguise, are we?"

He shushes me—with a finger to his mouth and all—as a carriage rolls past. A liveried servant rides a horse ahead of it. "Move along, move along!" the servant shouts, using his mount to force the traffic to either side so his lord can get to wherever he's going faster than the rest of us.

"Don't want to be caught mucking around with riffraff

before your peers?" My words are brisk and brittle. For a brief moment, outside the city walls, I had let myself forget that our stations are worlds apart. But now, beneath the grinning skulls of traitors, I am reminded that one well-placed whisper is all it would take for my head to join the ghastly chorus. Then I'd never get the money my family needs to survive. Hell, they'd never even know I had *died*.

Marlowe was right. Bloomsbury gambles not only with his life but with mine, and we both know who will be punished for defying the queen's orders.

"Let me down. We'll attract less curiosity this way," I say.

"Wait—"

I slither straight down the horse into a pile of dung.

Splendid.

Bloomsbury sighs like I've disappointed him. "Why must you make everything so difficult?"

I cross my arms. "I could say the same for you!"

He rubs his temples. "Is this how today shall end, Hughes?"

"Yes, and you'd better not lurk about the theater in disguise again!"

"As you wish." Bloomsbury nudges Ares into a trot.

I stab a finger at his disappearing back. *"And your disguises are terrible!"*

He won't even honor me with a look. Scowling, I stuff my hands deep into my pockets and continue the long, smelly trek back home, all the while cursing myself for letting Bloomsbury splinter under my skin when I expected nothing less from a bloody Cambridge boy.

# CHAPTER NINE

APRIL GIVES WAY to May, with naught but play rehearsals and Maggie's glares and Inigo's slow, but certain, recovery, until one day, there is a letter addressed to me at breakfast. Bloomsbury's manservant, Cooper, eyes the parchment as though it is a poisonous snake set loose in his master's house.

"I found this wedged beneath the door this morning," he says. But there's a question behind his words: *Who would want to contact you?*

The letter sits in my pocket, heavy as a stone. Only once we're back in the secure space of Inigo's chamber do I slide my fingernail beneath the wax seal.

The paper unfurls. Five pennies go rolling across the floor.

*I can explain. Meet me tonight at the Widow's Bull*
*alehouse in Deptford after eleven. Bring no one.*
*Kit*

I abruptly fold the note in half, hiding the words.

"Well, what's it say?" Inigo elbows me. "Show me—I haven't had much excitement these past few weeks, you know."

Reluctantly, I unfold the edges and let him and Maggie read over my shoulders, resisting the urge to snatch it from their eyes again. Inigo rubs his chin, his brows knitted together. Though the hollows of his collarbones jut far deeper than before, he's been able to walk small distances with the help of a cane. "By God, 'tis a strange request, no? Marlowe and you usually drink at the Seven Stars."

My face falls into my hands. "*That's* what strikes you as strange about this? The alehouse?"

"Is there something else strange about it?" Inigo says with a shrug. "You're always meeting him somewhere. I'm surprised you haven't seen him sooner."

I bite the inside of my cheek so hard, I taste blood. Inigo doesn't even know the half of it. Marlowe *shouldn't* have been able to find me here. Not in a noble lord's hidden house kept from city record. Why does Marlowe want me to meet him? I frantically think on everyone I've talked to and all that I've done since he threatened me. Have I somehow let slip his secret business—his business involving the queen—and am now about to pay the price?

"Will." Maggie's voice pulls me from panic. "Nothing good can come of this. Inigo's nearly himself again. Bloomsbury's play is opening soon. After, you'll be handed a plump purse. Why gamble with all that?"

Now that's a fair and persuasive point. There shall be no turning back from whatever Marlowe is about to divulge. It would be far wiser to tear up the letter and forget he ever tried to reach me. Better still to gather Inigo and Maggie and leave

London with its dark secrets behind entirely. To hell with Marlowe and Bloomsbury and all the other people who tug me into their dark intrigues and give me no lantern to light my way. I am tired of being left in the dark.

"You're right. 'Tis madness to go." I refold the letter and toss it into the fire.

Inigo and Maggie sag with relief. They move on to another topic, and I nod and respond in all the ways they expect, watching the parchment's edges curl and blacken before bursting into flame.

I don't need the letter anymore. I've already memorized the time and place.

After night has fallen, I sneak away to the Thames. A flock of small boats bobs in the shallows, their wherrymen reposing on the spindly dock. 'Tis so late that most of London's merrymakers have already returned from the brothels and alehouses and other entertainments on the south bank.

"Deptford, if you will."

The wherryman takes Marlowe's coins in a weathered palm without a word and pushes off.

The river is a black ribbon beneath the lantern at the boat's prow. Out on the water the silence is smothering. I grasp my cross and perch on the edge of my seat, ready to run. Not that there's anywhere to run out here. As we course eastward, the Tower of London looms into view. Waves flow beyond a rusted gate into the keep's darkened heart. Wisps of orange light flicker deep in the tunnel, like flames in a dragon's throat.

Rumor has it the Tower is where Queen Elizabeth's most treasonous enemies are kept. A shudder inches through me as we glide past the hulking walls.

Was coming here alone the right thing to do?

When the boat scrapes the river bottom just beyond the city's limits, my heart pounds in my throat. 'Tis rare for me to venture this far out along the south bank, and its reputation precedes it. 'Tis a place for swindlers and thieves, the sort who dress nice and are more like to knife a man in his back than in his heart.

The wherryman eyes me curiously. "Need me to wait fer ye, lad?"

I nearly tell him no and then think better of it. I'm all too aware I could be walking into a trap. Marlowe knows I've never once ignored a summons from him. Why would I start now, when my heart is burning with questions?

I head away from the docks, one hand clutching the cross in my inner pocket and the other clutching a dagger I nicked from Maggie. I walk briskly, shoulders hunched, until I spot a sign with a faded red boar upon it. Oily light pours from the building's windows, barely keeping the shadows at bay. I take a long, shuddering breath, set back my shoulders, and push open the battered door.

The room is occupied by a single stooped figure, who lifts his head hopefully when I enter.

Marlowe, his eyes red-rimmed, his hair unwashed.

"You came," he whispers.

I eye the empty cups around him and the two full ones

waiting, untouched. "Aye. Looks like you've been here a spell."

His lips twist. "Elias—"

"Don't." My hand drifts to my belt, toward Maggie's dagger.

Marlowe spies the movement and pauses. "You don't trust me."

"Why should I?" My stomach churns with fear and stress and chagrin, of all things. Though he certainly no longer deserves my trust, distrusting Marlowe feels so wrong, especially when he's sitting there looking like a man who's burned through all his luck.

"This is no trap. 'Tis an offer," Marlowe insists.

"You *threatened* me. With a knife I bought you. Why would I trust you at all after that?" I hiss, relishing his wince. "I haven't said a word to anyone, if that's what this is about."

"I know you haven't," he says, his words a fevered rush. "That's why you're here. I've been thinking about your offer to work with me. I was wrong to say no. I—" He swallows, throat bobbing. "I need your help. I thought I didn't, but I do now." He leans closer, words taking on a desperate edge. "What if I had a means to make all your dreams come true? To establish your family with luxury and riches for good, only for a summer's worth of work?"

I suck in a breath. His words tempt me like a pound coin on the street, bright and impossible and there for the taking. "I'd say you were addled by your own plays."

Marlowe lowers his voice further, even though, save for the barmaid, we're the only souls present. "'Tis not about my plays. 'Tis about the queen of England."

The word "queen" sets the hairs on my arms aquiver, makes me recoil with horror and disgust. Does anyone have any more blood on her hands than this woman? 'Twas soldiers who burned all my family ever had to ash, but it was Queen Elizabeth Tudor who sent those rabid dogs to take what we had. Who put my parents in a such a penniless place that sending their eldest off for the promise of a better life with strangers was more tempting than keeping him close.

And she has come for far more people than just my own kinsmen. She murders just about anyone or any group of people who would whisper against her. The queen of England has spilled such blood in her reign, 'tis a wonder the Thames does not run red with it.

I stand. The bench pushes behind me with a rending screech. "If she's involved, I'm out. You ought to have known that."

"But you haven't heard everything—"

"I've heard enough, Kit!" Treason and queens and murder and secrets. Good God, I'm a player, not a—whatever Marlowe is asking me to be. 'Tis too dangerous, too risky. All the gold in the world can't help me if I'm dead.

Marlowe reaches for me. "Wait—"

The door bangs open, and two men barge in. One short and laughing, the other tall and silent. Both their faces are startlingly white. Whatever their business is, it must not bring them into the daylight often, which seems about right for Deptford. 'Tis nothing out of the ordinary.

Except Marlowe's body goes rigid, his cheeks pale. Before I

can react, he yanks my cloak and pulls me closer. "Elias, you've got to leave, quick as you can, all right?"

I push my hair from my eyes with an unsteady hand, taking in the urgency in his expression, a hideous pressure building in my chest.

A shadow cuts over the table. One of the men is already here. "Mind if we join ye?"

Marlowe's expression shifts to sunshine at once—he's quite the player when he wants to be—and he gestures broadly to the vacant space. "Of course. My friend and I were just leaving."

The man's stare lingers on our full ale cups. "Don't seem like you're ready to go."

Marlowe's smile grows cloying. "We're quick drinkers."

I sink back on the bench, my legs jelly, pulse drumming in my ears. I remember the strange men from before. How the playwright's face blanched at the sight of them and he hurried me out the door. Now another dangerous man is seated beside me. All my instincts scream at me to run, except judging from Marlowe's tight smile, there's nowhere to go. *Keep it together!* I close my eyes, take a steadying moment, and reach for my cup. Except my shaking hands betray me, and I knock it aside instead.

Ale spills across my bench mate.

"Christ, boy, watch it!" The man leaps back with a snarl, and gold flashes at his belt. There's a sword at his hip in a gilded scabbard with a solar motif, the pommel itself a golden sun with piercing rays. It glitters in the candlelight, demanding to be noticed. 'Tis nothing like the blades the English nobles wear. No matter what angle I behold it from, the tiny sun blinds me. If I tilt my head just so, I can almost see a flame dancing beneath its surface. A sinister feeling smolders in my gut.

"My apologies, good sir."

The man catches my chin, forcing me to look at him. He smiles mockingly. "My face is up here."

A shout shatters the quiet.

Before I can process the sound, Marlowe dives across the table and shoves me to the floor. Above me, he and the two men brawl, bowling over tables and chairs like bandogs hungry for blood, great puddles of ale splashing everywhere. I scramble to my feet amidst the stomping boots, dagger drawn.

"Kit!"

My friend's attention snaps toward me, eyes wide. "Watch it!"

I barely dodge a swing from the tall man before the shorter man lunges at me with a knife. My horrified face is reflected in his eyes.

A weight collides into my side, pushing me away. Marlowe.

There's a feral scream—a thud—and then the barmaid is shouting at everyone to get out for God's sake, her apron a mess of dark crimson that looks like the pig's blood Henslowe uses for false beheadings at the Rose Theatre.

I scuttle on hands and knees, my heart thrashing. A slaughterhouse smell makes me dizzy. Through a gap betwixt the chair legs I spy the body sprawling on the floor awash in even more crimson.

His face is a great mess of blood, and only one glassy eye stares, open and unseeing.

I crawl beside the greatest playwright of London; an anguished sound rips from my throat, but there's no mistaking it.

Kit Marlowe is dead of a knife to the eye.

# CHAPTER TEN

"MURDER! MURDER MOST foul!" the barmaid cries over and over again.

I focus on a spot left of Marlowe's ear. I can't look at the wound again. When I try to, my vision blurs and my breath hitches.

"Kit?" I whisper, clasping his bloodied hand to my chest.

His lips part. A bubble of blood swells and pops. The hand falls away with a thunk, and the barmaid's screams begin anew.

He's already gone.

In the plays, people take eons to die. There are monologues and final confessions and curses, time enough for closure. In truth, death is quick as snuffing out a candle. Burning bright one moment and then dark and still the next.

No, Marlowe's not merely gone. He's *murdered*. And the murderer is still about.

My head snaps up.

The tavern is empty, the strange men gone. Ale dribbles slowly from the table's edge, the liquid drip-drip-dripping into the blood spreading from Marlowe's head in a grisly corona.

My shaking fingers search his pockets. I can't know—I'll

never know—what offer of his summoned me here tonight, but perhaps there's a chance, a *hope*—

The door bursts open. The City Guard.

The inside of Marlowe's doublet is still warm. My hand closes around a square of parchment and a smooth phial.

"You there! With the body!"

I seize the items and bolt, skidding out on the slick blood. The letter I found in Marlowe's pocket slips from my grip and tumbles—I glimpse my name, Will Hughes, on the paper—but there's no time to go back. The kitchen door yawns open. I sprint outside to the alley's safety beyond and press my sticky back against the building, trying and failing to control the sobbing gasps tearing through my chest. I ought to do something. But what? Marlowe is the one I'd turn to for questions like these, the way I turned to him for everything ever since he took me in from the streets as a terrified London newcomer, saying I reminded him too much of his younger brothers to ignore. This time I can't ask Marlowe because he's there, on the floor, with that great ragged hole in his face because I got in the way, and he pushed me aside, and now he's—

I stumble sideways, vomiting. Only when I wipe my mouth and look up do I realize something vital.

I'm not alone.

At the alley's end, a short man pauses while cleaning a bloodied dagger with the edge of his cloak, scowling as though he's been tasked with removing a particularly odious dead thing from his doorway. He stands beside a tall, somber man in a sweeping cloak, the hem trimmed in Marlowe's blood.

When he snaps toward me, I catch the gold flashing at his belt. The murderers.

For a moment, we all freeze, then their faces harden in recognition.

The shorter man sprints after me as I scramble over the woodpile blocking my escape. His blade tears through my cloak and pins the fabric, barely missing my leg and choking me. I frantically untie the cloak clasp and wriggle free. I clear the woodpile, landing on scattered logs on the other side, and start running, hurtling past the brothels and dockyards until I reach the darkness of the Thames. Each pounding step is loud as a heartbeat.

My wherryman reposes in his boat, nursing a cup. I sprint down the dock, ancient boards shuddering beneath my feet. "They're after me! *Make haste!*"

The wherryman startles so hard, his cup plummets into the water. With a stream of oaths and curses he pushes off before I reach the boat. I wave at him, shouting, "Wait, it's me! The lad who paid you to wait!"

But he does not stop.

'Tis only after the boat is well gone from sight I understand why.

On the mirror-dark surface of the Thames, I see that I'm soaked through with Marlowe's blood.

The sky already ripples pink when I curl up in Bloomsbury's empty playhouse beneath the creaking trees. I managed to lose the murderers hours ago, but I can't go back to London right now. It would be foolishness to be spotted on the daylight streets. I'm drenched in blood, the possessions of a dead man in my pockets. 'Tis not a good look and is sure to raise suspicions.

Bloomsbury finds me before noon. Just as I hoped he would.

The lord kicks down the door, flushed and out of breath. When he spots my huddled form on the stage, he sags against the doorframe. "For God's sake, I've been looking *everywhere* for you. Maggie was about to stab me."

I stand, Maggie's dagger in my hand. "And I've been waiting for you."

Bloomsbury freezes. He takes in the menacing angle of the blade and my bloodstains. His hand searches for a sword pommel that isn't there. Finding nothing, he drags a hand through his already disheveled hair and laughs, of all things. "Your form is utter rubbish, you know."

His laughter singes something in me, and I hurl forward, blade first. He barely sidesteps my wild lunge. I round on him again. He seizes the log that stands in as a swaddled baby in *The Most Lamentable Tragedy of Abelard and Heloise*. My dagger buries deep into the wood over his heart. He jerks the log back, near tearing the dagger from my grasp. I hang on tight and crash into the wall.

"Hughes, stop this!"

"*No!*" I fly at him once more.

This time Bloomsbury is ready for me.

He smashes the log into my chest. The wind squeezes from my lungs with an oof, and my limbs go numb. I swipe at him again, feeling less like a furious avenger and more like a kitten too clumsy to swat a fly, until I slump to my knees, then puddle across the floor, gasping.

Bloomsbury relieves me of my blade as gingerly as one might remove a pair of shears from a toddler's fist. He then straddles me, Maggie's stolen dagger clutched expertly in his hand. Damn it all, of course he's had training with a blade. Why did I ever think I could best him addled without sleep and mad with grief? Even still, I'll not go down like a coward.

I arch back, baring the column of my throat. "Kill me then!"

His brow furrows. "Why on God's green earth would I do that?"

"I questioned your honor. Why wouldn't you?"

His eyes grow stormy, something unfamiliar rolling in their depths. "I'm no monster, as much as you'd like me to be one." His weight lifts; I hear the clatter of the dagger tossed across the room.

Anger. That's what I'm seeing in him. For all my needling and teasing these past weeks, I've never made him angry before. The sight grounds me, and I remind myself that I'm very much alive and unharmed, even though I've assaulted a noble lord. Men are killed every day for lesser crimes than the one I've just committed.

I swallow and sit up. Bloomsbury appraises me with crossed arms and sleeves pushed past his elbows, the anger still lingering in the iron of his voice. "Out with it, Hughes. Where did you go last night? Why are you covered in blood?" More softly he asks, "Are you wounded?"

All at once the fire leaves me. I rub the aching space between my eyebrows, too exhausted and hurt and heartsore to fight anymore. "Did you hear the news from Deptford?"

He frowns. "Why would I know aught about Deptford?"

I bite my lip so hard, my mouth blooms with blood. Because that's the truth, isn't it? Kit's only another bloke murdered by knifepoint at an alehouse. A nightly occurrence in this blasted city. I wipe my eyes on my forearm and only succeed in smearing more filth on my face. "Christopher Marlowe was killed there last night."

Bloomsbury's whole demeanor changes. He softens, line by line, until he's no longer a lord but the lad I saw on horseback, the sun on his cheeks and the wind in his hair. "Oh, Will. I didn't—" He moves forward as though to comfort me.

I jerk away. "Is this your doing?"

"Me?" He clasps a hand to his chest, as though I could possibly mean anyone else.

"Aye, you! None of this trouble started until I met you and Marlowe told me you couldn't be trusted!"

Rather than pale with fear or grow red with rage, Bloomsbury simply sighs and drags a hand through his hair. I've never seen it mussed before. And he's wearing two different boots, like he left in a hurry. I stare at the mismatched colors as he speaks, batting aside a difficult feeling. "Marlowe. I—*zounds*. I'm sorry. I would never order the murder of a man." The pity in his eyes is overwhelming. "I know you don't trust me, but surely you know that, don't you?"

I squeeze my hands against my face. Hot, angry tears press

against my palms, stinging my cheeks as the awful truth crashes into me over and over again.

I couldn't save Marlowe. Just how I couldn't save Inigo and Maggie from the City Guard. Or the other kidnapped boys. I was *right there*, and I couldn't do a single thing. Hell, I was armed! If Kit hadn't pushed me away, if he had trusted me to mind myself for one goddamn time, then maybe he'd—maybe—

I take in a great, ugly sniffle and drag my sleeve beneath my nose. Bloomsbury holds out a handkerchief before I can wipe my hands on my filthy breeches. 'Tis a ridiculous thing, all frothy lace and embroidered flowers. When I don't take the fabric, he stuffs it into my hand even though I'm disgusting. I wipe my sniveling nose and think.

If Bloomsbury has not conspired to kill Marlowe, then who did?

"May I ask you a question?" he asks gently after long minutes have passed.

I shrug, knowing he'll ask regardless of what I say.

"Why did you leave to see Marlowe last night without telling a soul?"

I say nothing. Bloomsbury may have come here all half-dressed and urgent to find me, but it's not because he cares. It's because I'm useful to him. Without me, his play won't happen. Without me, Maggie will make his life a living hell, because that's the kind of friend she is. He doesn't deserve to know about the horror and shame wrestling in my gut, making me sick.

He clears his throat and twists his hands. "Hughes, I'm not

asking because I wish you harm. I ask because I . . . have not been entirely honest with you about why you're working for me."

I stare at his nervous fingers. Then his face.

Pink rushes into his cheeks. "Marlowe was right to tell you not to trust me. My family is in disgrace with the queen."

"Then why in God's name would you put on an illegal play right beneath the queen's nose? Surely disobeying her orders is not the best way to regain her favor." I knew Bloomsbury was keeping secrets, but I've no idea why he's bringing all this up now. Marlowe is dead, and somehow he's gone and made the event all about himself and the bloody queen.

Bloomsbury bites his lip and scoots closer, as if he needs me to believe him. "Based on what you've said—or rather, not said—and my own sense of the man, I believe Christopher Marlowe is involved in something sinister." He stares at me as if he expects a grand reaction—a gasp or a cry or some other measure of shock.

I roll my eyes. Obviously, Marlowe is—my heart clenches—was involved with something sinister. I have not yet considered what his murder means, but I know it means nothing good. He brought me well beyond city limits to tell me of a secret bargain involving the queen—and was killed minutes later. Is this daft lord only realizing this now? Perhaps Cambridge does a lot less book-learning than I had been led to believe.

Because Bloomsbury won't stop looking at me like a dog who knows his master holds a treat, and I know he shall not leave me alone until I give him a bone to gnaw on, I fish out the phial I found on Marlowe.

"When Marlowe was killed, he had this in his pocket. Perhaps you've seen something like it before?"

He holds the phial aloft. A shaft of sunlight catches the glass but doesn't penetrate the liquid. The thickness seems unnatural. The hairs on the back of my neck bristle.

"This"—he gives the phial a shake—"is likely poison."

A *spy*. That's what Maggie said Marlowe was, and after what happened last night, I'm starting to believe her. Who else but a spy would carry poison? Not to mention that the men who murdered Marlowe knew who he was, and, judging from the fear on Marlowe's face, he knew who they were as well.

Will the men who murdered him come for me next? They saw me in Deptford. Like a fool I went there as myself, nary a disguise in sight. Then there's the letter with my name on it. The letter I left sitting on the alehouse floor for anyone to find.

Aye, Will Hughes may not be my true name, but it's the name everyone in London knows me by. Dread threads through my ribs, hobbling my breath. How long will it take them to ask around and find the boy from the Rose Theatre?

A rattling sound spooks me, and it takes a moment to register 'tis my own teeth. My body shivers with sudden cold.

"Will?" Bloomsbury says in a way that implies 'tis not the first time he's called my name. "What is it?"

I shake my head. I'm not daft. Marlowe asked me about secret business involving the queen, and I'll not speak about the queen to a courtier in her royal court. I should keep my distance from Bloomsbury. But there's something in his concerned look that makes me want to tell him things—like he might truly be worried and not just because the mess I've stumbled into could sully his name as much as mine.

Bloomsbury speaks in a tone he must save for spooked horses. "You can tell me if you want. But it's quite all right if you don't."

Our eyes meet. The silence stretches until it's vast as the ocean. 'Tis the fact that he gives me a choice at all that undoes me. I nod once and spill the entire story, starting with the strange men Marlowe met in secret at the Seven Stars. I feel lighter at once, like the knowledge was a too-heavy satchel stooping my shoulders.

When I'm done explaining what happened, Bloomsbury is on his feet, pacing, his eyes still fastened upon that damn phial as though it is the answer to all his prayers, which is decidedly not the reaction I had expected. "So Christopher Marlowe asked you to help with something involving Queen Elizabeth, and he'd been meeting strangers covertly before. Except last night he was killed by different strange men who knew exactly when and where to find him. You think he might've been a spy." Bloomsbury gives me a knowing look, slick as a player. "Did he say if he was working for or against the queen?"

I open my mouth, except nothing comes out because . . . I don't know. I assumed Marlowe was working for the queen since working against her is a great way to end up dead. But when I think of Marlowe's cheeky, blasphemous plays, all the secrets he's kept from me, suddenly I'm not certain I knew anything true about Kit Marlowe at all.

And, because of me, now I'll never know.

"I'm not sure. He didn't say," I whisper.

Bloomsbury nods, half smiling. "That's what I thought. I think there's a way for us to find the answer. Help me solve this mystery, Hughes."

I choke back a laugh. Pursuing the matter further? Has this lord utterly lost his mind? "I think not. Minding your play is more than enough excitement for me, my lord." I heave myself to my feet and head to the door.

The damn fool runs to the door and throws himself against it, ruining my exit. His eyes have a glassy, wild gleam to them. "I'm stopping the play. If you want your money, you'll have to work with me on this instead."

At first I am speechless. Then anger roars through me. My fists ball. "Why, you lying—"

He holds up a hand. "I was supposed to pay you ten pounds for the play, yes? I shall pay you a hundred pounds if you help me with this instead."

And, just like that, I'm speechless again for entirely different reasons. *A hundred pounds?* Why, 'tis an unthinkable sum! What does one even do with a hundred pounds? Commission a gold statue of themselves? One thing I've learned from London is this: coin begets more coin. If I return to my family with this sum, we could do whatever we wished. Find a plot of land and live like kings and queens.

What could Bloomsbury want badly enough to pay this much for? To risk his life for?

I rub the back of my neck without making eye contact. "Why? One man is already dead."

His expression grows guarded, openness gone. "If my family were back in the queen's favor . . . it would solve more than one problem for me. Let us leave it at that. We could both get what we want if this phial holds what I believe it holds."

I cross my arms, pricklier than a hedgehog. "What makes you presume all I want is money?" I ought to keep my mouth shut—a hundred pounds is more than I could make doing anything else at all, more than I'd make in my entire life—but the thought of this lord thinking I'll do whatever he asks as long as the price is high enough rankles me for reasons I cannot put into words.

"I never presumed coin was all you sought." He holds my gaze for so long, I fight the urge to glance away. "You also want to know if you could've saved him."

I curl into myself so tightly, my joints crack. The guilt eats me alive like a sickness, growing bigger and more painful with each passing hour. Marlowe, pushing me aside, taking the blade that should've been mine. If I'd gotten there earlier—if I knew how to wield a dagger as well as Maggie can—it could've all been different. I wipe at my burning eyes with an angry gesture. "That's none of your damn business, Bloomsbury! You don't know me at all."

He stands, smiling sadly. "No, I don't know you. But I do know what it's like to feel as if you've failed someone you care about."

I meet his gaze again, looking for his judgment or pity, but there's nothing save grief. A memory he's reliving right there at the surface, hiding just beyond my grasp. Curiosity tugs at me—who has he failed in the past? Why does it still haunt him?

"So are you in?" he asks. "I can't promise you'll find the answers you want, but I can promise to make helping me worth your while."

Answers. The idea of them unspools the questions I've held fast. What was Marlowe involved in? And why did he keep it from me until the night he was killed? Am I in danger because I've rubbed elbows with the wrong playwright?

I swear softly. *Damn it, Kit. You were hurt under my arm.*

"Well?" Bloomsbury watches me with a keenness that borders on unsettling.

I should not trust him. It is the obvious and only path. And yet . . .

He has not given me a reason to mistrust him.

Of course, he's a noble, and of course he's keeping secrets from me, just as I keep mine from him. Except . . . each time he has given me his word, he has kept his promises. Which is more than I can say about most blokes, including myself. I wouldn't go as far to say I trust him, but he's trusted me, and that means a lot.

Finally, I shake out my hand and clasp his. "Fine. If poison is within that phial, then I'm yours."

## CHAPTER ELEVEN

FOR THE FIRST time, I am allowed into Bloomsbury's laboratory.

When I enter the forbidden room, freshly scrubbed and stinking of lavender, Maggie assaults me. "You promise-breaker! I told you not to go to Marlowe!"

Inigo tugs her off me. "Never mind her."

Maggie punches me with her free fist. "We thought you'd *died*."

"And Marlowe did die!" I snap, almost, but not quite, too exhausted to be angry. When I climbed from the washbasin and wiped my body dry, the cloth was pink. So I had to call for another bath, and then another, until my skin stung and the verdigris of Marlowe's blood was finally gone.

Bloomsbury's long-suffering sigh eases the tension. "For God's sake, what have I said about fighting in the laboratory?" Each word is punctuated by a stabbing finger.

Away from his theater, Bloomsbury has already returned to his natural state as a middle-aged man with a stick up his arse. Truly, I have never met someone who has so clearly missed his calling to become a schoolmaster for unruly boys. Though I shudder to think what sort of lessons a schoolmaster would teach in a room such as this one. Sharp instruments, made sinister by their strangeness, hang on the wall. Shelves sag with glittering crystal, small dusty bones, and a mess of glassware dripping shimmering liquids. Somehow, there's even more plants drying upside down than in the rest of the house. A rough-hewn table sits in the center of it all, a small work space cleared around Marlowe's phial.

"He hasn't figured out what the stuff is yet," Maggie says. "We ought to try it on something. There's a litter of kittens out near the woodshed."

Bloomsbury won't even give her the dignity of a scandalized look. "I am *not* a murderer of kittens."

Maggie is entirely unrepentant. "Fine, a rat, then."

Bloomsbury looks heavenward and sighs. "Very well. If you catch a rat, we'll see what happens."

"Excellent." Maggie has already pulled her leather gloves on. "Inigo, come with me."

Bloomsbury does not ask me to leave, so I make no effort to do so. I've not forgotten how his face lit up like midsummer when he saw the phial. Anyone would be rightly suspicious of someone who delights in murderous substances. He's let slip some of his secrets, but I'm not foolish enough to think he's spilled them all.

"Did you learn all this at Cambridge?" I gesture to the plants and instruments. "Seems like odd work for a playwright."

Bloomsbury frowns and uses a strange convex glass to examine the phial. "No, from my father. He used to conduct alchemical experiments for the queen. How to make fire burn brighter, weaken her enemies' blood through water."

My stomach flips, the hair prickling on my arms. "And that's what you're doing here? Making weapons for the queen?"

The glass falls from his hand with a clatter. "God no! The midwives in our local villages taught me about using healing plants, and my work is to combine that with alchemy to help people. I am *nothing* like my father!"

His voice is raised, the angry storm back in his eyes. I raise my hand placatingly and touch the healed spot on my head. "By the sounds of it, that's something we all ought to be grateful for. You say your father used to practice alchemy. What happened?" I shouldn't ask, not based on how the mere mention of his parent sent a vein in his forehead throbbing, but I can't help myself. Bloomsbury's secrets are like a locked treasure chest, and the more he hints at what's inside, the more I want to pick the lock and learn for myself what riches he keeps hidden.

A muscle flexes in his jaw. "Something went wrong. It's why the queen banished him from court."

I lean forward, as eager for details as a dog for table scraps. "Is that so?"

"They had disagreements over how the Crown should manage its vast empire."

I grip the edge of the table, hard. "Like what they're doing in the countryside? Pushing the common people from their lands and giving it to the nobles?"

Bloomsbury stills. His eyes lock on mine with an intensity I haven't witnessed before. "Yes. What would a boy from London know about the enclosures and riots in the commons, Hughes?"

Maggie barges in, startling us both. Behind her, Inigo holds a lid fast to a cooking pot. She shoves a great deal of Bloomsbury's instruments to the side and motions for Inigo to put the pot down smack in the table's center. She props her elbow on the pot, holding it firmly shut. Scrabbling sounds from within. "You promised us an experiment, your lordship."

"So I did," Bloomsbury agrees reluctantly, a queasy look on his face. "Though this will hardly give answers. We won't know where the substance is from or how it works or—"

Maggie makes a fart noise. "Just try it." She grabs the rat with her gloved hand, and it makes a tremendous clatter, all flailing limbs and snapping teeth.

Bloomsbury tilts a single drop of liquid to the rat's muzzle.

For a breath nothing happens. And then convulsions shake the small body. Foam spurts from the creature's mouth. Even Maggie lets out an oath and springs away. Within seconds the rat lies dead.

Bloomsbury kicks his chair back, face green. "It's poison, all right."

No one says a word, but I know we're all thinking it.

What would the most popular playwright in London be doing with a bottle of deadly poison?

And, more importantly, who was it intended for?

"We should tell the queen," Inigo whispers. "This is far above the likes of us."

Maggie rolls her eyes. "If we appear at Whitehall Palace

with poison, we'll be arrested and executed before we finish crying 'Wait!' 'Tis like I've been saying—many folks want to see dear old Elizabeth dead. Or did you lot forget?"

Indeed, I have not. I have heard whispers of gowns arriving to the palace parceled with sharp-toothed serpents, of foreign diplomats nodding off to sleep in their English beds never to wake again. Queen Elizabeth even murdered her own cousin, Mary, after she got wind of her Catholic cousin's ploy to dethrone her. It was said that it took more than one strike to part Mary's head from her neck, and when the executioner lifted her bloody head from its wig, it screamed curses in Latin.

Bloomsbury stands. He looks at all of us in turn, his gaze lingering the longest on me. Oh no. He's on the verge of administering a rousing speech. "A man is dead because he carried this phial, and I wish to know why. Maggie, Inigo, I shall pay you handsomely if you will assist us in uncovering this mystery."

Maggie bursts into a fit of laughter which quickly passes once she realizes Bloomsbury is entirely serious. She flutters the remaining fingers of her scarred hand. "The queen already got half my hand. I'll not give her the rest of me next."

"I won't go either," Inigo adds softly. "It's time to go back to our old life."

Our old life. Inigo says it as though there is an old life for me to return to, with the playhouses still closed for the plague and Marlowe dead and his secrets howling at me from beyond the grave.

*He pushed me out of the way.*

I keep replaying the moment when Marlowe could've saved himself or saved me, and he chose me. For all his lies and how he refused to share his secrets, Kit was still looking out for me after all. My throat aches. Surely, I at least owe him the dignity of discovering the reason behind his death.

I peer up from beneath my eyelashes to Bloomsbury.

Maggie spies the movement and groans. "No, Will, don't—"

"I have already given Lord Bloomsbury my word. I'm going to help him."

Maggie's sound of disgust grates on my ears. I don't have to look up to know Inigo is staring with round, tremulous eyes.

Bloomsbury bows his head. "As you wish. I shall give you several pounds with which to establish yourselves."

"We don't need your coin!" Maggie snarls.

"'Tis coin. We always need coin," Inigo amends in a small voice.

"*Fine.*" Maggie stomps her foot. "We shall take the coin and be on our way."

I watch them ready to leave, a curious helplessness stealing over me. I didn't expect them to say no, not after all we've been through, and the thought of losing someone else today makes my throat close tight. "I'll find you when I solve this mystery, I swear."

Maggie spins around and stabs her finger into my chest. "No, you won't. You'll be murdered following this lord's mad schemes, or you'll invent another reason for yourself to play the hero and abandon everyone who cares about you."

Her words strike a sudden hurt in me, as if I've bashed my elbow on the table. "'Tis not true! After this I'll find you and then finally find my family—"

Maggie laughs meanly. "Your family *gave you away*, Hughes. You were as useless to them as you were to us when we needed you!"

Her words open up a chasm in me. I'm eight years old again, calling for my mother that first night alone, crying for her to come back for me. How every night I'd fall asleep in tears praying the next day would be the one where my parents realized they'd made a mistake, that they'd appear on the horizon and take me back.

They never did.

"That's not true." Except my words wobble; my eyes burn.

Maggie sneers and bites deeper, sensing weakness. "You *know* it's true. If you wanted to reunite with them so badly, you would've left ages ago."

I swallow. "They need the money—"

She bursts into horrible cruel laughter. "If they truly care for you, they won't care about the bloody money!"

A roar tears from my mouth, something in me snapping, and suddenly I'm on top of Maggie, pinning her to the floor, tools and herbs falling all around me.

"That's not true!" I shout at her shocked face. "You take it back!"

"For God's sake." Bloomsbury pulls me away, his mouth a grim slash. "What did I say about fighting in the laboratory? Can any of you listen?"

Inigo helps Maggie up, his eyes wide as an owl's. "Will did save us this past time," he says, ever the peacekeeper. "I would've died without his help."

"Only after he used us like a chamber pot!" Maggie rounds on me again. "You've never cared for a single soul other than yourself. I doubt you even know *how* to care for anyone else, but you think you do and that's even worse!"

I grind my teeth and lunge at her again, but Bloomsbury's arm circles my waist, holding me back. Maggie sneers. "Now that you've latched on to this pampered prince's leg, you've no use for us. And *fine*. But I want to make one thing clear." She leans forward, baring her teeth. "This time you're not leaving us. We're leaving *you*."

And then she spits in my face.

I feel Bloomsbury's too-hot stare like a brand, watching how Maggie's words slip betwixt my ribs straight into the softest parts of me.

"You don't know a goddamn thing about where I'm from." I wipe the spit from my face with deliberate slowness, steeling my heart against the angry hurt that threatens to overrun it like the Thames spilling from its banks. Me and Maggie have fought before but not like this. This is a step beyond, a place we can't come back from.

Maggie's eyes grow wild. "I know more than you think!"

Inigo tugs her away. "That's enough now."

"Inigo—" I start.

He raises a hand, eyes on the floor. "Just—don't, all right? Not now."

Inigo's soft words cut through to my bones.

They're leaving. They're truly leaving me. My vision splatters with black spots, and I bite down on the soft part of my thumb as hard as I can, fighting the memory of those lonely nights, how the fierce, flickering hope someone would come for me dimmed each day I drew closer to London, until, eventually, the city snuffed it from me entirely.

I'm alone again.

Even though it makes my heart splinter, I turn away from Maggie and Inigo and everything else I know to Bloomsbury's astonished face. "I'm ready to leave whenever it pleases you, my lord."

# June 1593
## Westminster, London

*I saw and liked; I liked but lovèd not;*
*I loved, but straight did not what Love decreed:*
*At length to Love's decrees I, forced, agreed,*
*Yet with repining at so partial lot. . . .*
*I call it praise to suffer tyranny,*
*And now employ the remnant of my wit*
*To make myself believe that all is well,*
*While with a feeling skill I paint my hell.*

—SIR PHILIP SIDNEY,
from *Astrophel and Stella*: "Sonnet 2"

# CHAPTER TWELVE

"DO YOU PREFER the green or the brown doublet today, Lord Hughes?"

Late-morning sunlight blinds me as maids snap back heavy plush curtains. Another pours water into my washbasin from a long-necked jug shaped like a swan. A manservant peers up at me from the foot of the bed, eager to please as a puppy.

'Tis all rather too much first thing in the morning. "The . . . green, I suppose?"

The manservant bows and snaps his fingers. A maid fetches the green doublet, its sleeves, and chestnut breeches, and presents them to me with a flourish. Each of the silver buttons winking at me is worth my wages at the Rose Theatre for a month.

Before I can stand, the manservant is there with the washbasin, ready to snatch back my bed linens. I yank them to my chest. "I assure you, I'm quite capable of washing and dressing alone!"

I catch the bolt of confusion in the servant's eyes before his agreeable mask slips back into place. "But, Lord Hughes, it is my pleasure and duty to attend to your person."

Lord William Hughes, heir to Hughes Shipping in the port of Plymouth, is my most dangerous role ever. I've no script to read from and no stage directions to tell me when to smile or exit, or why I must give the Bloomsbury servants a show of my private bits each morning. Should I fail, the stakes are dire; impersonating a man of the noble class is a crime punishable by death. Though to be fair, most of the crimes in England are punishable by death.

Everything I'm doing here is the utter opposite of my rules for survival in London, and I still can't believe I let bloody Bloomsbury cajole me into this charade.

"Lord Hughes?" the servant prompts, menacing me with the soap. "Shall I begin?"

"I will wash *alone*, thank you." The maids curtsy and leave, but the indomitable manservant remains, still holding the soap. "You too," I add.

Bloomsbury decided investigating the likelihood of someone offing the queen would work best if I lived in his family's official London quarters. His household is now under the impression one of his school friends is visiting for business. The act is exhausting. I may be trussed up like a Twelfth Night goose, but I am still a street rat and used to slipping through life unseen. Here, before I finish a sneeze, a servant is there with a handkerchief. I wonder what happens when the queen sneezes; does the lucky servant stash her boogers away for good fortune?

I'm escorted into a vast dining hall, where Bloomsbury heads an ornately carved table set for twenty, an open book on his lap, perfectly combed chestnut hair hiding his face. Like every meal here, breakfast is a lavish and wasteful affair. There are two kinds of bread, five jars of preserves, and an entire cold roasted chicken with herbs stuffed beneath its skin. Best yet, there's not a single weevil in sight! A feast like this would feed my family for an entire week, and with a pinch of guilt, I wonder what they'd think to see me now. Would they understand why I'm working with Bloomsbury, one of the nobles who conspired to steal our land? Would they see how I'm only doing this for them? Or are some sins beyond forgiveness?

"Ah, there you are!" Bloomsbury snaps the book shut. "It's about time."

I seize a slice of bread and spread it aggressively with plum preserves, shaking off my dark thoughts. He might be at ease here, dining in the sight and earshot of at least ten servants, but I'm certainly not. "If I had been able to dress myself, I would've been here a whole lot faster."

Bloomsbury laughs loudly and leans closer. "Perhaps, but Lord Hughes would never deign to dress himself if he could afford not to," he whispers too softly for the servants to overhear. "Please do not draw attention to yourself by being quarrelsome."

His lavender scent washes over me. I wave it away like a cloud of gnats, scowling. "I can't help it. My very nature is quarrelsome. No one believes that I am a lord, my lord."

"They will if you stop calling me *my lord*. As I have asked you. Repeatedly."

It's only been three days, but Bloomsbury has made each

of them feel like a year. When he demands that his manservant, Cooper, ready the library for us again, it takes everything I've got left not to scream.

"Why don't we go back to the scene of Marlowe's murder?" I say as the library doors shut behind us. "We might actually learn something there."

Bloomsbury sighs as though I'm a very dimwitted hound who cannot find his own tail. "I've told you, sneaking and thieving is no way to solve a complicated problem. It's best if we examine the properties of the poison in the phial, *then* investigate which merchants sell its parts, *and then* we start talking to people who work there about their customers."

Zounds, if we do things his way, we won't get anywhere until winter! "My lord, I must disagree. Thieving and sneaking is exactly what this investigation needs!" I'm on my feet, pacing past the hundreds of books I can barely read, my fancy clothes rubbing me in all the wrong places. If I have to spend another afternoon in this frigid, dim coffin, I shall gladly hurl myself before the next carriage which clamors down the street. "Mayhap you're used to being the smartest bloke in the room, but you don't know a damn thing about the world Marlowe and I live in. If you make me spend another bloody day here, I'll die of boredom, and mark my words, I *will* haunt your ancestors forever, James!"

I freeze mid-step, my brain finally catching up with my mouth. Christ Almighty. There's quarreling with Cambridge boys for sport, and then there's *telling off a peer of the realm.* I've overstepped my boundaries so far, I'm halfway to France.

Like him or not, Bloomsbury is my patron. A single word from him, and I would be homeless and penniless on the streets of London again, all for opening my great gob of a mouth. If he wants to do a bad job with this investigation, that's his business and not mine. Even though I can't help but feel that the more time we squander shut up inside, the colder the trail of Marlowe's murder grows and the further we get from learning anything useful.

But when I turn to apologize, Bloomsbury is grinning like a damn fool.

"What's all this?" I say suspiciously.

His face dimples as he laughs. "It's just . . . that's the first time you've called me James like I've asked you to."

My skin prickles with itchy heat. I'm embarrassed and can't for my life lay a finger on why. "Forgive me, my lord. Your awful idea made me forget my place. Using your Christian name goes against my instincts. Noble lads like you often mistake me for a privy seat."

Bloomsbury's brow rumples. Then he stabs a finger in the air, his whole face lifting. "I've the solution for this!" He lifts a tiny silver bell and rings it.

I cross my arms and make a disagreeable noise. Of course he's got a bloody solution. Of course a noble lad would assume a single errant thought of his could undo centuries of unfairness. Someone ought to saint him.

A servant appears bearing two goblets and a full silver flagon upon a gilded tray. Bloomsbury lifts both glasses and stuffs one into my hand. "This enterprise will never work if you can't imagine yourself as my equal. Therefore, I propose that we become friends."

A strangled laugh escapes me. "Friends?!"

"Think on it. I am not *your* lord, merely *a* lord, and truly, I could not do this at all without your help. We are in a symbiotic relationship."

"I beg your pardon: We're in a *what*?"

"Symbiosis. From the Greek συμβίωσις."

Honestly, he is insufferable. "Oh, it appears I missed the day all the other street urchins took Greek."

"We're partners!" Bloomsbury exclaims. He takes in my suspicious face, and his expression dims. "Or, we could be, if you wanted."

Nobles and commoners are not friends. I have had the misfortune of drinking with the Cambridge boys enough to know that noblemen think the world, and all in it, is there for their taking, and if some people are worse off than others, well, that's just what God intended, is it not?

But thus far . . . Bloomsbury has not acted like that. I take in his bottom lip, caught between his teeth like he's nervous, of all things. A twinge that feels strangely like guilt goes through me.

I set down my glass and reach for the entire flagon. "There's a different way of making friends where I'm from. Let's play a game, shall we?"

He frowns. "What sort of game?"

I thrust the wine beneath his nose and shoot him a sly look. "A question for a drink."

His frown slinks into a razor-thin smile. "Are you playing tavern games in my library?"

I offer him the flagon with a flourish. "Gentlemen first."

He considers the bottle as though he's never seen one before, an elegant finger pensively tapping his chin. "You know, in my experience, such games are played when one is trying to strike up a romance with another."

It takes a moment for me to process his words. Then heat explodes across my body, a rush of annoyance following right after. I scoff to hide how his teasing words found their mark. "I can assure you that if I were flirting, you would know it. Are you going to play or not?"

He snatches the wine from me and drinks deeply. "Your friends said you don't care about anyone other than yourself, and yet you were willing to put your life at risk to save theirs." He tilts his head, serious eyes never leaving mine. "Why would they say this about you?"

The full force of his gaze is scorching. My chest squeezes uncomfortably. Zounds, he really went for the most personal things at once, didn't he? Even still, this was my idea, and I can't back out of the game on the first question. "I owe a debt to my family," I say, thinking of my mother's rough hands on my cheeks. "Maggie and Inigo don't understand it. Working with you brings me closer to fulfilling the promises I made."

Bloomsbury nods slowly, his gaze dragging over me, cataloging my restless fingers and bouncing leg. I stop moving at once. He ducks his head, his barely-there smile back, and I realize he's been watching me as closely as I've been watching him.

We're two rival stags, creeping through the woods, daring the other to come out fully. "What is the nature of this promise?"

I snatch the flagon from him. "One question for one drink. 'Tis the only rule, my lord." The claret is, by far, the finest thing I have ever tasted. I swallow more than might be advisable before asking, "Why work with me? Surely you've scads of noble friends from Cambridge who would be more useful companions in this endeavor."

His smile wilts. "Being the son of a lord disgraced does not dispose one well to making friends." Sheepishly he adds, "In truth, my younger sister is my dearest friend."

I nearly choke. Oh God, has he been lonely, of all things? Did he insist on dragging me to stuffy Westminster for companionship? The very thought sends a splash of dread through me. Whatever his family did to disgrace themselves must be terrible indeed if only his own sister will deign to keep Bloomsbury's company.

*At least he's got someone.* I push away the bitter thought along with the flagon. Except I push it too far, and it tumbles from the table's edge to the books below. With a horrified gasp, Bloomsbury catches it just as I do. Our startled eyes meet. His hands are under mine, his heat rushing into my freezing fingers.

"You're cold," he observes. "Shall I ask Cooper to throw another log on the fire?"

I pull away like I've been scalded by a cauldron. "No, I'm warm enough. And it's your turn again."

He swallows, wiping his mouth on the back of his hand

like a commoner. "All right, then. What's the story behind the cross you're always carrying in your pocket?"

I move to touch the object without thinking. His dark eyes spy the movement, and I stop; his words send a warning ringing in my ears. "I don't know what you're talking about."

He laughs. "Oh, come on, Hughes. You're attended to by the servants of my household now. You think none of them would find it and mention it?"

"'Tis a trinket. Nothing more," I say in a brittle voice. Bloomsbury is a peer of the realm; I am the son of rebellious rioters. Should he discover the truth of my origins and dislike it, the City Guard could arrest me on suspected treason, and that would be the end. Even still, I can't ignore the small, quiet part of me that's impressed he noticed.

The laughter eases from Bloomsbury's features, replaced by something which appears suspiciously like concern. "Hughes, I—I didn't mean to offend you. It seems important to you. I was only trying to be friendly."

Eager to end this talk of my past, I swipe the flagon and take a long, messy guzzle. "My turn. What's stopping me from taking the fine things in your house, telling the City Guard about your mad scheme, and running?" The words are hot and angry and impertinent, and I ought to curse myself for saying them, but Bloomsbury's question has knocked something loose in me.

"They wouldn't believe you."

"And whyever not?"

Bloomsbury's cheeks pinken; an uncomfortable look crosses his face. I lean in closer with a smirk and feel a burst of pleasure when he recoils from me. "Well?" I say, certain I've finally gained the upper hand in our battle of wits.

He looks to the ceiling. "Surely you do not think that the difference in our stations would go unnoticed?"

It takes me a moment to grasp his meaning. When I do, the smugness slips from me like water from wax. Of course everyone would believe Bloomsbury over me; he's got four names and I've got two, and, worse, should someone pry, they'd find both my London names to be utter lies. If I ever double-crossed Bloomsbury, there's no way I'd get away with it. The frustrated anger of a caged creature courses through me. I don't know whether to storm off or curse him six different ways to hell. I settle for a silence as bone-chilling as winter.

Bloomsbury watches my reaction with a rueful expression, his bottom lip betwixt his teeth. "I have one final question." He snatches the flagon from me and takes a sip before pouring more into each of our glasses. He clasps his hands and leans forward, eyes boring into mine. The stare goes on for so long, I fight the urge to look away.

"Can you trust me?" he says softly. "We don't have to be friends, but if we wish this investigation to be successful, we shall have to trust each other at least." His finger traces the arm of my chair, stopping inches from my clenched hand. "Can you try that?"

I stare at his hand. If I uncurled my fist, we'd be touching. "That's two questions. 'Tis not how the game works."

Bloomsbury quirks an eyebrow but says nothing.

I swill the claret in my glass, watching how the red liquid

catches the fire, all the while peering up at Bloomsbury from beneath my lashes. "Trust" is such a small word but such a vast, tender thing. The silence stretches into minutes, and still he does not break it. Anyone else would've prodded me or moved on by now. I don't know what it means, save that he keeps me constantly poring over the puzzle of him, wondering what's going on behind those dark, keen eyes.

I lift my chin and my glass. "No, I can't trust you."

His composure snaps with a groan. He drags a frustrated hand through his hair. "By God, you're impossible to work with!"

My chair scrapes as I edge closer, forcing him to pay attention. "I need you to listen to me instead. You don't know all there is to know, and when you act like you do . . . that's not what a partnership looks like, James."

I expected the sound of his name to perk him up, but no, he still sits there with one hand fisted in his hair, mouth glum. "So you're agreeing to be partners? Even if you can never trust me?" It feels as though he's asking me something else, his true meaning just out of reach.

I gesture to his house, the clothes on my body, the fact that everything I have right now I only have because of his goodwill. "I can't trust you *more*," I amend softly. "Trust is . . . difficult for me, and my entire life and livelihood are already in your care. But I will consent to being partners. For now. If you promise to start listening."

"You've got my word." Bloomsbury moves to clink his glass against mine, but I pull away.

"And, as my partner, you won't complain when I investigate Marlowe's murder my way."

His lips twist, but he knocks his glass against mine anyway. "I accept this, though I do not like it."

We decide to finish the claret, and, zounds, 'tis wonderful to drink something not brewed beside a privy. I pour another glass. Then a third. Somewhere between the third and fourth, I decide I'll head back to Deptford that very night.

"A marvelous idea!" Bloomsbury exclaims tipsily when I tell him. The entire landscape of his face really does shift when he smiles. 'Tis his most striking look, in part because the expression is so strange on him. Like he hasn't had a reason to smile often in a long, long time. "You ought to take notes afterward so we have a detailed record of all that you witness."

I snort so hard, I nearly fall off my chair. "Oh yes, let's teach your horse to sing next!"

"Why not?" He lifts a finger. "Ah, but of course! How forgetful of me." He holds out a quill and a shapely bottle of ink. "I'll have Cooper bring parchment to your chamber later."

I stare at the utensils. The realization that he's absolutely serious takes a long moment to seep into my wine-addled brain. "James—no. I can't write."

He frowns like he hasn't got two good ears with which to hear me. "You cannot write?"

I shake my head. "I've never even traced a letter."

"Why, come here, then."

Somehow we are both standing at the desk. Bloomsbury

readies a quill with ink as viscous as the poison in the phial. He writes *Will Hughes* in a curling script.

"Give me your hand," he insists.

I clasp my hands behind my back. "No. I have done quite well for myself without my letters."

He snatches my wrist and forces my fingers around the quill. Then he wraps his hand around mine. "Copy your name. I'll help."

'Tis not the first time we've touched, but this time it feels different. On purpose, not by accident. Helpful instead of meddling. I cast aside the thousand excuses welling on my tongue and give in to him because what's the worst that can happen?

His hand squeezes mine, and I make an errant squiggle beside the second *l*, and ink blooms sticky and wet across the page. I drop the quill at once.

"Oh, but you almost had it!" he protests.

I'm tippled on strong wine and with his monologues on the joys of friendship. That is the only excuse for what tumbles out of my daft mouth next. "Will isn't my name."

Bloomsbury goes still for a second. I half worry he's about to call for Cooper to dump me outside the door of his fancy town house and half worry he'll ask more questions I'm not willing or ready to answer. Instead he places the quill back in my hand and asks softly, "What is it, then?"

My heartbeat staggers unevenly. "Elias Wilde."

I've never seen my true name spelled before. Somewhere to the west, in a church of rough-hewn stone, lies a book in which my name is written in a crabbed vicar's hand. It is the only place where my true name is recorded in all the world.

Bloomsbury's hand steadies me into an approximation of the sound. Soon *E-L-I-A-S* glistens on the page.

I long vowed to keep my name secret. But as I stare at it, a wonderful rush of excitement floods my fingers and toes. 'Tis madness. I should be cross with myself for this moment of weakness, for sharing this intimate truth with Bloomsbury.

When I glance at him, his expression is thoughtful. "You're not from London, are you?"

"No," I whisper. "And if you tell anyone, I'll tattle to the magistrate about your damn brothel-playhouse."

The lord steps away and gives me the smallest of bows. "I shall hold your secret close, Elias."

And, though I've no reason in the world to do so, I believe him.

I believe him with my whole heart.

# CHAPTER THIRTEEN

TURNS OUT SNEAKING and thieving is exactly what the investigation needed.

I discover one of Marlowe's killers dining at the alehouse where he was murdered the very first night I visit. Not the man with the solar scabbard, but the one who tried to stab me. His name is Ingram Frizer, and the barmaid says he dines there every night.

He does nothing of interest at all the first week I follow him—so much so, Bloomsbury drops dark, sly hints about me learning Latin to help in the library—but the eighth day I'm posted outside his building like a shade in the wee hours of the night, Frizer's door opens.

Out sneaks the bloody murderer himself, wearing a terrible disguise.

I follow him through Southwark, where he pauses at a walled graveyard beside a church. Curling mist, feathered through with moonlight, fogs from the ground. At his touch, the gates open with a rusty scream.

*Oh dear God, please not this!* I pray. But 'tis too late; Frizer casts a furtive glance over his shoulder before disappearing into the darkness.

A shudder inches down my spine. I know graveyards are a place for peace, but every time I stumble upon one, all I can think of is the rotting corpses beneath my feet and how, on the Day of Doom at the Lord's call, they shall all burst forth from their graves and walk again among the living. I think of Marlowe's body and the bloody gaping socket of his eye, and guilt burrows into me like worms. Whatever became of his body? Was he laid to rest in a proper grave, or was he tossed out with the rubbish to be scavenged by the plague carts and dumped in a mass grave where no one will ever be able to find his body to wish his spirit well?

*One thing at a time.* That's what Bloomsbury's always saying in the library whenever I urge him to go faster. I inhale and exhale slowly, gathering my calm. I couldn't save Marlowe before, but I can help him now by getting to the bottom of whatever strange, tangled mess tightened around his neck like the hangman's noose.

The cemetery gates yawn open with a low keening, a wail I feel more than hear, inviting me inside its shadows.

I gird up my courage and slip within.

The graveyard has gone utterly feral. Crooked crosses list between knotted tufts of grass. Briars vine from mossy walls and curl about the twisted yews. Several mausoleums—private tombs for wealthy families—lord over the woodland snarl like slumbering beasts.

Though I know this yard is made of mortal things—men and wood, stone and earth—the moonlight silvers the scene into something sinister. Frizer is nowhere to be found, which is truly fantastic. My eyes rove, searching for something—*anything*—

BY ANY OTHER NAME | 127

There, a faint orange light, bobbing barely above the earth.

I stifle a scream. Only my player's constitution, honed by remaining in character through hails of hazelnuts and hisses, saves me from pissing my breeches. My breath comes out in short, hard bursts.

The light wavers and drifts, then disappears beyond the threshold of a mausoleum. Impossibly, the tomb's stone door has crept open.

I blow out a steadying breath and scamper to the mausoleum before my courage wilts entirely. Just as my back presses against the wall bordering the door, Frizer steps beside me.

My pulse goes jagged, and I bite my tongue so hard, I taste blood.

Frizer has not yet glanced to his side, else he would see me at once. His dagger is sheathed in plain sight inches from my hand. A too-loud breath or a creak in my knee is all that stands between staying hidden and my acquaintance with the aforementioned dagger.

I clamp my eyes shut and send my trembling fingers skimming over the mausoleum's stone wall. My nails bite into a crumbly bit of mortar. I worry it loose and carefully, *carefully* hurl the chunk over the mausoleum's roof.

Frizer whips his head toward the sound—the opposite direction of where I'm hiding. The stink of his meat-and-mead breath washes over me before I scuttle around to the crypt's back. His shadow slices across the yard, the wicked shape of his blade doubled in the moonlight.

I fixate on the curved shadow, the silence roaring. Following

Frizer was my idea, but I'm wondering if it was a good one after all. If I was not better off in the familiar library, surrounded by Bloomsbury's warnings not to touch the covers with spotty fingers and queasy with his too-strong lavender scent.

The shadow stays still for a long time. "Bloody rats," a gruff voice curses. His shape finally stomps away. I hold my breath until Frizer's bootsteps grow faint. Only when my straining ears hear the soft slam of the graveyard gates does my body loosen. I slip my hand into my doublet to clutch the cross and mutter a quick apology to God or the spirits or whoever else is listening before I slip into the unlocked crypt.

The air reeks. I pull the edge of my cloak over my mouth and nose and grope along the slimy walls with an unsteady hand, searching for something amiss. There's nothing.

Even though I truly, truly prefer not to, I slide all the way into the crypt and press my back against the far wall. My eyes slowly adjust to the scraps of moonlight filtering inside. Wrapped bundles flank me, freckled with phosphorescence. Pale mushrooms push through the cracked bricks, and my boots sink into mysterious wetness that appears to be oozing from the foundation. All it would take would be for someone to slam the door shut, and I'd be trapped here for God knows how long, alone in the darkness and cold, my voice muffled by the thick stone walls, where only the worms could hear—

I pinch the bridge of my nose and clamp my eyes shut. Panic is absolutely not what this situation calls for. I force my breath to steady before I open my eyes.

And then I spot it.

There's a stone angel in the crypt. An ugly one that looks not unlike a squatting toad. But it's the only thing not covered in mold or grave dirt.

I search the stone until—there, behind the wing—I pull out a folded bit of parchment.

"All right, Elias, you've done it." I tuck the paper away safely and wipe my sweaty brow. "Now let's get the bloody hell out."

Even though Frizer could still be here, by the time the gate looms into view beyond the final rows of graves, I'm sprinting. I fall upon the gates and try to wrench them open, not caring how much noise I make. I'll not be dying working for a rich Cambridge boy and his wild schemes!

But the gates don't budge.

Blast it all, Frizer's gone and locked them. Of course he has. 'Tis what any bloke with half their wits would do after leaving a clandestine message.

Which means . . .

Whoever the note was intended for has a key themselves and will know Frizer was followed when they find the parchment missing.

I give the gate one final rattle for good measure before slithering hopelessly to the ground, reminding myself of the most important thing; I found something.

My clumsy fingers fumble with the twine around the paper scroll.

*look to the red queen* it reads in a cramped hand.

I shudder as I recall Queen Elizabeth's thick red hair.

Could it be her?

A distant scream shatters into inhuman cackling. I startle and drop the parchment. It nearly blows outside the gates, beyond reach. I snatch it and tuck it safely beside my cross, sitting down, trying to imagine the hundred ways I shall lord this victory over Bloomsbury and not the hundred ways in which looking for answers in a musty library might be preferable to sneaking and thieving about after all.

The Bloomsbury servant who answers the door is shocked when I reappear the next morning covered in dirt and leaves. "Lord Hughes?"

I throw my filthy cloak at him, as the Lord Hughes, son of the wealthy merchant-lord, would doubtlessly do. "Of course. Were you expecting someone else?"

I stride down the vast corridor beneath the noses of Bloomsbury's venerable ancestors and give each and every one of them a terrible wink as I pass. Zounds, I can't *wait* to see the look on Bloomsbury's face when he sees what I have done! I am all but dancing when I reach the library, the note a hot ember in my pocket.

The manservant Cooper stands outside the library door. His eyes bug when he spots me. "My lord! We thought you'd been murdered."

"Not the first time someone's thought that of me." I breeze past him and push open the door.

Cooper gasps. "Wait, do not—"

The library is unrecognizable. All the books have been shelved neatly where they belong, and Bloomsbury's innumerable scribbles have been corralled into a tidy pile. The sticky plates and goblets spotted with finger-prints are missing.

But none of this is quite as strange a sight as the gray-bearded, wan-faced gentleman across from Bloomsbury. He dons an affronted expression as though someone has burst in upon him as he sits on the privy.

"I beg your pardon!" he sputters like I'm an awful surprise.

The feeling is mutual. 'Tis as though the rug has been yanked out from under my boots. Bloomsbury and I have near lived in this room a fortnight, and seeing all signs of our work and time swept and stacked away makes me feel like I did the very day I set foot in this too-tall, too-huge house. Like I've trespassed into a place that's got no room for me.

I slip back into my player's constitution and fall into a deep curtsy, only managing to transform it into a bow at the last moment. "I do apologize for the interruption, sirs! I am Lord William Hughes, heir to Hughes Shipping in Plymouth. Perhaps you have heard of my father?" I straighten to the lord's incredulous expression. "No? Very well then. You will hear word of him soon enough. He is doing big, important, and expensive things!"

"Lord Hughes is my guest," Bloomsbury says quickly. Twin splotches of scarlet sit high on his cheeks. He is wearing an enormous neck ruff that makes him look like a permanently startled cat. "We know each other from Cambridge. Will, may I introduce Lord Richard Middlemore?"

The lord's stern gaze takes me in very slowly, from the leaves snagged in my tousled hair to the mud caked upon my boots. "It is . . . a pleasure," he says in a way that implies it is no pleasure at all.

I bow again and dazzle him with a winning smile. This is not the first reluctant audience I have performed for. "I have heard nothing but great things about your deeds, Lord Middlemore, and I do apologize for interrupting this meeting . . . of pleasure? Of business?"

Lord Middlemore puffs out at my compliments. I have yet to meet a man who does not when he hears that other men think highly of him. "In truth, this meeting is about both. We are discussing Lord Bloomsbury's engagement to my daughter, Anne."

"Oh. How . . . utterly delightful." Zounds, somehow in the tumult of everything, I forgot that Bloomsbury was engaged. This Middlemore has not only taken out the rug from under me, but he's replaced all the furniture as well with ugly things from France. Bloomsbury must truly not like his fiancée, because he hasn't visited her once since I've been around.

Lord Middlemore nods, a nauseating paternal smile upon his face. "Yes. James is the man for overseeing my New World investments. Her Majesty has granted me a large parcel of land to cultivate so I may bring glory to her name, and mark my words, there's riches there for a man's taking if he's got the stones to try it!" He slaps Bloomsbury's shoulder with a boom of laughter. Bloomsbury winces, his false smile going crooked.

Investments? The New World? Where's all this coming from? I drop into a vacant chair, feeling as though I've tumbled from a wagon. "Is . . . is that so?"

"Indeed. After the wedding he is to accompany my daughter to America." Lord Middlemore has the smug expression of a dog that has nicked an entire ham leg from the table. "A firm hand shall be needed in the New World. 'Tis controversial to say, I know, but you're a man of industry, so you know sometimes you've got to get your hands dirty!" He chortles and elbows Bloomsbury. "Yes, James is what I need. Remember how your father—"

"Lord Middlemore," Bloomsbury interrupts. His entire face is rouged now, the pink against the enormous white ruff very pronounced. "Did you not say that you had something else you wished to discuss today?"

The two men move on, but my mind is still stuck in a rut. Bloomsbury is set to oversee whatever business Middlemore has in America? Where doubtlessly Middlemore plans to dig his English claws deep into the land and ransack its riches for England while leaving little to nothing for the people who already live there? The shock of learning this about my partner hits me like a slap, the surprise striking first, followed by the stinging pain.

I was but a babe when the queen's soldiers ousted us from our land. At first, they tried to budge us with words, and we did not move. Then came the unsheathed blades and hissed threats.

Then came the Burning Reaper.

He came in the night with torches, and the cottages bloomed orange like roses. He galloped down the street, a torch in one hand and a great sword in the other, killing all who fled their burning homes. My parents whispered us this story so we would know why the nobles can't be trusted. The lesson lingered with me in London, a way to remember that this is what the queen and her court mean when they speak of venturing to new lands: the broken bodies beside smoking, blackened homes. The gift of progress and civilization.

I cannot reconcile these different sides of Bloomsbury, the planter and bookish boy. I assumed Bloomsbury was his most honest self with me—we agreed to be honest, after all—but perhaps his so-called honesty, too, is just another side of him.

"When were you planning to admit you're going to the New World?" I demand bitterly when Bloomsbury returns from seeing Middlemore out. Anger simmers in my head, made more acidic by betrayal. I thought him good and honest because, why, he has been kind to me? Kindness does not make someone honest. He's still a noble, after all, and I know how nobles amass and keep their hoards of wealth. By stealing it from people like me.

*You're angry because you thought he was different from the rest of them.* The traitorous thought slithers in and makes me even angrier.

"Are you going to say anything?" The glassware jumps as I slam my hand on the table.

Bloomsbury undoes the great ruff around his neck and sets it on Lord Middlemore's vacated chair. He pours claret into a glass and downs it all at once. "Do you truly believe colonizing the New World is what I wish to do with my life?"

"Well, *you're* the one engaged to the daughter of a colonizer, so forgive me for assuming."

Bloomsbury suddenly kicks Middlemore's chair. I flinch as

it falls onto the bookcases, knocking the priceless tomes to the floor. I swear and duck my head like he'll round on me next, a prey instinct racing through me.

Anger crashes in Bloomsbury's eyes, his pupils going dark as a tempest. "Do you think I don't know what Middlemore is talking about? My father made weapons for the queen. Middlemore speaks of riches, yes, but I know he speaks of destruction and death. I am well aware of what happens when the rich and powerful want more of something, and I've told you, by God, I'll not be my father!"

Only after his final shout does he see how still I've gone, how my mouth has dropped open.

Revulsion and horror flick across his face. Inch by inch, he sinks into the chair beside me, unclenching fisted hands, his red-rimmed eyes on the floor. "Please forgive me. I—I have a bit of a temper when I'm vexed. I frightened you, and that was awful of me."

I swallow hard, the expression painful. "Middlemore's visit upset you."

"That's no excuse to lose control." His words writhe with self-loathing. "Middlemore was made a duke only recently. He craves a connection with my family's name and history to better secure his ties to the nobility. My father's disgrace has robbed our family's coffers, and my parents have arranged this marriage to reclaim their fortune."

'Tis laughable to imagine a noble family in dire financial straits. What does that even mean? That they dine on meat only every other day? They must—please, no!—wear their smallclothes a second time? Or—God forbid—perhaps they must stuff their mattresses with straw and not feathers?

"Stop looking at me like that," Bloomsbury demands crossly. "Like what?"

"Like I am the absolute worst scoundrel you've ever seen in your life." He pours himself another generous glass and squashes a hand into his furrowed forehead. "This is why this investigation matters to me. If my family's reputation is restored—and thwarting an attempt on the queen's life would certainly accomplish that much—then I can break off this hideous engagement and be free to do as I please."

Even mere days ago I would have laid into him, explained how his so-called problems are the result of too-rich meals and idle hands. And that's all still true, and we both know it. But, zounds, he looks so *tortured*, sitting there half-foxed before midday, his undone collar revealing the itchy red lattice pressed into his skin from the starched ruff. It shall accomplish nothing useful to remind him of all this now. He may be a liar, but he's no scoundrel.

I draw closer to him. "If you were free to do as you pleased, what would you do?"

He frowns at my knee, as if he can't believe I'm still here. "I would voyage to the continent and study medicine in the best cities of Europe. Amsterdam and Paris, Florence and Constantinople." He loosens a bit at the idea, going starry-eyed. "There's so much to *learn*. I could spend my entire life doing naught else and still barely scratch the surface. Think of all the possibilities! All the good it could do!"

"But if your family name is cleared, and you're your father's heir, would he even let you leave?"

Bloomsbury tosses back his—third? fourth?—glass of claret. "Oh, he and the court wouldn't like it a bit. They've never cared much for what I want. They only care about preserving our noble names or increasing the family fortune. I want to use my station to undo some of the harm people like Middlemore and my father cause."

Even though I resolved to be nice to him, a burst of annoyance sharpens my tongue. "Stop that. No one cares that much about bettering the world, especially not a rich man. Everyone's out for himself."

Bloomsbury stares, brow ascending. "What makes you so certain my sincerity is false?"

I've no answer save that I want it to be false. I duck my chin into my collar, quarrelsome through and through. "Because."

Because I'm used to dealing with swindlers and scoundrels. Not . . . whatever he is.

'Tis a brave and dangerous thing to go about this world having dreams. A dream is even more fickle and fleeting than a life. Bloomsbury shares his with me as if it's nothing, as though there's nothing to lose and everything to gain from being vulnerable. The more he reveals how different he is from me, the wider the hollow ache in my chest grows.

Bloomsbury's mouth twitches into that barely-there smile. "You drink with the best playwrights of our age and 'because' is the best you can do?"

And now I am blushing, and I hate that more than anything

else. I slam my goblet down and shout the only thing which will prevent him from smiling at me. "Because you have proclaimed us friends, but to most of the world the idea of a lord and a boy player as friends is the stuff of plays! The world you're speaking of—where people try to do what's best for everyone—it doesn't exist!" I gesture to my person. "I could be killed for playing the part of the lord, you know."

The smile slips from his face. Instead of triumph, the downward cast of his eyes floods me with guilt, as though I have played a sly trick on a trusting hound.

"Do you wish to be released from my services? I would not blame you if you did."

"No, I only wanted you to listen to me! Not everything needs be an oath or a declaration, you know."

My words have no effect on Bloomsbury whatsoever, who is thumbing his lip in a way which precedes him saying something I know I won't like. Before I can ask, he's on his knees before me.

"Elias, I shall protect you with all the power and might of my station." He looks up at me, jaw square, eyes dark and serious. A shiver shoots down my back.

"Zounds, what did I just say about oaths and declarations?"

One half of his mouth lifts. "Forgive me. It's amusing when you're flustered." And then that utter scoundrel *winks* at me, of all things, and I realize, far too late, he has played a jest on me.

I nudge him away with my boot. "Find yourself merry, do you?"

He winks again, and I am forced to confront a shocking realization.

I don't hate spending time with Lord James Bloomsbury.

He is witty and generous, which makes it difficult to dislike him. Doesn't hurt that's he's handsome enough to look at either. He's all fashionably long hair and dark, dreamer's eyes. Why, were he hired at the Rose Theatre and a nobody like me, I'd already be scheming how to get him in a shadowy corner after work.

The idea of kissing him is a thunderbolt. Sudden and deadly, too hot to handle. It makes me forget to breathe.

I groan and grab at my blazing face. God Almighty, what is *wrong* with me? Bloomsbury is a noble, part of the same group of people who stole my family's lands and left us scattered and homeless. His father *made weapons for the bloody queen*! I've no business having thoughts and feelings like this about him. Everything fun in England is illegal, and men kissing men is no exception. But a man who's got the sense to kiss only men of his own station usually goes unnoticed. Especially when he looks and plays the part of who the public world expects him to be.

A commoner kissing a lord is the opposite of subtle, the opposite of keeping to my class. Even the very thought of it feels like courting danger.

His eyebrow crooks. "Are you well? You look like you've got a touch of fever. Shall I have Cooper fetch my medicines?"

I flush even hotter and draw out the now slightly crumpled scroll I plundered from the graveyard, suddenly grateful the man can't read my brainless, traitorous thoughts with that penetrating gaze of his. If we don't hurry things along, it shall be years before I see a pence of the hundred pounds Bloomsbury owes me.

"Last night I found Frizer planting this note."

He brightens. "Why didn't you say so right away?"

We knock heads like he-goats as I unroll the scrap of paper.

*look to the red queen*

Before, the phrase felt full of possibility. But today I see it for what it is, a useless cryptic comment. The kernel of hope which lodged within my chest fades.

Bloomsbury lifts one finger. "Hold on now, this is good!"

"Oh, is it now? Marlowe already told us this plot involved Queen Elizabeth."

He taps the word "red." "What makes you think this is about her?"

"She wears those fearsome red wigs."

"But Mary, her Catholic cousin, was executed in the color red. It could be a nod toward her."

I throw up my hands. "It could mean bloody anything! It'll only make sense for the bloke it was meant for."

He nods slowly. "That's true. We ought to return to the church and see who goes looking for it."

Of course. Zounds, it was daft of me to leave. "But the vicar saw me. He'll recognize me again for sure." Unsurprisingly, midnight sojourning in the parish graveyard did not go over well with a man of God who said some very un-Christian things when he discovered my trespassing this morning.

Bloomsbury's eyes glimmer. A smile hides in the curves of his mouth. "I thought you were the best boy actor in all of London?"

# CHAPTER FOURTEEN

I'M WEARING THE most hideous dress and wimple covering my hair, neck, and sides of my face when we're outside the church once more and realize our scheme has one grave flaw.

"Elias, look," Bloomsbury says in a strained voice.

The bloody church is hosting a wedding.

The happy bride and groom and their guests pour from the church's double doors beneath the cheerful spire and parade down the street in a riot of celebration. There are so many people, the only way for Bloomsbury and me to avoid them is to turn back the way we came. But before we can escape, a burly matron grasps my arm and drags me after her.

"Come along now, you. 'Tis time for the feast! What would the vicar say if he saw you dallying with strange men?" She clucks her tongue and shoots Bloomsbury a sidelong glare. "Why, think of your mother's poor nerves if she spotted you with the likes of him!"

She's strong and walks quick. I look frantically to Bloomsbury to save me, but he's already lost in the crowd. The matron clucks her tongue again when she sees me looking for him and gives me a yank. I've no choice but to stumble after her, my eyes fixed on the cemetery gates growing smaller behind me. Is there someone within the mausoleum this very second searching for the paper I've already filched?

The crowd thins out in a flower-strewn square where lutes and drums play a lively tune. The market stalls are all shut up, and tables groan with simple food. The matron lets me go and presses a white rose into my hand with a decidedly unmatronly wink. I stare at the flower, unsure what to do. Then, with much giggling, the young people get up and create two rows: men on one side and women on the other. All the women clutch a flower like mine. 'Tis some sort of bride ale or another wedding dance custom I know not the rules for.

I ought to hitch my skirts and run, but there's Bloomsbury in the opposite line, stiff-backed and wide-eyed like he's on trial for high treason.

*What do I do?* he mouths frantically.

*Just follow along!* I try to say with my eyes, but 'tis too late; the dance has begun.

And that's when I realize there's a second fatal flaw in our plan: Bloomsbury is an absolutely awful dancer.

He brutalizes every slipper in his path. Watching him is utterly spellbinding. How is it possible for a person to be so awful at dancing? Don't nobles take lessons in this sort of thing?

A girl shrieks in pain, and Bloomsbury stammers an apology. He gives me a *please help* look. I'd snort with laughter were it not for the very real harm he's causing. If I don't get him out of here soon, he's going to ruin our cover when the guests realize none of them have seen this oafish dancer before.

Dancing pairs begin to peel away, all clutching hands and bashful smiles. A girl presses her rose into a boy's hand, and he kisses her cheek before joining the growing onlookers at the edge of the square. One girl offers Bloomsbury a flower, and instead of taking it, he spins her into an ale cask, perfectly oblivious. The girl's cheeks redden as she storms away, Bloomsbury staring after her with a stricken expression.

I glide over to save him.

"What—what's going on? I feel there's something I'm supposed to be doing!" he stammers, pupils wide with panic.

"You've got to kiss me. Keep it together, all right?" I hiss.

His face gets all shocked. And then his puckered lips swoop in on mine.

"Not yet!" I pull away at the last possible second. "Good God, wait, will you?"

We twirl again, and I press my flower into his hand. I lean forward until he stumbles backward and we're nose to nose. He's breathing heavily, like I'm about to stab him. Something in my throat squeezes.

"Now," I whisper.

He presses against me, hands curling about my waist. His mouth moves to catch mine, and I move to shove him away, but—oh. *Oh.*

Oh no.

He's all honey and smoke, like a stolen bite of cake whose sweetness is all the keener knowing it was never mine in the first place. A soft sound escapes me. My heads tilts to the side, letting him in, fingers catching on the rough fabric of his disguise. He kisses me deeper, and I swear, my soul leaves my body. How on earth did this strait-laced lad learn to kiss like this? Books? Zounds, if this is what book-learning is about, then I recant every vile thing I've ever said about Cambridge!

"Elias?" My name is a whisper, his lips brushing feather-light along my jaw. He holds my waist with the urgency of a man dangling from a cliffside. Like I'm the only thing keeping him from falling. "Do you think that was enough, or—"

Catcalls and cheering pull me from the moment quicker than a dog escaping a bath. Oh, right—there's the swarm of onlookers I managed to forget about in a moment of thick-headedness.

Splendid.

I pull away so quick, I swear there's a squelch. "James! It was supposed to be a *chaste* kiss. The vicar will be crying the banns for us after this!"

His dazed expression dissolves into one of outright horror. He lets go of me so fast, I nearly fall over. He opens his mouth, stammering, then shakes his head, words failing. He cannot even look within three feet of my person, face as hot as a blacksmith's forge.

I loop my arm through his and lead him back to a table amidst a fresh wave of jeers and cheers. It takes two cups of wine and the distraction of a far livelier tune for us to sneak away. As soon as we're out of sight, I rip off the ugly wimple and comb through my hair. "Well, that was a complete and utter disaster! We've learned nothing useful at all except that you certainly know how to make a spectacle of yourself."

Bloomsbury makes a strangled sound, his cheeks still poppy-red. "That's not true. I did ask the vicar if he's had any trouble in the cemetery, and he gave me a look and said, 'What's it to you?'"

"You said what?" I drag my hands down my face and groan. "Dear God. You've all but told him someone's been snooping in the cemetery! How are you so terrible at sneaking and thieving?"

"Well, you're the one who spent our time *kissing*." He spits the word like an ugly curse.

The way he says this vexes me. I slap him in the chest with my wimple, hissing, "You don't have to act like you've kissed a bloody toad!"

He sputters out a laugh, a hand easing into his hair. "No, kissing John Clinton Brooke was like kissing a toad."

I stop so quickly, it takes him three steps to notice. I go hot all over again. "You've kissed blokes before?"

He gives me an arch look. "Well, haven't you?"

I start walking instead of answering. 'Tis too much, too soon: the fact that he's like me and noticed it before I saw it in him. Men preferring men isn't an unusual thing in London, and I imagine 'tis not an unusual thing within the court, either. Except I don't know why he's telling me about this now. Unless—

No. I won't go there.

Bloomsbury hurries to catch up. "Please forgive me. I shouldn't have made a jest of things."

His apology rankles me more than it should. I tug at the too-tight stays in my sleeves and change the subject. "What a waste of a day! We're no closer to discovering who's looking for the message about the red queen now than we were before."

Which could very well mean our only lead has crumbled to dust. I expect Bloomsbury to assure me there's still a way forward, but instead we return to the Thames and board a wherry in silence. The river is bustling at the noon hour with skippers ferrying wares and people every which way and ships landing at the quays, their holds filled with goods for the markets.

A newly docked ship catches my eye.

Its make is foreign, sides salt-stained and battle-scarred, the sails tattered and torn. 'Tis the sort of vessel that hosts a hundred stories and makes a player itch to know them all.

But it's the flag snapping at her prow which makes me gasp: a red boar on a yellow background.

I stand upright for a better look, sending the wherry rolling side to side. The wherryman curses, and Bloomsbury snatches my leg.

I point to the flag. "That's Irish, not English!"

"So?" Bloomsbury tugs me down. "It's not worth drowning for."

Irish people are not uncommon in London. Not since Queen Elizabeth and her father before her began greedily settling their lands to the west, just as they did to the common lands of England which my family called home. By and large the Irish escape the Crown's notice by blending in and not drawing attention to themselves like I do. This ship bears a foreign flag proudly for all to witness. Likely the sailors on board have fought against the English occupation and would thusly be considered traitors. Why would they be here in London?

Our wherryman nods toward the ship. "That one rolled in a bit ago. Rumor has it the captain is some sort of sea witch." He gives us a squinting glare. "I reckon they're right. Have you ever heard of a woman leading a ship? Ain't natural, that's for sure."

As we draw closer to the north bank, the figures on the ship grow clearer—including the figure standing akimbo at the ship's bow overseeing the unloading of its cargo. A woman in breeches, her long unbound auburn hair curling and snapping in the wind. Glancing at her is like being blinded by sunlight on new copper.

The words of the secret scroll dash across my mind. And the sudden knowing squeezes my chest so hard, I fear my ribs may crack.

"'Look to the red queen!'" My hand snatches Blooms-bury's knee and sends the whole wherry wobbling again. "James, we've found her!"

# CHAPTER FIFTEEN

MAIDS HAVE A reputation as terrible tattlers, but it's an utter falsehood; the sailors and fishermen of London are the loosest-tongued gossips of all. We've not passed through the quays before we learn two facts about the mysterious woman captain.

First, she is called Gráinne Ní Mháille, and all of London has already taken to calling her the Pirate Queen.

Second, the Pirate Queen seeks an audience with Queen Elizabeth.

Bloomsbury is aquiver with excitement by the time we return to the town house. "The Pirate Queen must be what the note spoke of, I am certain of it!"

"But is she a friend or a foe? I can think of a dozen Irishmen who would be happy to slip a knife betwixt Queen Elizabeth's ribs."

Bloomsbury opens the library door and ushers me inside, his brow pinching. "Do mind the servants before you speak of regicide, won't you?"

I roll my eyes and flop back in a plush armchair. "We need to figure out *why* the Pirate Queen seeks an audience with Queen Elizabeth. Did you discover anything about her in your books?"

"You mean in my research?" Bloomsbury says, gesturing to his enormous piles of notes. "No. Of course not. Everyone knows the Irish bear no love for England. Our Pirate Queen, Gráinne Ní Mháille, is well traveled and has resisted English rule for years. Recently her forces suffered a great defeat. If she has come to London under her own colors, and if she so publicly seeks an audience with the queen, she comes here for diplomacy and not murder." He smiles smugly. "I assure you, this Pirate Queen is the red queen we've been seeking."

"But what if she's not?" I press, suddenly less certain of my own conviction that the Pirate Queen is involved in our plot. It could be stubbornness, the part of me that instinctually wants to counter everything he says, but I don't like how quickly Bloomsbury has agreed with me. There's a tremor in his smile, something he's not telling me. "For a bloke who's wasted a fortnight doing"—I crook my fingers around the word—"*research*, you suddenly seem eager to make haste."

"We're running out of time, Elias!" Bloomsbury bursts out, his smug expression vanishing. "If Queen Elizabeth dies, it's over."

I clear my throat. "I do not recall our success being a factor in whether or not you paid me. And before you get all sour, let's not forget that everything we've accomplished so far is *my* doing. 'Tis *your* fault things have gone slowly."

Bloomsbury's stare grows more intense. "Exactly. That's why I need you to go out tonight and learn more about her."

I choke out a laugh and stop when I realize he's not jesting. "Oh, come on now. It's been quite a day! It can wait." I've gone across the Thames twice today already, and the thought of my bed is the most heavenly thing I can imagine.

He does not crack a smile, not even the whisper of one. "I must insist you do it tonight."

I sit up straight, feeling the closeness we shared today easing apart. "Fine. But there better be plum-stuffed pastries for breakfast tomorrow."

Bloomsbury sags with relief. "I'll tell the housekeeper. And thank you."

I take my leave but hesitate with my hand on the door pin. Bloomsbury is still hunched over, scribbling madly. The fire is fading, catching upon threads of bronze in his hair. The light sharpens the lines on his face, which have not disappeared since Lord Middlemore's visit. *What are you keeping from me?* sits there on my tongue, waiting for breath.

But instead I push open the door and leave without saying anything, a weight sitting heavy in my heart.

'Tis an easy task to locate the pirate crew. All I must do is follow the hordes of whispering gossips who trail after them like the hem of a court lady's finest dress. Gráinne Ní Mháille and her men are holed up at the Gull, an absolute dump on an old ship slowly sinking into the putrid bankside.

Inside, the pirates delight in spinning tales for their fawning admirers: that they've seen tentacled beasts big as castles, that when lost at sea they resort to eating their kinsmen. I even catch Shakespeare among the onlookers, moon-eyed and rapt, ink splotches staining his fingers.

The sight tugs at me.

Marlowe would've loved this. The absurdity and the novelty of it all. He delighted in meeting new people and teasing out what part of them he could spin into a play, a poem, or whatever else he fancied to write at that moment. But of course—the thought sobers me at once—Gráinne Ní Mháille and her crew could be the very reason why Marlowe is lying dead in a lost grave.

The barkeep slides me a full tankard. I take a seat beside the smallest and wiriest of the pirates. A young man's tongue is looser than an old man's, and like Marlowe would have been, I am thirsty for stories tonight.

"So, you're with the Pirate Queen, aye? What's your name?"

The boy turns. He's about twelve but has the eyes of someone double his age. "Who's asking?"

"Will. Will Bloom."

I motion the barkeep to pour the lad a glass. He slides it over, and the boy snatches it with an appreciative smirk. "I'm Réamonn. That's all you'll be getting from me."

We clink glasses and drink. I set my tankard down and give him a rapt look. "What brings you to our port? I'm only a servant. I ain't ever left London before. I heard this ship has been to the edge of the world and back."

The lad's skinny chest puffs like a cockerel's. "Aye, we've seen some things you wouldn't believe. Places where color ribbons across the sky in the dead of winter. Sea-beasts put into the waters by the devil himself."

I let my eyes widen in starry awe. "And now you're here in boring old London."

"'Tis a little boring here," the boy admits. "But see, we've docked because Ní Mháille—"

"Will!"

I'm yanked away from my conspiratorial lean-in and into an unwelcome embrace.

Oh no, 'tis bloody William Shakespeare, here to ruin everything, like usual.

"It's been a while since I've clapped eyes on you, lad!" The older man's eyes sweep over me. "I suppose you've been too busy rubbing elbows with lords to grab a pint with your lowly player friends, eh?"

The pirate boy's eyes narrow. "I thought you said you were a servant?"

Zounds, I'm losing him. "I do both. 'Tis misery making it as a player."

"I didn't come here to listen to no lies, y'hear?" The pirate lad flashes me the dagger hanging on his hip and scuttles away.

I pinch the bridge of my nose. "Shakespeare. I'd say I've missed you, but we both know that'd be a lie, don't we?"

"Many people say that about me," the playwright says cheerily, helping himself to the sausage I've ordered. "Why, the last time I visited my wife—"

I cut him off. "What are you doing here?"

"Same thing you're doing. Trying my best to welcome our latest foreign guests." He sidles even closer to me. "They've given me the most excellent idea for a play. You see, there's these twins and a storm and a ship—"

I yank the sausage back from him. "I've not the time for this now. I'm trying to solve Marlowe's murder."

The playwright grows somber. "That was a nasty surprise. No one deserves to go like that."

His sincerity softens my temper. "No," I say quietly. "They don't."

Shakespeare lifts his tankard. I clink mine against his, both of us murmuring "for Kit" before downing the ale.

Guilt nips at me with sharp teeth: Does earning a hundred pounds along the way make my solving Kit Marlowe's murder less noble? What would my family think of the work I'm doing for them—for us? More importantly, what would they make of my working with Bloomsbury, one of the English nobles who stole our land? I push my food away, no longer hungry.

Shakespeare wipes foam from his mustache. "What's this you say about investigating the murder?"

Damn it all, I should have kept my mouth shut. "'Tis nothing. More of a lark than aught else."

He waggles his eyebrows at me. "Don't seem like a lark, with you here talking to all these corsairs."

Informing Shakespeare about my plans is a risk, but I know the playwright well enough that he'll hound me for the truth until one or both of us dies. "There's reasons to believe the Pirate Queen is involved in whatever killed Marlowe. I'm trying to talk with her. Something you ruined when you came over here and opened your great gob."

Shakespeare pillows his chin in his hand. "What if I said I could help?"

"I'd say you've never been helpful in your life."

Shakespeare dismisses my words with a wave. "I'll have you know that the Pirate Queen enjoys the theater as much as our own dear Queen Elizabeth."

"And?"

"*And*," Shakespeare says, shaking his finger at me, "she has requested to have a play performed on her ship by yours truly three days hence."

Now that perks me right up. "Can you get me in?"

Shakespeare flashes me, though it pains me to admit, a rather charming wink. "Don't be daft. I can do anything."

I hold out my hand. Shakespeare clasps it.

"Three days hence," he says. "I'll see you on Ní Mháille's ship."

# CHAPTER SIXTEEN

I N THE MORNING 'tis clear that something is very, very wrong.

I wake up alone with no manservant in sight.

Safely beneath the covers, I strain my ears for sounds of ringing steel or worse. There's nothing. It does not seem as though we are under siege, but one can never be too cautious. I slip on the clothes I wore yesterday, as well as a knife, and tiptoe into the hall.

Bloomsbury is there, also wearing yesterday's clothes and a wild expression. Everything around him is in an uproar. Footmen throw open windows to air out linens. The linens themselves lie in slumped piles on unmade beds. I have to flatten myself against the wall to avoid being run down by a fleet of maids moving a marble statue of a constipated-looking ancestor.

"Whatever you are about to tell me shall have to wait," Bloomsbury says before I can open my mouth. "My mother and sister are coming. The courier arrived this morning."

The news is a shock. It's been the two of us for so long, I've all but forgotten that Bloomsbury has family—much less that I'd be likely to meet any of them.

"They come for the queen's midsummer feast. It is two

days hence." Bloomsbury tears both hands through his hair, turning it to utter chaos. "I . . . forgot about it."

Following murderers in graveyards and drinking pirates' grog with rebel Irish sailors is one thing, but pretending to be a lord before Bloomsbury's bloody family? Zounds, if the servants suspect I am not a lord, there's naught they could do about it, but should two courtly ladies sniff out my secrets, I'd swing in the gallows of Tyburn.

"All right. Have a nice time with them. Find me in the lavatory—or whatever you call it—when your kin take their leave. We can resume our investigation then."

Bloomsbury yanks the back of my collar before I can walk away and presses me into a gilded corner. Everything about him is tense, the hunch of his shoulders and the sudden lines on his expression. He hovers over me like a storm cloud. "You can't go."

I cross my arms and glare, resenting that I have to look up at him. "Are you commanding me to stay, my lord?"

Something in his expression cracks. "Never," he whispers. "I'm begging you to stay."

The rawness in his voice disarms me. He does not look like a man about to host kin for a feast; he looks like a man who has been told he only has days left to live. I place a steadying hand on his taut forearm.

"What is this really about, James?"

He shakes his head once, swallowing. "We need answers to our investigation, and we need them soon. You can help me by staying and going to that damned pirate ship."

Before I can ask why, a servant calls for Bloomsbury. His face pales. "Oh God. They've already entered the city limits. We must ready to greet them."

The Bloomsbury ladies arrive in a once-fashionable caroche pulled by four red horses. The entire household assembles to receive them in their best clothes. I stand stiff-backed beside Bloomsbury and try not to dwell on the thousand ways this can go awry. Should I reach for the wrong utensil at dinnertime, it'll be over for me, and our entire investigation shall go down with me.

Bloomsbury's mother is helped out first. She is a pale woman with a severe expression and brocade skirts which weight her down like fetters. Another shorter figure barrels out without ceremony. She launches herself at Bloomsbury and fastens her arms about his waist. "James! I have missed you so!"

His face lights up like an Easter fire. He laughs and folds his arms about his sister. "As I have missed you, Catherine."

Lady Bloomsbury storms up the steps and grabs her daughter's arm. To anyone farther away it appears a friendly gesture, but up close I see how the girl winces. "Catherine, contain yourself. The servants are watching!"

Catherine pouts and sinks into a flawless curtsy. I see she's a few years younger than me, her features nothing like Bloomsbury's save for the same bright brown eyes. "It is a delight to see you again, lord brother."

Bloomsbury bites back a snort at her insolence, and his mother pretends not to notice at all.

Lady Bloomsbury extends her hand to her son: he bows and kisses it briskly. "James. Your father sends his well wishes." Her eyes slide to me, a question in them.

Bloomsbury introduces me as Lord Hughes, and I bow.

Lady Bloomsbury flashes me a cold, fleeting smile before turning to Bloomsbury. "I wasn't aware a guest was staying with you. We sent you here to complete the details of the betrothal. Not to lark with school friends."

Zounds, what a treat this woman is. No wonder Bloomsbury was dreading her arrival all morning. We'll never be able to carry on with our investigation under Lady Bloomsbury's hooked frown and beady stare. I tug at the ruff choking my neck, only to have Bloomsbury tread oh so surreptitiously upon my foot and say, "Lord Hughes is heir to a shipping company. We are in conversations about how he could help Lord Middlemore's New World colonies."

Lady Bloomsbury's appraising eyes search me with renewed vigor. "Oh! Well. How wise of you." She smiles and cups her son's chin, the first sign of affection she has displayed since she arrived. "You shall make an excellent overseer of the colony. Your father will be proud."

Bloomsbury's horrible courtly smile doesn't falter an inch, even though I know his entire heart is rebelling. His mother is far worse than I'd expected, and my expectations were already very low. 'Tis as though we've stepped into a tragic play where everyone dies at the end.

After the afternoon repast, Lady Bloomsbury claims she has a headache and goes to lie in her chamber. "You should join me, Catherine," she calls to her daughter as she leaves. "Rest improves one's complexion, and we are hosting guests tonight."

"Yes, Mother, I'll be there soon," Catherine says obediently. But when her mother disappears, the girl turns to James breathlessly. "Now we may be merry!"

"Is merrymaking an activity your mother would not approve of?" I say.

Lady Catherine looks between me and her brother, brow puckered.

"Will is a friend," Bloomsbury says simply.

"Then *yes*, Mother never lets me do *anything*!" The confession bursts from Catherine as though she has been keeping it in for quite some time. "And James has gone and left me with her for ages. He's been an absolute monster to me." She crosses her arms and jabs her brother with her elbow.

Lady Catherine is all of fifteen years old. I do not have much experience with women, much less if they also happen to be nobles. My eyes slide over to Bloomsbury, as though he'll help me, but instead he just shoots me a wicked smile and says, "Catherine, what would you like to do this afternoon?"

She pivots to me, hands clasped eagerly. "Lord Hughes, where is your favorite place in all of London?"

There are several answers to this question. Often, it is whoever's mouth my tongue happens to be in. Sometimes, 'tis at the bottom of an ale tankard. But it unexpectedly occurs to me that the Bloomsbury town house is far from the absolute worst place to be. In truth, if I factor in the plum preserves which the servants leave out for me every morning with sly smiles, then yes, this place makes my list. How mortifying! I must never let Bloomsbury know. "The Rose Theatre."

Lady Catherine's eyes become wide as saucers. Then they keep widening, and I am afraid they may plummet from their sockets. "Oh! Isn't that where Master Marlowe puts on his plays?" she says in this soft, reverent voice that punches the air from my chest.

Hearing Marlowe's name in this unexpected context bowls me over, and I can't bring myself to say he's dead. I square my jaw and look away. Unearthing Kit's connection to the Pirate Queen is what I ought to be doing—not larking about with nobles.

However . . . Catherine's expression is so sincere, her brow pinching with worry as she realizes she's said something that upset me. She can't be any older than my own sister.

I push a hand through my hair and blow out a hard breath. "Kit—I mean Marlowe—would be delighted to know a lady such as yourself enjoyed his work." There was little Marlowe loved more than the corruption of young minds. I wonder if he had any inkling that somewhere in the countryside a noble lass was making a study of his mischief? My resolve strengthens. "We should go to the Rose. Marlowe would have wanted you to see it, my lady."

Lady Catherine squeals and claps her hands. Bloomsbury whips toward me with an anxious look. "But the theaters are still closed for the plague," he says.

"Not if you know how to break in," I say with a grin.

An hour later, I've picked the lock to the Rose Theatre's double doors.

Lady Catherine bursts past us, hefts her skirts, and climbs onstage. There she spins in slow circles, her eyes filled with wonder as she takes in the towering timber-and-lath walls, the soaring balconies. "Why, it's gorgeous!"

Even though a noisy flock of rooks has taken up residence in the tiered seats and did Henslowe the help of carpeting the stage in shit, the Rose's quiet majesty remains untouched. I can picture the crowds, thick as cream, as I performed Cleopatra's and Bel-imperia's passions. Zounds, the missing of it all makes my throat swell! Two months ago the Rose was my entire world, and now I'm here in clothes that cost more than I ever made as a player, pretending to be a man that I am not, all in a desperate gamble that shall change my life or snatch away what little there is left to be taken from me.

Lady Catherine hugs one of the support beams and sighs, looking longingly at the wings where the players would gather. "Oh, it would be a dream to have one of my plays performed here!"

My head snaps toward her. "Do you write too? Your brother didn't mention his family had two playwrights."

Lady Catherine bursts out with a peal of laughter. "James, writing? Why, he can barely string a sentence together! Did you know he had me write all his letters to his betrothed?"

Wait.

Bloomsbury does not write?

If this is true—and judging from the burgundy flush

creeping across Bloomsbury's neck, it's very much true—then whose play was I managing before Marlowe's murder?

I fold my arms and level a sharp stare at the blushing lord. "Is that so? How *interesting*. He told me witnessing one of his plays performed before his wedding night was his dearest wish."

Lady Catherine is perfectly oblivious to our tiff. "I've always written, but Mother says I should take up the pin and not the quill, because no man would want a woman who writes. One day I shall prove her wrong."

Though I have only just met Lady Catherine, I find myself liking her already. She may be noble, but she has not let that capture and crush her spirit yet. I take her hand and plant a courtier's kiss upon her knuckles. "When you do, allow me to be the first to buy a ticket to your show, my lady."

She giggles and grins.

Bloomsbury clears his throat awkwardly. "We should go. Mother will wake up soon, and I'll have an earful of it if we're both missing." He pops over my shoulder as I lock the doors behind us, hands twisting nervously. "Could you . . . not tell Catherine about the rehearsals? It is one thing for me to risk my own reputation, but if word got out—"

"I shall not say anything. I promise."

His body relaxes. "Thank you." He wipes his brow and sighs. "You must truly think me a fool now."

"Whatever for?"

"For courting the queen's punishment and my family's ruin to make my sister smile."

"No," I say, the word slipping out before I'm aware of what I am saying. "I mean, yes it was daft. But it is also sweet." And it fills me to the brim with aching. Does my sister enjoy words like Lady Catherine? What of my brother? Though they are my closest kin in the entire world, they are also strangers to me. I haven't seen them for nine years.

The sound of scuffling breaks out, followed by a gleeful shriek. Bloomsbury and I look at each other and then sprint down the alley where Catherine has disappeared. The rankness of decay and piss grows so pungent, my eyes begin to water. But there, at the end, is Catherine, squatting upon the ground, heedless of all the filth seeping into her skirts. She turns at Bloomsbury's shout, clutching something dark and muddy in her arms. And—oh God, whatever it is, it's *wriggling*.

"I heard whimpering!" Catherine hoists up a droopy-faced puppy. It licks her face, and she coos. "Where are your mother and siblings, little one?"

Bloomsbury and I share another look. The breeze changes, carrying with it a strong whiff of carrion. Likely this pup is the offspring of one of the bandogs used in the bear-baiting pits. They've been closed like the theaters, and I know the pit keepers don't take good care of their animals.

"I am sure he can fend for himself," Bloomsbury says.

Catherine clutches the fetid animal closer. "James, this is a baby! Can't you see? He'll die out here."

The result of this, of course, is that the puppy returns with us, and we arrive back home irredeemably and inexcusably late.

Lady Bloomsbury herself waits in the stable yard. Were she

not so committed to the ridiculous rules of propriety which govern the sexes, I believe she would pull Bloomsbury's sword from its scabbard and behead us herself.

"Inside. *Now*," she spits through clenched teeth. When she takes in Catherine, with her wind-swept hair and ruined gown, I swear the temperature drops and hoarfrost creeps out beneath her hem. "And *you*. How dare you do this now. Tell me, does it please you to make a mockery of our family's name?"

Catherine takes a step behind her brother. "Mother, I—"

"The Middlemores are already here!" Lady Bloomsbury hisses so venomously, the chickens scatter. "I need you to go upstairs *now* and—"

"My lady?" Lord Middlemore is silhouetted at the door. Since last I saw him, some manservant has valiantly lost the battle to shape his great gray beard into something which resembles fashion. "There you are!" the lord croons, coming into the yard.

I glance over my shoulder—certain some new, nightmarish person has arrived—but no, instead Middlemore draws before Catherine, who seems utterly determined to never look at anything except the spot of the earth beneath her feet ever again. Though she is the one who ought to curtsy to Middlemore, because he outranks her, the lord drops to his knees before the girl and takes one of her dirty hands within his own. "I have missed you so, my dearest betrothed."

And then the man old enough to be Catherine's father tugs the puppy from her arms and presses a kiss against her clenched fist.

• • •

Inside, I pace beneath the wall of Bloomsbury's miserable-looking ancestors and try to make sense of what I have just witnessed. "Catherine is—"

"Engaged to Lord Middlemore, yes—"

"Who is also—"

"My betrothed Anne's father, yes—"

"So when you said you wanted to perform *The Most Lamentable Tragedy of Abelard and Heloise* before your wedding—"

"It was always about Catherine and her wedding, yes." Bloomsbury throws himself against the wall with a thump that sets the gilded portraits trembling and drags both hands down his face.

I walk back and forth across the polished floor, hands on hips. While I knew the business of marriage was little more than the transaction of livestock among nobles, it's another thing entirely to witness it. 'Tis a hard thing to be a woman in this world: everyone is a pawn or a plaything or both. Which one is it, I wonder, for Lord Middlemore, who aims to marry a girl younger than his own daughter? A wave of revulsion rises within me. I cease pacing and pivot to Bloomsbury. "This is why you want to discover the answers to Marlowe's plot as soon as possible. So you can spare your sister from marrying Middlemore."

A tendon cords in his neck. "Yes. If I could restore my family's standing with the queen, then—yes—Catherine would no longer be forced to wed this toad."

I shake my head. "I don't understand. Why did your parents

166 | ERIN COTTER

agree to have both you and your sister marry into this family?"

"Those were Middlemore's conditions. If my family was to receive his daughter's dowry, then my parents had to agree to the betrothal for my sister. Middlemore thinks . . . he thinks it'll make me more obedient to go along with his plans in the New World." He laughs helplessly at the absurdity of it all. "And he's right, because I'll do anything for Catherine! But if I can do the queen this service, if I can unravel this plot for her and prove that I'm a better person than my father is, then I shall ask her to intervene and stop my sister's marriage. I do not think she relishes the idea of Middlemore wedded to such a young girl, because she told me as much when she approved of my engagement. If the queen revokes her approval, Middlemore will have no choice but to listen to her. He'll have to find another bride."

I fight a cold shudder and thank God once more for not making me a member of the creepy nobility. "When is the marriage supposed to take place?"

His shoulders slump. "A fortnight from today."

So much of Bloomsbury's strangeness makes sense now. His urgency, his willingness to pay me so extravagantly. He's just a lad scheming desperately to save his sister. This is the secret he's been keeping cradled close. I suck in a soft breath, the hairs rising on my arms.

I've been drawn to him because our innermost selves are knapped from the same stone.

"Why didn't you say so sooner?" My whisper is swallowed by the huge high ceiling. "I would've understood. I could've done more."

Bloomsbury looks up at me from the curtain of his hair. Something unreadable flickers across his face. "I didn't think you'd care."

I duck my head, shame roiling over me. The noise of the household preparing for dinner grows so distant, it might as well come from another land.

"You were right before." The edge of my smallest finger traces down his, a feather-light plea. "But I care now."

The words linger between us like a physical thing. I can't take them back.

But when his mouth goes soft with surprise, I don't want to. I want him to know I mean every one of them.

# CHAPTER SEVENTEEN

THE NIGHT OF the Pirate Queen's play arrives.

'Tis also the day of Queen Elizabeth's midsummer feast.

As a guest of the Bloomsbury household, I am expected to attend the royal festivities with the family. But as a bloke in the throes of food poisoning sent from the devil himself, I am excused from the odious event.

In my chambers, I groan again and pour a slop of oats into the chamber pot. They make a chunky splat. I pour a bit of water in afterward for an extra tinkle.

Someone knocks. "Hughes? Is everything all right?"

I toss more slop into the pot and follow it up by blowing a tremendous raspberry. "Bloomsbury, I fear I have been taken ill!"

I can feel his sigh through the door. A wicked grin splits my lips. I saved this last bit especially for him.

"Does this mean you're, ah, indisposed for the night?" he says.

I blow another raspberry. "Oh my, I am afraid so! Do give all of court my apologies!"

Having overheard my illness, none of the servants dare

bother me. Once the rattle of carriage wheels fades, I change into the servant clothes stashed beneath my bed and rifle through the smallclothes drawer until my fingers caress something smooth and cold. The bottle of poison from Marlowe's pocket.

The liquid sloshes thickly, like congealing blood. Bloomsbury has insisted I take it along, hoping that the Pirate Queen's plundering will have acquainted her with whatever lies within the glass. I wrap the bottle in a scrap of linen and tuck it in my breast pocket alongside my cross. I steal through the house and exit out the scullery door, none of the servants any the wiser.

London has already begun its midsummer revels. Screams of laughter burst from the alehouses, and the street corners come alive with music and mischief. The whistle and pop of fireworks rend the air, and smudgy clouds of brimstone billow beneath the eaves. Shut up by the plague for weeks, now the entire city quivers like a starving bandog at the end of its lead, and I know not what would happen should the lead snap.

The jumble only grows wilder as I make my way to Gráinne Ní Mháille's ship. Even from the quay I can hear the roar of merriment and smell the funk of strong drink and the spice of roasted meat. I flash a wooden coin etched with the Pirate Queen's insignia to the pirate standing guard at the gangplank, and he lets me pass. The coin came tucked in a folded-up sonnet stuffed in the groove of the front door. Shakespeare came through after all. I wish he'd stop leaving me awful poems, but I suppose I can't complain about a free invitation to a private party.

Lanterns wink at the ship's sides like tethered stars as I climb on board. On the deck there are games and stories all spilling over one another in a dozen languages: ones I expect and speak snippets of after all my time in London, like Gaelic and Welsh and Cornish, but also stranger ones like German and Breton. I spot Réamonn, the pirate lad I met before, three tankards of ale around him, deep in conversation with Shakespeare.

"And it had ten arms and a beak like an eagle, and, I swear, when it looked at me with its eye, I saw Satan himself in there." The boy thumps his chest and takes a solemn swallow of beer.

"Interesting," Shakespeare murmurs, a dreamy cast to his eyes. Doubtlessly, he's already made it a plot device in some play. "How many legs did it have again?"

"At least a score," the boy says.

I skirt along the crowd—which is no small feat, considering how many people have forced themselves onto this blasted ship—until I spot the doors leading to its forbidden lower decks. My pulse quickens. I haven't seen the Pirate Queen yet, so she must be there.

I ease the door open. Just as I'm about to slip inside, a giant of a man bursts out from nowhere and seizes my shirt, lifting me to my toes. "Where do you think yer going? Trying to worm yer way inside, eh?"

I lie limp as a dishrag in the pirate's meaty paw. "The ale's all gone! Where do you lot keep the kegs?"

The sailor rolls his eyes and tosses me back into the crowd, roaring, *"Oy! Can somebody get this lad a drink?"*

Several tankards are thrust beneath my nose. Above them

a scarred hand emerges from the shadows and shoos the offerings away. Out from the ship's hold prowls the Pirate Queen. She's dressed like her men, and feral red curls shot through with silver cascade over her shoulders. She's far older than I thought—old enough to be a grandmother—but there's nothing matronly about the smirk she shoots me. "Here, pretty lad, take this." She presses her own tankard into my hands.

And then she winks at me.

I stare, flabbergasted, as she steps past.

*"Shakespeare!"* she bellows. *"You promised us a play!"*

The crowd scrambles as the players are pulled from their games, cups, and whatever else they're into. I press through the people until I'm as close to the queen as I dare to be and sit through Shakespeare's play for once as an audience member and not a performer, thank God. 'Tis something about twins and pirates and mistaken identities. I want to loathe it on principle, but its jests make me laugh. Shakespeare is a fine writer. With practice, he could likely be one day as good as Marlowe. Or—and at this thought my hands tighten—rather, with Marlowe gone, Shakespeare *is* the best playwright in all of England. I sorely hope no one has informed him of this fact, as it'll go straight to his head. Knowing Shakespeare, he's already thought of it himself and is telling anyone who will listen.

As the play ends, I wiggle past the last person who sits between me and Gráinne Ní Mháille.

*"Dia dhuit."* I hold out my arms so she can see that no dagger hangs at my hip. *"An féidir linn labhairt go príobháideach tar éis seo?"* My Irish is middling at best, so I spent most of the

past two days lurking in a tavern where London's Irish population lingers to get the phrase just so. It was Bloomsbury's idea. *Speaking their tongue shall endear you to them,* he promised.

The Pirate Queen gives me a cool sidelong glance. Then she nods once.

Something sharp pokes my side. The enormous bear of a man who hauled me up before grins. The edge of his dagger flashes silver in candlelight as it tickles my ribs. All right, then. Obviously the Irish was a shade too much. I bite back a curse against Bloomsbury and, before the applause finishes, I'm hauled off into the bowels of the ship.

The huge corsair tosses me onto a chair in front of a scarred table.

"Who the hell are you, and why are you on my ship?" Gráinne demands. Her gray eyes are flinty as a sea before a storm. "If you're a spy, you'll find no ally in me."

I do my best to appear charming and harmless. "I am no spy, my lady." Or at least, I'm fairly certain what Bloomsbury and I are doing does not qualify as spy work. "A friend was unjustly murdered, and I believe you may know something about it."

The storm in the queen's eyes spills over. She slaps the edge of the table and shouts, "I've nothing to do with any murder on English shores, you hear? Go crawling back to your master and tell him Gráinne Ní Mháille is an honest woman!"

The burly pirate lifts me from my seat. I kick out my legs and wrap them around the table's leg, holding myself fast. The sailor curses and pulls harder. My thigh muscles scream in protest. "Wait!" I tug the poison phial free. "Have you ever seen this before?"

Gráinne holds out a hand to stop her man, squinting. "Give that here."

She inspects the bottle carefully. Then she uncorks it and lifts it to her face. A warning cry bursts from my throat, but the pirate cuffs my ear.

Gráinne takes an appraising sniff of the liquid. She recorks the bottle and places it on the table, staring at it the way Bloomsbury stares at the tinctures in his laboratory. "It's been a long time since I've seen the likes of this."

I cannot tell if this is a conversation or an explanation. Between the steel in her eyes and on her person, silence seems most prudent. The pirate bloke leans over my shoulder for a closer look. "What is it?"

"'Tis a type of wolfsbane only found in the Pyrenees mountains," the Pirate Queen says. "The flowers are the most beautiful violet. Only a few people in the world can harvest wolfsbane without succumbing to the poison themselves." Gráinne turns to me; curiosity tempers her stern expression. "Where did you find this?"

"It was on a dead body. Corked and unused."

"Unused far as *you* know."

I squirm. It's been my assumption Marlowe has been the wronged man in all of this—but what if he wasn't? What if he's the villain, and I'm treading down this path ignorant of his misdeeds? Mayhap there was a good reason why someone wanted the playwright dead.

"You said the poison hails from the Pyrenees mountains," I hazard cautiously, as if I know where they are. "Does this mean it's not English?"

"'Tis Spanish." Gráinne begins to pace. "If a drop is placed in a glass, the drinker will dine and be merry for an hour before he drops dead. A nasty way to go." Gráinne stops and thrusts her face to mine, her lips a narrow line. "Which is why I want nothing to do with this. And if you had any sense, you'd want nothing to do with it either."

I'm losing her interest. I can feel it. When this happened on the stage, Henslowe told us to do something ridiculous, something the audience couldn't look away from even if they wanted to. But this cramped chamber is no stage, and my audience is armed and cares not to get their penny's worth of entertainment.

"Are you the Red Queen?" I demand breathlessly.

I expect a reaction. A widening of the eyes, a slip of the hand. Not Gráinne's bored sigh and the way she massages her temples like Bloomsbury does when I've asked one too many impertinent questions. "Brogan, remove him."

I only barely manage to snatch the poison before I'm hauled up by my armpits. "Why do you seek an audience with Queen Elizabeth?"

Gráinne smirks as she pours herself more ale. "If you can arrange an audience between myself and the English queen, mayhap I'll tell you."

"I could do that!" I shout over the pirate's shoulder before I am hoisted above deck. He drags me past the partygoers—

quite a bit drunker now than before—and past an astonished Shakespeare before he throws me onto the skinny board leading off the ship.

Pain bursts through my ribs, and I grab the plank to catch myself and avoid plummeting into the fetid Thames. A groan escapes me. Tomorrow I'll have a nasty bruise that will be difficult to explain to the servants. I crawl down the rest of the plank and lie on the dock like a sad starfish, one hand clutching the miraculously unbroken poison bottle over my heart.

"Oy!" The pirate lad, Réamonn, leans over the ship's side, cackling at me. "Better luck next time, mate!"

I make a rude gesture at him, and he cackles more, vanishing into the party.

I close my eyes and sigh.

It does not seem as though Gráinne Ní Mháille is the Red Queen.

But we do know where the poison is from, so there's that. Doubtlessly, Bloomsbury will consider this a massive win and embark on another tedious week of research, even though *everyone* knows Spain would love to see Queen Elizabeth dead. Ever since her father, King Henry VIII, tossed aside his Spanish bride like a toy he tired of, relations have been tense betwixt England and Spain.

An absolutely filthy sea ballad jolts me from brooding. Stomping boots cause the dock timbers to shiver beneath me. I will the sailors to pass without comment, but of course, God is not on my side tonight.

One sailor toes me with his boot. "You look long-faced,

lad. 'Tis midsummer! Come up on our ship and have a spot of fun!"

"Thank you, but I've had enough fun for tonight." I stumble to my feet, wincing.

Another of the men claps my shoulder. He reeks of something stronger than ale and, strangely, flowers. "If you've got women problems, I know where you can go." He pulls me closer. "We've just been to a brothel the likes of which you've never seen before."

"Full of English roses!" another man says, a look of wonder on his face.

I sidestep the first pirate's embrace. "I'm quite all right, thank you."

"'Tis called the Red Queen," he insists. "It'll make your night turn a corner, I promise!"

I freeze mid-stride. There's a faint ringing in my ears, as if a cannon has been shot too close to my person. I turn around slowly, hardly daring to hope. "'Tis called the Red Queen, you say?"

# CHAPTER EIGHTEEN

THE RED QUEEN is in Farringdon, a neighborhood where men with full bellies and fuller pockets live in elegant homes stacked like iced pastries in a bakery window. The brothel itself is near indistinguishable from its reputable neighbors. Only the single red candle flickering at its door gives away the true nature of its business.

I pound against the door with both fists. It flies open, and I nearly tumble across the plump feet of an elegant older woman.

"Sir!" Her eyes wander over me before settling upon my crotch. Her lips purse. "Is there . . . *an urgent matter* with which we can assist you?"

"Yes! Not like that, though." I shove my way inside, which is all shimmering silk and smoke. A far cry from the filthy dumps I pass by out on London's outskirts. "I'm—I'm looking to speak with someone here. Whoever it is left me a note in Southwark. 'Tis of utmost importance!"

The madam's eyebrows draw together in a disapproving slant. "I believe, sir, that you are foxed and lost, and I shall have none of this in my place of business."

From the perfumed shadows a figure eddies forth. "If you're looking for something to talk about, I could deliver, sir." She punctuates her words with a wink. Every detail about this woman is exquisitely arrayed. The curve of her white hand and the artful mussing of her mahogany curls. Not to mention the calculating gleam in her eyes.

She's no prostitute, but a player, like me.

I gasp and stagger, like a man utterly struck by beauty. "By God, you're like a dream." I take her hand and spin her around the foyer. She giggles.

There's a quick exchange of coin, and then the girl—Ester—leads me away. Suffocating fabrics and cloying candles choke the stairwells. I'm thoroughly lost by the time Ester pulls me into a room and shuts the door.

"Took you long enough," she hisses, all pretensions dropped. She roots through the top drawer of a skinny cupboard. "About as subtle as an oliphant, too." A bit of parchment is stuffed into my hand. "I've never seen you used as a runner before." Her gaze pans up and down my body. A smirk lifts her lips. "And I'd certainly remember you."

A brothel. Frizer's note led us to a brothel. 'Tis not what I expected—and Ester is *certainly* not what I expected—but it makes sense. Farringdon is a place for wealth, where rich merchants and nobles walk side by side, not as equals but something close to it. It's exactly the sort of place where a noble, or a hired hand, could place a message to make sure it reached the darkest, foulest corners of London without getting a single speck of dirt on their haughty hands.

I tear off the wax seal and read the message.

*They strike on midsummer at midnight.*

A hideous feeling chokes me.

*Tonight* is the midsummer's eve.

The hideous feeling sinks into my bones, my whole body going cold. I don't know who they are, or what this means, but my gut tells me it's not good, and my gut's the thing that's kept me alive in this godforsaken city.

"Do you work with a man named Frizer?" I ask.

Ester frowns. "Never heard that name before in my life."

The hideous feeling grows. If Ester says she has not heard of Frizer, then she is either lying or she and Frizer do not work together. Thus the note I found leading me to the Red Queen was meant to lead someone else here. Perhaps someone with a penchant for murder.

And if Ester says I'm late, then whoever her message was intended for was supposed to have been here days ago. Which means . . . the next step of whatever scheme we've stumbled into is unfurling tonight, and we've got no time left. God Almighty, our chance to act has all but slipped away unless I seize it by the tail and act now.

*I've got to get to Bloomsbury.* I roll up the parchment with unsteady fingers. He's always got a plan, even if it isn't a good one. He'll at least think of something.

"What's going on? Why are you shaking?" Ester says, suspicion on her face.

I stuff the parchment into my boot, already moving toward the door. "'Tis nothing. I must be going now."

"Who are you?" Ester demands, her expression darkening.

I hear, rather than see, the knife whizzing toward me. I gape at the quivering handle in the wall just beside my head, not prepared in the slightest when Ester knees the fork of my legs.

The world tilts sideways as I drop to the floor, agony ripping through me. Ester's blade kisses my throat right where my pulse leaps.

Someone knocks outside. "Everything all right?"

"Ooh, yes!" Ester giggles. Her knife breaks my skin, and I gasp. "We're having a marvelous time!"

Only when the madam's footsteps fade does Ester speak, her voice a growl. "I'll give you another chance. Who are you?"

Between Ester's blade and the throbbing in my balls, I'd sell out my own mother if it meant she'd leave me alone. "Will Hughes."

"And who do you serve, Hughes?"

"No one!" The knife bites deeper into my flesh. "Argh, all right! Lord James Bloomsbury! We're investigating the unjust murder of Christopher Marlowe!"

The knife's pressure eases. Ester judges me with an unreadable stare. "Are you for or against Marlowe's cause?"

*Finally* someone who knows what Marlowe's been up to. I consider how this knife-wielding viper softened at Marlowe's name before I answer. "Most certainly for Marlowe's cause, I assure you, mistress!"

Ester stands and motions for me to do the same. She wipes her bloodied blade on her skirt. "You tell me about this Frizer person now, or I'll take your bollocks."

I wince and tell her everything that's happened since Marlowe's murder, about me trailing Frizer and finding his note in the graveyard that led me here.

Ester rocks backward when I mention the note, eyes wide. "It's finally happened. They've found me."

"Who's found you?" I ask. Urgency crawls through me, the too-fast gallop of time making my feet itch to run to Bloomsbury. "Tell me."

Ester steadies her expression and sheathes her blade. "Oh no. I'm not telling you a thing. Seems like you'll find out for yourself soon enough. You're still bleeding, by the way."

I thumb away the blood on my neck, impressed, even though my crotch still aches something fierce. "No one's ever bested me like that before." I mean, Maggie has, of course, but she's half-feral and a thief, to boot.

Ester doesn't look at me. She re-pins the hair which has fallen from her twist. "'Tis easy to best men like you, Will Hughes." She touches her finger in a pot of dyed beeswax and dabs it upon her lips. "Men like you see women and see weakness. If a man admires a woman for her strength, 'tis because something about her reminds him of a man."

I open my mouth, ready to protest, but then I consider Maggie. The Pirate Queen. The rumors that Elizabeth has the heart and stomach of a king. She's got a fair point.

I bow my head. "I'm sorry for underestimating you."

She replaces the lid on the beeswax. "No need to apologize. I adore thick-headed men. It's what makes me dangerous and what makes you foolish." She turns to me, eyes smoky and lips stained with red. "Now go save the queen. I shall pray for your success." She plants a sticky kiss on my lips. Before I can react at all, she shoves me away with a wicked wink. "And *that's* in case you don't make it."

Whitehall Palace's brilliance shines bright in the distance long before I reach its walls. Somewhere in its belly is Bloomsbury with all the rest of court. Feasting and dancing and laughing whilst wild London howls outside the gates.

The tinkling of dice and laughter pours from the guard-house window overlooking a stone archway. No one minds the open gate. I slip through it unnoticed and enter the royal grounds. I keep to the paths lined by tall garden hedges and avoid the lawn dominating the massive courtyard. Distant noise, and the scent of spice, beckons me toward the great kitchen.

A fire roars in the enormous hearth. Everything is a riot of movement, servants bustling every which way, and the room blazes with a frantic desperation more befitting a battlefield than a feast. I press myself into a shadowed corner and watch the crush of people until I find what I'm looking for.

A serving lad sweating so nervously, he's got damp spots under his arms. He'll do quite nicely.

I stay hidden until he reappears with an empty mead jug. Then I yank him outside into a garden damp with dew and redolent of bruised mint.

"What's all this about?" he cries, tearing away from me.

The right thing to do would be to knock him out and hide the body. But this lad's closer to twelve than eighteen. And he's looking at me with these wide scared eyes that remind me so much of my brother, I can't do it.

I snatch the jug from him. "Why don't you go off and enjoy a bit of midsummer fun?"

"But Cook says we're all supposed to stay close until the queen dismisses us!" The boy glances over his shoulder, back toward the light and warmth of the kitchen.

I cup his chin and smile. My nails bite into the soft skin under his jaw. A warning. "If you tell anyone I came here, that would be most unwise. And I'll be needing your clothes as well."

A few minutes later, I stride back into the kitchen wearing trousers at least five inches too short and a doublet that doesn't close all the way, the poison phial nestled safely alongside my heart. Happily, everyone is too busy to notice my arrival. I fill my jug and follow the tide of servants deeper through the palace courtyard toward the open banquet hall doors limned with light.

If I once thought the Bloomsbury town house full of splendor, it is but a tarnished penny compared to Whitehall. The ceiling is so tall, I'm half-convinced God himself lurks in the rafters. A hundred thousand candles smolder above the coiffed heads of the nobles assembled below. The burning scent of camphor barely blots out the stench of bodies twisting in the summer heat. I stay focused on following the lad before me, but when I spot her, I freeze.

Elizabeth Tudor, queen of England, sits on a throne at the room's end.

Though I've not seen her before, I recognize the hawk-nosed profile which has been stamped on every coin fisted tight in my hand. All the hall's conversation and glances and noise pitch toward the queen, the point around which the whole room—the whole of England—spins. Her laugh cleaves through the clamor, the loudest sound in the room. The back of my neck sweats, and my throat goes dry. I know, should she demand it, any one of the men in this room would draw his sword and kill me without question.

Something slams into my back. My jug slips, and the sound of shattering pottery bounces off the walls.

Every pair of eyes in the banqueting hall turns to stare at me. Including *hers*.

All the terrible tales I've heard about the queen rush through my head. That once she plucked out a courtier's eye because his look displeased her. That she chops off the hands of pamphle-teers who dare quill a word against her. That she drowned the entire Spanish Armada with nothing more than a prayer.

A man whispers something into the queen's ear. She laughs, her eyes leaving me. Chatter resumes. The awful moment passes and takes a handful of years from my life along with it.

Someone shoves me. "You absolute dolt!" 'Tis the queen's cupbearer, both his exceptional beauty and the gold which threads through his livery setting him apart from the general staff. Seems a bit excessive to me, seeing as all the cupbearer does is serve the queen's wine. My work as a boy actor has acquainted me with this strange, extravagant, courtly role.

"You're the one who ran into *me*!" I protest.

"Go clean it up!" he hisses with another shove. "You're embarrassing all of us!" His gaze lingers on my unbuttoned doublet. I bend down before he can get a better look and pile the shattered pieces into what's left of the jug and mop up the mead, grumbling.

A shadow slices above me, and all at once, there's Bloomsbury.

"Hughes," he whispers, shock on every line of his face. "What are you doing here?"

He is absolutely resplendent in snowy hose and a copper-embroidered doublet and polished boots. In the queen's palace he is absolutely Lord Bloomsbury, and there's no trace of book-addled James to be found.

"Hughes," he says as if he's said it several times already. "Do explain."

I shake my head and cut my eyes toward the door. I can't explain with all these people about. Not when the Bloomsbury ladies could recognize me.

I toss the jug and wait for him in the gardens. Towering walls of ivy box in rows of budding roses. A pond lies beyond the briars, its surface velveted with duckweed. Even though the banquet hall and kitchen hum with noise, right here it feels as though I'm leagues away from the feast.

The shrubberies tremble, and Bloomsbury appears.

He smiles at the sight of me. Then his eyes snag upon my mouth. He flushes. "There's, ah, something on your lips."

I touch them, and my fingertips come away red. "Oh, yes. I was at a brothel."

He makes a strangled sound.

"Zounds, not like that! The Red Queen wasn't the Pirate Queen at all. 'Twas a brothel in Farringdon."

Bloomsbury groans. "Of course! My Cambridge class-mates went there. If only we'd thought to ask a single soul—"

"Bore me later." There's no time for Bloomsbury to lament his research process or celibate school years. I pull out the mead-sodden message from my boot. "Something's happening at midnight."

Bloomsbury rips the parchment from me. "Dear God," he whispers, the color leaching from his face as he reads. His eyes meet mine, huge with shock.

We've reached the next step of our investigation—but 'tis too much, too soon. Only this parchment reeking of liquor and the suspicions of a penniless player and out-of-favor lord compose our case. No one shall believe us.

Anxiety buzzes through me, like the murmur of the crowd right before the play begins. "You've got to do something or tell someone. They'll never listen to me."

"That's true," he agrees, too quickly for my liking. "You need to leave. You shouldn't even be here."

I roll my eyes. "Apologies for interrupting your royal evening. I imagined you'd want to know someone might be attempting to murder your sovereign—"

Bloomsbury seizes my shoulders and pins me against the prickly hedge. His thigh is betwixt my knees, holding me in place. The movement is so swift, so unexpected, I don't resist. His face blazes inches from mine, voice low and furious. "This is no game, Elias! You've trespassed on the royal grounds crying someone's killing the queen, and they'll arrest you for it, even if you're right. It doesn't matter what you say because you're nothing to them, and to me you're—" He pauses and takes a deep shuddering breath, and I swear, my heart stops beating.

"I'm what?" I whisper.

The anger in his expression fractures. His brow brushes against mine for the briefest moment, so quick, I think I dreamt it. "Not even my title can protect you here. You *must* leave."

I close my eyes as he steps away, heart jammed in my throat. "All right, then. I'll meet you at the house afterward."

He takes off into the darkness. Then there's nothing left except the rush of blood in my ears and a trembling in my limbs. I drag an unsteady hand through my sweaty hair. It feels like something dark and dangerous has whooshed past, leaving us unscathed only until it returns. I resist the urge to run after him, stay with him until the end of the night.

I don't want to be alone anymore.

Not out here, when every trembling shadow takes the shape of something sinister; every strange sound makes me flinch. Bloomsbury's reaction has unnerved me. I don't know if he's right about the danger, but if the pounding in my ribs is any indication at all, he's right about one thing.

I've got to go.

Something crunches nearby, so soft, I near miss it.

My vision spots with black, wild panic taking over.

There's more rustling, quieter, like a man trying very, very hard not to be discovered.

I'm not alone out here. Someone might have witnessed Bloomsbury's and my conversation. Or that damn kitchen boy might have gone and squealed that someone's infiltrated the palace grounds.

The pond beckons me, quiet and still. I creep through the roses—wincing when they cut, fighting the scream building in my lungs—and slip beneath the dark water just as a hooded figure steps into the garden alcove I've abandoned.

Ripples flutter on the water's surface, pointing exactly toward where my head pokes up among the duckweed. The damn pond's only a yard deep. I kneel awkwardly to hide in the shallows and scuttle backward, praying it gets deeper.

But the man doesn't look at the pond. Instead he kneels out of my sight, reappearing with two fingers beneath his nose.

My boots, sticky with strong-scented mead. I must've left wet prints on the stones. I hold my breath as the man's hood rises, following the prints until they disappear through the roses into the pond.

The man stares straight ahead—straight at *me*.

*Does he see me?*

I go rabbit-still.

Church bells chime quarter to midnight beyond the palace grounds. By the time the bells fade away, another figure has slipped into the garden.

The royal cupbearer who bumped into me.

"Is everything prepared as we discussed?" the shadowed figure says quietly.

The boy bows. "It is, sir."

"I can trust you to do your part?"

"Yes. The queen shall be dead before dawn."

The man hands something to the boy. A shaft of moonlight catches his waist, and I gasp.

A gilded solar scabbard hangs at his hip. The very same one the murderer wore the night Marlowe was killed.

The man cuffs the boy. "Stop making noise. Did you hear that?" He drops into a crouch, the sword flashing in his hand.

I clasp trembling fingers over my mouth and squeeze my eyes shut. *Don'tlookcloserdon'tlookcloserdon'tlookcloser.*

"'Tis the spit hounds. They're always underfoot," the cupbearer mutters sullenly. "Don't see why you had to hit me over it."

"That, dear lad, is why I am in charge and you are not," the man replies icily. "Now go."

The boy leaves.

The man does not. Without sheathing his blade, he stomps toward the pond. I take a deep breath and go supine under the water.

A blade stabs through the duckweed right where my head was.

I sink to the muddy bottom, lungs already burning.

The blade explores carefully, passing inches over my stinging open eyes. Then suddenly it thrusts deeper, sinking into the mud, a silty cloud blooming. Then it plunges again, grazing my arm. I grit my teeth against the fiery pain, tiny bubbles streaming from my mouth.

The blade stabs again, and I barely manage to scuttle away, chest all but bursting, more bubbles streaming out of my nose—

All at once, the blade yanks back.

I stay under until my vision spots and the pressure in my head nearly bursts, and then I explode out of the water with a heaving gasp. My heartbeat pounds all over my body, fiercest where blood oozes from my arm.

The garden alcove is empty.

Bloomsbury told me to leave, but he didn't overhear this. The cupbearer is the only person in the entire kingdom permitted to serve the queen's wine. Queen Elizabeth trusts her cupbearer and other personal attendants more than any treasonous blood relative or oil-lipped courtier. They guard her against situations precisely such as the one unfurling now. I can't fathom the wild promises whispered to the cupbearer to convince him to abandon his sacred oath, but I know the man with the solar scabbard must be powerful beyond imagination to make it so.

If someone does not act now, Queen Elizabeth will die.

Which . . . well, it wouldn't be the worst if she kicked it. But then I'd never see a wink of my hundred pounds. I'll trudge across the country to my family's cottage with nothing for them save the burden of another mouth to feed. Bloomsbury's spirited sister, Lady Catherine, shall be forced to wed that Middlemore toad, and Bloomsbury'll be sent from England, and I'll never see him again.

These unhappy futures play before me, warring against my instinct to run, to preserve my own skin before anything else. You don't survive in London by putting others before you. I know this. I've learned it the hard way again and again.

But is surviving the same as living?

I don't know. These past few months have stirred up all I thought I knew and made it unfamiliar. Is there even a chance I could escape unscathed tonight when I've trespassed onto the royal grounds and blood is about to be spilt not even a furlong away from me?

Feeling as if I've got no choice, I squelch into the banqueting hall as the bells begin tolling out midnight.

*Bong.*

There's a jester before me juggling apples. I push past him, and the apples tumble.

*Bong.*

Some lord crashes into me, his teeth stained red and breath wine-sour.

*Bong.*

The queen stands. All the heads in the hall snap toward her.

*Bong.*

I spot the cupbearer through the crowd, ahead of me, too far to reach.

*Bong.*

Nobles turn with black scowls; their angry whispers trail me like a flock of rooks.

A cry tears from my throat.

*Bong.*

The cupbearer kneels before the queen and offers the cup.

The queen lifts the goblet to her wrinkled lips.

*Bong.*

I launch myself at the queen.

The goblet spirals from her hands, flashing silver like a leaping fish. My ribs catch the floor, and pain bursts through me. Wine soaks my clothes and fills my nostrils with its cloying scent. I follow the spreading spill to where it stops just before a gilded white hem. The queen. And there, betwixt us, spins the bottle of poison, which has wormed its way from my doublet in the jumble to lie there like a bloody dagger proclaiming my guilt to a hundred shocked witnesses.

The queen stares down at me with eyes like black stones set in snow.

"Kill the assassin," she commands.

# CHAPTER NINETEEN

THE RINGING OF steel pulled from sheaths rends the air. I cringe and press my cheek to the stones, bracing for the blades.

*I'm going to die.*

And the worst thing is that everyone told me this would happen, and I was too daft to listen. Everything I've done to keep my family and myself far away from this bloodthirsty queen has delivered me right to her feet like a sow to slaughter. Do a person's eyes keep seeing after their head has been chopped off? If so, my last glimpse will be immensely disappointing. The queen's glare, sour as a crab apple. The slumped form of my own corpse, blood pooling dark and warm across the floors. I hope it takes them absolute ages to scrub the stains out.

"Wait! Stop!"

Wild footsteps echo, and a heavy weight throws itself over me. Lavender fills my nostrils. Bloomsbury. What in God's name is he doing?

"Your Majesty, this is not what it seems." Burgundy wine creeps up his lacy cuffs and soaks into his embroidered sleeves. My pride gives a feeble stir and demands that I stop allowing myself to be sheltered within another's arms. Instead the tension in my limbs softens. *Safe.* The word echoes over and over again, even though the swords pointed at my throat speak otherwise.

"Please, all can be explained, I swear it," Bloomsbury implores.

The banquet hall begins to buzz like a kicked hornets' nest. The guards' swords make no move to fall.

The queen towers over us. She is awfully tall, for a woman. The white lead powder on her cheeks has cleft and reveals the red flush of skin beneath.

And then finally, in a deadly whisper, she commands, "Arrest them both."

The Whitehall dungeon reeks of decay.

I draw my knees to my chest, shivering all the harder in my drenched clothes.

"You'd be warmer if you shucked those wet things," Bloomsbury advises from the other side of the cell.

"No. I'll not be caught by the queen with my breeches down."

Something sails into my face. Bloomsbury's opulent doublet. I hold it for a moment, unsure if I should hurl it back or not, then shrug into it. "It'll be ruined if I wear it, you know."

Bloomsbury laughs darkly. "Oh, we've far worse problems than ruined finery."

The heavy wooden door swings open with a thud. A man with a great ginger beard strides in, looking as though it would very much please him to shove us both from the palace walls and watch our bodies splat upon the street.

"Lord Robert Cecil of Salisbury. What a pleasure!" Blooms-bury says like this is all perfectly fine and we're meeting across a dinner table and not across a prison cell.

"I wish I could say the same." Cecil's eyes rove all over me. They linger for a long time on Bloomsbury's doublet. I gather it around myself like armor.

"There's a reason for all this," Bloomsbury insists.

Cecil flashes an oily smirk. "Let us pray it is a good one."

Bloomsbury explains the entire blundering mess, begin-ning with my murderous meeting with Marlowe and ending with my manful assailing of the queen's wine cup. Cecil's head is shaking long before the story's end. "Christ, you two are terrible spies."

"Well, the queen's still alive, isn't she?" I snap.

Cecil pivots, surprised, as though I am a rat that has some-how learned how to speak. "You poked your nose in a very delicate balance of information and have done untold damage to our networks, sirrah!"

"Apologies, who are you again, sir?" I say sweetly. "You must not be very important if you've been sent to squabble with prisoners."

The ends of Cecil's mustache quiver. "Why—you insolent nobody! I am the queen's spymaster!"

Bloomsbury slices his hand across his throat, motioning for me to shut up.

I barrel on, heedless of his warning. "Seems like you did a

rubbish job of spying, since we're the ones who saved the queen!"

Cecil stabs a finger at me. "I'll not be disrespected by the likes of you! I've drawn and quartered men for less." The cell door snaps shut, and the heavy bolt outside is slid back into place.

Bloomsbury and I share a long, exhausted look. Then he sighs and settles. "Would it kill you not to quarrel with everything that moves?"

I don't answer. My mind keeps going back to before, when I was certain I was about to feel cold steel bite into my neck and instead found Bloomsbury crouching over me, standing between me and the queen herself. There should be only one person in this cell right now.

"Why did you do it?"

"Do what?"

I drag my tongue along my cracked lips. "Come to my aid. You said you couldn't save me."

Bloomsbury tilts his head back against the wall, his freckled throat a marble column. The silence stretches for so long, I think he will not reply, but then in this soft voice he says, "I know. But I still had to try."

A shiver goes through me. He notices the movement, then shifts and clears his throat. He fists a hand in his hair and laughs helplessly. "Doubtlessly, my family's name is muddied beyond hope now. I imagine Mother has already died of shame and shall be haunting me any second."

"You regret saving me, then." I draw the doublet more tightly around myself, shivering harder.

There's a rustling from Bloomsbury, and then he's beside me. The warmth of his body is like a hot fire at the end of a long winter day. "When will you believe me that I value you for yourself and not for what you can do for me?"

His honesty disarms me. There's a hum in my body like a breath held for too long. I open my mouth, ready to argue, but no words rush to my arsenal. And, because it really is quite frigid and this could very well be the last bit of kindness I receive on earth, I allow myself to soften against him, eyes drifting shut.

The cell grows colder as my clothes dry. Only flickering torchlight limning the locked door from the hall beyond provides light. I've no idea what time it is. How long does Whitehall leave its prisoners to fester? Days? Months? Surely Bloomsbury's title earns him a respite from this hell. But does that mean they would leave me here? To rot amidst the rats and mold and God only knows what else? *I've drawn and quartered men for less.* I shiver again.

Bloomsbury's sigh breaks the quiet. "You should've left when I told you to."

"I figured you'd pay me more if I saved the queen."

I feel him almost smile. "That's not why you came back." he says, his head tipped to the side, his expression inviting me to say more if I like.

I bite my cheek, iron breaking on my tongue, and the last bit of resistance left in me dissolves. "I did it for my folks. Same reason I've done everything else."

Even though I once vowed to keep my history a secret, I suddenly find myself telling him everything. The cold gray sea and biting winds, our grubby cottage bright and tenacious as a torch. The tears in my mother's eyes as she kissed my forehead goodbye, hoping beyond hope she was sending me off with the lying men to a better life than the one she could offer me.

"'Tis why I wanted the money." I gesture toward the dank cell and the world beyond it, gold and glittering, entirely out of reach now. "We never had enough, and I wasn't old enough to help back then. But I am now."

And, zounds, I can picture so clearly what success would have looked like. Me, clambering up the last hill with heavy pockets. My family weeping with joy, their arms around me at last, holding together my splintered parts. The pain of the vision is gutting, and it takes all the resolve I've got left not to weep.

Finally confessing why I've been doing what I've been doing unclenches something tight in my chest. Keeping all this from him has made me feel worse instead of better like I thought it would. I take in a deep breath and marvel at how easily it comes now.

*I'm sorry.* The prayer is fleeting as smoke from a smothered candle. I hope some measure of it drifts to my family, and they will know what has become of me. *I did all I could.*

I open my eyes to Bloomsbury's aghast face.

"Elias—" He trips over my name. "What you've been through—it's absolutely awful. You know that, don't you?"

"Sorry if learning more about me displeases you," I say tartly. "Not all of us have stories worth putting into plays."

He shoots me a sullen, pitying look, as if I have said something so unfathomably witless he cannot bear to speak of it.

"James—"

He makes a curt motion, cutting me off. His eyes blaze like they did in the garden. "You are enough and have always been enough. To me, your kin, or anyone else, including the queen of England. Do you understand?" His voice is a wreck, and I realize too late that he's not angry.

He's weeping.

He's weeping for *me*.

The tenderness in me spills over, and I'm swept away in a torrent. There is a pounding in my rib cage which has naught to do with fear, but it frightens me more than anything the queen has in store for us. I twist to face him, take his hand roughly in my unsteady one, suddenly needing to know what this means, what this means to him all these weeks we've circled each other only to end up here, alone, together.

"James—"

The dungeon door bangs open, and Cecil is there. He smirks at the sight of Bloomsbury's tears, and I want to tear out his throat. "What's it to be, then?" I stand, arms crossed, legs apart, blocking his view of Bloomsbury. "Hanging or beheading? Either's fine with us as long as we've got a say in the last meal."

Cecil doesn't look as thrilled at the thought of my demise as I'd expect. "Come with me," he demands, and we've no choice but to follow. Bloomsbury and I walk side by side, so close, we're near tripping each other. Cecil leads us through a rabbit's warren of dank tunnels, pausing before a half-sized door. He knocks upon it once; an answering knock sounds back before the door swings open.

I blink like I've stepped out into the sun after a hard afternoon in an alehouse. We're in a marvelously appointed parlor, a chamber befitting any fine lord, save for one detail very much out of place.

A body dead upon the floor.

'Tis the servant boy whose clothing I stole. In death he is purple faced and reeking of shit.

Horror spreads through me like the bloodstains seeping through the exquisite rug. A few hours ago the boy was alive and well and rightly mistrustful of me. Now he is dead, and I have an awful suspicion 'tis my fault.

A quiet cough sounds. The queen stands in the gilded entryway, surrounded by a retinue of servants and guards.

Bloomsbury and Cecil immediately fall into low bows. A half second later I follow. A drop of sweat slides down my nose.

There's a rustle of fabric as the queen settles herself on a chair. "Lord Cecil. Lord Bloomsbury. And . . . *you*."

I rise from my bow to find the queen's black eyes piercing me.

"Will Hughes." I stumble into my deepest curtsy. "Formerly of the Lord Admiral's Men at the Rose Theatre." A hairsbreadth too late I realize curtsying is no appropriate manner with which to greet the ruler of England.

For a moment there's no reaction. And then the queen's cackle saws through the silence. It goes on for so long, Cecil joins in before he's silenced with a glare. The queen nestles her jaw upon a bejeweled hand. "And pray do tell us. How did the son of our disgraced Lord Bloomsbury form a partnership with a boy actor and thwart an attempt upon our life?"

My eyes are drawn again to the servant boy's body. I swallow several times before my breath steadies. "Did—did he drink the poison?"

"Did you ask us a question?" the queen says pleasantly, her words trimmed with danger.

Bloomsbury draws himself to his full height. Even covered in wine and filth and missing his doublet, there's a tilt to his shoulders and a depth to his chest I can only describe as aristocratic. "If I may be so bold, my queen, were it not for Mr. Hughes solving the final clues tonight, you would not be speaking to us right now."

Cecil's lips scrunch all together like an arsehole. "Your Majesty. These boys are foolish. I would have handled this much more delicately—"

The queen slaps Lord Cecil. The quiet that follows is so complete, I can hear the course of water passing through some distant channel.

"We did not invite you to speak," she hisses. "However, since you have already interrupted us, tell us again, Robert: Why was our cupbearer switched last night?"

Cecil presses a hand against the red splotch on his cheek. "The boy was ill, my queen, and the Dolley boy had served you as cupbearer before. Nothing seemed amiss!"

"And yet"—the queen inclines her head toward me and Bloomsbury—"here we are. This would've never happened under Walsingham, you know."

Cecil stammers and scoffs, paling.

I've got the disconcerting sense I've stumbled into a fight

I've no business hearing. Were I alone, I'd tiptoe out whence I came and latch the door behind me. But there's nowhere to go in the queen's decadently appointed chamber. My gaze bounces all over the gilt frames, tapestries, and other riches. How much blood that we can't see is in this room? How much of my family's blood paid for these fine things?

The queen stares at me like she can sense the anger growing inside me. "Elias Wilde. It is something to finally meet you."

The sound of my true name here, in the heart of the queen's palace, the most dangerous place in England, sends me reeling. Only Bloomsbury's touch at my elbow keeps me on my feet. "You—you know who I am?"

Queen Elizabeth snaps her fingers. Cecil lifts a thick letter from a gilded tray. The battered parchment is stained with a substance which looks terribly like dried blood.

"Christopher Marlowe was one of our best spies. He was pursuing our enemies when he was killed. He must've succeeded in catching someone if he had that poison on his person when he died. It was good of you to take it and continue his work. Marlowe always spoke highly of you, boy. So much so, he insisted we make you a spy in our networks."

Cecil lobs the filthy letter at me with more force than necessary. I slide my thumb betwixt the waxed seal and parchment, feeling light-headed when I recognize my own finger-prints smeared in the blood. 'Tis the letter he had in his pocket the night he was killed. The one I found alongside the poison phial and lost when I ran.

Though I'd long suspected Marlowe was a spy, the confirmation still sends a shudder through me. His every soft word and every gesture take on hidden meaning. I understand now how he got away writing audaciously heretical plays without consequence. Why his shrewd eyes would canvas a chamber before he settled in for a tankard of ale. How he always seemed to know something which everyone else did not.

Yes. Of course Kit was a spy.

But it makes not a bit of sense why he'd want me to be one too.

I did not make a secret of my unkind feelings for the queen with Marlowe. My previous words against the woman ought to send me swinging in the gallows of Tyburn as a traitor, not provision me with an offer of employment bearing her royal seal.

I force myself to meet Cecil's smirk. "How much do you know about me?"

"Oh, everything," he laughs. "Your true name. Every play you acted in. The sad town where your treasonous peasant kin live. What is it again, Thurlestone or Hope Cove?"

His words knife through me like a winter river, the cold cutting and threatening to suck me under for good. God Almighty, I've kept this secret so close, so guarded, only to have it ripped from my grasp here, where there's naught I can do to protect my kin. "Don't hurt my family," I say. "Please, they don't know, they've done nothing—"

Queen Elizabeth interrupts me, roaring, "They've done nothing except raise up arms against me, their queen, when I took back the land that was always mine!" Her royal calm fractures, revealing the entitled, angry old woman beneath the jewels and furs.

I drop my eyes. My nails bite into my palms. The silence stretches and knots like a hangman's noose. This is my end. I'm certain of it.

The queen goes on. "Today we shall not hurt your traitorous kin. We're here to help them. Or, rather, *you* are. The royal court is going on progress in a week's time."

The progress is the queen's tour through her kingdom. She travels with a retinue of courtiers and stays in her subjects' grand estates. Marlowe said the queen bankrupts whoever she stays with by feasting and partying every single night.

"Marlowe trusted you, Elias Wilde. And both of you have proven yourselves men of . . . unusual resource and fortitude. Our treasonous cupbearer has escaped London. We think that more attempts shall be made upon our life on this progress. I've need of a spymaster for this trip," the queen says like it's the most obvious thing in the world. "And I've chosen you and Lord Bloomsbury for the job."

I choke back an awful laugh. Us, spymasters for the queen?!

Lord Cecil's smirk washes away like piss in the rain. "My queen, you cannot possibly be serious. Think upon this. These are inexperienced men—boys, really—who happened to be useful once. We have a network of trained spies."

"Do you dare question our judgment?" the queen demands coldly. "Your men did not catch the threat until it was at the hem of our skirts. They come. I'll hear no more from you about it!"

205 ANY OTHER NAME | 205

Cecil bows. "Very well, Your Majesty." His eyes catch mine, and they sizzle with hate. Splendid. Exactly what I needed. A well-connected, noble, and rich nemesis who resents me for a job I never asked for.

The queen regards Bloomsbury and me with an expression that on anyone else would be called benevolent. "Is there no favor you wish to ask of your queen for your services?"

Bloomsbury bows again. "Nothing, my queen. It is an honor and duty to serve you in whatever way you wish."

The queen arches an eyebrow. "No one told us Lord Richard Bloomsbury's son spoke as pretty as he looked. But we know what you want, boy. What all of you want. Power and favors."

*And money,* I add silently, hopelessly. *We mustn't forget that one.*

"For you, young Bloomsbury, I will revoke my blessing of Lord Middlemore's marriage to your sister, Catherine. And for you, Elias Wilde, I shall make you a gentleman with a gentleman's estate."

I squint at the queen, certain I've misheard, until Cecil's disgusted groan confirms the truth of it.

A title and an estate would change *everything.*

'Tis a child's daydream conjured: the penniless player turned landholding lord. My family would not merely be lifted from poverty; our descendants would live richly for generations. But in my mind the idea sits like a plum cake maggoty with worms. The taste of a beloved sweet soured with decay.

I've been a traitor to the queen, 'tis fair to say, but I've not been a traitor to my people. Not yet and not ever. To be a lord, to come to Parliament and kiss the rings studding those bony fingers and smile and pretend that this horrid woman has not done her damnedest to pull my history up by the roots and burn it all—

"Keep your bloody castles!" I shout.

One of the guards gasps at the chamber's edge. Blooms-bury and Cecil turn to me, astonished.

The queen nibbles at a sweetmeat. "Your sister's name is Margaret, is it not?"

The name hits me like a crack upon the face. I've not heard it spoken by another for years, and to hear it from the queen's mouth with such cool menace undoes me.

"And your brother, John. A fine, strapping lad. It would be a shame for him to toil in the mines when he could've gone to Cambridge." Crumbs of sugar fall upon her wrinkled bosom, glistening with grease. "And what would your parents say if they knew you had the chance to change everything and you threw it away for foolish pride and vanity?"

Marlowe. Marlowe's told them everything about me. The anger of his betrayal burns in me hotter than a forge scorching the toughest ore. All my secrets, everything I tried to protect, wrenched from my hands and scattered to the wind. It takes all I have in me to drop to my knees at the hem of the queen's skirts and bow my head. "Leave my family out of this and I'll serve you." I hope she mistakes my quivering for fear and not the loathing raging through me like fire. She's given me no choice, and I hate her for it.

The queen smiles warmly and ruffles my hair. "That's more like it. I've no use for snapping peasant dogs in my kingdom."

Fear and shame and relief make war in my heart. Tears burn at the rims of my eyes, but I'm determined not to cry in front of this foul, murderous hag of a woman.

Bloomsbury's hand swims before me. I take it and pull myself upright.

Cecil bursts into laughter. "Are you two friends? Why, isn't this a touching twist!"

"Please don't," Bloomsbury begs in a whisper, his jaw flexed, his eyes on a point beyond my shoulder.

"Don't what?" Cecil goads.

Something is amiss. I feel it in the air the way fever hovers at the edges of London's poorest wards in the summer heat.

"Has he not told you who his father is?" Cecil looks toward me, and his obvious delight makes my hackles rise. He shoves Bloomsbury, forcing him to stumble into me. "I believe they called him the Burning Reaper where your folks are from. Quelling the Wilde rebellion was some of his most brutal work, if I recall. Something went wrong with the fires."

The Burning Reaper. The shadowy figure who torched my father's lands and scattered us to a cruel coast at the edge of a land that no longer counted us as countrymen.

The Burning Reaper is Bloomsbury's father.

No. *It can't be.*

Except . . . James made no secret of his father's savagery. He told me himself his father had made weapons for the queen, and I didn't think of what that meant. Didn't want to think of what that might mean. His father butchered my neighbors and uncles and aunts and took a torch to everything else. He told me he was the son of a brutal killer, and I didn't listen.

"James," I whisper. "Is it—"

A muscle twitches in his jaw. He won't meet my eyes.

And I know then that it's true. My knees wobble, and I grab the back of a carved chair to hold myself steady.

Cecil cackles again.

"Cecil. Do you mean for this investigation to fail before it begins?" the queen snaps. "Lord Bloomsbury has been punished for his deeds." Her anger turns to Bloomsbury and me. "Is this unfortunate history going to be an issue, gentlemen?"

*Unfortunate history.* She says it like it's a bad story we can close the cover on. Like what the Burning Reaper did has not haunted my life these past fifteen years.

"No, it shall not be a problem, Your Majesty." Bloomsbury's voice is heavy with defeat.

I duck my head, unable to answer. The blood from the dead servant boy has nearly crept to my boots, the stink of bile suffocating.

The queen sees what I'm looking at and smiles. As if she had been dearly hoping someone would notice. "I had him brought in for a bit of a lesson." She toes the body with her fine slipper. "Our guards found him attempting to scale the garden walls. Told some preposterous story about a boy who stole his clothes and told him to run and not say a word. Of course, what he should have done was tell our guards immediately that someone had infiltrated the palace grounds."

My blood goes cold. I might as well have drawn the knife across the boy's throat myself.

"For that treasonous act, we decided to try the phial you gave us on him. As you can see, it's quite poisonous."

I choke back a dry heave, finally caving and pulling my sleeve over my mouth and nose. "'Tis wolfsbane, Your Majesty. From Spain."

The queen reaches forward and cups my face with a cool hand. It takes every bit of my control not to flinch away. "Such a smart boy. You shall be an excellent spymaster, I know it." She glances at the body once more, still smiling. "The other reason I asked Cecil to leave this body here is so you both realize that the consequences of failing this mission would be quite . . . shall we say, *grave*."

The queen gives my cheek a pat before letting go. "The progress leaves two weeks hence. Lord Bloomsbury, your father's estate shall be the first stop." Her smile sharpens. "The Crown looks forward to your services."

# CHAPTER TWENTY

WHEN I RETURN to the Bloomsbury town house, I pour a goblet of the stiffest wine in the house and curl up in a chair. My brain has room for only one thought, which thrashes against my skull like a caged bird.

I am the queen's spymaster.

I, an out-of-work player, a nobody, am now responsible for ensuring that the person I loathe most in the world shall live, or my head will roll. And Bloomsbury. Christ. *He's—his father—*

A rattling startles me. My goblet dances in my trembling fingers. I set it down and sit on my hands until the candles cough and sputter and Bloomsbury invites himself into my room.

"Elias," he says in a traitorously gentle voice. "Is all well?"

All at once anger kindles in my temples—a tingling, fiery rush. "I've just learned your father is the Burning Reaper. The man who torched my family's land and destroyed our lives. How do you imagine I feel?"

His eyes slip to the floor. "I'm not my father." His words are so soft, I'm not sure if they're meant for me or him. "I apologize for not telling you."

"Shove off with your apologies! You—you *lied.* After all

your talk of friendship and honesty, you *lied* to get what you needed from me. As soon as I told you my true name, you knew who I was. You kept this from me on purpose!"

I should have known better. 'Tis the thing which galls me the most and fills my belly with cringing shame. I assumed Bloomsbury was not like other nobles . . . why? Because of his kindness or his earnest face or some other doe-eyed nonsense? Ridiculous. The first rule of dealing with lords is to never, ever trust them. *And you didn't only trust him. You—* The thought breaks off before it can finish.

Until now, I was handling all of it, the queen and Kit and the boy I've as good as slain, but Bloomsbury, teetering on tears, pleading for something which I cannot forgive, undoes the final knot lashing me to steadiness.

I've got to leave.

It was simple when I slipped away from the men who kidnapped me when I was a boy. One leg and then the other flung through the accidentally open window, then running steps stamped in the snow-covered street. When I disappeared, no one came to find me.

But God Almighty, I would be giving the slip not to a bunch of thieves on the outskirts of London but to the queen of England. She knows where my family lives. Their names. A frustrated scream kicks in my chest. Marlowe, Bloomsbury, the queen—each of them used me. They've wrapped their strings so tightly around me, there's not a chance of escape. I've gone from player to puppet. They all forced me down this path knowing I'd resent every step.

No, I can't run away from the queen unless I wish to bring the Royal Guard and their swords right into my family's parlor.

But I can run away from Bloomsbury and this moment.

He's still apologizing. "I didn't tell you because I didn't know how to." Shadows line his furrowed brow, his eyes red-rimmed and desperate. I see his earlier calm for what it truly is now, a mask to conceal the current of emotion always rushing beneath his skin. "I was afraid you would leave, and I didn't want you to go."

*I didn't want you to go.* His words sink in deep, past sinew and muscle, drawing blood.

I don't think about what that feeling means. Instead, I react to the pain, biting back and slapping his reaching hand away. "If you wanted me here, you shouldn't have lied!" He flinches, as though his lapdog has gone savage, and I cannot resist biting deeper. "You think you're better than the rest of those Cambridge boys, but you're not. You've used me as much as any of them would, except it's even worse coming from you because you think we're friends, when we both know you could ruin my life in an instant if you felt like it. You're no better than your father!"

He stumbles like I've struck him. The hurt on his face is so profound, my heart twists, even though I meant every word of what I said. *Apologize,* a voice in the back of my head whispers. *You don't mean it.*

I throttle the voice and stand. "I'm going. Don't try to find me."

The silence which falls is heavier than a November fog. Bloomsbury bites back a ghastly laugh and drags unsteady fingers through his hair. "As you wish, Hughes."

He says nothing else, not even when I storm out.

I know not what possesses me, but as I storm past Blooms-bury's quarters, I pause before the open door. The furniture is all dark wood and stiff curtains. The only spot of life is a single rose wilting and near dead in a delicate vase beside his bed.

My heartbeat crescendos. I walk over and pluck the blos-som from the vase.

A throat clears. The flower slips from my grasp and flutters to the floor. A maid stands in the doorway, carrying an armload of dripping ivory roses. "Did you lose something, my lord?"

I turn my back and leave. "No, I've got everything I need."

My second attempt to speak with Gráinne Ní Mháille could not be more different from the first.

"Make way for William Hughes, spymaster to the queen!" the dock-boy-turned-herald cries as he leads me through the quays. A visit to Whitehall Palace has outfitted me with a fat, tinkling coin purse and an elaborate feathered hat. The brim is so wide I can barely see beyond its circumference. I hope the filthy birds which swarm the Thames do not mistake my head for a fair place to roost.

When I reach Gráinne's ship, her corsairs are peering over its edge with expressions ranging from curiosity to hostility. The herald stops and tips a clumsy bow. "My good gentleman wishes to speak to the captain of this ship!"

A fiery head joins the others. Gráinne spits into the river and scowls. "Well. If it isn't *you* again."

Cecil has commanded Bloomsbury and me to assemble a

crew to assist our work on the progress. Since I can't stomach the thought of seeing Bloomsbury without my insides squirming with anger and something which feels suspiciously like shame, I have taken the task upon myself.

I dish out my most charming smile for the Pirate Queen. "My lady. The pleasure is all mine."

"Quit that fancy prancing and get up here," Gráinne demands. "Make sure he's not carrying more spy's tools with him, aye, lads?"

After a vigorous pat down, I'm escorted inside the ship's hold, the same burly man who tossed me off the ship Midsummer's Eve glowering over me. Were it not for the stiffness of my new clothes and the daylight creaking through the floorboards overhead, I would think I was reliving that night entirely.

"Spymaster to the queen, eh?" Gráinne says. "It seems you've moved up in the world quick." She pillows her chin upon her hand and takes me in. Lines carved from sun and sea frame her eyes and mouth. It strikes me that she's nearly Queen Elizabeth's age—threescore years. "What brings you here again? I've no time for courtly nonsense."

"I can get you an audience with the English queen," I say. "If you're willing to help me."

I hold up the parchment the queen gave me before we left the castle. The one that charters me to hire suitable persons to create my own network of spies. The Pirate Queen recognized Marlowe's poison at first sight and needs something from Queen Elizabeth. She is exactly the sort of ally I need right now.

Gráinne considers the parchment. "And what manner of help are you looking for, spymaster?"

I explain what's happened from Marlowe's murder until the night of Queen Elizabeth's feast. At the mention of the man with the sun scabbard, the Pirate Queen's face goes pale. Abruptly she stands, chair squealing. "You've no idea what you've stumbled into, do you?"

"What do you mean?"

"Few have stood against the Societas Solis and lived to speak of it. The queen and her men are setting you up to take the fall."

"I'm sorry, the what?"

Gráinne curses in Irish—too quiet and fast for me to catch—and then two goblets of wine appear before us. "Societas Solis is the name for an old order of trained assassins. Some of the deadliest killers in the world. Rumor has it they're based in Italy. Some even believe they report to the pope himself."

Oh, and now the bloody pope's a part of all this? I feel myself shrinking smaller and smaller, getting lost in the panic growing larger every second.

"Oh, come now!" Gráinne cries, seeing my face. "Surely you're not surprised? The pope's been saying 'tis fair game to kill Elizabeth for years. Ever since her family told His Holiness to get stuffed and declared themselves heads of the Church of England."

I leap to my feet, suddenly struck by a new dreadful suspicion. "How do you know Societas Solis is a part of this? What have you seen?"

She gives me a withering look, as though I am thicker than Bloomsbury's dullest book. "*You're* the one who's seen them, not me, lad. The sun is their mark. You saw it on Marlowe's killer."

The man with the sun scabbard. Splendid. An order of mysterious murderers is coming for the queen of England. And I—a penniless player with no previous experience with this subtle work—am the one tasked with stopping them.

"What else do you know about them?" I demand.

Gráinne holds out her arms. "I told you: they're assassins. Their entire business is murder and secrets. You won't be likely to find them renting a shop at the market. I only know of Societas Solis because a scallywag of a marquess told me all about how he hired one of them to off his brother-in-law."

Zounds, the assassin with the sun scabbard *saw me*. If he did not remember my face before, he surely will once I am trotted out at the progress. By naming me as the spymaster, and not one of their own, both Cecil and the queen have put a mark on my head. I am the bait in this blasted trap. And there's not a bloody thing I can do about it. A disbelieving laugh escapes me. I'd be impressed at how expertly they deceived me were it not for the dismay filling me up like water in the leaking hull of a ship stuck at sea.

Gráinne gives me a pitying smile. "The odds are not good for you. But I like a challenge. And I would like better yet to meet this English queen." She sips her wine with a satisfied sigh. "Me and my crew shall help you."

While Gráinne seemed like a great ally before, now I'm

no longer certain what good a pack of pirates can do betwixt me and a well-organized group of assassins. However, I'm in no position to . . . bargain. Or am I? *Bloomsbury would know what to make of all this.* The thought stabs me like a splinter.

Gráinne snaps her fingers, jolting me from my head. "I said, is there something else you want?" I shake my head, and she flaps a hand at me. "Get gone then, and try not to get murdered before we meet again—all right?"

There's this long awkward moment where I am not sure if she has dismissed me or not. But then the burly sailor nudges me from behind, and I scramble to my feet. "Yes, yes, of course." I smash my ridiculous hat back on my head and turn to go. But at the stairs I pause. "You once told me that if I arranged you an audience with the queen, you would tell me why you seek her. Will you tell me now?"

I have to know. Already Societas Solis has claimed several lives. Gráinne herself knows how deadly they are. Why would she be willing to risk it all for a single conversation with the queen of England—the greatest enemy of her people?

Gráinne shrugs as her goblet is refilled. "It's quite a boring story. I doubt a traitor like yourself would be moved by it."

Her words are briars biting into my honor. "Traitor?"

"Aye, you're a lad who harbors no love for your queen, but you're happy enough to live in her pocket. What else should I call you?"

I ball trembling hands into fists. "I did not willingly accept this role to help her. You ought to know that more than anyone!"

Gráinne props her boots upon the table and gestures to my person with her goblet. "Aye, I'm certain you're very eager to leave your bulging coin purse behind, as well as the power to make others do your bidding. Tell me, what did the English queen promise you to make you work for her?"

"It doesn't matter what she promised me. She threatened people I love, and that's why I'm here."

She sighs. "A title, then. Shouldn't have even asked. You're no better than one of those greedy English lords."

I stare at her, shame and resentment roiling in my gut. A traitor. I suppose that is what I am now, to someone like Gráinne. Now that my anger has faded, I can't lie and pretend Queen Elizabeth's offer of a title and estate isn't tempting. My childhood was far from easy. All five of us, stuck beneath one roof half the size of my chamber at Bloomsbury's. The single lump of bread painstakingly cut into five pieces and the angry pinch of hunger at night. Fear and uncertainty were also part of home for me. The queen's offer would banish the fear and uncertainty for good.

Except . . . I don't trust the queen. Not one bit.

"Aye, she offered me a title. But that doesn't mean I'm taking it."

This nabs Gráinne's attention. Her storm-wild eyes snap onto me like I'm a sea-beast she's never seen before. Slowly a sharp grin spreads across her weathered face. "Zounds, lad, you've got steel in you yet!" She stands and claps my shoulder. *"Déanaimid an méid a theastaíonn uainn le maireachtáil."*

I swallow nervously. "What does that mean?"

One side of her mouth crooks. "It means 'We do what we must to survive.'"

I gather my bottom lip between my teeth and nod once.

"We'll be at the progress," she says. "And for what it's worth, I think you've got a chance to outfox the Societas Solis. 'Tis slim, but 'tis there."

If I'm the bait in a blasted trap for an ancient secret society, then I've got a bit of groveling to do to get the two best knaves in London on my side. I stroll through all the bakeries until I spy a familiar curly-haired figure toiling in the kitchen.

"God Almighty, Elias?" Inigo exclaims. His eyes are on my exquisitely tailored clothing. "What are you doing here?"

"I need to talk to you and Maggie."

Inigo takes me home with him. I expect him to bring me to our old neighborhood, Moorgate, home of the vilest drunkards in all the city, but instead we walk to Cheapside, the market neighborhood beloved by Maggie for its residents' fat pockets.

"Surely not here?" I say as Inigo knocks on the door of a new building with impressive glass windows.

He gives me a wry look as the door swings open. "Things have changed."

The curtsying girl within brings us up three sound flights of stairs to a room overlooking the bustling market. The room itself is sparse and clean and utterly unlike the moldering hovel we rented before. The only thing not out of place is Maggie, who sits on the mattress paring her toenails with her favorite dagger.

"Will?" Her dagger clatters to the floor. "Is that you there beneath that goose?"

I doff my ridiculous hat. "At your service."

"Shall I fetch something for you and your guest, Mister and Mistress García?" the girl asks with another curtsy.

My head whips toward Inigo. "Mister and *mistress*?"

For the first time in her life Maggie blushes. "Ah, no, that will be all."

As soon as the door shuts, I fold my arms and glare. "You two got *married* and didn't *tell me*?"

"We did it more for the place than anything else," Inigo says. "They won't let rooms to unmarried men and women living together."

But it was for more than that. The quick smiles Inigo would dart at Maggie when he thought I wasn't looking. The way Maggie would only pick her toenails on the mattress when it was my turn to sleep on it. This madness has been a long time in the making.

"Yes, a few words spoken by a bloke with a book and suddenly it's all well and proper for him to be my chamber-fellow." Maggie rolls her eyes, punctuating how she feels about this bit of propriety. But then she grows somber, reminding me that we did not part as friends, but rather, with Maggie's accusations of me abandoning them for Bloomsbury, which, in hindsight, were not entirely unfounded. "What brings you here anyway, *Elias Wilde*?" Her eyes run judgmentally up and down my fine clothes. "Or shall I call you Lord Hughes these days?" she demands. "Honestly, how many other secrets have you been keeping from me?"

Inside, I wince that Inigo has confessed to Maggie my true name, but I know now is not the time to be sour about it. "My latest title is queen's spymaster, actually." I flash a tight smile. "And I've a job for both of you."

My friends (or rather, I *hope* they are still my friends) exchange a long look.

I shift from foot to foot, swallowing. "I . . . also wanted to apologize for how I acted before. You two deserved better than me lying and hiding my coin. I'm no good at trusting others, but I'm trying."

Something in Inigo's face softens. Finally, Maggie breaks the silence with a sly smirk. "That was a middling apology at best, but seeing as it's the first one I've ever heard you give, I suppose I'll speak to you again. Seems you've got quite the tale to share. I'll give you the chance to tell it over the luncheon you'll buy us."

Over an entire roasted chicken, I explain what's happened since we parted.

Maggie sighs when I finish. "Told you not to trust Marlowe—didn't I always say so? Now he's dead and left you with all his problems."

I make a noncommittal sound. I've hardly thought of Marlowe's betrayal—not when Bloomsbury's deceit aches so freshly. Marlowe warned me not to go prying in his business. Bloomsbury's lied through his teeth to me about his, all while making a great show of his honesty. I'll take the scoundrel who knows he's a scoundrel over the bloke who fancies himself a saint.

"Why should we help you if people are dead already?" Inigo says.

This is, to his credit, a fair point to raise. The hope in my heart dims but doesn't die.

"What if, rather than work in someone's bakery, you could own one yourself?" I gesture to my person. "There's wild riches in this—if we're successful."

The Maggie and Inigo I knew would've said yes in an instant. But Mr. and Mrs. García share another look, which makes my spirit sink.

"I dunno. Things have been pretty good lately. I can provide for us both." Pride puffs up Inigo's narrow chest. "Your Lord Bloomsbury set us up nice and pretty. I don't know if we're willing to gamble it all away."

Maggie's got a shrewd expression I know not what to make of. "What's Bloomsbury think of all this?" she asks. "Surely he's got thoughts about the society of whatever you called it."

Even though I've had the same thought myself every hour since the Pirate Queen warned me of the Societas Solis, Maggie's question fills me with a sour, sulky feeling. "I'm not his manservant. You can ask him yourself on the progress."

Inigo sighs and rises to his feet. "We won't help you, I'm sorry. 'Tis a good life we've got here. Quiet and safe and sound."

Oh God, this won't do at all. Next thing I know they'll start mooning over children. The thought of Maggie as anyone's mother is just about the most fearsome thing I can imagine. One shouldn't have to bribe one's friends. But I can see no other way beyond this impasse, and I need them on my side more than ever.

I untie the heavy purse at my waist and plunk it on the table. The coins make a delightful jingle. "Safe and sound is well and good. But what if I told you joining me on this investigation could change your entire life?"

"How much is that?" Maggie demands breathlessly, eyes huge. Inigo elbows her, and she elbows him right back.

"Let's count it, shall we?" I upend the purse's contents. Shillings roll every which way across the table. The pile is huge and audacious and more money than any of us have seen in one place.

Maggie rakes her fingers through the coins as if they are wont to disappear. "This much, then?"

A slow grin splits my face. "No. If you agree to help me, then consider this your first payment."

# CHAPTER TWENTY-ONE

I WAIT A WEEK to call on James Edmund Bauffremont of Bloomsbury, son of the Burning Reaper.

I could have stayed in Whitehall Palace and avoided Bloomsbury entirely until the progress left London. Cecil offered it to me, the way a highway robber offers to relieve a man of his purse. But I supposed I owed Bloomsbury an explanation for the very strange crew I have assembled for our even stranger mission. Then we can get on with the spymaster business, and afterward I'll never have to see or speak to him again.

Except when I imagine never speaking to Bloomsbury again, something cinches in my chest.

It feels an awful lot like sadness.

Ridiculous. I've only spent two months with him, not two years. I've been longer acquainted with the fleas in my linens than with Bloomsbury.

*You've never met anyone like him before.*

I push away the unwelcome thought with a growl. 'Tis all the more reason for me to look forward to the day we part. The sooner we get through this business, the sooner I can forget him. And I'm not hurrying things along by lurking outside his family house in the sticky evening air.

I rap on the town house door three times and wait. Cooper answers and gasps when he sees me.

"Lord Hughes!" he stammers. "We—we did not expect to see you again."

"Whyever not? I was away for work. Where is Bloomsbury?"

Cooper still stares as though he has never seen me before. "He—he has gone to Lord Middlemore's. I do not expect he will be back until after dark."

Irritation pricks me. While I have been assembling our crew for the progress, Bloomsbury has been dallying with his wretched betrothed and her father? Likely as not they've carved the whole bloody New World into little parcels of profit by now.

"Fine. Draw a bath for me in my chamber, then."

Cooper's throat bobs as he swallows. "Ah, I do apologize, but that is simply not possible. Lord Bloomsbury ordered us to close up the chamber—"

My voice shoots up an octave. "He booted me from my chamber?"

"We—we didn't think you would be back, Lord Hughes!" Cooper stammers, his cheeks pink.

I sag against the doorframe. He's removed all trace of me in less than a week. 'Tis a little hurt in the grand scheme of how else he's betrayed me, but this small action makes the pain of his betrayal rush all through me again, like a scab splitting open.

He doesn't want me here anymore.

And that's fine because I don't want to be here anymore either.

I shall tell Bloomsbury of my plans and then return to Whitehall Palace until I'm forced to see him again. The time we spent outrunning highwaymen and inviting ourselves to strange weddings and, yes, even sitting before the fire in his quiet, sleepy library was all for work. It was never more than that. I shake off the unsteadiness and draw myself up to my full height, ironing out every speck of feeling when I meet Cooper's concerned look. "Fine. Where does Middlemore live? I shall find Bloomsbury myself."

Soon, I'm heading to Cheapside where the Guild Masters live. Apparently, Lord Middlemore's title is so new, he has yet to build a grand home among the noble houses. The shame he must feel to be neighbors with my barely reputable friends pleases me greatly. Perhaps I will ask Maggie to make his life more miserable by stealing all the laces from his breeches.

Yet when I reach the address, my blustery flight from the Bloomsbury town house seems foolish. There I could have at least drunk and dined myself into better spirits while waiting for Bloomsbury. What am I supposed to do at Middlemore's? I certainly do not wish to be invited inside and watch Blooms-bury's fiancée sniff at me as though I am a pile of dung dropped by her horse.

Muttering curses, I slink to the mouth of the alley to wait. The stables are back here, and if Bloomsbury has ridden his red stallion Ares over (which I know he has), then he will pass me by. I settle into a dark corner and compose indignant speeches in my head.

As the sky purples, candles flicker to life, one by one, in the glass windows. The streets are empty, save for a bloke nursing a pipe in the crook betwixt two buildings across the street. When the sky grows darker and swells with big-bellied clouds, still the man does not move.

I worry my bottom lip. 'Tis likely nothing. A mere coincidence. But after all that I've been through, nothing feels like a coincidence anymore—especially not with the rain pattering on shingled eaves and the scent of damp soil, like a fresh grave, all around me.

There's a wink of light, and a clatter of hooves sounds in the Middlemore stables.

The other man jerks up, rapt as a hound with a scent.

Out comes Bloomsbury on Ares, the stallion a smudgy smear of crimson against the rainy gray streets.

And the man follows.

I bite the edge of my thumbnail so hard, it breaks. Gráinne's warnings of Societas Solis howl in my head. She said I was the bait in Cecil's trap.

But what if she was wrong?

What if it's Bloomsbury?

I loosen my dagger and stalk after them.

Bloomsbury parades down Cheapside toward Westminster as the rain thickens. The suspicious man is a wraith flicking from shadow to shadow. He moves like someone accustomed to moving unseen. I worry if I blink, I'll lose him in that single instant.

Bloomsbury pauses before a crooked alley snaking behind a row of alehouses. 'Tis a shortcut we've used often enough returning from the city proper back to his town house. To his left stretches the road to Westminster, luminous with torches burning halos in the mist.

*Don't do it, don't do it, don't do it—*

He takes the blasted shortcut.

I curse and hurry around the dark corner.

A tavern door bursts open as Bloomsbury goes past. Two men stumble against each other, mouths bubbling with laughter. A pair of drunks. Far from an unusual sight, but I catch the subtle look they share as Bloomsbury passes them.

Another man laughs boisterously at the alley's mouth. He steps aside to let Bloomsbury pass. Only when the lord's back is to him does he draw a sword from his side.

I hurl my dagger at the assassin, a cry tearing from my lips. "JAMES!"

The assassin's sword sparks against the stone wall inches from Bloomsbury's head. His startled face catches mine, pale with the shock. Ares panics and rears, sending Bloomsbury tumbling off the horse into the mud. The stallion charges down the path and sends the pair of drunks scrambling away with curses and oaths.

I sprint down the alley and launch myself at the swordsman before he can swing again, my arms noosing about his neck. He gurgles horribly, sword slipping.

I slide down his back, snatch the blade from the ground, and level it at my adversary.

The long blade quavers in my arms like a jelly. Inch by inch, the sword sinks earthward until its tip plinks to the ground. Zounds, being a player has not prepared me for this lifestyle.

The swordsman cackles as he witnesses my struggle, unsheathing a knife. "Need a hand, lad?"

Bloomsbury shouts and bashes a rock into the swordsman's head. He staggers away, blood pouring betwixt his fingers. Bloomsbury's wide eyes hold mine for a moment too long, like he can't believe what he's seeing. Another man converges on him, dagger flashing.

Bloomsbury screams and collapses.

Red spots my vision. With a roar I heft the sword and swing it as hard as I can. Its weight sends me windmilling until the blade sinks into something with a sickening wet thunk.

Another cry of pain, another body on the ground. 'Tis the man who has been following Bloomsbury, scarlet blossoming from his leg like a goblet of wine filled to the rim and running over and over.

The original swordsman braces himself against the wall and observes the sword trembling in my grip, the feral snarl on my face.

He runs.

I drop the weapon and go to Bloomsbury. He curls up small, both hands pressed against a slice in his side. Dark liquid beads up around his fingers and streams to the ground, mixing with the rain.

I cup his face with unsteady hands. "Are you all right?"

His eyes swim in their sockets before latching on to mine. "Wh-why are you here?"

"I was waiting for you." My hands are scarlet with blood. His blood. Something plummets within me at the sight. My vision goes dark and narrow at the edges until red is the only thing I can see. My fault. It's my fault just like always. If I hadn't left him, if I had gone to Middlemore's instead of sulking outside—

He coughs, and there's a gush of warmth over my lap. Is the blood getting thicker? I frantically tear off my doublet, rip a strip from my chemise, and press it against the wound. "James, is this how you stop the blood?"

He doesn't answer. His eyes flutter shut, lashes half-moons against purple skin. Panic explodes through me. Is he dying? I haven't seen enough mortal wounds to know and now this is the most important question in the world and the only person who can answer it is drifting away to unconsciousness in my arms. God Almighty, I already lost Kit. I shall not lose James as well.

We need help.

I move to stand, but Bloomsbury seizes my wrist, his words slurred. "You were waiting—for me?"

"You're bleeding out and that's your question?"

A dreamy, vacant smile eddies across his face. I shake him roughly, snap my fingers near his ear. "No falling asleep—stop that!" He can't fade away. Not here, not like this. Not when our final conversation was venomous with anger and hurt and all the other bad things and none of the good.

He speaks, his words a whisper. "Why were you waiting?"

"I had to tell you something." *That you're a dolt. An utter dolt for lying to me and then going and getting skewered in this alley before I could tell you off about it.*

His expression dims. "Is it that you despise me?"

It's such a thick-headed question that only one response is proper.

I gather him in my arms and press my lips to his.

After a single, shocked second, he kisses me back.

The world rushes past our still spot in the midst of the storm.

When I finally draw away, 'tis as if all the stars in my sky have shifted, the constellations I once used to guide my way home rearranged, all leading to the boy before me.

Against all sense and reason, I have lost my heart to a lord. I ought to be angry with myself, but instead all I feel is a softness too tender to put into words.

I lay my brow against his. "Does this answer your bloody question?"

He smiles against my skin. "Thoroughly."

Relief knocks the last of my strength from my limbs, turns my last panicked breath into a shuddering sob. Thank God. If James is well enough to kiss, then he must be well enough to live.

"Will you be all right?" I should pull away to give him space, but my arms won't move.

James slips a hand between us to investigate the wound, once more the bookish alchemist. He winces. "We . . . ought to call for someone, but yes."

A scraping sound interrupts the moment. The man I've injured has crawled several lengths down the alley. Ares stands over him with a flicking tail and a low head like a guarding hound. He blows several snorting breaths, as if chastening me over what's taking so long. I push down every bit of lingering gentleness in me into a hard, tight knot of anger. "Come, let's get you home and show Cecil our new prisoner."

# July 1593
## The English Countryside

*I grieve and dare not show my discontent,*
*I love and yet am forced to seem to hate,*
*I do, yet dare not say I ever meant,*
*I seem stark mute but inwardly do prate.*
*I am and not, I freeze and yet am burned,*
*Since from myself another self I turned.*

*My care is like my shadow in the sun—*
*Follows me flying, flies when I pursue it,*
*Stands and lies by me, doth what I have done.*
*His too-familiar care doth make me rue it.*
*No means I find to rid him from my breast,*
*Till by the end of things it be suppressed.*

—QUEEN ELIZABETH I,
from "On Monsieur's Departure"

# CHAPTER TWENTY-TWO

THE SKY ABOVE Queen Elizabeth's progress is a shade of blue all but royalty is forbidden to wear. Her court parades through the countryside on fine palfreys and carved carriages, a splash of silk and jewels against the fleecy green fields. The image is grand, but among the nobles it's all empty laughter and smiles laced with poison. Their false love for the common people who shout blessings for the queen is the icing on a sweetmeat swarming with weevils.

Already, I've woken to find a rude image and the words *back to the wilde with thee, treasonous cur* scratched in my saddle. The porters refuse to say who did it, but I've no doubt 'tis Lord Robert Cecil's doing.

The queen's former spymaster hates me the way a barkeep hates bathing—passionately and without good reason. I've never seen anything like it before. He despises me so much, I wonder if he'd blow my cover as Lord Hughes against the queen's wishes just to see the rest of the court jeer and mock me. Passing as a lord on the progress allows me to observe the nobles and wonder who stands to benefit from the queen's death enough to work with an order of deadly assassins. If the secret of my identity is discovered, the job my life depends on would be far harder, and there's no doubt Cecil wishes to make life harder for me.

The progress jolts to a halt when a fine gray rain starts falling somewhere outside Rochester. The queen and her ladies take over the only inn, whilst the rest of us are left to impose on the poor townsfolk. The court will doubtlessly eat and drink the town's larders bare in the span of a night.

"I'll keep an eye on old Elizabeth tonight," Gráinne whispers as she passes me by. She is riding astride, like a man, her long red-and-silver hair uncovered and bound up in a dozen braids. The English nobility regard her with a strange mix of awe and scandal. When I brought her the parchment sealed with Queen Elizabeth's wax insignia, Gráinne's eyes flashed like I had offered her a chest of rubies and emeralds. I do not know what the two queens spoke of at their meeting, but whatever it was has redoubled the pirate's dedication to my mission.

"All right. Find me if you spot something." So far, I have no suspects among these empty-headed lords. But that does not mean that Maggie and Inigo, traveling ahead with the other servants and queen's retainers, have not discovered a suspect among the people too lowly to be seen traveling in the queen's company.

I find a barn on the outskirts of the village. The crofters' farmhouse shines with light at the edge of a garden swollen with summer crops. If Lord Hughes knocked on the door, the family would be forced to accommodate me, feed me, and sleep in this barn themselves.

Instead, I duck inside the barn and tuck three shillings

beneath a milk pail. The distant pulse of music and scent of food carries on the air. *If there's a feast, you ought to be there. What if something happens?*

My stomach knots guiltily, but I do nothing. Surely no one would think to murder the queen tonight. A summer storm is afoot, and this stop was unexpected after all. I laugh bitterly. Zounds, this is exactly the kind of thinking that would get the queen murdered. I dearly hope Gráinne is as good a shot with her crossbow as she has been boasting all day.

A figure holding a candle appears at the barn door.

My hand fumbles for the new sword strapped to my hip before the light catches the figure's face.

James.

My heart slams against my breastbone. "What are you doing here?"

He steps inside. The candlelight catches upon the raindrops in his hair, silver on bronze. "Looking for you."

I swallow. I'll choke if he keeps speaking, give it all up and perish right there in the hay. "Well done, you found me! You can go back to the inn now." The note of finality in my voice is undoubtedly a dismissal.

Instead of leaving me in peace, James sets the candle down and sits cross-legged right there on the floor. "Why are you avoiding me?"

"Avoiding you! What a ridiculous idea!" I force out a laugh. "We are co-conspirators. We've been sharing looks all day."

His brow furrows. "You know I am not speaking of work."

My skin pebbles with gooseflesh, the lump in my throat growing bigger. James isn't wrong. I have been avoiding him and doing a most excellent job of it. We haven't had a moment alone since his near murder and my ill-advised kiss. 'Tis easy enough to avoid him given the court's interest in the handsome, young Lord Bloomsbury, savior of the queen. His family's transformation from pariah to progress host has endowed Bloomsbury with an air of thrilling mystery. Simpering admirers of all sexes attend to James as dutifully as the manservant Cooper.

I watch them all with a jealous glower, fighting the urge to snap when they draw too close.

Unlike me, they do not notice the bulge of the bandage around his ribs. Nor how it takes two servants and five minutes for him to dismount from his horse, his face twisted in pain. James has no place here—not while someone has already tried to kill him once and Cecil could learn nothing from James's would-be murderer except that he was paid to kill him with Spanish coin. He ought to be home, away from all the murder and intrigue that follows me like a curse, until he's well again.

But every time I try to tell him this, my tongue grows thick as pudding.

Even now, I sit in stubborn silence until he breaks it.

"The night I was attacked—"

My insides surge at the thought of what he might say next. "What of it? You saved my life once, so I saved yours."

"I never got to thank you," James says quietly. "So, thank you."

I can only nod once as heat crawls up my neck, stealing away all my words and composure. If I speak, I may start to cry. He doesn't have to sleep with the image of his body in the mud, the howling fear of thinking I'd lost him for good. I wipe my eyes brusquely, refusing to meet his gaze. Zounds, I was once the best boy player in all of London, and now I am undone by a single sentence. Henslowe would fire me in an instant.

"May I ask you a question?" he says.

"It appears you are already asking, so please, go on."

His smile lingers, but his eyes grow guarded. "Did our kiss mean anything to you?"

Once again, James has proven himself the lord of idiotic questions. Every time my eyes drift shut, the memory of our damned kiss is right there, tormenting me all hours of the night, making me feel things I'd rather not feel. Embarrassment, regret. The rash desire to do it again, as soon as possible. I resent that I care for him, but I can no longer pretend that I don't.

I've kissed plenty of lads before, and it's never lingered with me like this. Worse than wanting to kiss James again is the other want behind it, the one that craves his company even if we aren't kissing. That's what frightens me the most.

"'Tis not my habit to kiss men who don't mean something to me," I say, being half-honest even though I should lie. "'Tis a good way to get a belly full of steel, as you might imagine."

He falls quiet and traces patterns in the dirt, all tangled hair and shy, soulful eyes. "Then where do we go from here?"

The thought of what shape those deft hands might trace on me upends my brain. "I think it best if we not do anything at all."

My feelings for him snuck up on me the way a dire illness does. First just sniffles and coughing and insisting everything's fine and dandy until 'tis too late for the doctor, and then, whoops, you're a corpse thrown out with the rubbish. I've no doubt my feelings for James are as deadly as a disease. Especially if they go any further than this. 'Tis one thing for me to kiss boys of my own station in the reeking London alleys; 'tis another thing completely to kiss a lord of the queen's court. We could never be. Not without gambling with both our lives and the lives and livelihoods of everyone depending on us. Of all the lads in the entire kingdom I could've fallen for, he is the very worst choice.

His hand drifts to mine, smallest finger grazing my own. "What if that's not what I want?"

I snatch my hands away and cross them safely over my chest. "Have you truly considered what could happen if we were discovered? The punishment for sodomy is death. Your title and wealth would be repossessed by the Crown. All you've ever loved and worked for would be forfeit should the wrong person witness a kiss between us and tattle. Is that what you want?"

James does not quail from my furious stare. "Yes, I am aware. You're not the first lad I've kissed, Elias."

Heat gathers in my belly, and my fists clench. He takes in my restlessness and silence with an intensity that makes me certain he's seeing right through my flimsy excuses to the feelings I'm desperate to keep hidden. "We've talked an awful lot about me," he finally says, an edge to his words. "What is it that *you* want?"

I know he's not talking about the usual things—shelter and safety and a return to my family. But I don't want beyond that. Wanting is for people who know they have a future, and the future is a dangerous gamble if you're not certain where your next meal is coming from.

But as I look at James from beneath my eyelashes, there, in the most secret corner of my heart, I wish for this wild, fey thing between us to bloom, the wide world spread out before us like a blank curl of parchment. A great ache fills my chest and pushes out everything else.

He leans closer, feather-light touch on my leg. "Tell me," he whispers, the words soft with hope.

A gust of wind snuffs out the candle, plunging us into near darkness. Flashes of angry light dance on the curves of distant clouds. I am like the sky, with pinpricks of light all over me, but I can't find the shape of the words I wish to speak.

"I want us to forget this happened," I say firmly. "And finish the work we came here to do before someone else gets hurt." I banish all the wanting to the hinterlands of my heart. It matters not what I want—not when there's a history of the people nearest to me getting hurt or killed and we're playing with intrigue and murder.

"Very well then." His hand is still on my thigh, tracing those same damn patterns as before. "But that's not what I want."

"No?" My voice shoots up an octave.

"No. I propose a dalliance. Only until the end of the progress, of course. Who says we cannot work and be merry?" A rakish smile tugs on his lips. "What say you to that?"

I stare at him, repeating his words to myself. Willing them to make sense.

After murder, the second surest way to get killed on this progress would be us doing exactly this. Hiding a scandalous secret, the lord dallying with a commoner imposter in the queen's court. Us, biting our thumbs at all of England's petty rules and laws about who's allowed to do what with whom. Zounds, what a half-witted plan! Absolutely not. That's the only answer to this wild question.

But I don't know how to handle James like this—all bookishness gone and replaced with a heat that boils me alive from inside out. Being near him now turns my brains and all my common sense to mush, allowing the reckless, secret part of me that wants this with him to slip its lead and run wild.

That must be what makes me growl out a "yes" before I fall upon him.

Our kiss is different this time—eager and frantic. My hand tangles in his lovely hair; he tugs me into his lap, and I remind myself, over and over, *Take what you can get. 'Tis only for now.*

I can't handle his *Where do we go from here?* because there is no future and there is no us. We both know that at the end of this, he must marry and make heirs and fulfill all the rest of his lordly duties, and I—well, I must return to my family and the life that waits for me there. But him and me and now? I can do that. That's all I've had with the other lads I've kissed, and it's worked. This can be the same if I make it the same.

I can do this.

When we pull away, we're both breathless and dazed. "I suppose I should go," James says with a bashful laugh. "I promised Gráinne a game of dice. She must be wondering where I've gone."

His blush turns me ravenous. I tip him a clumsy wink that makes him laugh harder before I pull him back to me. "Tell her you've found better games, then."

Just as we're about to kiss again, a shadowy figure runs across the front of the barn.

James and I both stiffen like hounds on a foxhunt.

"Did you—"

"I did."

My former thought—*surely no one would think to murder the queen tonight*—feels like a hideous jest now. This is what I get for snogging on the job. "Let's go."

James is already beside me. "Carefully, now."

My just-dried clothes are soaked immediately in the downpour. We tiptoe around the barn, staying to the shadows, lest a bolt of lightning point to our presence. There's no one here. Perhaps it was only the son of the crofters checking on the cattle and leaving us in peace.

But then James touches my elbow and points.

Across a field tender with summer green is an orchard.

We stand and stare, getting wetter and wetter in the driving rain. Right when I'm assuming we've gotten it wrong, a shadow streaks out from the trees. A flash of lightning reveals someone on horseback, heading eastward down the road, away from London and farther out into the countryside.

Another figure appears, cloak drawn and steps hurried as though he would rather not be seen.

And he's headed right toward us.

We both freeze, backs against the barn, hardly daring to breathe.

The figure draws closer and closer until he gets right to the garden's edge. A flash of lightning illuminates the face within the cloak's hood.

Lord Cecil.

James gasps beside me as the queen's former spymaster continues toward the glowing inn where the queen's revelries are doubtlessly continuing.

Only when the man is well out of sight do we turn to each other with stunned expressions, and James says, "Who in God's name is he meeting with out here in the middle of the night?"

# CHAPTER TWENTY-THREE

CECIL WILL ADMIT to nothing the next day when I confront him.

"Last night seemed very quiet, did it not?" I say, sidling up beside the former spymaster.

Cecil glares as if I am a squashed toad on the bottom of his boot. "What would you know of it? I didn't see your face among the revelers last night."

"I was patrolling the outskirts of the village for suspicious activity. I witnessed something."

"Did you?" Cecil says in a bored voice.

"Yes, a clandestine meeting in the orchard. Does that not strike you as strange?" I ask, all innocence.

Lord Cecil's face remains still save for a tic in his jaw. 'Tis an impressive bit of playing. Doubtlessly, Henslowe would welcome him with open pockets into the Rose Theatre. "If you did not see the man's face, then you saw nothing." He kicks his horse into a gallop and abandons me.

Cecil is keeping something from me. Irrevocably and absolutely so. But why? What's his motive? I would assume he plots against his queen, but why would the queen's former spymaster plot against her? I think back to our last meeting, how the queen was angry at Cecil after her treasonous cupbearer escaped. Perhaps he is conducting his own investigation separate from ours, eager to outwit us to end up back in her good graces to humiliate me and James the way he was humiliated.

Something else is going on here, but all the court playacting in the world hasn't prepared me for parrying minds with an actual member of court. Thinking on it makes my brain ache and fills me with the panicked certainty that I'm in far over my head.

The progress reaches the Bloomsbury estate at midafternoon.

The once-proud castle lurks at the forest's edge like a felled giant, its foundation fuzzed with green, ivy plucking at mortar betwixt the stones. The ancient trees scrape hungrily at the walls, parts of the castle completely hidden by their twisting branches. It appears as though the earth is doing its best to wrestle the estate back into the wildness one cracked stone at a time. While the castle is an intimidating sight, it's not what makes me suck in my breath with dread.

In the shadow of the keep's walls, dozens—nay, *hundreds*—of tents bloom like enormous white flowers.

"What's with all this?" I whisper. "I thought the queen said only a hundred nobles were on this progress? There's scores of people in those tents!"

"Only a hundred nobles *are* on the progress," James says. "But they brought their servants as well."

"And they've all brought a household of servants with them?"

Bloody hell, I knew Maggie and Inigo were posing as my

servants and were traveling ahead with the queen's servants, but I hadn't counted on every courtier bringing their ten favorite maids and picketing an entire town's worth of people right outside the castle gates. Why, anyone out here could be working for the Societas Solis. Our suspect list has quadrupled faster than fleas on a dog's arse.

I'm swept through the castle gates into the courtyard, where my hopes of sneaking off and finding Inigo and Maggie among the tents are dashed. Servants wearing the Bloomsbury colors line the courtyard, cheering for the queen's arrival. Lord and Lady Bloomsbury and Lady Catherine stand waiting on the threshold of their home to welcome their queen.

Queen Elizabeth emerges from the gossamer curtains of her carriage, resplendent in white and diamonds. "Lord Richard Edmund Bloomsbury. It is our pleasure to stay in your home."

The Burning Reaper looks exactly like James three decades from now, right down to the barely-there smile. My chest clenches at the sight of it, and I curl my hands into fists. *You're doing this for your family,* I remind myself fiercely. *Make it through this progress and you'll never have to see him again.*

"It is our pleasure to host you, my queen." If James's voice is the summer breeze whispering through the fields, his father's voice is rock cracking in the mountains. I shiver and wonder if this horrible noise was the last thing my parents heard before the whoosh of fire consuming all they ever possessed. It takes all my willpower to bow to the man as I cross the threshold into his home instead of spitting at his feet.

*You deserve nothing but evil,* I think as he inclines his head benevolently, a vacant smile on his face. *Nothing but the very worst which God can send your way.*

After greeting the Bloomsbury hosts, we are shown to a banqueting hall where already the tables groan with enough food to feed a city-sacking army. Each seat is marked by a noble's name and titles written on good, creamy parchment. I search for my own name until I find it jammed at the very end of a table adjacent to the kitchens. If I squint, I can barely make out James seated near the queen at the high table along with the rest of his family. Worse, my tablemates are all gray-bearded and appear to have only three teeth betwixt the lot of them. The servants have already started to spoon-feed broth into their gummy mouths.

Christ, how am I supposed to learn anything useful here? Just as my despair sinks to a new low, a man clutching an enormous book slips into the final chair across from me. 'Tis Lord John Foxwell, according to his place card. A scraggy beard grows upon his chin like a patch of weeds starved for sunlight, but he's closer to twenty than two hundred, so that's a start at least. I summon up a winning smile and lean closer to him. "I can't believe they'd seat two outstanding lads such as ourselves near these old men!"

He looks up, frowning, and I grin more brightly.

"They must've been worried we'd be too much fun for everyone else—aye?"

"Fun?" Foxwell cries. "I'm not quite sure what you're doing on this progress"—he squints at my name tag—

"William Hughes, but I am certainly not here to have fun. None of us are."

I take in the tables bursting with food, the musicians, and the laughter shaking the rafters. "So we're *not* here to have fun?" I say, to be certain I'm understanding Foxwell correctly. Because it very much appears as though we're in the midst of fun.

"Foolish young man. Did you truly imagine you'd spend the next six weeks feasting and being entertained?" Foxwell harrumphs and crosses his arms. "We are here to impress our sovereign, our *queen*," he says like it's the most obvious thing in the world. "If we can impress her, then perhaps she will shower our families and houses with good fortune and riches."

Zounds, the queen expects her entire court to both feed her and keep her entertained for six weeks? Would it kill her to have a quiet night at home for once? If the Societas Solis doesn't make a move soon, all the progress's feasting and merrymaking may kill the queen before they get a stab at her.

"That is why I requested to be seated in the quietest part of the hall," Foxwell says. "So that I can prepare to show her my New World herbarium."

"You're showing the queen your what?"

"My dried plant collection."

I mock gasp. "Now that sounds *very* fun."

Foxwell sniffs and hugs his book protectively. "Plants are nothing to jest at! Why, planting the wrong crops can ruin a town's entire livelihood." He taps the book, which I can now see has bits of dried grass and stems poking out from betwixt the pages. "I'll have you know the plants discovered in the New World are just the thing to turn England into a real farming force in Europe. Sunflowers, potatoes, tomatoes, pineapples . . ." His eyes grow glassy with desire. "Just *imagine* the possibilities!"

"I doubt there's a person here who could."

Foxwell's expression sours. "What's a lord doing so far from his home if he's got no money or talent with which to impress his queen?"

Everything about Foxwell is boorish and prim, and I should absolutely not let him get under my skin. And yet. "Who says I don't have talents? Maybe they're just not the sort you plaster in a book and bore people with."

His eyes narrow. "Your place card says you hail from Plymouth, yes? I'm waiting on a very important plant specimen from Spain, and it's lost. Last I heard, it was rerouted through Plymouth port. Perhaps you can be useful and tell me whom I must write to find it?" There's a knowing gleam in Foxwell's eye I don't like at all—like he's in on something I'm not.

Before Foxwell can insult me again, I push back from my seat. "What a wonderful idea. I'll write to my contacts about it right now."

I storm through the crowded banqueting hall, not caring whose chair I bump or whose foot I squash along the way. In the cool hallway, I demand that a startled maid show me to my quarters.

My bedchamber is a large room with deep windows looking over the forest. The leaves press so thick outside, the entire room is greenish. I realize someone nimble as Maggie could shimmy up a tree and leap into the grounds with a dagger betwixt their teeth or poison in their pocket, which is really fantastic. There's hundreds of people in this damn castle. How am I supposed to investigate every one of them? All while being Lord Hughes among lords when I don't know the first thing about the court? Queen Elizabeth knows where my family is. She never said she's hurt them, but she also never said she wouldn't. What if I don't work fast enough? What if she doesn't like my work? Will she send men to drag my brother screaming from our home, or will she find a way to bring him here, force me to watch?

A tentative knock at the door startles me. I spin around, hand on dagger, until I realize what's happening. "For God's sake, I can undress myself!" I shout to the servants, tearing the lace cuffs off my sleeves.

"Are you certain?" a sly voice answers.

I nearly trip over myself in my rush to wrench the door open.

James stands there, dressed in naught but his chemise and breeches, his doublet and sleeves dangling on a hooked finger over his shoulder. Zounds, have his collarbones always had such an elegant sweep to them? It seems unfair I haven't noticed until now.

He cants his head to the side. "Spot something you fancy?"

I drag my eyes up to his face. "You know quite well what's on my mind."

He steps in. The door shuts behind him, and then his hand

slides about the small of my back, the other cupping my nape. He smiles wickedly. "Why don't you tell me about it."

And then we're kissing against the closed door.

For all that this plan is reckless and stupid, I can't say I have any regrets when his teeth tease my blessedly bare neck. A groan pushes through my clenched jaw.

He smiles against my skin. "Hush now, or I'll stop it!"

*It only takes one rumor.* The servants and nobles stroll beyond the door to the night's entertainment, utterly oblivious to the scandal occurring within.

James is fire and I am gunpowder; an errant spark could destroy everything. All it would take is one ill-timed gasp, one enterprising servant with a grudge, and the entire court would know of our torrid affair. I should worry but I can't, because when we kiss, all I can think is *dear God please let us do more of this.*

But, far too soon, he pulls away with a wry smile, tucking a curl of hair behind my ear.

"You ought to be careful," I grumble. "Anyone could've seen you walking in here. We don't want to make people talk."

"Well, it is a good thing I wasn't seen, isn't it?"

I bite the inside of my cheek, resisting the urge to kiss him again. His confidence should make me want to stop, not keep going. "You can't know that," I say. "There's absolute scores of people here. We're never going to find the assassin."

"We've hardly even started looking," James reasons, cupping my chin with a tenderness that feels more dangerous than anything we've done so far. I soften into his touch, relaxing for the first time since we arrived. "Banish those lines from your face. All shall be well, I promise." He kisses me again, sweeter and softer than before.

Right when the door to my chamber bursts open.

We pull apart too late; Maggie and Inigo stand there, gaping in their servants' disguises.

"Goddamn it, Elias!" Maggie throws her washbasin to the floor and plants fisted hands on her hips. "We were gone for *a bloody week*." She turns to Inigo accusingly, like he's to blame. "I told you traveling with the other servants was a mistake! Now look what's happened."

"I take it I am not his first ill-advised lover?" James asks innocently.

"You are the *worst* ill-advised lover of them all!" Maggie snaps. "Gamble with your own lives, sure, but you pull all of us into it as well."

Guilt nips at me, chasing out the reckless rush in my veins. How could I have forgotten about Maggie's and Inigo's and Gráinne's stakes in all this as well?

*You didn't,* part of me reasons. *But it did nothing to stop you.*

My eyes meet James's across the room. He smiles, only for me, and something hooks and pulls tight in my gut. Perhaps I should think more of everyone else involved in this. Perhaps I should dwell more on the danger. But 'tis mighty hard to think of duty and danger when every moment I'm with him feels bigger and brighter than all the others before it.

"Besides"—Maggie's somber tone draws me back to the conversation—"someone's already dead. You best pull your gobs apart and follow us to the church."

• • •

The Bloomsbury chapel is attached to the castle, a space softly lit and silent despite the pulse of activity in the castle walls. The body is wrapped in bedclothes in a candle-filled alcove off the side of the nave. Gráinne already waits for us there, her mouth grim.

"Yer man said to meet you here. Took you long enough," she grumbles.

I do not look at James and pray his blushing face does not give us away. "Well, we're here now. Let's take a look."

I fight back a wave of revulsion as the Pirate Queen saws through the fabric over the corpse's face. 'Tis a young woman, still dressed in her Tudor servant's livery, her eyes closed and her neck at an unnatural angle.

"She was one of the queen's chambermaids," Inigo says as Bloomsbury and Gráinne inspect her broken neck more closely. "They found her dead in the orchards this morning and said she probably fell from her horse—"

"But why would she be on a horse if she was supposed to be preparing for the queen's arrival?" Maggie finishes. "Something's off about it all. That's why we told the vicar to wait before performing her burial rites. Said our most noble lord would want to make sure the death was natural." She rolls her eyes mightily, showing me what she thinks of being forced to act as my servant for the summer.

I wince as Gráinne rips the funeral shroud all the way open. "Let's see if someone murdered our lass a different way, then."

Gráinne and Maggie inspect the body while Inigo, James, and I look away. I've seen more naked bodies of all sexes than

I can count, but Inigo insists on it for propriety's sake. In the Bloomsbury family chapel with the weight of the castle pressing on us, I'm happy to give the poor servant girl a measure of privacy.

"Why would someone murder her and make it appear an accident?" Inigo says.

"If one of the queen's servants is dead, then she'd have to be replaced," Bloomsbury says slowly. "Which means . . . someone could make sure their own person was hired instead."

I dig my fingernails into my thighs. "So the Societas Solis could be trying to place their assassin at the queen's side."

The three of us share a grim look.

But a half hour passes, and neither Gráinne nor Maggie find any other injury—external or internal—which might explain the girl's cause of death aside from her obviously broken neck.

"'Tis right uncanny," Gráinne says, covering up the body once more in the linens. "You best be telling the queen to mind who her housekeeper wants to hire. I agree the servant's death is mysterious, but there's nothing else to learn here."

I listen, but I cannot stop staring at the corpse before me, feeling like there's something about her death we're all missing. The others are already leaving, arguing over who gets to investigate what. I rub my eyes and yawn. "Go along—I'll catch up. I'd like to pray for the dead girl for a moment."

Maggie frowns as she slips out of the chapel—likely remembering I've never been to church a day in my life—but no one else seems to think anything is amiss. I wait until their footsteps have vanished before caressing the cross in my doublet and praying for forgiveness. Then I tear open the girl's funeral shroud again and investigate her body myself.

She's young, younger than I thought, and the knowledge fills me with guilt. This girl must've excelled at her job to be included in the queen's personal attendants. Her family is still in London, and they have no idea their daughter or sister is dead. Whether her death is murder or not, I know she does not deserve to have her corpse pawed at by the likes of me.

The body is neat and clean—save for the fingernails. They're short and jagged, bitten to the quick in places. I wonder if the girl gnawed them thinking of all the stress and excitement of the progress, never realizing that she'd be dead before it barely began.

There's dirt under her nails too.

I stare at them, a faint ringing in my ears.

I've seen nails like this before.

When the men who kidnapped me would bring new boys to their house, sometimes the boys' nails started to look like this too. Jagged and broken from trying to claw their way to escape. I remember the bloody stubs scratching under the doors, pleading for someone to free them, hating myself for scurrying away because I knew freeing them meant sentencing us both to death or worse.

I turn the servant girl's hand over, observing how one nail is cracked and broken, the blood carefully mopped up. How the skin under her nails is pushed back oddly in places and flecked with dirt.

The girl may have died of a broken neck, aye, but there was a struggle beforehand, and someone went through great pains to be sure signs of the struggle would be hidden.

I think of Cecil's midnight rendezvous in the rain, the second figure who left the scene on horseback. That they found the girl this morning. How, in the hustle and bustle of the queen's arrival, there would have been plenty of time for a murderer to receive a message and drag a girl, kicking and screaming, into the woods to end her life and leave a saddled horse to spread lies about how she had died.

Did Cecil send the order to kill a servant girl last night?

And, if so, what secret had she discovered, and why was it worth her life?

# CHAPTER TWENTY-FOUR

BUT, DESPITE OUR best efforts, we can find out nothing more about the murder of the queen's servant, and the lead crumbles to dust. So, too, does every other rumor and whisper we investigate. Scandals and mysteries the progress has dragged into the Bloomsbury estate twist and turn like the vines crawling outside the windows. 'Tis impossible to tug one loose without the entire wall of ivy collapsing. I spend a few days trailing a suspicious porter only to find out his secret is meeting up with one of the queen's manservants in the stable hayloft every night for a spot of fun, and I can hardly fault the lads for that.

"So you've seen nothing, learned nothing, and have nothing at all to report to us. Is this true?" Queen Elizabeth's black eyes bore into me from her throne beneath a pavilion. She's hawking today, a merlin perched on her hand. Other hooded birds of prey gobble globs of bloody meat from servants' hands. Some of her closest courtiers—including Cecil—are seated beside her. Most of them pretend James and I are not standing before them speaking, but at the queen's jab, Cecil flashes us a sharp-toothed smirk.

I grit my teeth and resist the urge to slap the smirk from

his face. "There's the servant girl who died under mysterious circumstances. One of *your* servant girls. I wouldn't say that's nothing."

The queen sighs like she loses a servant girl once every fortnight. "Why are you wasting our time?" She addresses the bird on her hand. The tiny falcon cants its head to the side, its sharp eyes unblinking and primal.

"Because . . . you told us to come here?" Bloomsbury says helplessly, which is true. The summons came this morning, upon a scrap of red velvet in a gilded tray. But judging from the way Cecil's smirk is growing wider and wider, I wonder if embarrassing ourselves before the queen was his doing. After all, we still don't have enough proof of his guilt to know the servant girl's death was his fault, and I'm certainly not going to accuse him groundlessly in front of the queen. Not when her soldiers are stationed close by with sharp pikes.

Queen Elizabeth scoffs and dismisses us with a wave of her hand. "Perhaps we were wrong to trust the two of you with this mission. Learn something useful and report back to us quickly before we change our mind about having you involved in this!" She whistles sharply, and her merlin takes off faster than a crossbow bolt. At the forest's edge, there is an explosion of feathers and a fearsome tussle in the grass. The merlin soon appears again, its talons drooping with something heavy. One of the servants lays a white cloth over the queen's gloved hand. The merlin drops a dead songbird in her palm, its feathers bloodied and neck twisted. She passes the carcass off to the waiting servant with a pleased smirk.

I wince and bow, the dead servant boy and girl in my mind once more. "Yes, Your Majesty. We won't fail you."

"There must be something we missed," I say desperately as James and I stalk through the too-green halls back to his chamber. The dead servants are still with me, except this time they're my brother, my sister.

"Elias." James takes my arms right outside my door, his voice low. "There's still time. There's no need to fret."

"You don't know that." His calm adds to my panic like more kindling to the fire. I shrug out of his grasp and go into my room.

I've summoned all the crew into my chamber—Maggie, Inigo, James, and Gráinne along with her terrifying tiniest crew member, the pirate lad Réamonn. Back in London, he seemed youthful and full of swagger when he told me and Shakespeare of his swashbuckling adventures. But here he seems young, too young to hold his own in Queen Elizabeth's thorny court with its poisoned glances and violent intrigues. I want to tell him to leave. Ask Gráinne what she's thinking, dragging a child into all this, but a warning stare from her stops me. "Are you certain there's nothing more we can learn about the dead girl?" Gráinne says.

"The vicar's only buried her a few days past. I'm sure if we asked him to dig her up, she'd be quite fresh still," Maggie suggests. Everyone ignores her.

"We could have the dogs sniff something of hers. Have 'em track her," Réamonn suggests.

Bloomsbury sighs wistfully and shakes his head. "That is a fair idea, and I wish we'd thought of it sooner. All the servant's personal items have been given away already. We're too late to start a hunt with scent hounds."

"We assumed the girl had no reason to leave the castle, so we've been searching for the murderer here," Inigo says. "But what if we're wrong?" He turns to James. "How close is the nearest town?"

James stops raking a hand through his hair, expression brightening. "Knoxbury is closest. The progress passed through it on the way over."

I have vague recollections of the place. Great slate roofs and cheerful flower boxes, the narrow main street lined with welcoming crowds.

"Maybe whoever killed her was staying in town," Inigo says. "And that's why we can't find him."

"'Tis worth a look." Gráinne strokes her chin. "Me and my crew'll go tonight. I'm getting bored of all the fancy-prancing among these English nobles."

"Aye!" Réamonn agrees with a shout. "And if they won't talk, we've got ways of making 'em talk!" He bares his teeth in what I'm assuming is supposed to be a smile, but the expression could just as well be a snarl.

James's cheeks flush pink. "Erm. Perhaps you and your men should not be the ones to go, my lady."

Gráinne's scowl deepens. "Why not? Is it because we're frightening?"

I take in the iron rings braided into the Pirate Queen's hair and the way she always stands with her hand upon the hilt of her knife.

"Aye," myself, Inigo, and Maggie say all at once.

"No." James stands, bracing his hands on the table. We all look at him, and I cannot help but notice that the scarlet in his cheeks has crept down his neck and under his collar. "I have a—ah—special relationship with the people of Knoxbury."

Gráinne tips her head sideways. "Special enough that common folks'll spill their secrets to the son of their Lord Bloomsbury? I've never met a commoner who trusted a lord enough to tattle on a fellow commoner—not unless there was something in it for himself."

James's mouth hooks into a sly smile. "Trust me. I have my methods."

"So to be clear, your methods of winning over the townspeople primarily involve gifts."

Early the next morning, James and I lead an oxcart laden with food and medicines down the dew-flecked road stretching from Bloomsbury Castle to the heart of Knoxbury. It took me and him and Inigo near an hour to carefully portion, bottle, and move the tinctures and poultices he brought from London into the cart, James chiding us gently the entire time if we let so much as a single drop splatter.

"Of course there's gifts! People need to eat and be well." He grins. "That's how I won you over, after all. So you know it works."

I grumble good-naturedly, and he laughs again. The more

steps we take away from the castle, the court, and its sharp smiles, the more joyous he becomes. More than once, I nearly ask him what dark secret he thinks we'll discover in Knoxbury, and every time, something in his smile or the sun on his cheeks or the wind tousling his hair stops me.

'Tis like before in London, when it was me and him and no one else and we were investigating Marlowe, except this time we actually like each other. I tuck the moment away beside the others of us, the memories growing as familiar as the family cross against my heart. I don't think about what it means when I relive them late at night, what this might mean about me.

We round a hill and discover a group of boys frolicking in a sparkling stream.

They gasp.

I whip my head over my shoulder, certain something hideous must be lurking behind us—but no, there's nothing—only to turn back to find the lads rifling through our cart and tugging at James's sleeves.

"Lord James! You're back!"

"You've brought us things again!"

"It's been too long!"

My eyes zip from the cart to James to the lads and back again. "What's all this?"

The labs sober up at once—all clasped hands behind backs and bare toes scuffing the dirt. They peep shyly up at James. One of them has latched on to his lace cuff.

James's grin is so wide, I can see his perfect molars. "Why, this is Lord William Hughes! My dearest friend in all the world."

The lad holding James's cuff yanks harder, forehead scrunching with suspicion. "Last time you were here you said I was your dearest friend in all the world!"

I've never much cared for children. In the streets of London, the little urchins were as like to snatch my meal as a magpie, and the ones too small to steal from me cried until I felt so bad, I gave them my food anyway. The lad clutching James like a nursemaid is a good head and a half shorter than the rest of the lot. He defiantly shoves his free thumb into his mouth when I kneel to his level.

"I promise you, you're certainly a better friend to Lord Bloomsbury than me. I'm terribly disreputable."

Then I tip him a saucy wink, which makes James mock gasp and the lad squeal with laughter.

The boys follow us all the way to the market square, where mothers and older sisters mill about and shout greetings to James and ask after his health. I watch him wave back and greet the village folk by name, all the while working to unload the oxcart and pass medicines and food into waiting hands.

"I don't understand," I whisper helplessly as I unload the goods. "Do you know all these people?"

"Of course. They're tenants on my land. I grew up with these families. It was here where I realized I wanted to spend my life working with medicine," James says.

I watch him pass off a jar of something odious to a pregnant woman. They smile and chat about people I don't know, about places I've never been to. 'Tis a side of him I never suspected was even there. I thought he despised all his courtly duties.

"Why here? Did a villager teach you the ways of healing?"

He frowns, the first time a vestige of gloom has touched him all morning. "In . . . a sense. A fever ravaged the village when I was younger. A lot of people fell ill, including the midwife. She was the closest thing this town had to a healer. She's the one who told me what herbs to gather and how to boil them for tea as she was dying."

I tug at my collar uneasily. I've a terrible feeling I won't like where this is going at all. "So she's the one who taught you, then."

James shakes his head. He's stopped unloading the cart, his stare blank and focused on some distant memory I can't see. "I thought I could do better than her. I'd found a different and better way to extract the healing properties from the herbs in my laboratory. My father said it was a waste of time. It wasn't our concern if the villagers were dying. That I should focus my talents on doing things that would make a difference. He forbade me from helping anymore, but I didn't listen to him. I made the drink stronger and snuck back. A farmer's young wife volunteered her husband to try it. He was close to unconsciousness, and no one had woken up who'd fallen asleep at the fever's peak. I fed it to him with a spoon—" His voice catches, throat bobbing. "I fed it to him, but it didn't work. The dose was too powerful. He died in terrible agony, screaming the whole time. Right in front of his girls."

I stumble backward, seeing it all. A heartbroken younger James at the bedside, the cries of the children. I take in a deep shuddering breath, steadying myself, even though inside, my heart cracks. I know a thing or two about the heaviness of guilt, how your soul curves about the burden as it crushes from within. Guilt is a river. It drowns at first, but given enough time, it cuts stone.

I want to cradle his head in my hands, push back the curtain of his hair so he can see my face. Know that I mean every word of what I'm saying. "You were barely more than a child. You didn't mean any harm."

"His wife and family did not blame me, no." But the lines of his body stay rigid; his face stays hidden.

His hand is ice, the only part of him I can touch without anyone noticing. I can't stand seeing him like this—tormented and doubting, blaming himself for something that wasn't his fault. "I don't understand. Was your father angry for not listening to him?"

He finally turns to me, agony ripping across his features, his words a tortured whisper. "No, he was proud of me for it. He wanted me to show him how to make the poison so he could bring it to the queen. I destroyed all my research that very night, broke all my tools so he couldn't recreate it himself. He beat me for it."

I remember the riddle of the scars on his shoulder. I had assumed his marks came from childish playing and jesting, the way all mine have. I swallow back a guilty lump.

"You're nothing like your father. I'm sorry for saying so when I was cross with you."

He shakes his head, fists clenched. His hair slips over his shoulders and hides his face. "You don't know that. When my calm leaves me, I can feel his rage right beneath the surface. If I ever lose control—"

My fingers slide under his jaw, forcing him to look at me. His eyes are red-rimmed and wild, nostrils flared like a spooked horse.

"I've seen you lose control," I say quietly. "And there is no one in this world more careful and aware of his power and privilege than you when you're angry. I would not still be at your side if you were like your father. All these people in Knoxbury would not rejoice at the sight of you if you were like him."

He closes his eyes, lines easing from his brow, cheek pressing into my palm for a moment. "Thank you for saying that."

"I'm only speaking the truth."

We stand like that for a moment longer before I pull away. Awkwardness clings to me like ill-fitting clothing. For all the kissing we've been doing, we've not spoken this honestly since that night in the barn. Every time I learn something new about James, it makes me revisit the whole idea of him. Brings me closer to reckoning with the stinging pang of our time together coming to an end.

I want to see what he does and where he goes after this. How exactly he brings his dream of doing good to life. Except I can't—and I never will—because even if he escapes that ship headed to the New World, there's no place for me in his world and none for him in mine.

"I bet your father is absolutely delighted that the townspeople love you," I say, needing to make a jest of things before he sees how cracked my composure's gotten. "Gives them his best gooses for Michaelmas. Says the prayers and everything himself."

James laughs as I hoped he would. "The fact that the villagers like me more than my father is not *not* a reason he's decided to marry and send me off to the New World," he admits. "My father is a man who enjoys control and cruelty. He dislikes that I get with ease what he must get by force."

I shudder, thinking again of the Burning Reaper's grim voice. "And what's that?"

James gestures to the town, and all beyond it. "Our people's loyalty and trust."

Another crowd of curious villagers approaches, and in minutes, the oxcart is near empty and the crowd vanished. But their warmth lingers in the tipped heads and smiles folks give James as we head toward the two-storied timbered inn standing sentinel at the other end of the town.

A realization sneaks up on me—too curious and strange to be unwelcome.

I didn't realize a lord could do good for others with his life and position.

Could I have made a difference like this if I had accepted Queen Elizabeth's title and estate? I'll never know, since I've no need for the people's loyalty, trust, or a tether yoking me to the bloody queen. But imagining this future makes me feel peculiar and aching, like I've lost a tooth and can't help worrying the hole it's left.

James nudges me. "You know, it's not unusual for lords to

visit each other's lands and learn from one another. I could visit yours when this is over if you wanted."

His question trips me up like a rock in a footpath. Though he stares straight ahead, I sense he's watching me carefully. Assessing my reaction.

I may have forgotten to tell James that I have no plans to accept the queen's reward. I may have done so on purpose, worried the truth would crush the tenuous thing growing betwixt us.

Which is reason enough for me to tell him now. To come clean before that feeling grows stronger, its roots too deep to yank up.

"I—I thought we agreed we wouldn't see each other like that once the progress was over?"

His dark gaze slides to mine, stopping me. "That is what we had agreed on, yes."

*What do you mean?* my mind screams. But there's no time for me to respond to his cryptic comment, for we've already reached the inn, and the innkeeper throws open the door before we can knock. "Lord James Bloomsbury!" She's an ample woman in neat skirts with graying hair. She gives James a wink, and I like her at once. "Hope you saved something for me in that cart of yours."

James hands the oxcart reins to a stable boy. "Everything left is yours. Give it to the people who need it most."

The innkeeper pats James's cheek. "You're a good lad, my lord. I'm glad to see the queen finally recognize it, if the rumors from the castle are anything to listen to."

270 I ERIN COTTER

"Queen's business is what brought us to town today," James says as he follows the innkeeper into a well-kept banqueting hall. The room is filled with wooden benches which are all worn smooth, the tables dressed with wild roses. The lush scent dances with the bread baking in the kitchen, and for a half second I'm back at my family's cottage in the summer heat.

The innkeeper raises her eyebrows. "And what would the queen want with Knoxbury?"

James lowers his voice, leaning closer. "There's been a mysterious death at the castle. There's reason to believe the murderer may have stopped over in Knoxbury during the past week. Have you seen or heard anything strange?"

The innkeeper blows out a breath and settles herself on a stool near the fire. "A murder? My goodness, no, Knoxbury is not the sort of place where these things happen." Her hands clutch on her lap, twisting in the apron. "The entire progress has been something quite strange. There's been lots of people out and about I've never seen before."

"Perhaps someone who was heavily armed?" James presses. "Or acted in an unusual manner? Went back and forth between the castle and the village? Perhaps traveling with a servant girl who seemed to be traveling . . . against her will?"

The innkeeper's laugh is uncertain. "Why, that's half the people in the town and half the people in the castle now."

I should've told James not to lead with the murder, but 'tis too late now. I can sense we're losing the innkeeper. Especially from the sideways look she shoots me when James blinks. Like I'm someone she can't speak freely in front of. I give her my most winsome smile and bow elegantly. "There's no need to be alarmed, mistress! My friend is being coy when we should be upright." I laugh and punch James's shoulder—harder than I would if I were truly jesting—and after a beat he nods with me. "No, I know exactly who the person behind this horrible deed is. You would have seen a sun upon their person—perhaps a sword, or a ring, or something of that nature. Definitely a sun, though."

To my shock, the innkeeper claps her hands together. "Why, I know the man you speak of!"

James gives me a confused look. "You do?"

She nods. "Yes, he carried a sword in a strange scabbard embroidered with suns."

The words set off something slow and deep in me, the trembling spreading outward to my hands, which I clasp behind my back. Christ Almighty, the man with the solar scabbard—the man present at Marlowe's murder—is here in Knoxbury!

"He left four days ago after helping me prune the rosebushes." She gestures to the tabletops.

I frown at the thoughtfully arranged pitchers of flowers, unable to imagine the man who I last saw with his cloak trimmed in Marlowe's blood stooping with garden shears.

"The girl was found dead three days ago. Did the man receive any messages while he was here?" James says. If he left four days ago, his timeline matches up with when Cecil sent his secret message.

The innkeeper shakes her head. "No, and even if he did, he never gave me a name."

My shoulders slump. Zounds, we're so close! And as much as I'd like not to run into the man again, the fact that he was here means something, even if we don't know what yet. Where our investigation has been floundering in darkness, I'm starting to see shapes in the shadows, secrets coming into the light.

"I know where he went, though," the innkeeper says.

Both our heads snap up. "You do?"

"Aye, he was headed to Wickden."

"The town's only a half day's ride away!" James turns to me with a grin. Like the thought of confronting a known murderer in a tiny town is the most exciting thing he can imagine.

I face the innkeeper with a furrowed brow. "How do you know this?"

She steeples her fingers, giving me a wink. "Why, because I asked, and he told me."

# CHAPTER TWENTY-FIVE

JAMES AND I barely return to the castle in time to ready ourselves for the evening's feast. As Inigo dresses me in my fancy clothes—his duty as my manservant since I can't lace the sleeves myself without dislocating my shoulder—I fill him and Maggie in on what we discovered in Knoxbury.

"The man with the solar scabbard was here?" Inigo cries, dropping my sleeve to the floor.

"Unless 'twas some other man with a gold sun scabbard," Maggie quips from where she's sitting cross-legged on my bed. "Heard they're all the rage in Rome this summer."

"The scabbard worries me some," I say, ignoring her jest. "Why wear the scabbard out and about if he's the assassin? 'Tis a rather distinctive ornament. Anyone who sees it would recognize it. 'Tis almost as if he wants to be spotted."

Something about this sits uneasy on me. For all his book-learning and research, James has learned distressingly little about the Societas Solis. He tells me it's rumored that Jack Cade, the leader of Cade's Rebellion, kept the mark of the sun about his person when he came to kill the king on the London Bridge in 1450. And that the craftsmen who revolted against the *Signoria* in Florence in 1382 scrawled suns on the city's walls. He says it seems whenever there's trouble with people in power, the sun always appears on the side of the commoners. Which doesn't make any sense at all if they're hired assassins. Common folks don't have much to spare.

While James finds this observation very interesting, I don't see what it does to help us now. Truth be told, I know not why he squanders his time with his books, confirming what we already know: Societas Solis is dangerous and powerful. It seems unlikely that myself, a player whose greatest talent is his looks, would outsmart them so easily. I shiver and caress the cross in my inner pocket, its familiar shape failing to take the edge from my unease.

"Are you going to Wickden tomorrow, then?" Inigo asks, fussing with my other sleeve.

"Aye, and you're coming with us." 'Tis the plan James and I agreed upon. He and I and our manservants will go to the small village of Wickden. We will question the innkeeper and other persons of standing in the town while Inigo and James's manservant, Cooper, sneak through all the hidden places where the man with the solar scabbard may be lurking.

"Me?" Inigo says. "You ought to take Maggie. She actually knows her way around a blade."

I twist my hands nervously, dreading what I have to say. "Wouldn't do for a lord to travel with a lady servant." Maggie pins me beneath a smoldering, furious stare. I swallow and go on, knowing with each word I flirt with danger. "It . . . would be improper. And people might notice and talk."

"God forbid we do something improper!" Maggie spits. "I suppose I'm to sit home and scrub your underthings with all the other maids." She crosses her arms and hitches up her shoulders. "You ought to take one of Gráinne's men instead. They have the proper bits *and* know their way around a blade, no offense, my love." She pats Inigo's cheek once before glaring at me some more. "I'll wait here for the big, burly boys to come home and make me swoon with tales of their heroics!"

I wince under her fierce look. I should've thought of taking one of Gráinne's men myself. I'm cross she thought of it before me.

"'Tis not like that, and you damn well know it! I'm playing at being a lord and you two as my servants. We've got to follow their rules while we're here," I say.

Maggie's eyes narrow. "The longer this goes on, the less it feels like you're playing." She hops from my bed. "Enjoy your bloody feast with the queen. We'll be eating cold gruel outside if you bother to search for us afterward." Maggie yanks the door open and stomps away, the slam sending the portraits on the walls shivering.

I turn to Inigo. "Zounds, what's gotten into her?"

Inigo finishes tying my sleeve and steps away, his eyes dropping to the floor. Even the godforsaken rugs are green here. "I ought to go after her. I'll see you tomorrow, aye?" He smiles, the expression not reaching his eyes, and leaves.

I stare at the closed door, worrying a loose thread on my cuff. Maggie's words leave a sour, twisting feeling in my gut. The three of us are here to find the queen's would-be assassin, stuff our pockets with gold, and afterward do whatever we please, rich as jewel thieves. Simple as that.

So why do I feel like something's changed? And why do I have the nagging fear it's somehow my fault?

I leave to fetch James so we can head to the feast together. As the heir to the house, he's got an entire suite of rooms to himself that I've become mightily acquainted with over the past few days: a parlor, antechamber, bedchamber, and an attached library. The door to the parlor is already ajar, so I let myself in, the knot of tension unraveling in me at the thought of seeing him, sharing my worries—

But we're not alone.

James sits beside his betrothed, Lady Anne Middlemore, on a high-backed settee I've never seen him use before. His doublet is sleeveless and undone, his face frozen into a ghastly rictus of a smile. Lady Anne is dressed in an exquisite pink gown, dark brown hair scraped back from her temples so tightly, I can see the skin pulling. Her pale face is powdered with so much white, she looks like a ghost. James himself certainly looks haunted.

Lord Middlemore looms over the pair like a raven doting upon a carcass, deciding which morsel to snap up next in its greedy beak.

"Are you sure you cannot consider being married on the progress?" Middlemore says, dropping a hand to his daughter's shoulder. "It is all my dearest Anne desires."

Lady Anne simpers. "Nothing would make me happier, my lord."

My stomach sinks to near about my boots.

Even though I know the spark of our dalliance can't burn

beyond this progress, even though I know they're betrothed, seeing Lady Anne seated beside James still sours my mood. A gag forces through my throat, the sound causing everyone to turn toward me.

"Oh, it's *you*." All the mirth vanishes from Middlemore's face at once.

I plaster on a courtier's smile—all teeth and no sincerity. "Oh, I do apologize! It appears I have a knack for stumbling into you at the strangest times, Lord Middlemore." His face purples, and I can't resist goading him further. "I was so sorry to hear that the queen ended your engagement to James's sister Catherine. I know you both must be terribly disappointed!" The happy letter containing this news was waiting for James and his family the morning after the queen's arrival. Lady Catherine's shriek of glee was so loud, I swear, it shook all the birds from their nests in the ancient forest.

"It appears you have a knack for inviting yourself to meetings which were supposed to be private," Middlemore growls savagely.

*He knows we're up to something.*

The thought knocks the breath from my lungs. I force out a laugh, like his jab is a jape and means nothing at all to me.

"Shall we go to the feast, then?" I ask the room, but my eyes are on James.

Lady Anne whips toward him, sulking already. "But you said you had to work tonight! Even though there's to be dancing and you know how dearly I love dancing."

"Yes, I really must be working," James says—more than a

bit desperately. "Perhaps Lord Hughes can escort you to dinner, my lady?" His eyes practically shout *Please save me*. Even though I'd rather strangle myself with my own stocking, I offer my elbow to Lady Anne and bow. "It would be my pleasure."

Lady Anne scrunches her face and takes my arm like it's something slimy, and we leave, her father lumbering behind us like a pit bear.

I know I should say something to Lady Anne—compliment her dress, or speak well of her fiancé, or ask her what her favorite flower is—but I can hardly stand to look at her, knowing her hand on my arm shall soon bear James's ring. That *this* hand will be the one he reaches for when the sea storms shake the vessel that carries him to the New World.

"Lord Hughes, you're shaking," Lady Anne remarks. "Is there something amiss?"

I grit my teeth and will the images away. "Of course not, my lady."

I part with James's odious fiancé as quick as possible in the banqueting hall and escape to my table like a man fleeing the City Guard. For once, I'm grateful to be seated with senile old men beside the kitchens. A nervous, helpless energy bubbles though me, spoiling all the rich food on the table. I'm so out of sorts, even Lord Foxwell notices.

"Stop bouncing your leg—it's jostling my plants!" he grumbles, setting down his herbarium.

"They're already dead, Foxwell!" I snap.

He puffs himself up like a cock in the hen yard. "I'm presenting them to the queen at the talent exhibition tomorrow,

I'll have you know! Just because you have nothing of consequence to share, it does not look good for you to sabotage the success of other men."

I've been forced to endure talk of the talent exhibition for days. An event where people like Foxwell can parade their strange work and hobbies before the queen like slobbering, simple hounds bringing dead birds back to their masters for a pat on the head. I won't be bored with it again tonight.

I mutter a wholly arsed apology and excuse myself. 'Tis long before it's an acceptable time to abandon the queen's revels, but I can't bring myself to care what anyone will think of my leaving. By their own will, my feet carry me through the near-empty castle until I'm knocking at James's door again.

"Oh! Elias." He's all ink smudges and mussed hair and the soft-eyed look which means his mind is turning over some problem. "I'm—I'm rather busy. I've got to finish parceling these medicines for Wickden."

"I'm not here to snog you, if that's what you're worried about."

He relaxes ever so slightly. "Then why are you here?"

I bite the inside of my cheek. "I can go, if you'd rather."

"No," he says quickly. "It—it would be nice. If you stayed. But only if there's nothing else you'd rather be doing."

Zounds, I'm reaching the point where I'd watch James scratch his teeth with a tooth-scraper. It unsettles me, how much I want to linger here with him, doing nothing. With other lads, I'd be gone as soon as the kissing was over. Which is why I shouldn't be here at all, why I shouldn't be pulling up a stool alongside the candlelit table, ignoring the part of me whispering *'Tis not supposed to be like this.*

My hand finds his and traces patterns across the knuckles. We sit in silence, with the snarl and shift of the fire, or with him murmuring some explanation about his medicines I can't follow. If I close my eyes, I can almost imagine we're back in his library in London, surrounded by his damned Latin books.

I wonder, when our summer fades, how long it shall take him to forget me? For the details of my face to blur and grow soft in his memory. Perhaps one day, when he coddles his grandson upon creaky knees, even my name will become a mystery, like a scrap of song he can recall hearing, though the words are long vanished.

"Do you still mean to marry Lady Anne after this?" The question slips from me unbidden.

James smiles wryly but does not look up from whatever he's writing. "What makes you ask?"

"She's only interested in you for your money, *and* her father is awful. Can you break off the engagement if our investigation is successful? Or can the queen? I know that as a lord, you're expected to marry, but you ought to be with someone who's nicer to you."

His quill slows and stops. I realize I'm gripping his hand far too tightly, but I can't find the will to let it go. James is silent for so long, I worry my great gob has said too much, wonder if I should take it back and pretend it was all a jest.

"Men used to love other men openly, you know," he finally says.

I feel ambushed by his strange confession. "Wh-what do you mean?"

"Greek men took other men as lovers. It is something Cambridge tries not to teach us, but it's right there in Plato."

My heart knots painfully. "Why are you telling me this?"

"I—I thought you'd want to know." James tugs his hand from mine and places it on the table. Tremors shake his fingers, but his expression is steady, alive with a growing fervor.

"Elias . . . have you considered that this doesn't have to end when the queen's progress is over? I am a lord. You're going to be a lord. With us as equals, fewer people will pay attention to us. We both know rich, powerful men can do as they wish. We can continue this, if you want."

His brown eyes are so wide and warm with hope, it kills me. I pull myself back, forcing out the truth I haven't been able to admit to him. "I'm not going to be a lord."

"What do you mean?" His brow furrows, like he's certain he misheard me. "Of course you'll be a lord. It's what the queen promised."

I've had days on this progress to observe first-hand the society I would enter if I became a courtier in the queen's court. The cold welcome I'd be granted and the unsatisfying work I'd have to do to make sure an old woman never, ever had reason to doubt my loyalty to her.

"Queen Elizabeth's greed drove my family from their lands, and her indifference lets poverty and death run unchecked for the common people. Why would I want to be a part of that world? I'm going to take whatever else the queen gives me and run. To hell with her poisonous gifts!"

He looks at me like he's never seen me before, brow furrowed and helpless. "But . . . that'd be spurning the royal family's favor. They'd consider you a thief. A traitor. You could never go anywhere in England again. If someone recognized you, you'd be dead."

"Aye, that's right."

"But, Elias—"

I tear my eyes away from his pleading face. "I've witnessed the world you live in, James! 'Tis a gilded cage, its door threatening to snap shut and trap me. You knew what I am and who I was the moment we met. This isn't my world, it's yours, and I don't want a place in it."

The longer I play at being Lord William Hughes, the less I feel like Elias Wilde. The less I know what's right and what's wrong and what I can live with and what I cannot. The queen's offered title is a shackle, not just for me, but for all my kin. I'd have to marry a woman I couldn't love. I'd have to bring children into a world that doesn't care for children unless they've got the right sort of parents.

James slumps like a man scooped from the sea, half-drowned and pale. "Then . . . it wouldn't matter if I stayed here or went to the New World or married Anne or not." His grief is a knife slipped through my ribs. "I'd never see you again. Not unless I went with you."

My throat tightens. "You can't do that. You'd be giving up your title." My eyes sweep across the room, taking in the bottled medicines and precious manuscripts, a fortune's worth of knowledge. "Your work."

*But what if you did?*

The terrible want whispers from the darkest part of me, awful hope wrapping spiked ropes around my heart and squeezing tight. *What if, what if?*

"My sister." He falls back, swallowing hard. "Catherine would be at our parents' mercy for whatever terrible suitor comes along next, wondering why I left her behind." His expression grows glassy and unfocused, and I know he's thinking of the person closest to him in the world, the one he'd never see again if he left with me, and all at once I'm as helpless and small as a young child, glancing over my shoulder at my parents and siblings while a strange man leads me away to London, whispering promises in my ear he's already broken.

I square my jaw and look away. He can't leave with me. Of course he can't. I knew it already, but realizing it again is a burning pain in my chest, the hurt too deep to fix. I shove all my secret wanting away, ashamed of myself.

He straightens and gestures to the space between us, voice unsteady. "So your plan is to run away, find your family, and pretend we never happened?"

I go perfectly, absolutely, still.

His words scrape at my deepest, most secret fear.

What if my family doesn't accept this part of who I am? In my memories they are as I left them—my brother and sister beneath my chin and my arms barely around my father's waist.

But in truth they've grown and changed and lived as much as I have, and I've never let myself think of it before. Each time I kiss James, each time I lift a cup and toast the queen's health in the Burning Reaper's hall, I wonder, *Will my family care for the person I've become?*

"Don't insult me by pretending I could ever forget you." My voice is hard, but brittle. One more soft word from him and I'll shatter. "You can't give up your family and title, and I can't accept the one the queen would give me. The world isn't made for lads like us." He moves to speak, but I hold up a hand, gritting my jaw to stave off the burning in my eyes. "Please don't make this harder."

The silence roars. I can't bring myself to look within an inch of James, too cowardly to witness whatever's there.

He stands, each movement slow and deliberate. I peek at him. There's nothing on his face but a terrible gentleness that sets my pulse skittering. "People believe everything has always been a certain way, but that's never been true. Anything can change—men loving men, England ceasing to take lands which are not its own."

"'Tis a gallant idea. But that's not the world we live in."

His hands are on my face, forcing me to look at him. "But it *could* be." His dark eyes spark with fire. "You're always saying what the world is like as though there's nothing to be done about it. Except you're wrong. The world can change for the better. *We* can change things, if we took the chance to be together."

An unbearable feeling sweeps through me. I am undone, body and soul, by this man and his damned heart and imagination vaster and wilder than anything else. Of course he believes things like this. Someone like him really could change the world, and that's exactly why I've got to leave him behind. "James—"

"No, I won't have you arguing with me, Elias Wilde." The fire of his conviction rages, hot and unchecked. "Not this time. I'm—"

I silence him with a kiss. He's got to stop before the heat catches and we burn together, taking everything down with us. 'Tis a savage kiss, tempered with something deeper and unnameable which frightens me. His hand cups the back of my head, and I am somehow sitting on the table and the books are dangerously close to the candle—

"James?"

The whisper is louder than the crack of a cannon.

His sister, Lady Catherine, stands at the doorway, her eyes huge and fathomless.

I scramble away from him so fast, I take out the chair behind me. It falls to the floor with a tremendous clatter.

"Catherine." James freezes halfway between me and his sister. "How did you get in here? The door was locked."

Catherine swallows and holds up something small. "You gave me a spare key, remember?" She drops the key to the floor, and the metallic *plink* feels louder than the slamming of prison doors.

James stares at it, at her, his face white. "It is—this is— what I'm trying to say is—"

There is no possible explanation which could neatly explain away why Catherine's brother had his tongue in the mouth of his best friend. The longest, most awkward silence in all the world falls, and I dearly wish I were anywhere else but here.

Catherine points to her brother. "*You*." Her finger swings to me. "And *him*."

"Unfortunately, yes," I say. "'Tis all a bit of a mess, but—"

Bloomsbury silences me with a scorching glare.

Catherine rights the knocked-over chair and sits in a most unladylike fashion. She takes in our guilty faces, the mussed papers, the fact that she now possesses the knowledge to utterly destroy our reputations and lives for good should she choose to whisper to the right person. She glances between the two of us, a finger on her lips. "Is it . . . love?"

And now James and I cannot force ourselves to look at each other at all. He addresses the toe of my boot, his face ten different shades of pink. "It—it is—something like that, yes."

*Something like that*. The words nestle deep in my chest, like a bit of coin squirreled away against the harsh winter, shiny and secret and all mine.

Catherine tips her head to the side, brow furrowed. The expression is so much like her brother's, it takes all my self-control not to say so. "I don't understand why you're doing it and fear it might be foolish."

I nod slowly, nails biting into my palms, because curse it all, isn't that what I've been saying? But still, hearing it confirmed by Catherine sends a pang through me. Whether as a lord and a commoner, or as lords both, whatever James and I are doing is rash and thick-sighted. I should have stopped this ages ago. Never mind the fact that the thought of ending things feels like strangling the most vibrant part of my soul.

I'm courting danger and perhaps even death, but zounds, if this isn't the most alive I've ever felt.

She stands and takes James's hand. "But I understand that love is good, and if this is love, then . . . it must be good."

James sighs with relief and presses a kiss to her knuckles. "Thank you. Please don't tell anyone."

"I won't, but be careful, *please*," she says, face pinched with worry. "The court doesn't care for things it cannot understand."

I sink into James's chair, too unsteady to stand. The relief knocks the breath from me like jolting awake and realizing the nightmare wasn't real. Except this *is* real, every single moment, and I know it's real because I'm not capable of dreaming something like this.

Catherine is good. She thinks *we're* good. She accepts us.

James hugs his sister close, the top of her head tucked beneath his chin. "We shall, I promise you a hundred times over." He rocks her back and forth, eyes squeezed shut. I swallow and turn away, my heart twisting. Will my family accept this side of me the way Catherine has? I cannot even imagine, and the thought leaves me aching.

"Why are you here, anyway?" James says in his usual tone. "You know I'm not supposed to be disturbed unannounced."

"I knocked on the door *several* times before entering," Catherine says pointedly. "And I'm in need of your books. The queen has given me permission to write a masque, and I must check some classical sources."

James looks stricken. "Oh, but I'd rather you didn't take them out of the library."

I clear my throat very obviously. "James. I believe we have no choice but to do as your lady sister demands at this point."

Catherine tips me a curtsy. "Yes, thank you, Lord Hughes. At least one of you is reasonable."

James helps his sister gather the books she needs. The stack is so tall, I can barely see the girl over it. Clearly, bookishness runs in the family.

"Keep food and drinks away from them, will you?" James pleads. "Oh, and dogs. And hair. Everything, really—"

"Good night, dear brother," she interrupts. "I hope you . . . well, enjoy yourself."

Lady Catherine leaves whilst her brother sputters with shock, but then her head pops back in the doorframe. "Oh, and Will?" It is the first time she has even used my first name. The smile she gives me is all wicked sweetness. "I never wanted Lady Anne Middlemore as a sister. She's ponderous as a funeral."

The door shuts behind her before either of us can say anything at all.

James and I both stare at it, incredulous. Then he smiles smugly. "See, there's space in Catherine's world for people like us."

I fight the urge to roll my eyes. "She's only one person."

James shushes me. "And one person is where it all begins." His brow presses against mine, thumb tracing my bottom lip. "We're not done talking about this. I'll change your mind yet."

I pull him closer. "Fine. As long as we're done talking for now."

# CHAPTER TWENTY-SIX

THE RIDE TO Wickden is as sobering and unpleasant as a bucket of cold water after a night of merrymaking. James and I were up half the night kissing and the other half finishing parceling the medicines we'd spent the first half of the night ignoring. The pirate lad Réamonn and James's manservant, Cooper, follow us with the laden oxcart. Their judging stares are the only thing keeping me upright in the saddle. I strongly suspect they both know what James and I did last night, and I know not how to feel about it.

'Twas foolish of me to ever think our relationship would go unnoticed—but the circle of those who know is growing, and I worry what will happen when someone who is not our friend discovers what we're doing.

James, too, is worried and wan this morning, his hair half-escaped from his queue and a furrow in his brow.

I nudge his boot with mine. "At least we'll not have to see Lord Foxwell's herbarium today, aye?" My dreary dining partner was busy during breakfast, already sweating through his chemise, and approximately a dozen new dried plants trembling before him.

James laughs, the sound like a flash of sun in a gray sky.

"'Tis not too late for you to go back and attend the exhibition, if you're curious."

"I'd rather scoop my eyes out with spoons."

Wickden is quieter and smaller than Knoxbury. Grubby one-story buildings press against the dusty road, and the women gathered around the well in the town square stop and stare when we pass. No one calls James's name. A trickle of unease goes down my spine.

The innkeeper waits for us outside the largest building, his round face screwed in a scowl and arms crossed defiantly over his stomach. "Lord James Bloomsbury," he says as we dismount before him. "To what do we owe this . . . pleasure."

I age a year in the long pause it takes him to find that final word.

James smiles brightly, the expression strained. He gestures to the oxcart. Réamonn and Cooper pull back the canvas sheets, revealing the glimmering phials of medicines and fine salted meats. "I come bearing gifts for you and the people of Wickden, as a thank you from my family and in celebration of Queen Elizabeth's arrival to our fine lands."

Silence.

Réamonn and I share a nervous glance, and I bite back a thrill of panic. What do we do if the man refuses to help us? Réamonn taps his hilted dagger and waggles his eyebrows suggestively.

I roll my eyes heavenward and shake my head. I dearly wish again Gráinne had been willing to loan me an actual pirate man and not a bloodthirsty pirate boy.

The innkeeper finally sighs, the sharp angles of his posture softening. "Fine. Let's go inside, then."

He stomps into the inn and shouts for his staff to help unload the oxcart at the stable. James gives me a small nod, and we follow the innkeeper into a dark dining hall with a smoldering fire. The tables are empty despite the fact that it's near midday.

"What's all this really about?" the innkeeper demands, squinting suspiciously at James. "Don't pretend there's not something else afoot behind these gifts, sir."

James explains what's brought us here—the servant girl's murder, the man with the solar scabbard. He shares everything save the fact that the man may be conspiring to kill the queen of England. The innkeeper's scowl deepens. "Oh, aye, I've seen that man before. Just ran off this morning without paying me. Destroyed the chamber and everything!"

James and I share a charged glance. "Can I look at where he was staying?" I ask breathlessly.

The man frowns. "Don't know what good it would do ye."

"Please let him look," James implores. "We want to get to the bottom of this mystery before more people are harmed."

"Seems a mighty bit of trouble for a dead maid."

The innkeeper's words strike like a slap. James's hand brushes my elbow, warning me to bite back the angry retort I'd like to lob in the man's face.

"I strive to keep all my people safe. Not just the rich ones," James says, standing taller.

The innkeeper sighs at the reminder of what he owes James

as his liege lord's son. "'Tis time for the midday meal," he grumbles. "Would you . . . care to join me while your friend looks upstairs? I can tell you all the man did while he was here, but I'll tell ye again there's not much to say."

I'm shown upstairs to the chamber. The bedclothes are twisted and scattered. The remains of a dinner plate lie on a small table, crumbs buzzing with flies. The washbasin's kicked over, water pooled and sinking into the wood floor.

My mind spins, turning over what we know, trying to make sense of the puzzle.

The man with the solar scabbard fled Wickden without paying, room ransacked, like he'd left in a great hurry. In Knoxbury he told the innkeeper where he was going next. In both towns he made no effort to hide his remarkable scabbard nor to keep himself out of the public eye. I think of what I told Maggie, a sinking feeling taking hold in my gut. *'Tis almost as if he wants to be spotted.* But why?

I begin tearing through the drawers, the bed linens, and search the corners for rubbish, a loose thread, anything. I pick up and shake the pillow, feeling something hidden within the straw.

A letter addressed to me.

*Elias Wilde.*

My shaking hands struggle to pry the parchment open, clumsy with dread. This was left for me to find, under my true name.

He knows what we're up to.

Something flutters to the bed. A spray of dry purple flowers, leaves shriveled and curled. I examine the letter itself, but there's no further text. No hidden message at all, save for the flowers and my name.

I turn the plants over with the edge of the parchment, careful to avoid ruining such delicate evidence with my unsteady hands. I haven't seen anything like them before, which isn't strange, given that most exotic plants are grown by nobles behind garden walls and iron gates.

Except . . . the purple flowers drag out a memory. I'm in the dim hold of Gráinne's ship, the Pirate Queen turning over Marlowe's phial in her curious fingers.

Downstairs I hear the murmur of voices, the clink of silverware.

And it all snicks into place.

I bolt into the hallway, tearing down the stairs into the dining hall.

*"Don't touch anything!"*

I crash chest-first onto the table, sliding down its length. Ale and bread and cheese go flying. The innkeeper shouts and runs.

There's James at the head of the table, inches from my face, a goblet at his lips. I smack the goblet away. Dread chokes me, gruesome and cold.

"Did you eat anything?" I seize his chin and see myself reflected in his huge eyes: wild-haired and feral, dripping with ale. Like a wolf he found in the forest's dark heart. I clench my fist, resisting the frantic urge to pry his mouth open.

"Elias, what—"

My grip tightens. *"Did you eat anything?!"* Already the

poison would be coursing through his veins, taking root in his center, nothing I could do about it.

James pales. He shakes his head once, and I let go, supine with relief.

"He's poisoned the food," I say tightly.

"How do you know—"

"I'll tell you later." My head whips toward the kitchen, where the door is still slowly swinging shut. I scramble to my feet, freeing the knife from my belt. "Get that man."

The kitchen empties into the garden, where already the innkeeper struggles in Cooper's and Réamonn's hold. He gasps when he sees us, red-faced with terror. I prowl over and sneer, holding my knife where he can see it. "All right. Let's try that whole asking-you-questions thing again, shall we?"

We tie the innkeeper to a chair in his own dining hall, and I place what's left of the ale and the dried flowers I found before him. I've pocketed the parchment, not wanting the innkeeper to know my name.

The man flinches as James drops to a knee beside him, but James's face holds nothing but kindness despite the fact that the bloke tried to murder him not five minutes past. "I'm not telling my father or the queen what you've done if you answer our questions truthfully. All right?"

The man nods furiously.

"Good. Tell us what happened."

"The man—he never told me his name—he said the Bloomsbury boy would come looking for him with another boy. He gave me a phial and said to make sure Bloomsbury drank it." He swallows, his gaze skittering away from James. "He said if I slipped it in the ale, you'd never notice."

I frown. "He didn't tell you to poison me?"

He shakes his head.

I know not whether to count myself offended or lucky. It doesn't make sense to poison James but not me.

"And where's the phial now?" James says.

The innkeeper tips his head to the kitchen door. "Behind the flour."

I nod to Réamonn, who leaves and returns with a horribly familiar-looking phial. It's near empty, but the few drops clinging to the phial's bottom are the exact consistency and color of Marlowe's poison in royal custody back in London. This is a different phial, no doubt, but it clearly comes from the same place that the other phial came from.

James sighs and runs a hand through his hair. "How much did he pay you to do this?"

"Five pounds, my lord," the man says softly. "And another five afterward, as long as you died."

"He was never going to pay you." I get to my feet, the parchment with my name burning hot as a coal in my pocket. "He set you up. He knew I'd know what you did when Bloomsbury stopped breathing, and he was going to let you take the blame for killing him." I take out the parchment and show it to James. He sucks in his breath softly, seizing my wrist heedless of the company.

"What's it say?" Réamonn whispers, his eyes huge.

"'Tis my name," I say softly. "My real, secret name."

My mind whirs faster than a hawkmoth's wings. *Someone knows what James means to me.* The poison was only meant for him, and the letter was only addressed to me. A chill creeps down my spine.

Our investigation's been found out in more ways than one.

The innkeeper sits up straight in his bonds. "Maybe he was gonna pay me; maybe he wasn't. You two figured it out before it came to aught, so I don't see what it matters anymore."

I pinch the bridge of my nose, praying for patience. "You know, for a man who just tried to kill his lord's heir, you're not very penitent."

"There's something you're not telling us, isn't there?" James says.

The innkeeper grins viciously. "Aye, there might be."

"Out with it, then!" I snap, arms crossed, dread pooling in my gut. "Sir, you are tied to a chair, and only our silence will prevent your death or dismemberment for the crime of *attempted murder*."

James brushes past me and holds out a golden pound. The innkeeper eyes the coin hungrily, but James snatches it back. "You'll remember our mercy when I or someone else from my family needs something from you in the future, all right?"

The innkeeper grimaces but inclines his head. James slips him the coin and motions for Cooper and Réamonn to untie him. The innkeeper stands and rubs his wrists. "The man with the strange sword met with another man at the inn last night. From the looks of it, he was a noble at the castle." He nods toward the dried wolfsbane on the table. "They whispered all night, and then the lord bought something from him that looked an awful lot like those dried flowers."

"What'd this nobleman look like?" I half expect the man to say *A pompous windbag with a ginger beard*, describing Cecil.

"He was an oddly tall one, his face full of spots." The innkeeper frowns at the memory. "He didn't stop talking about plants once. Not even when I'd ask him if he wanted more ale or wanted to pay up. They talked about plants for bloody hours. Christ Almighty, it was a bore to witness."

James and I turn to each other, and from his wide-eyed look, there's nothing more to be said. There's only one man in all the progress who fits the description the innkeeper's just given to us.

And Lord Foxwell is presenting his poisonous plants to the queen right this very moment.

# CHAPTER TWENTY-SEVEN

WE THUNDER TOWARD the castle. I clutch the saddle for dear life, more or less plastered to my horse's shoulders. "Why must it always be poison?" I cry over the roaring wind. "Can't the Societas Solis find a new method of murder?"

James is hunched low on Ares's neck, his hair tangling with the horse's mane. "Hurry—I fear we may be too late!"

We explode into the castle courtyard, our horses foaming at the bit and sweat streaking their sides. The exhibition is still in full swing, lords and ladies gathered around tables covered in meringue animals and gilded portraits and gleaming blue-steel weapons. Musicians pluck merry tunes in the corner, drowning out the conversation. I search the crowd. There is Lord Cecil, whose face is puckered as a rotten plum, and there, beyond him, I spot Lord John Foxwell.

The man sits alone at his exhibit, shoulders high with hope. The herbarium is open on the table, dried plants tucked betwixt pages with painstakingly written Latin explanations. Guilt near slays me at the way his eyes brighten as James and I near—people approaching to finally admire his plants and applaud his knowledge! I swallow back my guilt and stab a finger at Foxwell. "Guards! By the power invested in me by the queen as her spymaster, I order you to arrest this man!"

The music screeches to a stop. Foxwell startles and glances behind him, as if I could not possibly be speaking of him. The guards mutter among themselves, sharing shifty looks. They obviously don't believe me either, and I can't say I blame them. I barely believe it myself.

James claps his hands. "You heard him! Arrest the man!"

The guards move forward, pikes raised, but Foxwell flaps them away like a swarm of irritating flies. He tuts and crosses his arms as if James and I are schoolboys who slipped frogs into his shoes. "There must be some sort of mistake."

The queen bustles over in a fury of brocade, a retinue of curious nobles and guards trailing her. "What's all this?" she demands. "We were enjoying the exhibition. It would be a shame to ruin such merriment." In her voice is both a reproach and a warning. *Don't waste my time again.*

James bows. "My queen, we have found the man who would kill you."

"Or he's at least worked with a known murderer," I add hastily, not wanting to condemn Foxwell outright, since we have yet to hear a word from the man himself.

Low mutters and raised eyebrows break out among the nobles. Only the queen remains impassive to our announcement. "Is that so?"

"This man met secretly with the killer of Christopher Marlowe last night. The very same man who tried to poison you at midsummer."

Foxwell snorts at the accusation. "Your Majesty, these boys are addled. You can't possibly think I mean my sovereign ill will!" He laughs, quickly stopping when no one else joins in. "Do you truly think me involved in a plot? To murder *my queen*?"

"We have it on very good word that you went to Wickden to dine and drink last night with the known murderer. A man with a golden scabbard covered with suns," I say.

"Thomas Walter?" The indignation eases from Foxwell's features, replaced with puzzlement. "Why, I converse with him all the time. 'Tis a bit odd he's this far out of London, but when he sent me word he would be close to the Bloomsbury estate, I had to go meet him. He has the best plants."

Wait.

Foxwell *knows* the man with the solar scabbard?

The guards step closer, pikes raised. Foxwell sucks in his breath sharply at the movement. "This is outrageous! Robert, tell them so. You know what kind of man I am." He speaks to Cecil, and I swallow a groan, because of course the two worst people on all this bloody progress are on a first-name basis with each other.

But Cecil isn't sneering for once. He's simply staring at Foxwell, expression unreadable.

"Hughes and Bloomsbury. It's quite serious to accuse a member of the nobility of such crimes." Cecil turns to us, arms linked behind his back. "What evidence is there of this injustice?"

"The innkeeper said Foxwell bought something from the

murderer last night. They talked together for hours," James says.

Cecil turns to Foxwell. "Well. Is this true?"

Foxwell gapes, like Cecil's speaking in a foreign tongue, but at a nudge from a guard he scoffs and picks up his herbarium. He flips through the huge leather-bound manuscript. "As I mentioned, I know Thomas. We share a passion for botany. He told me he had something special for me." Pressed plants fly from the pages, and for once Foxwell makes no effort to be gentle, even though he's accused me more than once of sullying his collection just by breathing too loudly near it.

Foxwell stops at a page, the flower freshly pressed to the parchment. A horribly familiar spray of dried purple flowers. "'Twas this. A rare form of wolfsbane."

I stare at the wolfsbane, wondering if this is all a terrible jest. The man with the solar scabbard knows Foxwell and sold him the very same poisonous plant he left for me. After a beat of hesitation, I reach into my doublet and pull out the carefully wrapped plant from the Wickden inn. "That's the same plant the murderer left behind for me to find."

The queen's cheeks pucker, and her eyes darken anew as she takes in Foxwell. "Tell me why a loyal subject such as your-self would have this plant if you did not mean to do your queen harm? Is this poisoner swordsman working for you? Creating your poisons, perhaps?"

Foxwell pales. "No, of course Thomas doesn't work for me. I met him because I thought—I thought my queen would be impressed by such a plant. That she could use it on her enemies!" He shakes his head desperately. "This cannot be happening. I've known Thomas for years. He's no murderer. He would never . . ." He trails off, as though realizing the more he speaks, the deeper the grave he's digging for his innocence grows.

"The man with the solar scabbard tried to kill our queen once already." James jerks a thumb toward me, mouth a grim slash. "He witnessed it."

Foxwell laughs, the sound utterly feral and unhinged. "Oh yes, well, if the *Hughes* boy saw it, then it must be true." His eyes rove over the assembled crowd, latching on to Cecil and narrowing. "You told me to keep an eye on Hughes! You said this lord was untrustworthy and up to no good. Now you would take his word over mine?"

Cecil flushes pink as the queen's attention snaps to him.

"Is this so, Cecil?" Her words crackle with anger. "You would distrust our faith in this boy and Bloomsbury once more? After we explicitly forbade you from tampering with their work?"

Cecil's face cycles through a spectrum of colors before settling into a mottled purple. The sidelong glare he gives me is filled with hate. "I merely asked Foxwell to tell me if he witnessed any strangeness. I never told him to mistrust Lord Hughes."

Foxwell gasps with outrage, and James starts defending my innocence. The queen hisses and raises both hands, demanding silence. "Hughes has made this accusation, so he may continue to show us the proof." Her focus snaps back to me so suddenly, I flinch. "Get to it, boy! We've not all day to waste."

I swallow and drop to a knee before Foxwell. I feel the eyes of the entire courtyard on my back, itchy and hot as the sun. "Didn't you say you were waiting for something from Spain to be delivered to you?" Foxwell nods frantically, and I say, "This type of poisonous wolfsbane is only found in the Pyrenees mountains of Spain. Are you trying to tell us this is all a terrible coincidence?"

Foxwell's breath comes in short, startled gasps. "It—it is not what it appears. I bought something from Spain, yes, but it was seeds! Seeds from the New World from explorers!" His voice drops to a whisper. "Please, you know I speak the truth. I told you about the tomatoes."

The quiet is so intense, I can hear the old stones groaning in the castle walls, the roots burrowing deeper into its foundations.

"We shall see if this object from Spain arrives at all," the queen says in a bored voice, already half-turned back to the exhibition. "Hughes, break his hands."

I whip my head toward her, certain I've misheard. "But we don't know for certain that he's done anything wrong yet!"

"It seems hasty, Your Majesty." Even Cecil is on my side for once, his features ashen and drawn. "Think of the consequences. His father's influence—"

The queen ignores her former spymaster entirely. "If Foxwell cannot use his hands, then he certainly cannot get up to any wrongdoing." Her black eyes bore into mine. "If you're certain of his guilt, you will do as we say. Unless . . ." Her voice lowers, only for me. "Don't make us ask twice, peasant dog."

Her gaze drops to my hands. I clench my fists and fight the urge to hide them behind my back.

Bloomsbury steps forward, half shielding me from sight with his body. "Please, let me—"

"We did not ask anything of you, Bloomsbury!" the queen snaps.

Cecil yanks me up and shoves me forward, and then it's me and Foxwell and the guards restraining him alone on the wide grass lawn. The crowd is a hazy smear at the edges of my vision, a riot of color and noise, all spinning around me. The queen's presence is a fire at my back, and my entire soul shouts at me to run, but there's nowhere to go.

The guards push Lord Foxwell closer. He falls with a startled cry. He is not much older than me, and fear makes him younger. His fine white breeches are soiled at the knees. His ruff is askew.

It could just as easily be me on my knees. Foxwell might be a lord, but he's not much more than a boy: a boy who could very well be innocent.

But . . . I know the price I'd pay should I refuse to carry out the queen's bidding before all of court. I hate it, and I hate myself for thinking it, but if it's to be me or him, I know who I've got to save. I shake my head and withdraw into the darkest corner within me. The place shaped by hungry winter nights and weeks without pay. The place I'd hoped to never visit again.

With unsteady hands, I take out the dagger at my belt. I smash the hilt down on Foxwell's outspread hands, choking back bile as his protests become screams.

The queen tuts behind me. "That was nothing. Do it again."

So I do, again and again, until my own hands are covered in blood as much as Foxwell's and he stops screaming entirely. The lord lies limp as guards drag him away, his broken hands two shore-splintered crabs.

My blood roaring like a waterfall, I fall back on my haunches, face in my hands. But I can still see beyond my trembling scarlet fingers. My eyes won't shut. The courtyard is a disaster. One older woman, who bears an uncanny likeness to Foxwell himself, sobs as her friends console her. The other courtiers whisper and edge away from me. As if I'm the man they shouldn't trust. As if I'm the person to fear even though I've just arrested the man who tried to kill their monarch. Already the queen has drifted away in a cloud of her courtiers now that the thrill of violence is gone.

My bloodied dagger falls to the dirt. Nausea surges in my throat at what I've done, and I vomit so hard, tears come to my eyes.

I've maimed a man.

I don't think a soul comes back from something like this. I didn't want to do this, but Queen Elizabeth ensured the blood, the sin, would be on my hands, and not hers. She has already made me her dog, her spymaster, her torturer. What else can she take from me? A sob catches in my throat. I imagine my family recoiling in horror at my red hands. I imagine the queen over my family's red, slain bodies. Was her plan always to take everything from me so there would be nothing left? Was there ever a hope of escaping this nightmare?

306 | ERIN COTTER

"Elias?" James's hands are on my shoulders, his voice tight with shock and rage. "Say something. If you're hurt—"

"I want to be alone, thank you." I shove past James, his wounded expression digging a fresh splinter of guilt into my chest, and run to my room.

Except on the way, in the too-green hall, something trips me, sending me sprawling.

Lord Cecil.

He stomps like an angry bull, bellowing. "By God, you'd better be right about Foxwell! Or I'll tell everyone what you and Bloomsbury have been up to when you think no one's watching."

*He knows.*

I stand, commanding my limbs not to tremble, my voice to keep even, while inside, my nerves are fraying. "Go ahead. There's not much to see." I bluff coolly, even as my pulse staggers. My friends. James's sister. The assassin. And now Cecil. How much time do we have left before the queen knows? Before she discovers she's got a fresh way to shorten my leash, to force me to do her bloody bidding no matter the cost?

I believed James and I were safe as long as the wrong person didn't discover our secret. Now the very worst person who could have found out is threatening to take the last good thing I've got left and turn it into something ugly, a cudgel he can use to hurt.

A shadow cuts over us. James. He glances betwixt me and Cecil, and I cross my fingers behind my back. *Oh God, not now, please don't try to lie.*

"Will?" he says, his terrible liar's voice giving him away at once. "Do you . . . want to talk? Somewhere private, perhaps?"

I clench my fists, keeping my expression steady. Cecil chuckles at my forced composure, ignoring James and his confused look. "Perhaps there's not much to see betwixt you two, but there's an awful lot to *hear*, if you're listening."

And then he storms off with a swirl of his cloak and leaves me alone and bloody in the gorgeous gilded hall, feeling sicker and more anxious than ever before.

# CHAPTER TWENTY-EIGHT

ECIL'S THREAT—*BY GOD, you'd better be right*—weighs heavy on me.

Even after two days of questioning Lord John Foxwell, we're no closer to learning the truth. Neither threats nor bribes nor anything else will get the lord to stop spewing the same story.

To Foxwell, the man with the solar scabbard, Thomas Walter, *is* innocent. Marlowe's murderer is his friend, a botanist himself, with useful connections to Spanish explorers and the plants they bring back from their journeys. Foxwell insists on this so strongly, I'm beginning to realize that only two options are possible: either Foxwell is a goddamned good liar, or he truly believes what he's saying.

And then there's my connection to the man with the solar scabbard. He left that note, addressed to my true name, a name he should not know, because everyone who knows Elias Wilde on the queen's progress is either here with me or dead.

These dark thoughts circle me like wolves, and I can't shake the sense there's something we're missing. Something huge and obvious just beyond our sight. But what?

"There's no point fretting over it now," Maggie says when

I share my doubts with the group for the hundredth time. "You've arrested Foxwell. The man with the gaudy sword is missing. There's nothing else for us to learn right now."

My co-conspirators and I are sprawled listlessly in James's library, our search for the man with the solar scabbard an utter failure. 'Tis as though he's vanished from England itself, even with Gráinne's men roaming the countryside looking for leads.

"Then we'll look again in all the places we've already looked," I say firmly. "We need to know if Foxwell's telling the truth or not." *Before the queen tortures him more.*

"If you were so worried you had the wrong man, why did you tattle to the English queen first thing?" Gráinne says, crossing her arms. Her cold stare sweeps over us, lingering on me. "It's not the way among the *Gaedhil* to imprison men without justified cause, as it is among the *Gaill*."

The Irish word for "outsiders"—*Gaill*—runs through me like an icy wind.

I stand and thrust a finger beneath the Pirate Queen's nose. "Quit questioning my honor! I did what I did because I had to, all right? I won't accept the queen's title and become her savage dog. I'm out when this is over." I trace the shape of the cross inside my chest pocket. "I'll not bring my family closer to her evil court."

The dagger Maggie cleans slips and thuds into the floor point-first. "What? You're giving up our reward?"

"Not your money," I say quickly. "I'll make sure you'll still be getting paid. But I won't accept the noble estate. I'm ditching the court and finding my family after this."

Maggie groans and buries her face in her hands.

Inigo, bless him, has the grace to only look bemused. "But . . . why stay at all, then? You could leave and let us finish up the rest of this. You could run away now and spare yourself the trouble." He glances at the maps and papers strewn across James's desk, all our failed efforts to try to make sense of the mystery. "Spare yourself a heap of trouble."

I smack the desk, making him and everyone else jump. "I'm seeing this bloody progress through so that we all get what we want from this, all right? If all I want to do is disappear afterward, 'tis nobody's business but mine."

James meets my furious glare, and it takes all in me not to snarl at the sadness in his eyes. Ever since Cecil's threat, I've avoided him, no matter how many imploring words or glances he sends my way. Not that it's made me feel any better. *Why can't you see this is how it must be?* I want to shout. *Someone's tried to kill you twice, and it's my fault.* The memory of the poisoned goblet at his lips shakes me awake at night. 'Tis Marlowe's murder all over again, but this time, I'll not let James be hurt under my arm. I'll do anything to protect him.

He starts to speak. "Elias—"

"That's the spirit, lad." Gráinne claps my shoulder, blessedly cutting James off. "See the job through and then do whatever the hell you want. That's what I always say." Her teeth flash as somewhere deep in the castle a horn bellows. "Now let's get ready for the last bloody feast in this place, aye?"

• • •

Tonight is the progress's final night at the Bloomsbury estate. Tomorrow Queen Elizabeth's court shall pack up and bankrupt a different noble castle, and we will resume our spy work in a new place, with new places to hide, and new ways for everything to go spectacularly sideways.

For the final courtly feast, ancient plum orchards beside the forest have been transfigured into a fey wonderland. Garlands of wildflowers stretch beneath the canopy, their edges rouged by the smoking braziers. The setting sun paints everything rosy as the court arrives in costume. The ladies are like birds from a distant land, gemstone-bright and sparkling. The lords are in a half state of undress, rude and crass, and I'm suddenly glad I had Inigo linger to ready me just so. I'm in all black, from my high collar to my polished boots, save for a silver-and-ivory half mask in the likeness of a wolf. When I join the crowd of courtiers, I imagine making my entrance on the Rose Theatre's stage, and for once I pay their looks and whispers no mind. Rancorous laughter already rings out from the heart of the gilded forest, and somewhere a barrel of mead is already flowing. This is the queen's court unlaced and unbuttoned, all its stifling rules lifted just for one night.

"It is a sight. Is it not?"

I turn toward James's voice.

And stare.

His hair falls past his shoulders under a crown of antlers. Beneath an embroidered emerald coat he wears nothing at all, and divots upon his bare torso beckon to me like a map to a forbidden kingdom. Around his ribs is an angry, healing scar, the bloody souvenir of our first proper kiss.

James laughs nervously and adjusts his coat so it hides the healing wound. "I know. It is utterly ridiculous."

No. He is Apollo brought from myth to earth. I swallow and force my features to remain smooth. "Tell me again why we had to dress up?"

"Catherine has written a masque," James says.

I heard Marlowe speak of court masques. They are like plays without a stage wherein nobles must act in specific roles. "She's gotten a play onstage after all," I say.

James smiles ruefully. "Yes. Though I do rather wish that she had not cast me as the prince of the forest. She's done it to embarrass me."

A sudden sadness cuts through me. I know not how many more nights we'll have together. Each day that passes brings us closer to the last one, and even though I need James safe—even though I know the end of whatever's betwixt us is the best thing for both of us—the feeling still makes me want to dig in my heels and scream. As if stubbornness alone were enough to make time slow, stop.

I lift a hand, second-guessing myself all the while, and gently tuck an errant length of hair behind his ear. "You play the prince's part magnificently."

His dark eyes warm before he steps away. "Then I must go to my stage. I'll find you afterward—all right?"

The nobles wait around a roaring bonfire as darkness swallows the world. I wait with them and attempt to wrestle my anxieties into submission. No one has seen nor heard nor smelled any mischief since Foxwell's arrest. But until his guilt is assured, I cannot relax, not completely. For if we're wrong—

Well, Cecil's made his threats clear. He'll tell everyone about me and James, and it won't matter at all whatever good we've done, because unveiling a scandalous affair—especially if it's between two lords, especially if one of those lords is engaged and the other isn't a lord at all, but a vicious nobody who's used his wits to lie to every noble in England to carry out the queen's dirty work—is more than enough to ruin both of us.

Trumpets blare, and the queen emerges from the castle courtyard to a swell of music. A froth of diamonds spills over her bust and flows down into an ivory gown. The crown she wears is a twisted snarl of silver and quartz. Her face is powdered, her lips two holly berries amidst the whiteness. The crowd hushes at her appearance.

And then James appears, and my throat closes at how beautiful he is, gilded in the firelight. He bows before the queen and offers her a scepter upon a tasseled pillow.

"Oh fair moon, our faerie queen, please accept this gift from my father's hall and know that, tonight, we only live to please you."

Queen Elizabeth holds the scepter aloft. A fortune's worth of jewels winks in the firelight. If Maggie were here, I know she'd already be plotting how to steal it. "Then I declare a feast for all my subjects! Come forth, faeries, and tend to your mistress!"

The musicians burst into a merry tune, and acrobats come gamboling from the trees, tumbling over the fire and capering from bough to bough. The nobles gasp and cheer at the sight, falling onto one another, a third of them already drunk and roaring with mirth. Servants bustle by with sweetmeats and wines and more delicacies than I've seen before. Unlike all the other courtly feasts I've been forced to attend, this one . . . actually seems fun. Despite all else on my mind, I smile.

At this masque, this final night at the Bloomsbury estate, there are a thousand and one things I ought to worry about. Whether or not Foxwell is innocent. My shortsighted feelings for James and how at any moment Cecil could expose our affair to the entire court.

But, with James approaching through the crowd, his delighted expression only for me and my body full of stars because of it, I decide to let it all go just for tonight. Just for him.

Because while I've got the rest of my life to worry about what might come next, I've a feeling I'm only getting one night like this.


We feast on roasted boar drenched in honey and currant-stuffed goose, followed by tarts filled with sugared cream and plump berries foraged from the woods, not to mention the wine.

Dear God, there's a lot of wine.

James lingers at my side. The candlelight catches the copper in his hair, and the affection in his gaze for me is more intoxicating than all the wine we've drunk, which is really, truly saying something.

He traces patterns on the small of my back. "Come away with me after this."

Every spot where his fingers touch is a flicker of fire. "What if someone sees us?"

He smiles mysteriously and leans closer so that we're nearly brow to brow. "I have something to tell you in confidence."

The promise of a secret lights my heart like a candlewick. "Can't you tell me now?"

His whisper grows teasing. "No. You shall have to wait. 'Tis worth it, I swear."

A throat clears. "Bloomsbury."

Lord Middlemore towers over us. Upon seeing me cavorting with his future son-in-law, he scowls. "I have a moment to discuss the topic which you asked me about. Do you have time?" Middlemore's eyes sweep over me with disapproval, as though daring me to interrupt their meeting once again.

James stands and *smiles*, of all things. "Yes, of course!"

I snag James's wrist as he follows Lord Middlemore. "What are you doing? Have you lost your senses?"

He spins around with a grin and a raised finger, nearly pressing it to my lips. "You'll know soon enough. I assure you this is a good thing!"

I am not assured at all. What else could James possibly have to say to Middlemore? He has been seated near him every night, as a nod of respect to their soon-to-be kinship. It fills me with a sour, sulky feeling. Who knows how many moments James and I have left? Must Middlemore spoil one of them?

A figure thuds beside me onto the vacant bench. Lady Catherine, James's sister. "What did you think of my masque? As good as anything at the Rose Theatre?" She is flushed, her eyes aglow as she takes in the elaborate costumes around her, the decor. All of it is part of her masque. She is the creator of the entire evening and surveys her world like a pleased goddess.

I smile and tip my wolf mask over my eyes. "I like it very much."

She laughs and claps her hands, the very picture of delight. "So does the queen! She enjoyed this masque so much, she has asked me to write another." Her voice drops to a conspiratorial whisper. "I'm starting tonight, so I'll be needing the key to James's chamber."

I choke on my wine.

Catherine continues undeterred. "Please, I know he gave the one I had to you. He's hoarding the books I need for research. I've got to get them before the progress moves on."

Zounds, what's with these Bloomsbury children and their love of research? I take in Catherine's keen stare and eager posture. Then I reach for the key with a sigh. "Careful, all right? You know how he gets about the bloody books."

She squeals and rushes off. I stare after her, half smiling.

Another figure slips beside me, supple as a shadow.

"I did not realize you and Lady Catherine were so close," says James's betrothed, Lady Anne. She's dressed like a cat, the embroidered half mask hiding all her face save for a razor-thin smile.

The hair prickles along my neck, a warning for me to watch myself. The woman has never deigned to speak to me alone before. She usually settles for scowling and glaring from a distance. "Catherine was asking me where her brother was. Nothing more."

Lady Anne helps herself to a candied plum from my platter,

nibbling daintily. "How unusual! I know how protective my dear betrothed is of his sister. It is odd that she's on a first-name basis with a lord I've never heard of until this summer."

My stomach slips lower.

Lady Anne helps herself to another of my plums, smiling. "Remind me of your title again? I fear I've forgotten."

"You know damn well who I am." The words lash out before I can stop them.

Lady Anne's smile turns simpering. "Oh, I meant the name of your family's estate. It must be *very* small if I've never heard of it before."

I sneer right back at her. "I knew you'd never win Bloomsbury over with your personality, but it appears your manners won't be winning him over either."

Lady Anne giggles as though she is in on the jest and not the subject of it. "My mother told me and my sisters to beware honey-tongued men like you."

"Your mother sounds like a wiser woman than yourself."

Her pleasant courtier mask slips away. "I know what game you're playing. You're a man with nothing who stands to gain everything by keeping yourself in Bloomsbury's pocket."

I tut. "Is this any way to speak to your betrothed's closest friend?"

Lady Anne's eyebrows become angry slashes. "Jest all you want. You're not the only person aiming to get something from a rich man, and mark my words, I'll win this game and you'll be left with nothing!" She stands and storms away, her words cutting through my wine fog straight to my fears from before. Does she suspect our relationship? Or does she resent our closeness? My muddled senses can't tell, can't summon up the will to do what's right and safe when the night promises forbidden luxuries.

"Hughes!" And then suddenly James has returned, his joy a tangible thing. His smile is silly and vacant and likely the result of more than a little wine. "Isn't tonight an absolute *delight*?"

"Speak for yourself. Your fiancée's been hideous to me," I grumble.

"I know," he says. "I was waiting for her to leave."

I elbow him, and he elbows me right back, grinning. He takes in the sweep of my neck and the cut of my clothes, hunger flicking across his face. "Let's go somewhere else."

An answering heat rises up in me beneath his look. I tilt my head to the forest behind us.

When we step among the trees, I see that the court's bacchanalia has spilled into the secretive shadows beyond prying eyes. Soft sighs and giggles spark through the air. In the snatches of torchlight through the tree trunks, I catch a slip of petticoat, a dash of wrinkled hose, figures supine on blankets and cushions.

Here's the other thing Marlowe told me about court masques: they're an excuse for all sorts of debauchery. A chance for people to do whatever they please under the guise of being someone different for an evening.

I push James against a twisted trunk, my fingers finally tracing the currents of his chest, heedless of who watches. Tonight, we shall get away with whatever we wish under the guise of the queen's faerie court masque.

His breath is warm on my neck, my name ragged in his voice, and I'm crushed to know this is the only time we can be together like this. Here, in the open, where no one looks and no one cares what we do.

To everyone else, tonight is a game, a jest.

But for us it's everything. A moment that gestures beyond how things are to what things could be, if everyone agreed tomorrow that this night did happen and there was nothing strange in it.

He pulls away. "You're crying."

I make no move to scrub the tears away. "I wish we had more than this." I whisper the truth like a curse, the thing I've been holding in for days.

He settles my head over his heart, the unsteady beat loud as drums. The masque eddies around us, churning into a higher pitch. I close my eyes and breathe him in. How shall I ever pass by a garden redolent with lavender without stopping, dragging my fingers through the flowers to crush the fragrance to my nose? An unbearable feeling scrapes at my ribs, reaches for my soul.

James's antlered crown is askew. I move to right it, and he catches my hand, his fingers lacing through mine. "You promised to come away with me."

"To where?"

"My bedchamber."

A strangled noise escapes me. Cecil's threat—*there's an awful lot to hear*—returns at once. 'Tis one thing for us to be seen together out here; inside the castle is a different world. "I don't know—"

His grip tightens. "Don't fight this. Not tonight."

The scent of him mixes with the wine sloshing about my head and overrides all my sense and reason.

We tiptoe back to the castle. The candles have burned themselves to puddles, and several lords are snoring in various corners throughout the halls. James unlocks the door to his chambers and pushes it open gently. Within is the antechamber, and beyond, the bedroom door is ajar. The moonlight reveals a figure curled still and small on James's bed, surrounded by a spill of books.

"Catherine?" he whisper-hisses. "What's she doing here?"

I wince. "She—ah, bullied me into giving her the key to your chamber. She needed the books."

James stares at her, worrying his bottom lip as though he has entrusted the care of his firstborn to a hungry lion. He sighs and gently closes the bedroom door. "She drools when she sleeps. Let's hope *Foxe's Book of Martyrs* isn't her latest victim."

I swallow back a wave of disappointment. "Does this mean we're to abandon our plan?"

James gives me a daring smile and begins to undress. For one heart-stopping moment I think he means to fool around in the antechamber with his sister sleeping one door beyond, but then he blessedly pulls on a chemise before shrugging on his doublet again. "No. I only came here to change. We're going somewhere else."

Now this is a twist I did not expect. "But where?"

James turns to me with a shy smile that makes my heart stop. His thumb skims over my wrist before he takes my hand. "Trust me."

# CHAPTER TWENTY-NINE

I AM ALONE IN the forest with James, the laughter of the masque replaced by hooting owls and the scuttle of things beneath the leaves. A strange stone structure emerges in the torchlight, half-buried in a hillside, plush moss velveting its sides. I stop and stare. I've never seen anything like it before. Time has stooped the stones like an old man's spine. A trickle of smoke pours from the crooked top, which ought to be cause for concern, but instead James gives the smoke an approving look.

"It's a ruin. Not a broch, but quite similar," he explains. "It's been here longer than my family's been alive. No one knows who built it or why."

He ducks into a dark stone passage and gestures for me to follow. The structure is open to the sky, and a fire burns before soft cushions. Bread sits on a silver tray beside a jar of what can only be plum preserves.

At the sight of it all, my heart clenches like a fist. "Is this for us?"

James kneels to feed a fistful of leaves into the fire. His smile is as bright and tentative as the first star in the sky. "Do you like it?"

This breaks every rule. All the careful lines we've drawn betwixt us and betwixt the world to keep ourselves safe. This is no tryst in a dark corner within a locked room. This is something meant to be seen. A declaration, a promise.

Pressure fills my chest like a scream. "You know we can't do things like this."

James snags my wrist, keeping me from bolting. His face is full of calm determination. "You must hear what I have to say."

"No. I don't want to hear it."

"Elias—"

"Did the wine addle your ears?" I jerk away from his touch and whatever else he's trying to say. "I don't want this. 'Tis too much and you know it."

He perches on a toppled stone, hands clenched on his thighs, chin downcast. Like he's finally recognized me for the snapping stray that I've been the entire time. I bite back the apology I want to give, knowing 'tis better he sees me for what I am rather than what he wants me to be.

After an eon, he speaks. "You're right. It was too much." He looks up, all the stars gone from his eyes. "I can't go on with you like this anymore."

All my anger blows away, something small and scared left in its wake. *This is what you want. 'Tis how things ought to be.* I keep my features composed. Calm. Giving away nothing of how my stomach churns, how it feels as though he's finally pushed me off the ledge and I'm falling into the nothing below.

"Good. I—I suppose we're in agreement, then. I'll—I'll head back to the castle and gather my things from your chamber."

I move past James, but he slams his fist against the stone wall, blocking my passage. The world goes impossibly still. It narrows to nothing except his arm and my escape just beyond and how he trembles.

"You didn't let me finish." His hair hides his face save for the muscle moving in his jaw. "I'm leaving it behind. All of it."

I'm snared like a rabbit. "What do you mean?"

He gestures beyond, to the castle and its grounds. "I don't want any of this if you're not there. Let me go away with you."

The words stop my heart like a knife. If his face was not right before mine, his eyes more serious than I've ever seen them before, I would refuse to believe what I've heard. "You don't mean that. You have—" *A family, a title, a future.* I close my eyes and take in a shuddering breath. "You have everything."

"It means nothing without you."

My entire body begins to shake like I've seen blood, vision going fuzzy. My mind feels as though it is somewhere else entirely, floating far above us. This is an impossible dream, a cruel joke. I have been witched if these are the words I am hearing. "Stop jesting. Real life is no play. We can't just run away."

"I mean it." James kneels on the ground, taking both my hands in his own. "I mean every word. I've already booked our passage to Antwerp."

I bite my tongue so hard, iron floods my mouth. The fuzzy feeling grows. He swims before me like a painting, like he's not fully there. I want to escape, but my body's turned to stone. If I take a step, I'll stumble.

"I know—it was hasty of me," he says as though he has not utterly knocked my world from its moorings, as if his hands are not the only things holding me upright. "I thought we'd want to see your family first, get them settled. I wasn't certain what you wished to do afterward—if you'd wish to stay with them or go somewhere else."

"What of your sister? Your engagement? Your work?" There's a buzzing in my ears, so loud, I can barely think over it. God Almighty, why is he doing this? Why must he always argue with the impossible and make everything harder for me along the way? Anger simmers under my skin, hot and painful.

He presses onward, his eyes never leaving mine. "I have told Lord Middlemore I'm reconsidering the engagement entirely and it may be best for Anne to set her sights on other suitors. It's why I was speaking to him tonight. And once we're settled on the continent, I'll send for Catherine. She's the only part of my life I can't live without. Everything else can go. As for work, I've some money of my own. We won't live like lords or gentlemen, that's a fact, but I can promise we'll live better than how you were living in London." His words are a passionate rush, a Puritan preacher screaming of fire and brimstone in the streets. My bones are crushed in his grasp. "I'm going to take care of you. I know other people have promised you this and broken their word, but I won't be one of them. I'm going with you, Elias. If you'll have me."

"*No!*" The shout claws from my throat, an animal tearing from a trap, heedless of its mortal wounds. "I don't believe you! Stop lying!"

There's a moment of appalling, offensive silence. Even the forest goes quiet.

"Why are you fighting this?" he finally asks, so soft I nearly miss it.

"My own family didn't even want me, James!" The confession rips something loose in my soul, tearing down the steep walls I built to safekeep the tenderest part of myself. "They sent me away because I wasn't enough for them." A dim part of me recognizes that I'm crying.

If my own family never wanted me, why would he?

I don't remember falling, but his arms are here, holding me together as I shatter. "That's not true. They were lied to and misled by those men who stole you as a boy, but you can't blame them or yourself for that. They believed they were sending you somewhere better, I know it."

I shake my head, hot ugly tears spilling down my cheeks. The lies I've told myself like bedtime stories flash before me. My folks sent me away because I was too young to work. They sent me away because there were too many mouths to feed. They couldn't say no to a chance for me to get an education. But beneath the lies, the awful, certain truth always stalked the dark hinterlands of my heart.

I can't save the people I care for.

That's why my family sent me away. Why I left the other stolen boys behind. Why I hid money from my friends who desperately needed it. Why Marlowe and the queen picked me from everyone else in the world to be their bloodthirsty dog.

A self-serving darkness lies at my center. Hidden deeper

than flesh and bone and having nothing to do with who I love. My family saw it first and abandoned me before I could harm them, too. There is not enough goodness in me worth loving.

"I'm a liar and a coward. The people close to me always get hurt. I ruin lives, and I'll not ruin yours next!" The shuddering, shameful words are a broken, lonely howl.

I expect him to leave, recoil at the fierceness of my feeling and the awful truth. But he doesn't. He presses closer, his body a bulwark. "No. You had to do those things to survive because the world is an awful, unfair, and cruel place. You're more than your actions. Do you have any idea what I see when I behold you? Why I want to upend everything in my life to be with you?" His fingers slide along my neck, thumbs brushing my jaw, and then I'm looking into his perfect face. The one I can't unsee, not even when I'm asleep. His expression is gentle, so very gentle, I want to cry all over again.

"I see someone who sees the injustice around himself and isn't afraid to name it. I see someone who values doing the right and honorable thing no matter the cost to himself. I see someone who feels more deeply than anyone I've ever known thrust into a world where having a caring heart feels more like a curse than a gift, but you, Elias, by God, you are a gift." His hands run down my shoulders, holding me tightly, bringing us brow to brow. "Zounds, if you could see yourself the way I do, you'd understand why I love you."

All the noise in my head stops. "You—you love me?"

"Yes, that's what I've been trying to tell you!" he cries. "Let me fulfill the promises I want to make you, for God's sake."

Both his knees hit the ground, chest heaving. "Unless you don't wish to have me because you don't feel the same."

My voice is gentle, incredulous, body zinging with shock and something else at the sudden turn this has all taken. "Of course I want you." How . . . has he not known this? How has he missed the way I've looked at him? How every time he's near, I'm pulled toward him unwillingly, like the sea to the moon? I take up his hands, press a kiss to each knuckle, a swelling in my chest building like a wave. "I, zounds, James, I *love* you, but I didn't want to ruin your life. I couldn't bear that. I thought if I kept my distance, then I couldn't."

"By all means, please ruin me." He catches my hand and presses my palm to his cheek, looking at me like I'm the last thing on earth. Then he flashes me that barely-there smile.

I crash into him.

Our bodies become a tangle of limbs and jagged breath. We kiss until our lips are swollen and our limbs grow heavy and we're both gasping and there's no choice but to slow and stop, to settle into something more tender and sweet. The quiet cocoons us, and it feels as though a thousand doors are open, that endless possibilities are here just waiting for us to seize them.

"What now?" he asks, curling around me.

A jumble of thoughts and feelings spins through my head, not one of them quite ready to be put into words. I try anyway, twisting a lock of his hair about my finger. "I don't know . . . if my family will accept us. They never got to see this side of me. Not like Catherine has." I swallow back a sudden bundle of nerves. "I worry they won't."

He kisses my throat, fending off my doubts. "Then we'll go to Antwerp."

I've never heard of the place. "Why there?"

He smiles against my neck and kisses my collarbone. "The Low Countries are different from England. They're less interested in overseeing what folks do with their lives. People like us have a space there."

*People like us.* The phrase kindles a flame betwixt my ribs, fills me up with something that feels suspiciously like hope. "You mean . . . lads who take other lads as lovers?"

"Yes, exactly. We can make a different life there. I could pursue my work with alchemy and medicine at the university, and you . . ." There it is again. His slow, full smile that first sent my heart soaring all those months ago at the river. Anything is worth the treasure of that smile. "Well, you'd be free to do whatever you pleased. Anything at all."

I turn over to stare at him, my pulse rioting. His plan is absolute nonsense. Utter madness. An impossibility so far beyond the edges of my imagination, I can barely picture it.

And yet.

*Yet.*

It . . . might just work. Me and James, together, far away from English eyes and laws and politics. I thought my place was back with my family, living the same life we always had, but then again, I assumed there was no other place for me. I never imagined I could create my own place instead of forcing myself into the small space the world offered me. Maybe my world is far vaster than I ever allowed myself to dream. Perhaps I can be more than one thing in it.

James sees the realization lighting up my features like a new dawn and moves to kiss me. I hold up a finger, stopping him.

"Do—do you mean this? You would give up everything you have for this mad fever dream?" I need him to say it once more to know it's all real and true.

His mouth quirks up on one side. "No, Elias, I'm giving it all up for you, because I love you. I will do anything to forge a life where I can love you the way you deserve. I've never been more certain of anything in my life."

I take in a long, shuddering breath and relax into him. "Then yes," I whisper into his chest. "Yes. That's what I want."

He makes a low, heart-wrenching noise and gathers me to him as though I am something tender and precious. As though I may disappear if he lets go.

As if I could ever leave him.

# CHAPTER THIRTY

**M**ORNING ARRIVES, ALL brazen and loud and entirely unwelcome. I groan and hook myself about James's back. "I think spending the rest of the progress hiding here sounds rather excellent, don't you?"

"Don't tempt me." James attempts to rise, but I catch him about the waist and tug him down again.

"Elias," he says, laughing. "We cannot be late!"

Except we're late anyway.

By the time long-shucked clothes have been found and a modicum of respectability has been restored to our appearances, the sun is high in the sky, feathering through the forest branches in bursts of bronze. Someone has definitely noticed we're missing by now. Maggie shall give me a tremendous lecture, and I don't care at all. My delight is an overflowing cup of wine; I am drunk upon it, and nothing can puncture the perfect sphere of happiness in which I'm dwelling.

Once at the castle I expect we'll be able to lose ourselves amidst the crush of wagons and carts and baggage and horses all getting ready to move onward to the progress's next stop. But when the familiar ivy-clad castle peeps through the woods, there's nothing at all. Not even a lone outrider reining in an impatient horse. The stones are still and silent as a cemetery.

"Well, this is odd." James drags a hand through his hair. "Perhaps . . . you ought to go through the servant's entrance." His bottom lip snags between his teeth, and all at once, my joy scatters like dandelion seeds in the wind. It would take a mighty disturbance to hold up the queen's progress like this. Something's gone wrong. Very wrong.

I squeeze his hand. "Nonsense. Wherever you go, I'm going too."

The gates to the castle courtyard are open and unguarded, like some ancient monster has finally climbed from the forest's dark depths to tear us trespassers from its home. We charge through the gates, my hand tight on the hilt of my dagger, panic a tight knot in my throat, but a bloody courtyard is not the sight which causes me to stop short.

In the courtyard the Burning Reaper, James's father, is on his knees, weeping.

I look away, as though I am the first to have come upon some accident so terrible, the sight is too much to take in. This man has felled whole clans the way a farmer's wife slaughters her chickens before the first frost. Now great, shuddering sobs cleave his body. No man ought to make sounds like that. Not even the Burning Reaper, who deserves to more than most.

James is already at his father's side. "What's happened?"

The Burning Reaper stills beneath his son's arm. Whispers a word I cannot hear.

James's face blanches. His lips part in a soundless scream.

And then James is stumbling, his father's blow catching

332 | ERIN COTTER

him so fast, I've missed it. The Burning Reaper towers over his cowering son, a wildness in his features that frightens me. Time lengthens and bows, and I know when it snaps, there will be a before and an after, and there will be no coming back from this moment.

"Murderer!" he screams.

The word ripples like ice through the courtyard and through my body, freezing my bones brittle.

Only then do I notice the guards ringing the courtyard. They bristle with blades as if they've been waiting.

Waiting for *us*.

The truth slams into me like a portcullis. James and I conspired to commit more than a few crimes last night, but I'm quite certain murder wasn't among them.

"James Edmund Bauffremont of Bloomsbury." James's father hitches himself to his full height and regards his son with a terrible expression. "By the decree of myself and the queen, you are under arrest for the murder of Lady Catherine Bloomsbury."

A horrible moan comes from James, the last sound of a slain beast. He collapses to his knees. His glassy, shocked eyes circle his father, me, the guards, frantically searching for any sign that he's misheard. That it's an awful misunderstanding. "Catherine?" A trickle of blood runs from his mouth. "N-no, I saw her last night. She was in my room. She was sleeping!"

I take one step backward. And then another. I keep going until I crash into the wall. The news takes up all the space there is within me—growing larger and larger—until I cannot hold anything else at all.

Catherine, dead?

The thought spins through me, the only dancer on an empty floor. Catherine, dead? Catherine, who welcomed me into this world when no one else would, who loved plays and dogs and was only fifteen years old?

Two white spiders flex on my thighs, and I nearly scream before I realize they're just my hands, my hands with their nails biting into my skin, my body rocked with a dry sob.

It can't be true.

But as my gaze ricochets from the grim-mouthed guards to the faces pressed in the windows dotted all overhead, I know it's the truth, and horror and helplessness pummel me over and over again until I, too, am on my knees upon the dirt. No one would lie about this. This is no nightmare I'll wake from.

Catherine was alive and well last night, and now she's dead.

No, that's not right. *Murdered*. Just like Marlowe. Just like the queen's servant girl, who'd done nothing at all.

I scrape the tears from my cheeks and straighten. The word "murderer" reverberates through me until it beats like a second heart. Though everything in me screams to run, I pull up all my power and courage and march right to the astonished Burning Reaper and prod him in the chest. "Your son is innocent! Can't you see? Would a man capable of murdering his own kin act like this?"

James is limp as a fish in his fetters, the half-moons of his eyelashes fanned across bloodless cheeks. No matter how much the guards prod him, he won't stand. I cannot tell if he's conscious or not. 'Tis as though someone has scooped out his spirit with a ladle and left him dry and empty. I want to take him in my arms, mourn with him, but I can't. 'Tis my turn to be the strong one.

The Burning Reaper gives me a hard stare, his face—James's face decades from now—a rictus of grief and rage. I stare right back, refusing to back down.

"And how do you claim to know his innocence? Catherine was found in his chamber."

I puff up my chest even more. "Because I was with—"

James suddenly throws his shoulder into my shin. "Leave it alone, for God's sake." His words are a hoarse cry, drenched in agony, but the keen look in his eyes is all for me. *Say nothing. Go. Leave me to this.*

Only then do I realize how close I've come to being arrested with James for the second time. And if we're both in prison, who will fix everything that's gone wrong?

I suck in a hard breath beneath the Burning Reaper's suspicious glower and force myself to speak to the man who destroyed my family, the man who looks everything like and acts nothing like the boy I love. "Because your son is not that kind of man. Anyone who knows him knows this."

The lord's eyes snap with anger and anguish. I stay put beneath the look, chin high.

He turns away first. "Take him away," he says, gesturing to James.

I roar and kick the ground, my hands fisted at my sides, heart thrashing at the injustice of it all as a limp James is dragged away, my limbs quivering with the effort of staying still, to not rush after them and rip their hands off his body. Someone has framed him for this hideous crime. That much is certain. I've got to figure out the why and the who of it before 'tis too late.

I turn and go nose-first into a guard's chest. "You're supposed to come with us. Queen's orders."

I hide my unease at his command behind a glare. "Can't. I'm quite busy. Haven't you heard a girl's dead?"

He squeezes my shoulder so hard, I wince. "You can walk, or I'll drag ye. Your choice."

I'm dragged away from the courtyard into a cellar hall reeking of onions.

"Ah, Will Hughes. Just the man I wanted to see." Lord Cecil steps from the shadows. For once he is neither sneering nor glaring, and this makes the glow of triumph in his eyes all the more sinister. "It's been a goddamn disaster since you've left."

I growl and push past him. "Not now, Cecil. James has been framed for a crime, and the murderer is still afoot."

I move toward the stairs—where I can be useful, where I could learn something to help James—but rough arms drag me back. *"Lord Bloomsbury,"* Cecil says firmly, "must answer for his crimes. You, as the queen's spymaster, must fulfill your duties."

The guard shoves me through an open door flanked by two more guards. The earthiness grows more pungent. Within, a thin figure is huddled on a threadbare blanket betwixt piles of onions. Lord Foxwell. Imprisonment has not agreed with him. He's gaunt as a skeleton, and I swear there's white in his scraggy beard. His hands are still bandaged. He gawks at me, eyes all but popping from their sockets. "You!" he finally—and literally—spits out. "Cockled toad! Ill-mannered villain! You—you utter pox of a person!"

I wipe spittle from my face, unease and annoyance clashing in me. What has bloody Foxwell got to do with anything when James is imprisoned, when he needs me to figure out what's behind this awful accident? "Cecil, why is our prisoner bedfellow to onions?"

"Enough with the theatrics, both of you!" Cecil snaps. "This is not the South Bank. The box, please."

A small wooden crate is thrust into my hands. A package. Its sides are stained and splintered as though it has traveled a great distance. A heavy feeling settles in my gut as I lift the busted lid. A gush of wood shavings falls out, and then there, in the very center within a linen bag, is something soft and fragile.

I dump the tiny seeds into my palm. I bet they're bloody tomatoes. Exactly what Foxwell said he had bought from Spain. Seeing them fills me with a sick, sinking feeling.

Lord Foxwell crosses his arms. "I suppose this means I am free to leave? Truly, Cecil, I cannot believe you listened to a word out of this lying fool's foul mouth. Whatever inspired you to sully your good name by letting this vexed creature boss you about—"

There is a resounding smack as Cecil slaps Foxwell. "Are you questioning the queen's judgment, Lord Foxwell? It was she who demanded we invest this"—Cecil's eyes zip to me—"aborted hedgehog with authority."

Foxwell shakes his head vigorously, his hand over his reddened cheek.

"Good," says Cecil. He tosses the empty strongbox at the lord. "As you were, then. We apologize for this disruption in your affairs."

Foxwell snatches the box with a wince and scrambles away. Once the slap of his footsteps fades, Cecil turns to me with a thunderous look. "Guards, seize him!"

Before I can react, I'm held tight to a guard's chest, my arms twisted behind me. I struggle, but 'tis no use. The man's stronger than an ox, and his comrade's scowling at me with his sword half out of its sheath even if I did escape. My breath leaves me in short, panicked bursts.

Cecil sneers. "Because of your own incredible incompetence— you have been relieved of your duties as spymaster. Starting at once. Let's go."

I'm dragged outside, not whence I came, but through the servants' doors, past the castle gardens and chickens, into the forest's edge. "What's the meaning of this?" I demand, suddenly no longer certain that the queen really sent for me at all.

Cecil makes a gesture, and the guard throws me against a tree, crushing all the air from my lungs. The other guard draws his sword. Away from the cellar's gloom, I see they're not wearing the livery of the queen, but rather of Cecil's noble house. I think of the mysterious message Cecil sent from the road before we arrived at the Bloomsbury estate, how he was waiting for me when James and I returned from the forest, and a ghastly premonition sweeps through me, like remembering too late the lit candle left beneath a thatched roof. How it's too late to stop the fire.

Cecil's been playing his own game this entire time.

His smile curves like the edge of the cutlass. "Did you ever truly think you could best me? Christ, to think the queen would have made you a knight!"

The other guard draws his blade, and I speak quickly. "If you kill me, the queen will know you've disobeyed her orders. Is that any way to regain her favor?"

Cecil's smirk grows more sinister. "Bloomsbury is the son of a lord. He'll be imprisoned until the queen decides whether he's guilty or not. You, however, are nothing and have always been nothing. Filthy dogs like you don't deserve to live. I'm doing Her Majesty a favor."

One of the guards swings his blade.

Bits of bark fly. I only just manage to roll out of reach. The guard swings again.

Cecil's really trying to kill me over his lost job as the queen's spymaster. It ought not to surprise me, but it does. Is pride truly such a valuable thing that it's worth killing over? Can pride feed you, clothe you? Make you feel as though life is worth living?

Perhaps it can, for someone who's never struggled to survive.

"Don't let him escape!" Cecil roars, pure fury.

My pulse beats a frantic jig as the other guard seizes my

doublet, hoisting me to my feet. If I'm going to save James, I've got to escape. I kick him where it counts—right in the fork of his legs.

He releases me with a howl, and I take off into the brush before the other guard can snag me. I may not be strong, but I'm quick, and that's saved my arse more than once in London.

Cecil's bellow of rage shakes the trees. "If I ever see you again, I shall not hesitate to have you murdered. Remember that!"

I run faster, heedless of the branches slapping and tearing my skin. The roar of blood in my head so loud, I cannot hear anything else. Everything promised to me has been snatched away.

My family's money. My safety.

My future with James.

Gone.

The sudden loss shudders through me, cracking what's left of my composure, and sucks me down to a place deeper and darker than I've ever been before. There was always a chance I might lose my life in this wild venture, but instead they've taken away something far more precious.

Everything worth living for.

# CHAPTER THIRTY-ONE

I FLEE TO THE orchards. Wilting garlands of summer blooms crunch beneath my boots. 'Tis impossible to think that only last evening we were here—*Catherine* was here—and I foolishly let myself hope that all would be well soon. 'Tis as though God himself is playing a gruesome jest on me. *Oh, you think you might finally be happy? I'll show you, then!*

James and I were hoodwinked. Plain and simple. And we fell into the snare like rabbits, not feeling the noose until it cinched about our necks.

The man with the solar scabbard set Lord Foxwell up. We were meant to find the false evidence and accuse him. And Catherine . . . what if her murder was an accident? I imagine it all in vivid detail. The assassin, knowing the entire castle would be attending the masque, could have easily slipped into the empty room, blade ready. Waiting for James to return, dizzy with drink and dance. If we'd retired earlier that night, if we'd beaten Catherine to the room—

A shiver jerks through my body as the nightmare slams into me again: Kit's hot blood soaking my clothes, the red corona spreading about his head. A single glassy eye staring at nothing, the other a meaty dark pit.

Me, too useless to do anything save scream and hide.

'Tis Marlowe's death all over again, but this time, I'm not helpless. The true assassin is close enough to consider us a threat, and all we've got to do is flush him out before he gets to the queen. Then James's name will be cleared. As much as it pains me to still give a rat's arse about Queen Elizabeth's life, the only foolproof way to prove James's innocence is to catch the true assassin before he gets to the monarch.

When stars sprinkle the sky, I sneak through the servants' tents outside the castle walls until I find the tent I'm looking for.

The canvas panel twitches back at the scrape of my nails. "Elias?" Inigo takes in every detail of my appearance, as though he's not quite sure it's me. "Where have you *been*?"

I barge inside without waiting for an invitation. "What word is there of James?"

Maggie and Inigo share a look. She slips the knife she's been cleaning back into its hiding place. "He's been imprisoned. Rumor has it the queen's taking the court to Dover next for his trial and possible execution. They're leaving the day after tomorrow."

*Execution.* It seeps through me like poison, cold and dreadful and paralyzing.

They plan to *execute* James.

I collapse into the only chair, a keening in my ears. I move to speak—to give shape to the anger and fright and frustration raging in me so fiercely, I feel strained at the seams, but I can't. 'Tis even worse than I feared. The court doesn't care if James is innocent or not. Killing him gives the appearance that the ugly problem of an innocent girl's death has been solved, and God knows how the court cares about appearances.

"Elias," Inigo says hesitantly. "Don't take this the wrong way, but . . . why are you here?"

I give him an odd look. "I've come here for help." Of course I did. Where else did they expect me to go?

Maggie and Inigo remain silent. I picture myself as they must see me: sticky with filth and sweat, hair tangled, fine clothes stained and torn beyond repair. The very part of a madcap. Then a hideous thought occurs to me. "Why . . . do you think *I* had something to do with Catherine's murder and James's predicament?"

Inigo looks to the ground, and Maggie goes pink.

"We didn't know!" she bursts out. "You never returned to your chamber last night, and you and Bloomsbury are always disappearing together without a word to us, and what else did you expect us to think when the girl was dead in his room and you two were missing?"

"You didn't tell us anything," Inigo says softly. "You haven't told us much for a while."

I gape at them, hardly believing they would think something so terrible of me.

I want to be angry—the old me would be, I'm certain of it—but . . . a part of me thinks they have a fair point. I've let my damned feelings for James get in the way of everything else. And now, because we weren't around last night, his sister is dead and someone's framed him for the crime. My chest constricts painfully. While we're innocent, who would ever believe us after this? I know if I can't get Maggie and Inigo to believe me now, then no one ever will.

I take in a shuddering breath and explain what's happened. I expect a chorus of gasps, or a widening of eyes. But no. Both my friends remain stone-faced throughout. The chill in my bones grows colder.

When I'm done, Maggie pokes Inigo. "We agreed you'd do the talking."

Inigo scrubs his neck and clears his throat after yet another poke from Maggie. "I'm sorry, but . . . I dunno what you expect us to do."

Zounds, that sounds an awful lot like no, and that won't do at all. "What do you mean? James is innocent. Haven't you been listening?" I leap to my feet indignantly. Inigo has the grace to look guilty. I try to use it to my advantage. "James saved your life! Surely you owe him something for that."

"He did, aye, and I'll always be grateful. But we failed, Elias. Foxwell isn't the assassin. Two girls are dead. What else is there to do?"

"Why, doing anything is better than nothing at all!" I make a fist and catch it with the heel of my palm. Neither of my friends will meet my eyes. I laugh disbelievingly. "God, maybe I'd expect this from Inigo; I've never known you, Mags, to back down from a fight."

"All right, that's enough of that." Maggie storms over and prods me in the chest. Hard. I fall back onto the chair. She hovers over me all hot air and fire, like St. George's dragon, and I realize, rather too late, I've taken things too far.

She lays into me. "We've spent this whole time waiting on you and doing chores while you and Bloomsbury go off snogging and whispering everywhere. Now his sister's dead, and he's imprisoned, and suddenly, you've got need of us again. Well, we're through with being the people you go to when things get bad. We only said yes to all this for the money!"

I stare at them in turn, not understanding. "But we agreed to do this together! I'm one of you."

Maggie squares her jaw. "No you're not. Not anymore. You're—you're some sort of lordling-in-waiting who puts on airs and thinks he's better than everyone else. All because a few lords with clinking pockets thought you'd be useful to them. You've changed, Elias. You're one of *them* now. Or you'd like to be, which is far worse."

Panic kindles in me. The single loose ember of it I've held smoldering all day now catches into a roaring fire. Maggie and Inigo are the only people who can help. What am I supposed to do without them? "If we don't act, James might die—"

Maggie interrupts with a fart noise. "He's the son of a lord. I'm certain he'll be fine."

"I care for him!" I cry. "Can't you understand?" I ought to keep quiet, but my heart is pounding like a rogue stallion, and I will not rein it in. "I won't abandon him. I—" The words snag in my throat, but I can't force myself to say them. *I can't fail him the way I failed Marlowe and everyone else.* I swallow back the wave of rising bile, fists clenching. "I won't leave him alone. All right?"

Fear. That's what's choking me. The fear that I won't be enough for the hundredth time in my life.

Maggie cants her head to the side. "Are you so sure Bloomsbury would save you if you were in his position?"

Inigo glances at his wife with shock, as though only noticing now she's a stone-hearted monster. "Mags—"

"No. Let him answer."

I recall the softness in James's eyes when he says my name, like it's a prayer and he is the church's devoted subject. How he believed I was always enough for this world, even when no one else did, not even myself. He's a fire at the end of a winter day, a lone shilling in the street you don't deserve—endlessly generous and giving even when there's no reason in the world for him to be this way. I open my mouth and try to explain, but my throat swells shut. Even if I had hours and days, I could never explain. "I'm certain he would."

There's no sound but the clatter of the servants' camp outside. Maggie and Inigo share another damn look, and then Inigo stands and begins rifling through a knapsack. He tosses a kitchen servant's livery into my chest. "Maggie stole this for you. You're rubbish in the kitchen, but hopefully no one will notice."

Understanding dawns on me. "You two are running away from the progress."

"Aye, we're going back to London before someone remembers you and James weren't working alone," Inigo says. "And I've given you a way into the castle." He gives me a wan smile, and, for a moment, 'tis like old times, when it was only him and Maggie and me against all of bloody London. But Maggie's right about one thing. This summer has changed us all, and we're not the people we once were.

Or mayhap I'm not the person I used to be, and they saw that before I saw it in myself.

I consider it from their side, how I forced them to be the people I needed them to be and not the people they are. I swallow back an unexpected lump, shamed at how I've treated them and realized it far too late. "I'd rather you two were staying with me, but . . . I understand, and I'm sorry. I wish you all the best, I really do."

I've got to do this alone.

The thought ought to tear what's left of my composure to ribbons. Instead, it makes me feel patched. Stitched together. I reckon part of me always expected I'd be alone at the end.

Inigo sniffles. Maggie smiles ruefully, like she knows something I don't, and clasps my shoulder. "Keep your well wishes. I've a feeling you'll need them more than we will."

# CHAPTER THIRTY-TWO

THINGS GO WELL for, oh, about a day.

Then, the first night, there's a sharp pressure at my neck. I jolt out of sleep, panicked in the dark kitchen's quarters. A line of warmth trickles down my throat. None of the sleeping servants around me stir at the commotion. It would be so easy to wake them—

The knife bites deeper. An unfamiliar voice growls. "Don't even think of it."

Seeing no choice, I lift my hands and let myself be forced from my pallet, mind spinning.

Someone discovered me. But who would think to look here, the farthest place in the castle from the noble quarters? If someone recognized me at once, why wait until the candles were snuffed to apprehend me? Cecil made his threats pretty clear. Fear webs through me. I'm missing something huge and obvious—I'm certain of it—but I can't for the life of me figure out what it is.

In the dim torchlight of the castle's passages, I see my assailants number not one, but two, both cloaked and hooded. They hustle me outside. The navy sky is shaded periwinkle to the east. A wagon harnessed to a single horse waits at the roadside. The sight makes my heart clench. Soon, it shall be morning, and the entire progress will be rolling out again to Dover Castle, with James as their wronged prisoner, and if I'm not with them, I won't be able to protect him.

"A carriage ride. How romantic. What's the occasion?" I say, trying to mask my rising panic.

"Weren't we supposed to gag and blindfold him?" the knife-wielding bloke says.

There's a storm of feminine cursing, and then I'm shoved around, fabric pulled tight over my eyes. The woman comes at me with the gag next. I lunge blindly, my teeth sinking into her flesh. I growl and tear at her hand like a spit hound relishing a meaty bone. Blood wells about my teeth. A slap strikes my face, and the world goes sideways.

The man whistles appreciatively. "Zounds, I see why your lord wants this one gone."

"Shut *up*," the woman hisses, voice tight with pain.

The gag goes over my mouth again, and I'm shoved forward. The whiff of leather and horse grows stronger. Someone knees me, and I go sprawling painfully into the wagon's back seat.

"Here he is. Now where's our coin?" the woman demands.

"It seems as though he has caused you a bit of trouble, mistress." A new voice speaks, a man, and gooseflesh spider-walks across my skin. I've heard this voice before.

But where?

Something smashes down on my littlest finger. A howl tears from my throat. I grab my shaking hand and find bent bone and blood. The wound throbs in time with the terror spiking through me, all the bravado I felt before washed away like piss in the rain.

"That's for your trouble from me," says the horribly familiar man's voice. I register the jingle of coins through the splitting pain. "That's from Cecil, as promised," he says.

I hear the clink of counted coins before the whisper of a purse slipped into a pocket. "He's a feisty one. Best to deal with him now, I think."

"An excellent idea," the familiar voice agrees pleasantly.

Before I can parse what this all means, something collides with my skull and all goes black.

When I come to, the world's hazy with hurt, and it feels as though something has made my mouth its grave. I groan and clutch at my skull, only to have pain splinter all through my hand when it catches on the ropes tied about my wrists. The carriage jolts over every rut and rock in the road, threatening to make me sick into my gag.

"There, there. Only a day's journey to London now," my captor consoles me with an evil laugh.

Zounds, a day to London? That means we've been traveling all night and, judging from the light pressing against my blindfold, through half the day as well. The progress will have long since moved on from Bloomsbury Castle, and I'm two days' journey from James at least.

But I'm not dead, which is good. And better yet, if I'm being taken to London, someone very much wants me to stay alive. At least for now.

*Cecil*. The name stabs through my aching head with sudden clarity. They said his name last night. The lord told me if he ever saw me again, he'd kill me, and I've no doubt he meant it. So why would he go through the trouble of taking me to London? There's more going on here than it seems.

I shout as best I can through the gag.

"Quiet," my captor commands.

I drum my heels on the floorboards in the most vexing way possible.

"Quit that!" he snarls.

I rise to unsteady legs only to be yanked down by the bottom of my doublet. Rough hands fumble with the knot of my gag, and the fabric falls away.

*"What do you want?"*

"I've got to piss!"

"You can piss in London."

I twist my legs and do a bit of a caper. "But I'm absolutely bursting! D'you want me to piss back here?" I know we're both imagining the stench: urine-soaked wood baking in the sun.

The man gives a disgusted grumble, and the wagon lurches to a stop. I am hoisted up by the armpits and set upon ground. "There you go."

I hold up my knotted hands. "I can't undo my breeches like this!"

Cold steel feathers betwixt my wrists, and my bonds fall away. I graze the knot on my blindfold, but I'm slapped away before I can untie it.

"None of that now," the man growls. "All a man needs to piss is his prick and his hands." He shoves me, and I stumble away. "Get on with it, then!"

I attend to my business. I've not managed to rid myself of the blindfold yet, but I did manage to loosen it enough to see. There's yellow-and-green thatched fields all around us. The road is a thin trace of flattened grass and dirt. Probably thumped down by some shepherd boy once each day as he goes to check on his flocks. Thick, fleecy clouds scud overhead. If I were not kidnapped and manhandled, it would be a glorious summer day for picnicking.

The wagon we ride in is similarly unremarkable. Not much to observe about the man, either. He's pale skinned and balding with the joyless air of a Puritan about him. Completely unremarkable save for the—

My pulse skitters, and I nearly piss upon myself.

A gilded solar scabbard hangs from his hip.

'Tis *him* again.

The man I saw at Marlowe's murder. And saw again at Whitehall Palace moments before Queen Elizabeth was nearly poisoned. Lord Foxwell's odd plant chum Thomas Walter. He's personally ferrying me across the countryside back to London, and none of this, absolutely none of it, makes any sense.

"Oy, lad, you nearly done?"

I finish my business right quick and lace up my breeches with uneasy fingers. I lurch toward the voice, but my feet tangle, and I go sprawling into the dirt.

The man gives a long-suffering sigh and hauls me up by

the collar. He slams me back on the wagon bench and reties my hands, making sure to give the rope a good yank against my broken finger. A pained hiss whistles through my clenched teeth.

"I want to hear nothing else from you now, understood?" He snaps the reins sharply, and the wagon rolls out once more.

For once I am obedient. My mind is too full of thunder for words.

What if Cecil is also part of the Societas Solis?

Cecil is the only common link betwixt all this. I assumed he and Marlowe were working for the queen because Queen Elizabeth had told me so. But what if he's played us and her for fools the entire time? Attempts on James's life only started happening after we met Cecil. And we never discovered why he was meeting strangers in the woods when the queen's servant girl was killed. He's known about almost every step of our investigation and could easily work against us if he chose to.

I can see the shape of his plan now. Instilling himself as the queen's spymaster so she would trust him irrevocably. Planting false evidence about Foxwell so we would assume we had won. Trying to kill me so I would not whisper a word of my suspicions to anyone. Taunting me only enough so I imagined his bitterness came from jealousy and not the burgeoning triumph of a man well on his way to winning a much bigger game.

And I know his mind well enough now to see his next move. He'll let James be tried and—my stomach churns with bile—*executed* for Catherine's murder, the one Cecil himself must've committed, and then, in the chaos, Cecil shall strike for the queen's heart like a vicious serpent. Marlowe always said the nobles had the most to gain from Elizabeth's death.

A terrible excitement courses through me, crowding out the pain and everything else. 'Tis not too late. I might be a hostage in the back seat of a wagon headed in the wrong direction, but there's still time to stop Cecil and save James.

I just have to escape first.

When the assassin retied my bonds, I kept my elbows pointed away from my sides. Now I bring them together, and my wrist binds slacken ever so slightly. I shimmy my hands to loosen the rope further, though each movement sends a shrill pain through my busted finger. Soon the ropes slip off. I kick them overboard. Then I untie my blindfold.

Cecil's henchman sits before me, swaying gently with the wagon's movement. He's nearly bent double on the cramped bench, eyes resolutely on the road. He's hasn't noticed anything's gone amiss in the back seat yet. His shiny bald pate winks in the sun.

I lift the rock I kept hidden in my hand after my fall and smash it upon his crown.

His bellow of pain shakes a flock of rooks from a nearby tree. Our horse spooks and explodes into a gallop.

Yanking us and the cart right along after it.

The assassin swings around to face me with a hate-filled snarl. Blood pulses betwixt fingers clasped to his skull. He lunges with his free hand. I hop to my feet to avoid his swipe. The cart strikes a hole too fast and goes airborne.

I lose my balance and tumble.

I crash sideways onto the front bench beside the assassin.

The carriage wheels churn and churn inches from my head, sending up a spray of skin-scorching gravel.

He grabs his sword. Metal hisses as the blade slides free—

I smash his hand with the rock. He lets go with a howl, and the sword slips back into its scabbard.

I scramble for the blade, grab the hilt, and yank it out.

The man reaches for me and I swing.

The sword thunks into his neck with a meaty squelch.

His eyes pop with surprise. I fall back on my arse, the wet blade angled between us. A high keening pierces my ears. It takes me a moment to realize I'm the source of the sound.

The man reaches for me with grasping hands, movements slowing. Then he tumbles off the bench. I clamp my eyes shut and hold on for dear life itself as the wagon runs over the body. There's a sudden jolt and crack as something beneath the bed gives way.

The wagon jerks to a stop.

Dust fogs the road, turning the light tawny. A great lump lies motionless in the dirt. The man with the solar scabbard. One of his limbs is twisted at a grisly angle. Beneath the smell of earth and horse lies the cloying sweetness of blood.

I force myself from the broken wagon on wobbly colt's legs and vomit all over a patch of wildflowers. The sick burns my nostrils, and already my ears ring with distant shouting.

Someone's witnessed what I've done. If they catch me, I'll be taken for a highwayman. But when I attempt to heave myself up, I blunder sideways and am sick again, the unsettling truth knocking into me again.

I've killed a man.

I've seen plenty of bodies—who hasn't, in London?—but 'tis another thing entirely to see one and know that I am the cause of it. I've done loathsome things to save myself before, but I've never fancied I'd be adding *murderer* to the list.

*Oh God, James, what shall you think of me?*

The shouting draws closer. I wipe my mouth and shove myself up. I lift the sword from the weeds and then force myself to go to the assassin's body and unbuckle the solar scabbard. I fasten the belt on and slip the weapon into its scabbard. It's too big. The weight of it tugs on my hip and wrenches me off-balance.

Men rush toward me from the fields. In another few minutes they'll be upon me.

The only way I can outrace them is with the horse. I frantically unsheathe the sword and saw through the cart's traces and press the creature's sweaty cheek against mine. "Steady there now, girl, all right? You get me through this, and I'll make sure you eat apples every bloody day for the rest of your life."

The beast snorts. I decide to read it as a yes.

By the time the fieldsmen reach the wagon, I'm already streaking off down the dirt road from whence I came, my desperate heart lodged tight in my throat and the truth of the queen's would-be assassin lighting up all my veins like a fever.

# August 1593
## Dover Castle, Kent

Long have I longed to see my love again,
Still have I wished, but never could obtain it;
Rather than all the world (if I might gain it)
Would I desire my love's sweet precious gain.
Yet in my soul I see him every day,
See him, and see his still stern countenance.
But (ah) what is of long continuance,
Where majesty and beauty bears the sway?
Sometimes, when I imagine that I see him,
(As love is full of foolish fantasies)
Yearning to kiss his lips, as my love's fees,
I feel but air: nothing but air to be him.
Thus with Ixion, kiss I clouds in vain:
Thus with Ixion, feel I endless pain.

—RICHARD BARNFIELD,
"Sonnet 16"

# CHAPTER THIRTY-THREE

GIVEN THE STATE of my affairs—broken finger, bruised skull, penniless because I'd not the foresight to take the dead man's coin *and* his sword—it takes four days to ride and scrounge and steal my way to Dover Castle.

The castle is England's first bulwark against invasion, built atop chalk cliffs knifing over a navy sea. Scarcely beyond the water lies Antwerp. The city where James and I were supposed to leave all this behind. The slenderness of that horizon, how I fancy that if I squint just so, I can see that other side, makes my chest ache.

The queen's Tudor rose flutters above the castle's keep, which is all but hidden behind the baileys. The walls rise from the earth like great molars, green fuzzing along their foundations. The distant clamor of an arms practice clashes against my ears.

Dover Castle is no cozy, peaceful home for lords.

Drunken ballads have well acquainted me with the castle's history. 'Tis said that only God himself can smite the walls. That when we are all worm's meat, the castle will still stand sentinel upon the English shore. Immovable. Impenetrable.

Impossible.

A big breath catches in my chest. I hitch the stolen satchel upon my back even higher. The sheathed sword within presses upon my spine. Aye, perhaps Dover Castle is impossible for golden armies and prancing lords. But it won't be for me.

The helpful inn girl in the town told me that James has not yet been tried. I also know from the selfsame girl that at least once a day a great wagon filled with plucked chickens, summer vegetables, and sweating cheese rumbles through the heavily armed gates, right over the moat, beneath the walls, and straight into the kitchens.

Right on time, the wagon rolls over the hill, pulled by two huge oxen. I hide until the driver passes and hurl myself into the wagon behind his back. A hand clasps mine, pulling me aboard. The inn girl grins at me, and I give her a wink. She ushers me into a spot right behind a pungent stack of Dover's best cave-aged cheeses and then piles great heaps of cabbages atop my person.

The wagon jolts to a stop outside the castle gates. Around the cabbages, I spy a soldier outfitted in the livery of the Cinque Ports. He browses the wagon's contents, drawing closer to my corner. The soldier palms a cabbage right over my face. I hold my breath and squeeze my eyes shut. There's a yell—my pulse spikes—and the wagon lurches forward once more. I exhale so hard, dirt rains onto my face from the cabbages.

Safe.

Suddenly the cabbage disappears, replaced by the pinched face of a guard.

"*Oy*, I said there was something strange down there!"

I explode up from the vegetables with a shout.

The guard is so shocked, he stumbles backward. His fellow gatekeepers mill about the cart, gaping at me as cabbages roll every which way. Before anyone can shout for reinforcements, I kick a cheese wheel as hard as I can.

My foot goes right into the hollow center.

Hornets, angry from having their nest shoved into a scraped-out cheese wheel, swarm out from the hole. The guards scream and curse as the insects assail them.

I leap off the wagon and run.

The inner castle yard is all a cramped mess, like the inn girl said it would be. I flatten myself against an outbuilding and watch armored guards sprint past, their pikes readied. I wait three breaths after they pass, then stroll out and gape at the guards wailing and flailing at the outraged hornets.

In my nicked peasant's clothes, I'm just one more shocked onlooker, lost in the crowd.

The girl who helped me orchestrate my scheme sidles beside me, grinning. "It *worked*!"

I cannot bring myself to return the smile. "Of course it did. Remember, my horse is yours if you've the sense to not tell anyone you've seen me, understand?"

The girl beams brighter and places a finger to her lips before racing away.

I stare after her, a bad feeling in my gut. The girl may not talk, but what if someone else does? What if she's in the wrong place at the wrong time, like James's sister? The servants? How many more people will be hurt or killed before this is over?

I lose myself in the bustling Dover kitchens, a cap pulled low over my recognizable silver-blond hair. I know that just because no one's looking, doesn't mean they're not seeing. Cecil's spiders could be anywhere, sending whispers to their master even now. And all I've got proving Cecil's guilt are second-hand words and a sword which doesn't even belong to him. Goads me to admit it, but the queen's former spymaster has played his game well.

Which means I've got to play mine better.

I keep to the shadows betwixt the kitchen and scullery hall, smiling to any who spare a word to me until I spot what I'm looking for.

There. A scullery maid, her hand tightly bandaged.

Though every nerve in me wishes to confront her right now, I wait until she finishes her work and ducks into the servant-women's dormitory alone. I follow her in despite the great old sign on the door that says AWAY WITH THEE, LADS.

"Excuse me, sir!" the scullery maid snaps, her voice full of outrage. "This is the women's quarters. You cannot . . ." She trails off when she gets a good look at me. Then the blood drains from her face, and she stares as if I'm the dead come back to life.

I kick the door shut and storm over, fumbling at the bandage on her hand. She hisses and tries to stop me, but I'm already squeezing her naked hand tight, the marks from my bite livid against her lye-chapped white skin.

Sure enough, 'tis the maid who helped Cecil's man kidnap me.

"Miss me?" I ask in my best Lord Hughes voice.

The maid snarls and yanks her hand back. "You're supposed to be dead."

"Seems I missed the cue for my exit."

I press forward, widening my stance, and let loose my most wicked expression. She flinches, glare growing sharper.

"You're going to tell me what, exactly, Cecil said when he sent you after me," I say.

The slightest line dips between her eyes, so fast, I nearly miss it. "Cecil. He—he said that you were catching on. Causing him problems. He needed you gone."

The hair prickles along the back of my neck. I've been a player long enough to recognize a badly delivered line when I hear one. "You're lying."

The girl's face flushes pink, and I know I am right. "If you do not leave this instant, I shall scream! I'll—"

I grab her shoulders and throw her against the wall, followed by my forearm against her windpipe. She cries, fear finally lighting upon her face. I press harder. "Tell me what really happened," I demand through gritted teeth.

Tears well in the girl's eyes, but all she does is spit in my face, most of it getting on her and not me.

I sigh and release her.

The girl slumps to the floor, her wide eyes incredulous. I slowly kneel down to her level. "Please. I don't want to harm you. But something horrible may happen to you, me, and England itself if you do not tell me who sent you after me."

The girl's face blanches. With a trembling hand she reaches into her bodice and presses something into my hand.

'Tis a perfectly shaped gold sun. I turn it over with unsteady fingers, a Latin inscription, *Veritas Loquor*, catching the brazier's light.

The girl talks. "She—she told me to make sure you heard Cecil's name. She said I could keep this as payment. 'Tis real gold, y'know. I thought at the next town I could sell it, maybe get a few pounds for it or . . ."

The words trail off. My head rings as though a musket has fired too close to my person.

*She?* There is a she in all this?

"What—what did she look like?"

"I did not see her face." The girl lifts her unbandaged hand and slowly traces an *x* over the two smallest fingers. I stare at the gesture, uncomprehending.

"These fingers in her glove were limp," the girl explains. "Like she was missing fingers."

Her words take a long moment to sink in and settle somewhere low and deep within me. From the abyss rises a single, impossible name.

Maggie.

Zounds, she's talking about *Maggie.*

She's the one in the Societas Solis.

I wobble back on my heels. Blood pumps through me in staggered, shocked bursts. The world narrows to the golden sun clenched in my fist. Like if I squeeze it hard enough, it'll disappear.

No. Surely not. The Mags I know is no assassin. I can picture her smirk, lighting up the attic like a spike of sunlight when she'd unveil her stolen spoils after we'd gone hungry. She lived with me. She pared her toenails on our only bed. She's my friend.

Yet. *Yet.*

I bite my lip, tasting metal. When the scraps are stitched together, it makes a horrible sort of sense. More so than Cecil, Maggie knew what was happening with our investigation. Who we suspected, what our next move would be. She was one of only two people who knew I was disguised in the Bloomsbury kitchens. She was also one of the few who knew I suspected Lord Foxwell. And—my heart goes colder—she saw Marlowe's desperate message summoning me to Deptford.

She must be the one who sent the order to kill Kit.

*Someone will catch you.* 'Tis what I always told Maggie about her hand.

I never thought I'd be the one catching her.

I press a shaking palm against my mouth, squeezing my eyes shut. The truth knocks into me like a fist to the teeth: Maggie has outsmarted me every step of the way since the very beginning of all this. Christ Almighty, she was only able to commit her crimes *because* of me. Like a daft fool, I trusted her and led her exactly where she needed me to take her for months.

And—worse—if I had not obstinately trusted Maggie, Kit Marlowe and James's sister Catherine would not be dead. James would not be imprisoned for a terrible crime he didn't commit. My hand may not be the one which has locked whatever cage he's trapped in now, but I've played a role in placing him there every bit as much as Maggie. Mayhap even more than her.

Maggie murdered Catherine, and she only could because of me.

*There is no reason for him to love you. Not after this.*

The thought opens me up like a chasm. I crush my hands against my face, pushing back the tears and the shame and the desperation howling within me.

I must confess, part of me wants to run. Running was how I dealt with all my problems before, and 'tis only a matter of time before James knows the truth. He's going to despise me when he learns what I've done, but I can't dwell on that now. There's still a chance, slender as it is, for me to save him and right this one wrong in a season where everything, literally everything, has gone wrong.

My shoulders straighten. I suck the snot and the shock and everything else back within me. This entire time, the maid has watched me like a spooked field mouse wondering when the kestrel's claws will strike. "M-my lord?"

"I'm keeping this." I pocket the sun and stand. "Thank you. You've helped Queen Elizabeth and me more than you'll ever know."

Her eyes bulge so wide, I fear they may plummet from her skull and roll across the floor. "You're—you're working for *Her Majesty*?"

I unsheathe the hidden knife at my waist and flash a sharp smile. "No. I'm here to save the lad I love. And you're going to help me do it."

# CHAPTER THIRTY-FOUR

WELL AFTER MIDNIGHT, when Gráinne Ní Mháille leaves the progress's nightly revelries and returns to her chamber, I'm ready for her.

The Pirate Queen pushes open her door and freezes. Her eyes dart from the crossbow I've trained on her to the maid tied and gagged in the corner. Then she sighs like I've disappointed her, of all things. "Cruelty doesn't look good on you, lad."

My stomach clenches. I ignore it and heft the crossbow higher. "Won't be a good look for you, either, when another girl's found dead, this time in an Irish pirate's lair." I knew Gráinne agreed to come on the progress and work with me for her own reasons, but I never learned what they were. Now I'm realizing, far too late, that perhaps I should have asked more questions. If Maggie has played me this entire time, there's nothing that suggests that Gráinne hasn't too. And if I need someone else's help to free James—which is very much the case—then Gráinne is my only hope in all of Dover Castle. If I can trust her.

Gráinne's gaze goes flinty at my threat. "What do you want from me?"

"Answers. Why are you here? We both know there's no love lost betwixt you and the English queen. There's no reason for you to spend half the summer capering about with her and her court unless there's something in it for you. If you're the reason James is—"

Gráinne lifts a hand, stopping me. "I've nothing to do with what's happened to that lad. Ain't right with me how they've treated him. Anyone can see he's no kin slayer."

Something in me starts to soften, but I keep the crossbow steady. "You never did tell me why you sought an audience with Queen Elizabeth."

Gráinne's expression grows guarded. "As I've said, 'tis a boring tale."

I make a great show of making myself comfortable where I'm sitting on her bed. "Well, we've got plenty of time."

Gráinne's nostrils flare. "It's my son. He's been captured by the English. I came to bargain for his freedom. Are you satisfied yet, *Lord Hughes*?"

Someone calls the Pirate Queen mother? I imagined Gráinne was like Queen Elizabeth, whose power draws from her unwillingness to tie herself to any person. Queen Elizabeth has neither husband nor heir, nor anyone else close enough to call kin. No one at all truly knows what thoughts flit behind those fathomless black eyes.

But Gráinne does not hold back among her people. I can picture it: a less salt-worn version of this ruthless woman. Her hair more auburn than silver, arms strong and rippling with the effort of heaving a toddler in and out of his seaside cradle.

Somewhere in the background is a deep-voiced man, his hands on her shoulders, smiling.

The image threatens to make my throat swell. I tamp down the feeling. "Have you secured his freedom yet?"

"What do you bloody think?" the Pirate Queen snaps. "Do you imagine you and Bloomsbury have been the only two men affected by his sister's death? Elizabeth is mistrustful of everyone now. Including me. 'Tis only a matter of time before Cecil tells her to arrest all my men." She crosses her arms and glares at me. "If you're looking to pin blame with that crossbow of yours, you've come to the wrong place."

I ought to feel bad for putting Gráinne and her men in this position, but I don't. Not even a little. If the queen doesn't trust Gráinne or me, and we both need something from her, then it makes the wild plan I'm trying to hatch all the more possible. "What if I told you I know how to fix everything that's gone wrong?"

Gráinne looks deliberately betwixt me, the crossbow, and the captured maid. "I'd say you're a madman." She yanks over a chair and spins it the wrong way. She straddles the seat, arms crossed over its back. "But I'll listen anyway."

Our eyes meet, and for once, there's nothing we're hiding from each other. Gráinne hasn't been honest with me, but she hasn't been dishonest, either. After a beat of silence, I set down the crossbow and untie the maid's gag. "Tell her what you told me."

The maid glares but obliges me.

Gráinne listens to the story of Maggie's deception with

neither comment nor expression, only stirring to examine the golden sun and the sword I pull from my bag. By the time I've neared the end of my tale, my throat itches. "Maggie thinks everyone who would thwart her is gone. If I were her, I'd be readying to strike right about now."

The Pirate Queen nods slowly, though her face remains close-lidded as a treasure coffer. "When do you think Maggie would kill the English queen?"

I ransack what I know of Maggie. Even though we lived side by side for months, she never told us much about her past. She said she was maimed for thieving and left for dead. Broken bone and torn sinew. My stomach lurches at the memory of her grisly wound. No, she wasn't lying about that. But perhaps she was lying about getting caught as a thief. Maybe she was tangled up with murder and intrigue well before I knew her. Perhaps she's been playing me for months, part of the Societas Solis the entire time. Just waiting for someone to give her an opportunity to strike. Waiting for *me*.

Gráinne snaps her fingers under my nose. "Don't make me ask a third time, lad. When will she act?"

Maggie is slick as a newly netted fish and possesses the cunning of a fox. I think of the showiness with which she'd pick pockets and her endless jests and japes. Aye, there's a bit of a player in sly Maggie, more than she knows, I'd wager.

"She's got a flair for the dramatic. Her first attempt to assassinate the queen was at midnight in a court banquet hall. And whenever she did a big thieving job, she'd get all dressed up." I run my thumb along my bottom lip. "She'll do something flashy. Something no one can miss."

"There's to be a grand naval battle the day before Bloomsbury's trial," Gráinne says. "A reenactment of the English queen's defeat of the Spanish Armada." She jerks her chin toward a squinty slit of a window. In the distance there's a serene lake. "My crew and I were asked to play in it. 'Tis set to happen the day after next." She laughs bitterly. "We're just a troop of hired players to bloody Elizabeth now."

Excitement lights me up like a spark. "That'll be when Maggie will strike. Right when the queen is reliving her greatest victory, I'm certain of it! We'll spring a trap for her during the battle."

Gráinne laughs again. 'Tis no small thing—she throws her head back and wheezes. It goes on for so long, the hair rises on my nape, and I reach for the crossbow again. "You come in here with a kidnapped girl, threaten my person and reputation, and now have the audacity to ask a favor from me?" She wipes tears from her eyes and sobers when she sees I'm armed once more. "I don't trust you an inch, Elias Wilde. You're always playing someone you're not. Playing some game no one understands but yourself."

My body goes hot. Indignation moves me to speak, but she silences me with a gesture. "I'm not interested in why you're this way. I've known plenty of false men. Wouldn't go as far to call myself an honest woman, either. My question is this: Why should I trust you now? You've already lost this game. You had a chance to leave all this behind. Your life would be easier if you had."

I square my jaw. "An innocent man shall be on trial for his life. You are the one who told me that it is not the way among your people to imprison men without justified cause. Is that not enough of a reason?"

Gráinne pillows her chin upon her fist, head tilted. Her storm-gray eyes study me for so long, I fight the urge to fidget. "Ah. I see you've found something to care about which isn't yourself." Her eyebrows wiggle audaciously. "Perhaps something to do with a certain royal prisoner?"

There's simply not a way to respond which does not disclose the fact that I have fallen witlessly in love with the worst person I could fall for. So I say nothing at all as my cheeks pinken.

The Pirate Queen laughs and slaps her thigh. "Zounds, you're among the most obstinate lads I've ever met. 'Tis a pity your parents planted you in such weak English soil. You would've made a fine member in my crew." She tilts her head again and considers me closely. "Are you absolutely certain about Maggie?" she says. "If you're wrong, the Bloomsbury boy will be beheaded."

It was not so long ago I would have said no. 'Tis a hazardous claim to make, its evidence threadbare and patchy as an old cloak. But instead, I let slip the ropes on my doubts. I've spent my whole life waiting until I knew more or had more to make a move. I'm done with waiting. "Yes. I would bet my life on it."

"Good. You may well lose it before this is over." Gráinne

steeples her fingers on the chair's back. "All right then. I'll disguise you as one of my crew without telling your queen. But in return, you'll take the blame if things go wrong, or I swear, I'll cut your bowels from your belly myself."

I don't like that the Pirate Queen has something over me, but I know if Maggie thwarts me again, I'll be dead no matter what. Dead at Gráinne's hand is likely better than whatever Queen Elizabeth and Cecil would have in store for me.

"What about me?"

I jerk toward the kidnapped maid. I nearly forgot about her, and, judging from the look she's giving me, she knows it. "There's nothing stopping me from telling Queen Elizabeth what's going on," the maid says primly. "You're both traitorous shagrags, as far as I'm concerned."

Gráinne opens a drawer on her table and pulls out a clinking bag. She upends it on the maid's skirts, and I spy gold and silver coins from more kingdoms than I ever knew existed. "If you shut your mouth and leave, you can have all this." The Pirate Queen glances at me, a brow arched. "Unless you think killing her would be better?"

The maid blanches. Gráinne considers her fear and runs a finger along the knife at her belt. "Could cut out your tongue instead, love, if dying doesn't suit your fancy."

I recall the soft snap of Foxwell's bones when Queen Elizabeth commanded me to maim him. Easy as river rushes snapping beneath my boots. Something lurches in my belly. "No, she can leave with all her bits."

Gráinne sighs. "If you say so." At my nod, she slices through the girl's bond. The maid takes her booty and scrambles, leaving me and the Pirate Queen alone.

Gráinne crosses her arms and stares, a smirk lifting her lips. "I must say, Elias Wilde, you've surprised me."

At once I'm on guard. "Is this a good thing or not?"

Her smirk widens. "We shall see, won't we?"

# CHAPTER THIRTY-FIVE

ANY CONFIDENCE I had about outsmarting Maggie wobbles the day of the battle.

Today, when the great navies of England and Spain clash on the green-spotted lake, corsairs shall number among the players. Amidst wooden swords and blasting powder lurk real blades. At the first sign of wrongdoing, the person who spots it shall cry *God save the queen!* and everyone shall grab their weapon and rush to the queen's defense. 'Tis a slippery plan, and it makes me nervous. Too much hinges on Maggie's first move. What if we fail? What if she escapes?

Someone elbows me. "Oy—what's wrong with your hands?" 'Tis Réamonn, the swashbuckling pirate lad. He prickles with knives like an adorable, bloodthirsty hedgehog.

"Why are you out here? Shouldn't Gráinne have left you in the nursery?" I ask, clasping my shaking hands behind my back.

He smiles, the expression all teeth. "You won't be saying that when I save your arse out there. Then you'll owe me a blood debt." He leans closer, ghastly expression growing wider. "Then you'll have to do whatever I ask!"

I won't be unmanned by a boy who's no taller than my

shoulder. I look heavenward and sigh. "Let's hope our work leads us to no blood things of any kind, shall we?"

Wooden ships twice the size of horse carts bob on the lake's surface, their freshly painted sides bleeding into the water. The ships bear English and Spanish colors and trappings—all of it an homage to England's defeat of the Spanish Armada in 1588. On the shore, Queen Elizabeth herself is a blanched silhouette behind snapping silver curtains on a raised pavilion. The nobles are seated on a tiered dais to the side. But it's not the court that I'm worried about for once. Instead I scan the faces of the hired players on the opposing shore.

Gráinne says she personally oversaw the guards who questioned and searched each and every man who stepped within the castle walls. While no player seemed suspicious, knowing this brings me little relief. There's no certain method to uncover a man's secrets. And secrets are far deadlier and more pointed things than blades.

The queen's herald, who has been boring us with the story of the Crown's great naval victory, winds up to a sputtering, red-faced finish. "Let us return to that great, glorious day in Her Majesty's reign and witness the splendor of England's might and power!"

Two cannons boom beside the water. A roar goes up from the crowd.

My chest tightens as the battle begins.

All the so-called sailors scream and clamber from the shores onto the ships. I only barely manage to fling myself aboard before servants shove the ships away. Already, gunpowder flashes and roars, smudging the air with smoke. How am I supposed to search for Maggie if I cannot see a damned thing?

*"Begone, Spanish dog!"* A wooden cutlass whirls from the frothing smog, followed by a snarling face. The player's weapon catches me in the gut. I wince and yank the play weapon away.

The player's scowl wilts. "Hey! You're supposed to slump into the water all dead-like. 'Tis what we practiced."

With a single push of the cutlass, I send him splashing into the lake and take up his post.

"Sorry, mate. I'm playing a different sort of game!" I call to his shocked face as the English ship cants away.

The ship's mast cuts through the smoke overhead. I scramble up the ship's rigging and brace my boots on the yard, fingernails biting into the mast for dear life. A cannon goes off so close, my teeth rattle. My eyes squint against the burning air, and there, betwixt plumes of purple smoke, I spot an armored figure standing at the prow of a ship. Masses of red hair cascade from the back of the helm. Paper and wire wings sprout from the back of the costume. The player is unmistakably dressed as Queen Elizabeth, transformed into the Goddess of Victory, and the crowd leaps to their feet and roars all the louder when they see her.

Well, Gráinne failed to mention this melodramatic bit of nonsense was in the plan.

The gaudy queen distracts me so much, I don't see the Spanish ship barreling our way until it's too late. It catches us with a mighty boom, and our ship breaks apart like an empty wine barrel. The mast shudders beneath me. For a moment, nothing happens. Then, with a groaning, shivering crack, it breaks, and I'm falling.

The water swallows me whole. Grasping weeds pull at my legs, tugging me deeper. I grapple with the clasps of my billowy costume before it can drag me under farther, cursing the nobles who watch me struggle for sport every which way to hell.

*Is this how it ends?* I wonder, flailing at the lake's surface. Gráinne's plan sounded absolutely wild when she shared it, and now that I'm half-drowned three minutes in, it all seems like a farce.

My hand catches on another swimming sailor. I'm about to apologize to him when the man turns, and the words die in my throat.

'Tis one of Gráinne's men. The one eye he's got left is wide open and glassy with fear.

Only me and Gráinne's men are armed with real blades out here. One of her men dead means someone else is armed too. Someone who's not supposed to be. My intestines go to mush. *Maggie is here.* But where?

Smoke wreathes across the water. Belches of fire cut through the gray. I fight to keep my head above water and shout, "God save the queen! God save the queen!"

But no one hears me over the din of battle.

A wave sends me into the murky darkness again as a ship nearly brains me. Something clamps down hard on my arm and wrenches me upward.

I scramble over the ship's side and collapse on the deck,

choking on water and dripping blood that isn't mine. The sailor who hauled me from the water inhales sharply at the sight.

"Christ, can you not swim?" Réamonn's expression is a strange mixture of horror and curiosity. "You can't swim, and you decided to take part in this? You should've left the work to me! I would—"

I grab his narrow shoulders and shake him. "Réamonn, we've got to do something. The assassin's here!" I gasp out the words between heaving breaths.

"Ooh, how frightening! Someone better go tell the queen," another voice cackles.

Cold ripples through me. I turn toward the voice.

And stop.

Maggie grins and gives me a saucy wink. "Speak the truth. Were you surprised it was me?"

The pirate lad unsheathes a too-big knife and rushes her before I can stop him.

Maggie sidesteps. Réamonn sails past her. I see her hand move to her belt as he rushes her again.

With a yell I'm between them, blade barely in my hand before parrying Maggie's strike.

My dagger goes spinning into the waves.

Réamonn watches beneath my elbow with wide, quivering eyes. Only my block saved his skin.

And now I'm unarmed, facing down the deadliest person I've ever met.

"For God's sake, get out of here!" I shout to the boy as Maggie turns to me.

380 | ERIN COTTER

"You always did have to be a hero, didn't you?"

I stumble away from Maggie's swipe, the crowd's roaring in my ears.

"You killed Kit and Catherine and that maid!"

I drop to my knees, dodging another lunge. Maggie sneers. "Marlowe was onto me. The other two were in the wrong place at the wrong time." Her faces pinches with something akin to regret. "I made sure it was quick."

Réamonn is nowhere to be seen. Good.

When Maggie swipes again, I explode up from the deck. The small knife I keep hidden in my boot opens a red line on Maggie's chest. She hisses and rounds on me with renewed fervor.

My second blade goes flying into the water. Before I can react, Maggie tackles me, pinning me to the deck. She kneels on my stomach, one hand on my chest and the other around her dagger. The water churns and boils just beneath my head, soaking my hair and flecking her wild face with foam. Her blade presses into my throat. The roar of the crowd has reached new deafening levels. I wonder if they can see how real this is—that nothing about this is a game for us.

I bare my throat. "Kill me like you did all the others, then. Catherine was only fifteen, you know."

Her eyes narrow. "Don't make this harder than it already is."

"You're the one making it hard!"

The knife digs in deeper—hard enough to make me gasp. *She's really going to kill me.* I'm more certain of it than anything else. The thought makes the world go fuzzy and my heartbeat hitch. All the nights we slept back-to-back when it was too cold for warmth. All the times we broke bread together. It was everything and nothing. It led us here, to Maggie's bared teeth and her knife at my throat and my eyes squeezing shut because even though death's been nipping at my heels this entire time, I'm still not ready for it.

Will anyone even know I'm dead?

Will James know I tried?

With a disgusted sigh Maggie shoves me overboard.

I somersault into the cold water, floundering before finding my way to the surface again. Maggie's ship has already disappeared into the fog.

I scramble toward land.

The other "dead" soldiers pepper the shore festooned with foul lake rubbish. I swipe a knife from an unsuspecting pirate's belt as I squelch past them to the noble stands and, ignoring the scandalized looks from the ladies, force myself to the top tier.

Up here, the damn gunpowder smoke is more vapor than fog, and I've a far better view of the lake. The queen's flagship duels valiantly with two Spanish ships which, judging from the many swooning, heroic deaths, are more manned with players than pirates.

Maggie is on the English flagship, fighting beside the costumed queen.

She's a proper seadog, poking and hissing at would-be enemies, scrapping twice as much as anyone else. A punch straight to the face takes out the final Spaniard on the second ship. The crowd screams triumphantly.

I start running along the very back of the stands, yelling for all I'm worth, *"God save the queen!"*

The nobles turn to look at me. Some with disdain, some with amusement.

"God save the queen?" someone else takes up in a timid voice. Oh God, 'tis one of the nobles. He catches my eye and gives me this bashful, knowing wink and tries it again, rising to his feet. "God save the queen!"

The cursed chant spreads faster than the plague.

*"God save the queen! God save the queen!"*

They stomp their feet. The ground trembles, and still no one moves. Why is no one moving? Where is Gráinne? None of this is happening as it should! I plant my hands atop the skulls of two chanting fools and launch myself from the stands toward the queen's pavilion.

The queen's ship floats to the middle of the lake to confront the final Spanish ship. Their sides crash together, and men from both ships mill over the sides to fight. Wooden swords fly: ribbons of scarlet unfurl from limbs. Queen Elizabeth as the Goddess of Victory pushes the last Spaniard into the water. The queen holds her sword aloft, and her brave English sailors brandish their painted wooden blades and join their points to the queen's blade. The crowd's hurrahs grow thunderous.

Except the blade held by the gloved figure sparks in the sunlight. 'Tis real steel. *Maggie.*

*"God save the queen! God save the queen! God save the queen!"*

The chant is a solid gale all around me. I sprint to the royal pavilion.

The final English ship draws close. Queen Elizabeth stands to greet her likeness. One sailor breaks form and hurls himself at her with a shout.

The queen screams.

I clamp my knife between my teeth and jump with all my might.

*God save the queen* sputters out with shocked gasps and screams.

I land on the pavilion, but 'tis too late.

A knife already quivers in Queen Elizabeth's heart.

# CHAPTER THIRTY-SIX

TOO LATE TOO *late too late.*

Everything blurs together, smeared ink on parchment.

Queen Elizabeth sputtering, falling backward.

Guards shouting and scrambling closer.

Me, launching myself at Maggie.

A whoosh of air and weight, unmistakably real and passing just over my head.

And Maggie thudding to the ground in a scarlet slick.

I fall beside Maggie and know not whether I should spit upon her or call for fetters. There's a crossbow bolt buried in her thigh. Ragged breaths tear through my lungs at the sight of blood.

"Why—why did you let me escape?" The question bursts from me.

Maggie throws me a sharp-edged smile. She lifts a hand—a fresh gush of blood sinks into my breeches—and cups my chin with a bloody palm. "You should have run when I gave you the chance."

A shadow cuts over me. The English ship has nosed into the queen's pavilion and knocked everything askew. The player queen jumps onto the stage and rips off his helmet.

The crowd gasps again—shocked into fresh scandal.

Beneath the helm is no man—but Queen Elizabeth herself.

I stare, utterly flummoxed, until the seated queen heaves herself to her feet.

'Tis Gráinne, the Pirate Queen, and an ugly slash through the bodice of her dress reveals the battered breastplate beneath it. Maggie's dagger only pierced the steel, not the beating heart beneath it. A very familiar crossbow dangles in Gráinne's hand. She tosses it to a shocked guard and rubs her hands together. "Christ Almighty, what a romp this has been!"

None of this, absolutely none of this, was part of the plan. Why is Gráinne here? Why did the queens change places? Why do I appear to be the only person surprised by this turn of events?

"What the bloody hell is going on?" I demand.

Gráinne laughs merrily. "Did you truly think I would fall for that cock-and-bull story that Maggie was the assassin and you knew how to get her? Not that you were wrong." Her eyes dart to Maggie, who spits at her name. The guards brandish their pikes toward us, and I suddenly see myself as they must: a lad huddled beside the girl who attempted to put a knife through their queen's heart.

I stare up at the two red-haired queens. "You cannot possibly think, after all this time we've worked together, that I am part and parcel to this plot?"

Gráinne's expression twists with something that touches regret. She bends her head and whispers in my ear. "I liked you, lad. You would've made a fine pirate. But I don't believe you were working with Maggie for this long and didn't know what she was. I'll do whatever I must to save my son, even if it means protecting the bloody queen of England."

Gráinne's been loyal to Elizabeth the whole time. I was only her means to get to Queen Elizabeth, same as Maggie. Worse still, Gráinne makes a fair point about my actions. *I'm* the one who trusted Maggie and brought her into the progress and the royal court. Unknowingly, I have been an accomplice to Maggie's crimes. Not a single person here thinks I'm innocent.

My eyes snag upon the magnificent points of Queen Elizabeth's boots. They trace up the fine silk hose and pass over the gold-threaded doublet and sparkling breastplate until I reach the black, black eyes which behold me with nothing but coldness and contempt. Something about all this feels dreadfully familiar.

"Arrest them at once."

For the second time in my life I am imprisoned. Except instead of being locked in a dismal dungeon, now the mighty white cliffs of Dover press against my back. The cliffs are so tall, the very tops are hidden even when I crane my neck so far back, it hurts. Before me blue waves shimmer in the cheerful sunshine.

That's right. We've been marooned on a bloody beach. Already high tide licks at my boots. Judging from the high-water mark on the cliff, we've not got much time before it smothers us completely.

"There's worse ways to go, you know." Maggie pokes my

calf. "'Tis lucky for us, really, the queen decided drowning us like rats was less embarrassing than the mess of an execution—"

"*Stop it.* Will you?"

Maggie's been relentless as a magpie, and I can't take it anymore. She made jests the entire time two stiff-lipped guards led us down to a naval dock and onto a boat that appeared about as seaworthy as a thimble and then abandoned us on this godforsaken spit of land.

"Fine, then." Maggie purses her lips and leans against the cliffs, her wounded leg outstretched and bleeding sluggishly. The wound is above her knee, a dark hole that makes me skittish to stare at for too long. 'Tis hard to believe so much blood can come from one injury. By the time we were dumped from the boat, a puddle of blood already sloshed in the prow. Every time she moves her injured leg, something ropey that absolutely should not be seeing the light of day flexes wetly. A wound like this looks fatal.

Maggie catches my morbid stare and arches an eyebrow. What's been hidden yawns between us like a chasm. Weeks— no, *months*—of secrets and betrayals hidden behind sly quips and lopsided smirks.

"You used me," I finally say.

Maggie's jaw tightens. "I had to."

"That's not true."

"What do you want me to say? That I regret it? I don't. You were the person who could lead me to the queen. And if you had simply let yourself be kidnapped, we wouldn't be here right now."

I laugh darkly. "Oh, yes. Do blame *me* for all this."

Maggie snarls and leaps to her feet only to fall back with a cry of pain. I'm half-standing before it crashes into me that this is how it's always worked, Maggie tricking me into doing exactly what she wished me to do. I sink back on my heels and watch her breathe in sharp, painful bursts, both hands red on her wound. 'Tis wrong, I'm certain of it, to sit here whilst another person is in pain and not do a thing, but I shove the feeling aside. Instead I ask in a cold voice that sounds nothing like my own, "How long have you been with the Societas Solis?"

At first I think she won't respond. But when she does, her voice is low and steady, as though she's unfurling a long-bottled confession. "As long as I've drawn breath."

I imagine a nursery of tiny assassins, each one pricklier than the last. "Really?"

"Of course not. I was five years old, and someone was offering to feed me. I hated the queen more than the devil for creating a kingdom that left me out in the gutter. Societas Solis gave me a home and cared for me when no one else would. Isn't this what Marlowe did for you?"

"Enough with the japes!" I shout so loud, seabirds startle from the cliffs. "We both know Marlowe never raised me to be a spy or a killer. He—"

"You *are* a killer, though," Maggie says. "No better than me. I know what you did to get to Dover Castle."

My stomach curls in on itself, outrage curdling into a mess of guilt and shame. The man with the solar scabbard. Thomas

Walter. I can still feel the jolt through my bones as the cart crushed his body, that hazy scent of blood in the summer fields.

"That was different. He was going to kill me."

Maggie's mouth is a downturned slash. "No he wasn't. He was supposed to bring you to London and let you go. It was our arrangement."

A horrible pinch of understanding goes through me. "You . . . tried to save me?"

"No, I tried to get you out of my way," Maggie growls, gesturing to the broad sky and the water lapping ever closer. "And you've gone and mucked *that* all up. Should've figured you would, though. Your heroic streak is the worst thing about you. Could've been a fine spy if you didn't have that. Marlowe thought so too."

"Marlowe? What's he got to do with this?"

Maggie looks surprised. "Why, everything. He and I were playing cat and mouse for years. Societas Solis wanted him dead. He was one of Elizabeth's most infuriating spies, and he kept sniffing out our schemes to kill her before they came to anything. I was the best person to do the job once I fell in with you and Inigo."

Shame splinters through me. Marlowe. Catherine. The servant girl. The kitchen boy at Whitehall Palace. Maggie's henchman, the man with the solar scabbard. And James, especially him. "They're all harmed because of me, aren't they?" I know this, but I need to hear her say it—admit that I'm the only reason she could ruin so many lives.

There's a flicker of something almost like guilt across her

face. "When Marlowe sent you that note from Deptford . . . I knew what I had to do. But he knew what line of work he was in, Elias. He was lucky to live as long as he did. You said so yourself already—I used you to get to him and then, when it was useful for me, Queen Elizabeth." She thuds against the cliff face with a sigh. "Zounds, and I was so close! Months of work, unraveled in an instant. Framing Foxwell, making sure you lot thought it was my man with the solar scabbard behind everything. Letting Cecil make himself suspicious simply by being there and being jealous of you. By the way, his secret letters were all to his cronies trying to oust you from your spy position. I investigated it. Elizabeth was right to trust you over him. He's an awful spy."

Even though I'm furious with Maggie because she, of course, also ruined my life, curiosity still gets the better of me. "Why did Societas Solis want to kill Marlowe? Or Queen Elizabeth for that matter? What's in it for them?"

Maggie is quiet for so long, I fear she won't answer. Then she takes a steadying breath. "You once told me you thought the world would be a better place if Queen Elizabeth were dead. Can you truly tell me your heart has changed?"

The ocean roars. The biggest wave yet rolls in and soaks over my boot, filling it with cold water. Stuck betwixt the white cliffs and our impending watery doom, I am forced to confront an unpleasant truth.

I've been trying to blame Maggie for all this—but this isn't her fault. Not entirely.

Queen Elizabeth's laws hold James prisoner when his

innocence is plain. Her laws also sent the Burning Reaper to my family's lands, tearing out our history and livelihood at the roots. If Queen Elizabeth and those in power were not hungry for more of it, if they were not so determined to steal all the world's riches for themselves, then people like me and Maggie would not be left to thieve and murder and lie just to survive.

Maggie continues. "Bloomsbury, even though he's a bloody noble himself, was always right about one thing. The world can change. England is a poison that must be stopped. Societas Solis thinks so, and so do I. That's why when the Catholic Church was willing to pay to kill the heretic Queen Elizabeth, head of her own bloody Church of England, we leapt at the chance. Mark my words, one day this earth will be sorry we failed to end England's power now, when we had the chance."

I don't know if Maggie's right. Not entirely. But there's something about her words that nestles deep within me, feeling right and true. Just as the rich shouldn't take everything the world offers for themselves, James and I shouldn't have to change our names and flee the land and, quite possibly, leave behind everyone who's ever known us just to be.

Maggie knocks her foot against mine as I turn over her words. "Say it. Just say it."

I heave an enormous sigh and scrape both hands over my scalp. "Has anyone ever told you what an absolute monster you are when you're right?"

"I never tire of hearing those words." She kisses her fingers. "*You're right!* is the finest phrase in all of English!"

"But you didn't have to take me and James and everyone

else down with you," I add harshly, shutting her right up. "You killed innocent people and ruined our lives, Mags!"

The waves splash to my ankles now. Won't be long before the water plucks us away and tosses us out to sea. I imagine the burn of water choking my lungs. The final, salt-stinging sight of the waves before I am carried under. Dark, slimy creatures tearing into my bloated flesh, my body washed up on the beach, and the gulls plucking at the dark sockets of my eyes until they burst and empty and—

Bile spews from my lips. I wipe my mouth with shaking hands, trying and failing to bottle up all the fear and anxiety in me. James shall never know what became of me. He'll think I left and never tried to save him. He'll never know I died thinking of him. My eyes squeeze shut until I see stars. I see our first and last night where we were truly ourselves, the bright, glimmering future we dreamt of. I see it all slip away into the darkness waiting for me.

Maggie shoves a torn bit of her chemise into my fist. Something that appears suspiciously like chagrin tempers her expression. "Elias," she begins softly. "You can't thwart the nobles by pretending to be one of them. You've got to play the villain. Be what they expect you to be and they'll stop looking for you."

"What are you talking about?" I dab at my leaking nose.

"'Tis how you'll save James, if them catching us hasn't cleared his name already. You've got to play the villain."

I bark out a laugh. "Don't be daft. We're three hundred feet below the cliffs on a beach—"

"There's a dock," Maggie says. "About a mile from here around the bend."

"Oh, you mean the one we left from flanked by armed guards? Aye, I'm sure they'll be *thrilled* to see us again."

She rolls her eyes. "'Tis a different dock than the one Dover Castle uses, farther away and near falling off the cliffs. But the soldiers don't know about it, which is what counts. It belongs to an old fisherman and his wife. I suspect he's a smuggler."

I must be giving her an odd look, because she crosses her arms and dons a scowl I know all too well. "You don't think Societas Solis pays me to sit around and look pretty, do you? I'm a great assassin and I do my work! Of course I explored the place and found all the escape routes should things take a turn for the worse, and well"—she gestures to the cliffs behind us—"seems like they have, haven't they?"

"If there's a way out, then why haven't you left me behind already?"

She sighs through her teeth. "I'm not leaving."

"You'll drown if you don't."

She plucks something from a pocket. "Not if I off myself first." In Maggie's hand there's a phial half-full of a dark and familiar liquid. Wolfsbane. More of the same miserable substance I found on Marlowe's person, which launched me on this wretched journey. Zounds, Societas Solis must have an entire cellar of it somewhere.

"What did I tell you about making jests?"

"'Tis not a jest." Her eyes meet mine, and for the first time, something wavers within them. She more falls than limps through the knee-deep water and clasps the phial between both of our hands. A dark shadow billows from her injury and turns the water dark as wine. "Escape isn't certain. 'Tis a long and tough swim to that dock for someone without a busted leg. Even if I did escape, I've failed. And the Societas Solis—" Her voice catches. She swallows and laughs darkly. "Well, let's just say that they don't take kindly to failure."

She's utterly serious about this. A hundred lifetimes pass as we consider each other honestly for the very first time. I tug the bottle from her grasp and uncork it. Maggie gives me an encouraging nod. I nod back.

Then I hurl the bottle straight into the sea, where it sinks into the waves with a plink.

Maggie groans. "Should've expected that. Honestly, do you have any idea how rare and expensive that stuff is?"

"I won't leave you here to die." I snatch her wrist and attempt to drag her away. "I'll help you, and then—then you can go away and leave us alone forever. That's how you'll make it up to me—to us."

Maggie tugs me closer, her dark eyes solemn. "Elias. I've already swallowed the poison. 'Tis a matter of time now." She squeezes my numb hand and guides me to sit beside her in the water.

"But why?"

"I've been in the business of killing long enough to know when someone's worm's meat." She gestures to her leg. "Death by my own hand is better than death by anyone else's. We both know that."

"But—but—" I cast about for a reason to stop her. "'Tis a sin, killing yourself. No one can bury you in the graveyard now."

Maggie's lips part. And then she's throwing back her head, laughing. The sound is so unexpected that all I can do is stare. She wipes tears from her eyes and says, "They wouldn't put my body in a graveyard, I can assure you." Traitors' bodies are buried at the crossroads. Burying a body at the crossroads means that the dead's soul shall never find peace. The thought of a soul wandering lost and unmoored sends a shudder down my spine.

"Why are you helping me escape?"

"Christ," Maggie says softly. "Because despite it all, I meant it when I said you and Inigo are my friends. That's why I couldn't kill you, even though I damn well should've." She points to a distant bend in the cliff. "You'll see the dock just beyond there." I notice the trembling in her hands, the way her veins stand livid against her skin. "Go on, before the current is too strong to swim in."

I nod once, throat tight. Before I overthink it all, I wrap my arms around Maggie. At first she stiffens like a cat wrestled in from the stable but then relaxes the longer I hold on.

"Tell Inigo—tell him—it was real every second." Her whisper is so quiet, I barely hear it over the waves. "All right?"

I hold her tighter. "Of course."

Even though she urges me to go, I stay at Maggie's side as her body quakes, her pulse gallops, until finally, her hand slips from mine into the water gushing about our hips.

I gently close her eyes and place her in the waves. Already, the ocean rushes, spreading her dark hair like a nimbus. A hundred memories flash through me. Maggie, a black shadow on white, pushing the snow from our thatched roof before the ceiling buckled. Maggie shoving a fragrant and warm roll into my hands along with the month's rent we were always short on. Maggie easing closer to me during the coldest nights. Her hooked smirk and unsavory jests. Aye, she was a murderer—there's no disputing that—but she wasn't all bad either. A tender feeling lodges in my chest.

Maggie deserved better from the world.

Seeing her still at last, felled by something as lowly as an arrow, I've got the sense some deadly beast from the deepest waters has just rushed past, choosing to grace me with its presence and not smash my skiff to smithereens. A fabled, powerful creature out of a pirate's tale, impossible to believe in had you not witnessed her with your own two eyes. My hand finds the cross in my doublet, and I whisper a soft prayer. By the time I am done, tears course down my face and drop, one by one, into the water.

Maggie did not find peace in this life; I dearly hope she shall find some measure of it in the next, even though she's far from deserving of it.

But my time on earth is not yet done. I glance at the distant bending cliffs and slowly stand. The water tugs and pulls at my thighs, threatening to drag them out from under me.

James is still waiting.

# CHAPTER THIRTY-SEVEN

I COULDN'T TELL MAGGIE her lifeline was a hangman's rope.

When conditions are good, I'm a rubbish swimmer at best.

And when conditions are bad?

I gasp in a ragged breath before another swell punches me under. Salt stings my eyes, my lips, every cut and scrape. The muscles in my arms and legs scream like I've been swimming for hours, but it's only been minutes. Swimming out farther into the white-capped waves makes my body heavy with dread. The cliff is no closer. In fact, I'm fairly certain I'm being carried back to the underwater beach, closer to Maggie's watery gravesite.

Perhaps the ocean decided she shouldn't sleep alone.

Next time when I'm pummeled underwater, it's a gray blizzard. I push toward the lattice of light above, except something slams into my side, sending me spinning deeper into the swift current. Bubbles burst from my nose, the pressure in my chest building. Just when I'm about to break, when my vision goes spotty and I know I've got to breathe, I pop out on the surface like a cork.

I take in a huge, shuddering breath, blinded by the massive

glittering expanse around me. It's so bright, I must squint to see the mighty white cliffs of the shore. My spirits plummet. I've been dragged farther out to sea. Weariness worms into my bones like a sickness, and the very thought of swimming is more than I can bear. I've survived this long. But to what end? Even if I made it back to Dover Castle, I'd have nothing—truly nothing—to work with. There's no one in those walls who can help me. Not after Gráinne's betrayal.

A dark smudge floats on the horizon, right where the sky meets the shore. I think of the pirate's tale of what dwells in the deep waters—creatures with tentacled limbs, great, fanged beasts big as boats—and a spasm of fear tightens within me.

I set my gaze on the distant shoreline and start swimming.

But the smudge grows closer. So close, I know it's no shard of my imagination playing tricks.

'Tis real.

A boat.

Hope blossoms in my chest, so huge and painful, I may burst.

*"Over here!"* I shout, flailing my arms.

The boat is a slate arrow slicing through the water, right toward me. But then I recognize the figure at the oars, and all the hope seeps out of me.

'Tis Réamonn the pirate lad.

I splash in the opposite direction quick as I can.

"Stop getting further out!" His voice is tinny and far, and it redoubles my efforts. But there's no outswimming a boat, and soon he's right behind me.

"For God's sake, did Gráinne send you out here to make sure the job was done?" I shout, frantically kicking the boat's hull. Like that will make any difference at all.

"No, I came here to save ye, you dolt!" The boy slaps one of his oars before my face, glowering down its length. I glower right back up at him and wipe my hair from my eyes. Does he mean well? Because the last time I trusted a pirate's word, I was tricked and left for dead on a rocky shore.

The pirate lad sighs and jabs my chest with the oar. My breath wheezes out in an oof. "Come on, then! 'Tis this or drowning, and drowning's a nasty way to go."

I don't trust him. Not a bit after what's happened. But I don't want to drown, and if he's rowed all the way out here for me, I can't lie: curiosity makes me want to hear what he has to say.

Gritting my teeth, I grab the oar and drag myself on board, sending the entire boat shuddering. It's tiny, barely bigger than one of the wherries on the river Thames.

"Are you certain this thing will make it back to shore?" I ask Réamonn darkly.

He gives me a sharp-toothed smile. "You certain you weren't heading to France? Because if you kept swimming along with the current, that's where you'd land."

I say nothing. His expression grows smug as he begins to row back to land, going the opposite way of where I'd been swimming.

"Why did Gráinne send you?"

"She didn't. I sent myself. I'd be another dead body in the

lake if it weren't for you." Something grows softer in his fierce look. "I owed you a blood debt. You saved my life, so I had to try and save yours. Wouldn't be right for me to ignore what I owed you. That's how a man loses the favor of his gods."

I snort and cross my arms. "And what's your fair Pirate Queen going to do with you when she finds out you did this?"

Réamonn shrugs. "Nothing, I reckon."

My suspicion must still show, because he curses and punches my arm softly. "Gráinne doesn't care about you and never has. She came here for her son. She'll do anything for him, including making the English queen happy for a summer. And let's be honest, if that Maggie girl truly is the assassin, it doesn't reflect well on you, with the two of you being friends and all."

I bite back a dry laugh. No, it doesn't look good that Maggie was my friend. I doubt there's a single thing I can do to convince Queen Elizabeth we weren't working together at this point. Not when Maggie even managed to fool me and James all those months.

*James*. Even the thought of his name lights me up like a fire. "What word is there of James? Is he . . . ?"

Réamonn shakes his head. "The trial's happening tomorrow." His voice is hedging, careful.

I fix him under a quill-sharp stare. "And?"

His throat bobs. "Might be more like execution, I mean. If the gossip is anything to go by, all this is heading toward a beheading."

I let out a long, shuddering breath and lean back against the hard wooden rail.

*A beheading.* I think of the rotting skulls spiked atop the London Bridge. The dead traitors and criminals James and I walked under all those weeks ago.

They want James to join them.

Nothing's changed. It doesn't matter that the entire court saw Maggie attempt to kill Queen Elizabeth. They still think James is guilty. And why wouldn't they, I suppose, after Queen Elizabeth hustled Maggie and me off to that beach before anyone could hear a word from either of us?

*Save him now, before anything else happens.* I could find where his cell is. Then I could bash open the lock, lead him out of the darkness back into the light.

But what would we do next? Two traitors to the Crown, stuck in the most heavily defended castle in England. We'd be lucky to escape at all. And if we managed to make it beyond the castle walls, within a day the entire countryside would be swarming with searchers after the hefty reward the Crown would surely offer for our return—whether we were dead or alive.

No, in order to save James, I've got to clear his name of his crimes. Only then will he be free of the trouble I've caused him.

*Play the villain.* Maggie's parting words light like a spark in the sky.

And an idea catches within me.

"Do you know of a way for me to get into the castle?"

A pause. Réamonn knows what I've asked him to do. I'm asking him, a foreigner protected here only under the word of a brutal queen, to bring me, a known enemy of the Crown, back into her castle. I'm asking him to risk himself for me. His lips twist as he continues to row, nothing but the murmur of the waves breaking the silence.

"Aye, I know something about that," he says. Our eyes lock. He's got the stare of a grown man who's seen things I'll never see in my life. But behind it, there's still a glint of childlike mischief. He grins slowly. "Don't breathe a word of your scheme to me, though. I want my surprise to be real when it happens."

Dover Castle is like a cauldron the day of James's trial: hot and stuffy and threatening to overboil at any moment.

The great hall deep in the castle's heart has been readied for the trial, long tables pushed aside and every chair in the castle brought within. Nothing matches, and the nobles crowd in elbow to elbow. An enormous candle-branch dangles overhead, each of its dozen arms tipped in fresh fat candles. The entire affair would seem a great feast were it not for the impatience which eddies up to the vaulted ceilings like a foul stench. Whispers scutter in the corners like rats.

*"The queen would rather save face than admit she was wrong."*

*"Zounds, when are we leaving this dreadful place?"*

*"This is no way to treat a lord."*

Hope nudges its way into my heart like a rivulet punching through banks of snow along the winter street.

This might truly work.

When Queen Elizabeth sweeps into the room, a hush falls over the crowd. Nobles scramble out of the circumference of the black skirts which snap out from her waist like a storm cloud. Six guards escort the queen inside and then lock and flank the doors. At the sight, my heart gives an unmanly flip.

I'm clinging to one of the giant wooden beams that arches over the hall, looking down on everything. It's been hours since I scrambled up here in the middle of the night, and my muscles scream with pain, but I fight it. All it takes is for one person to look up, and the plan is ruined.

But when the heavy doors scrape open and James is brought before the queen, I can't hold back a gasp.

He looks awful.

His back is bowed as an old man's. Great shadows stamp the hollows of his cheekbones. When the guards force him to his knees before the queen and the snarls of his hair fall back, his face registers nothing at all. 'Tis as though the spark of life has already left his eyes.

Rage—wild and hot—pours through me.

The queen did this to him—she and Cecil and everyone else who thought one man's life was a fair price to pay for a queen's peace of mind.

"James Edmund Bauffremont of Bloomsbury, you are here today to stand trial for your sister's murder. How do you plead?" Lord Cecil sneers.

"I have told you time and time again I did not do this thing." James's tone is civil enough, but his words are filled with iron. "Clearly it matters not what I have or have not done."

Whispers break out like the buzz of a hornet's nest.

"You would proclaim your innocence, then?" Cecil says down his nose.

James inclines his head. "I would. Even if this court has no interest in truth."

The whispers grow fiercer among the nobles. Tendons bulge on the queen's hands where they clutch the throne. "Insolent boy. Do you care nothing for your life?"

James meets the queen with a stare that could level a mountain. "What else could you possibly take from me?"

The crowd's murmuring grows louder. My heart swells with savage pride. That's my cue—or as good of a cue as I'm going to get.

I touch the cross tucked against my chest and stand. The ceiling beam shivers under my feet. Someone beneath me starts to look up.

I step off the beam into nothingness.

For a single, heart-ending moment, I fall.

Then I land on the candle-branch with a scream of rending metal. Candles singe my clothes, and hot tallow scalds my skin. The candle-branch swings wildly. Nobles scream and churn beneath me.

I launch myself from the ceiling fixture and land in a crouch right before the queen's throne.

*Play the villain.*

I brush a smidge of dust from my shoulder and bob a curtsy. "My queen, we meet again. I can assure you the pleasure is all mine."

Queen Elizabeth's black eyes widen.

Fresh screams bellow from the assembled nobles, who all but trample one another in their haste to leave. As they very well should: an assassin is back from the dead and here for blood.

"You—you're dead!" Queen Elizabeth shouts, gnarled hands white on her throne. She looks to the guards posted at the closed doors. They're too far away to reach me in time, and we both know it. "My men watched you drown themselves!"

"Did they now?" I draw a stolen sword from its scabbard. "Or did they tell you they watched us drown, and you believed them?" The queen's eyes cut over to Cecil, who's gone pale as milk. I give him a wink, and he flinches deliciously. "See, that's one difference between your people and mine. When Societas Solis decides to kill someone, we make sure the work is done."

The queen's eyes dart to James, whose expression is as shocked as anyone else's.

I cackle at the sight. "Did you truly believe this gullible man was a part of our scheme? He thinks the best of people— aye, even ones like me and Maggie—and we tricked him into bringing us into his home. To bring us to *you*."

Maggie may have told me to play the villain—but the time for playing is long past. If I end it all here, if I manage to convince Queen Elizabeth I was a part of the plot and finish the assassination Maggie started, then no one else has to die.

James will be free.

And me?

Well. There was never a good way out of this mess for me. I'll finally be the villain they always imagined me to be.

At least I'll have been slain doing something that matters, something that changes things for good. They'll chronicle my name in histories and plays, and breathless crowds will press into the theaters of London's South Bank to witness my deeds onstage for years. Zounds, even my family, distant as they are, will hear what I have become.

*Queen killer.*

There's a rather nice ring to that—isn't there?

"Elias." My name soft as starlight on James's lips. His eyes are shining and so very wide, as if he's never seen all of me before. "Don't. Please."

'Tis his hand that nearly undoes me. A lifting, helpless gesture, an attempt to stand betwixt me and the horrible decision I'm about to make.

But I must do this. And I'm doing it for him and Maggie and my family and everyone else who has been wronged by brutal, cruel England and its black-hearted ruler.

Our gazes lock for an endless moment. Even though the rest of court seems tricked by my speech—some of them even rise to pull James away from me, the killer—nothing in his heartrending expression wavers. He believes in me.

He always has.

*Remember me.* The wish is a beat of blood.

I rush to sheathe my blade in the queen's chest, proving James's innocence even as I condemn my own.

A sudden crack sounds overhead. Some animal instinct urges me to move, and I barely somersault out of the way before the candle-branch crashes down and the great hall goes crimson.

Flames kindle along the queen's wooden dais, leap to

hastily vacated chairs. The stink of singed upholstery already burns my nose even though only a breath of time has passed. Panic sharper than an axe blade slices right through me.

*Fire.*

More than the plague, there is nothing deadlier in all of London than fire. A flicker, catching, spreading, consuming entire blocks before the bells toll the next hour.

I've put all our lives in danger.

Nobles fight to escape and trample the guards frantically unlocking the great double doors. The queen writhes on her throne like a stuck shiny beetle, shouting for her guards and court to come closer, to free her, but the flames stand betwixt her and everyone else.

James. Where is he?!

I scamper atop an abandoned chair, frantically searching for his familiar silhouette, but the room's gone dark as twilight and there's nothing to see. *He could be anywhere.* Crushed under the crowd, trapped beneath the candle-branch, choking in some corridor. There's no time to find out. Already the smoke eddies to the rafters, hiding the ceiling from view, and more and more soldiers pour in with shields and stones to smother the flames. Either the fire or their blades will get me should I linger. My plan has slipped its pen like an angry bull determined to crush all in its path.

I feel for the wooden cross against my chest. *Please keep him safe.*

And I run.

The entire castle shudders in the stampede. Smoke pours

down the white halls in a black rush, scorching my eyes and burning my throat. The crowd is a seething, frantic mass. No one recognizes me for now, but I know when the fire's contained, that won't last.

A hallway branches off on my left; I tear down it and vault up the stairs. I wrench open the first door I find and slam it behind me. The din grows quieter, and I double over in a fit of coughing.

A throat clears.

James's fiancée, Lady Anne Middlemore, stands behind me, her face the very portrait of shock.

"Lord Hughes. I thought you were dead."

"A common misconception," I choke out, before another cough overtakes me. God Almighty, I managed to duck into the bedchamber of one of the only people in all of Dover Castle who would recognize me through any disguise? I grope for my sword, belatedly realizing I've dropped it in the fray.

"Did you save him?" Lady Anne says, something unreadable in her pale eyes.

"I—I *tried* to."

Somewhere deep in the castle, a fresh wave of screams begins. A gush of warmth pours beneath the door, reeking of burnt hair. Lady Anne tips her head. "I take it this is your doing?" she asks brusquely, as if soot-stained would-be assassins drop into her bedchamber all the time.

I shrug, neither confirming nor denying my guilt.

She stares at me for a long moment. Then all at once she sighs and shakes out her hands. "Right then. Let's get out of here."

My head snaps up. "What?"

She's already fastening on her cloak, as if she's going on a fashionable promenade and not escaping an actual fire. "Your ears still work—do they not?"

"Why are you helping me?" I've been at the unlucky end of a too-good-to-be-true deal before.

Lady Anne's lips twist. "Because I need Bloomsbury—all right? You've seen what kind of terrible man my father is. Imagine calling him kin. He'd make me wrestle bears in the pits if he thought it would secure his fortune and title." She turns with a snap of her cloak, voice bitter. "A marriage would be my surest escape from my father's house. If your little stunt is persuasive enough to clear Bloomsbury's name—which I'm assuming it shall be, since you've somehow managed to set the castle on fire—then we'll be free to marry. I don't love him at all, but he's kind, and that's rarer than diamonds and gold in the queen's court."

Her cold practicality makes my skin prickle. "You're asking me to let James go so he can marry you. What makes you think that'll work?"

She inclines her head. "I know he'll follow through on the wedding because I'll have saved you, and I know he cares for you more than anyone else." She smiles, the expression barbed. "I can assure you, marrying a man would not be my preferred way out of this conundrum, but I imagine setting the castle aflame was not your preferred solution to your own problems either, was it?"

There's a splintering sound, followed by a roar. She jerks

her head toward the door. "We've got to go. Unless you'd rather be burned to death or have me turn you in to the guards?"

One of her three choices is obviously better than the rest. "Ready when you are."

She purses her lips at the sight of me. "Not like that you're not."

Lady Anne turns to her chest and then shoves a pile of lace and silk into my arms. A dress. She meets my stare over the fabric, one brow quirked. "I understand you are familiar with such garments, Master Hughes?"

For the first time since I can remember, a real smile tugs at my lips. "Aye, you could say that."

In the end, not even Marlowe or Shakespeare could make up an escape quite like this. Me, sneaking through Dover Castle disguised in the skirts of my beloved's betrothed. Lady Anne doesn't stop when we get outside, either, but instead brings me straight through the milling crowds and beyond the impenetrable castle walls.

"Don't say anything. The less we speak, the better." She must see the questions in my eyes, for she adds, "Please shut up."

The whiff of manure and straw oozes from the closest outbuilding. 'Tis the stables. Lady Anne glances over her shoulder before opening up a servants' door and shoving me inside. "Stay here. You'll be able to steal a horse and leave after dark. Don't do anything ill-advised between now and then." She looks my person up and down. "I know that'll be difficult for you."

I manage to stick my boot betwixt the sill and the door before she can slam it in my face. "No! I need to know what's happened to James. I won't leave without knowing!" He could still be imprisoned by the queen. He could be injured. He could be dead.

Lady Anne rolls her eyes. "If he's dead, 'tis your fault."

I growl and press my shoulder against the door, wedging it open farther. "Then I'll go back and look for him myself!"

She throws up her hands in defeat. "Fine! Hide here, and I'll learn what I can and return. All right?" We stare at each other for a long moment. Something of the fear and anxiety and exhaustion in me must reach my face, because she softens. "I didn't say this before. Thank you for doing your best—"

"Thank *you* for finally saying that—"

She interrupts me with an arched brow. "But let us hope your best is good enough, shall we?"

She kicks my boot away, and the door slams shut.

# CHAPTER THIRTY-EIGHT

THE STABLE RAGES with rumors all the next day, each one more fantastical than the last. Spain has sailed up the Thames, and London is under siege. The devil set fire to the great hall, and his hoofed prints are burnt black against the stone floor. Some go as far as to swear that God himself placed his hand over the queen's heart so that neither fire nor blade could pierce it.

And I am left wondering: Is this how history is made? From a patchwork of whispers and murmurs which buries the single scrap of truth so deep that none can recognize it?

I think on this and more from my hiding place in the stable's hayloft. It's been a day, and there's been nothing from Lady Anne. It would be easy to imagine I dreamt her involvement in the entire event, were it not for the lady's clothes shoved in the loft's farthest corner. God Almighty, why did I ever listen to that girl? More than once last night I crept to the stable door and twisted the handle to behold Dover Castle glittering like a full moon where the land met the sky. It would be so easy to do it, slip outside this time to see for myself if James is well or not—

The barn door creaks open, so soft, I nearly miss it.

I cautiously peer over the edge. 'Tis late enough that no one ought to be here. In the aisle betwixt the horse stalls is a man holding a lantern.

My heartbeat crescendos as, step by step, the figure draws closer. Then I recognize him, and my heart all but bursts from my chest.

*James.*

The sight of him alive and whole brings tears to my eyes. I wipe them away with an unsteady hand, but they come too fast. *He's alive.* The overwhelming certainty of it steals my strength, pinning me in place.

He walks carefully, his earnest face holding the expression of a sleeper newly awakened, desperate to hold on to the last dregs of a dream. I nearly call out to him, but the dread knocks the words right out of my lungs. *If you talk to him, you'll have to tell him what you've done.* That it's all my fault his sister is dead and he's been imprisoned, because I trusted Maggie.

After all that's happened, I cannot bear to see the light leave his eyes when he looks at me. He's alive, and that's what I needed to know. I'd rather him remember me like this, a maybe-there shadow, one that flitted across his life so quick, he will hardly be able to know if it was real or a dream years from now.

I draw back from the edge of the loft, every inch farther from James more difficult to stand, but then—traitorous boards!—a squeak in the loft gives me away.

"Elias?" James's whisper is soft with hope. "Are you truly here?"

My name on his lips is like a summoning spell. Beneath me is James, my James, all full of tenderness even after all that's happened to him.

I clamber down the ladder, the thud of my boots like each pulse of blood in my temples. He's *there*. Just in the lantern light after all this time. I trip on the last rung and fall into him. He catches me in his arms, the lantern handle sliding down to nestle in the crook of his elbow.

We drink each other in for a single, stunned moment, and then he crushes me to his chest. "By God, it's really *you*."

This close 'tis easier to spot the gauntness of his cheekbones, the fingernails bitten to the quick. All the scars my work has left on him.

I squeeze my eyes shut and cling to him fiercely. He's alive; he's really here in my arms. Flesh and bone and that wild, beating heart I think of more than anything else on earth. There's a hundred things I want to tell him, but a sudden shyness scrambles the words all up, and instead I can only murmur, "I missed you, too."

We stand like that for a long time before pulling away. He traces my jaw with his thumb, his expression filled with wonder, like he can't believe what he's seeing. "I knew the assassin couldn't be you. But when I saw you there with that blade and the look on your face—"

I swallow hard and catch his hand. Here it is, the moment I've been dreading. "I played at being the assassin. But Maggie—it was her. She was part of Societas Solis. Everything terrible that's happened is because I trusted her."

James slips from me and shudders with revulsion, the movement going through every part of him. I keep waiting for my heart to shatter, but instead a stark calm fills me, like throwing open the shutters on a frigid day. He finally knows. I no longer have to carry this secret like a dead thing, heavy and rotting upon my back. The lightness is almost unbearable.

James clenches his fists and forces himself to look at me. "I know."

"I—what do you mean?"

"I know," he repeats. "Do you think the guards of Dover Castle do not gossip? They are men, and they have tongues. I knew of Maggie's betrayal and your involvement even before my trial. It was all they could talk about after the battle, and none of them could answer my questions about you. I was so worried." His touch skims gently down my arms, catching my hands in his. They're trembling.

I stare at his raw, bruised knuckles. I was braced for his hate and his anger and, aye, even his tears, which would have undone me utterly. "Then why aren't you furious? 'Tis my fault all these terrible things happened. Catherine was killed because of me."

He takes me into his arms again. His brow nudges against mine. "They said you had been cast into the sea. I thought you'd *died*, Elias. I thought I'd lost you and Catherine both. And it broke me." His hand catches in the curls at my nape, so tight, it hurts. "When I saw you in the great hall, I thought I had died and by some dark miracle we were together in hell." His voice takes on a raw edge. "And I was *happy* about it because I never thought I would see you again in this life."

I press myself closer to ease the anguish in his expression, to banish the fear in his gaze as he lingers in his bleak memory. "A hell with you is better than a heaven without you, to be certain. But there's no reason to fear anymore, love. All is well now."

My words coax a faint laugh from him, and I feel the tension leave his body. "I suppose you're right."

A giddy brightness in me catches and spreads, blotting out all else. Against all odds, we survived. And if that's not a bloody miracle, then I don't know what is.

I bury both my hands in his hair and kiss him with everything I've got. "Then let's away now, before something new and dreadful happens. Why, we could be in Antwerp before sunset tomorrow!" I grab his hand and drag him toward the horses. I can already see the Flemish city spreading like an ink-blot at the edge of the sea. Our ship, nosing into the harbor, church spires poking over the city's walls like crooked fingers beckoning us beyond the gates.

But James doesn't budge. When I turn back to him, his eyes shimmer strangely. The sight sends something cold through me. "What is it?"

"Lady Anne told the queen about us and about my feelings for you. The queen has pardoned me. She believed your act and thinks you and Maggie were behind everything, including pulling me into your schemes unknowingly. But she also says that my affection for you blinded me to my senses and my duty to Crown and country. To prove my devotion to the queen, I am to marry Anne and go to her father's New World lands as soon as possible, or my life and yours, should they ever catch you again, shall be forfeit."

*Exile.* The word rips through me like a rapier. James is being sent to rot an entire world away. "When?" I gasp out, staggering sideways.

"I'm to be married a month hence." He swallows, a hard knot moving down the column of his throat. "Then I—or we, I suppose, are to leave for the New World in the months following."

The air crushes from my lungs. James is exiled to the New World—a place so far, it might as well be the sun. It is not death but the next closest thing.

No. Too much has been taken from me. I'll not let him go too.

My fists clench. "There must be a way to escape this."

"Elias."

"I do not jest! It can be fixed, we—"

"Elias—"

I pound my fist into the wall and relish the hurt as my knuckles split. "Zounds, James, why are you trying to stop me?"

He cups my face in his hands, stilling me, forcing me to look him in the eyes. "Because I thought you had died once, and I never want to feel that way again. I've already lost my sister. If you go now, I'll know you're safe." Tears spill down his cheeks. "I promised to keep you safe."

I try to argue, but he shakes his head, stopping me before I even begin. I see it in his expression, the terrible grief that has carved hollows in his cheeks. There's nothing I can say to persuade him. He's come here to say goodbye.

A terrible sob splits me wide open because he's right. I know he's right, and I hate it more than I've hated anything in my entire life. Stories like ours do not have happy endings. I have always known this, but I let myself forget for one wild, strange summer night. Saving James always meant letting him go forever. Our stars were always cursed.

We sink to the dirt, so tangled up I cannot tell where he ends and I begin, nor whose tears dampen my face.

"Have courage, beloved." He traces the curve of my spine over and over again like it's an arrow to some secret shore only for us. "When Elizabeth is dead and gone, I shall sail back from the New World and find you."

'Tis a lie.

We both know this is true.

But ofttimes a lie is not a lie but a fiction we must tell ourselves to make life bearable. To move on instead of staying stuck forever in what-could-have-beens.

I catch his chin and kiss him once more with everything I've got. But there's a bang and scuttle—the sound of shock and someone slipping away. Over James's shoulder, I see the barn door swinging gently, and a chill grips me.

Someone's seen us. 'Tis only a matter of time before more prying eyes come.

I reach up and try to smooth the lines on his brow one last time. "Can you help me escape?"

His breath catches. "Now?"

I nod, my throat suddenly swelling.

He tilts my face up to his, his thumb stroking my jaw. He

does it for so long, the moment grows tender and aching. "I hate the thought of you striking out alone."

"I have started over before," I say, voice cracking.

His thumb stops moving. "Elias—"

I pull away. I can't let him break too. If he does, I'll never be able to leave him, and then the goddamned queen will find us, and this time, we shall not escape.

"I want you to have this." I drop my cross into his hand.

His eyes widen. "I cannot take this."

I fold his fingers over it and shove his hand away. "Please, just keep it."

The last thing my mother ever did for me was slip me her cross as a reminder of home and the love that went with it. If James is to be exiled—if he's truly to go across the world from me—then I know he has more need of it than I do now.

He tucks the item away, his hand lingering on the small object a moment longer than necessary. "Then I insist on giving you something as well." He unlatches one of the stable doors and lets out the beast within.

'Tis his horse, Ares, saddled and ready to go.

"What's this?"

"What does it look like? I am giving you a horse."

"But he's your favorite horse."

He shoves the reins into my hand, almost laughing. "Yes. Please do not sell him if you can help it."

We share a wan smile, but it fades at once, the light moment not enough to overtake the dread that hangs from me like a waterlogged cloak.

We venture into the star-filled night. No one stops us. I press him into the wall and kiss him desperately, finally, my hands roving across the lines and angles of him. I know not if the stars are the same where he is going. But beneath me, his body is a constellation—points and curves of light I'll never forget.

When we pull away, both of us are panting and damp. The sky blushes blue to the east, and not too far beyond is the murmur of men's voices. The castle is waking up.

His hands cup into a stirrup. "Hurry, before someone comes."

I consider his hands for a long, long moment. Then I place my foot in them and heave myself into the saddle.

James stares up at me, his face shining and familiar and so unbearably lovely. I take in every plane of it, knowing the memory will grow soft and faded over time and this final look must last me forever. "I love you. More than I've ever loved anyone else before."

He leans his brow against my thigh—the tallest part of me he can reach. "And I you."

More words catch in my throat. I swallow them back and instead take off toward the glittering town of Dover below. My gaze is forward, into the rushing black unknown, so that I never witness the only boy I've ever loved disappearing behind me.

# Eight Months Later
## April 1594

*It lies not in our power to love or hate,*
*For will in us is overruled by fate.*
*When two are stripped long ere the course begin,*
*We wish that one should lose, the other win;*
*And one especially do we affect*
*Of two gold ingots, like in each respect:*
*The reason no man knows, let it suffice,*
*What we behold is censured by our eyes.*
*Where both deliberate, the love is slight:*
*Who ever loved, that loved not at first sight?*

—CHRISTOPHER MARLOWE,
from *Hero and Leander*

# CHAPTER THIRTY-NINE

APRIL IN LONDON is a sharp-eyed sparrow hopping forth to see what all the fuss is about, cold dampness giving way to a tentative warmth. The rain lingers, heavy and lush, and if I close my eyes and breathe deeply, the whole city falls away, if only for a second.

I sprint down Cheapside, late, and pass by a notice board whose posters mold and peel in the rain. I tear one off and stuff it in my pocket.

Already a queue snakes out the door of my destination. I shoulder through the crowd inside.

"Oy, no leaping the line!" One moon-faced maid scowls at me. "I been waiting half an hour for this bread!"

Inigo's bakery, it turns out, has been quite the success.

He has called it, somewhat unwisely in my opinion, Maggie's Revenge. When pressed why pastries and vengeance go hand in hand, he only shrugged and said, "Pastries and vengeance were Maggie's favorite things."

It is a most treasonous bakeshop, and I hope the queen never hears of it.

The bakery opened only a month ago, and already Inigo can barely keep up with the demand. I go to the kitchen and exchange my cloak for an apron. Inigo is already there, shoveling loaves into the oven's belly with a wooden paddle. I take the paddle from him and push him toward the front.

"About time you got back here. The customers have been grumbling all morning."

"I was wrenched away."

Inigo plucks something off the floor. "Wrenched away by this, were you?"

The crumpled poster has tumbled out from my pocket. 'Tis a fair likeness of my face emblazoned with the words WANTED, REWARD across the top.

"You know, the more of those you take down, the more Lord Cecil and the queen will suspect you're in London," Inigo says.

"I know." But the thrill I get from prodding the monarch and spymaster just a little more each time I remove a poster is worth the risk for me. As a wanted criminal in the most populous city in all of England, it isn't as though I have many other thrills to chase. Until the bakery opened, I rarely ventured outside in daylight. Even now, the cheerful sun feels like a blade tickling the back of my neck. Stealing Cecil's posters is a small freedom I allow myself in a city that has become my prison.

Perhaps Maggie was not the only one who enjoyed vengeance.

While Inigo and I work side by side all day and sleep in the same room overhead, we rarely speak of what happened last year. He carries his pain in his own way—how he throws himself into discovering new recipes, or how he has recently started to linger too late at the alehouses. We do not speak of it, because there is nothing to say. We both live around the shape of people who used to be in our lives. We go on because the only other option is to give up.

I only tried to see James once.

Unsensible fool that I am, I went to the church on the day of his wedding.

The September roses hanging on the gates were redolent with a rot. The church bells tolled out merrily, but to me their song was a funeral dirge. The church itself—all white with peaked spires like whipped cream—was an absolute dream.

I sat on my horse, Ares, a fair distance away as the guests all came out and then, finally, the bride and groom in a shower of flower petals.

James was smiling. And that was all I needed to see.

Aside from Inigo, there's only one person in all of London who knows I've returned. And when I find him leaning against the bakery's wall after the morning rush, too earnest and clutching that blasted play again, it takes all the patience in my soul not to scream.

"Shakespeare," I hiss. "What'd I tell you about hanging around here?"

"Please, Hughes, you've got to audition for Juliet. We can hide your hair under a wig and change your name. No one needs to know it's you!" The playwright brandishes the script, and *The Tragedy of Romeo and Juliet* nearly pokes out my eye. "You've simply got to audition! You and that Bloomsbury boy inspired this one!"

I turn away. Hearing his name unexpectedly scalds me like an ember. "'Tis a play about a rich boy and girl who fall in love. Not seeing much of myself in that tale, I must say."

Shakespeare waves my complaints away. "'Tis more exciting when they're nobles; we both know that. And no one wants to see men fall in love. What they want to see—"

His words stoke the anger that's always smoldering in my belly. Before he can finish, I grab the playwright—play and all—and shove him out into the street beyond. "My acting days are over, Shakespeare! Find some other lad to play your lass."

A flash of a cloak whipping about the corner catches my eye. When I return inside the bakery, I spot the cloak and its owner sitting in a corner, eating a pastry and pretending to look outside. 'Tis the third time I have seen him this week.

If he did not linger during the lull between the morning and evening rushes, and if he swapped out the fancy cloak once in a while, I may have never noticed he was there again.

I groan. Lord Cecil should know better than to send novices to spy on me.

I go to the kitchen for Inigo.

"The ginger lad is back. He might've heard me booting Shakespeare out again."

He lifts his head and sighs. "Would you like me to ask him to leave?"

I drum my fingers against the doorframe. "If you did, it would only remind Cecil that you're still in London. As far as his spy lad here would know, I have hoodwinked you into harboring a known criminal and enemy of the Crown. But

Cecil would know my being with you is no trick or accident."

His brow puckers. "That. . . does not seem ideal for business."

"It does not."

There's a long pause. Inigo drags a hand through his dark curls. He gnaws on the bottom of his lip. I wait patiently for him to spit out whatever's on his mind.

"Elias, you know you have a home with me as long as you please . . . but perhaps it's time to go find your family?"

I have procrastinated this for months. At first I told myself it was because I owed it to a grief-stricken Inigo to help him open his bakery. Then I told myself it was because winter is a dangerous time to travel. Then I convinced myself the roads were too damaged to set off in the spring.

However, I can no longer hide the truth from myself: I lingered because I was hoping—daring to hope, really—that James would pass by Maggie's Revenge and know I was here. That he would come find me. Even though it goes against all sense and reason and would endanger both of our lives, I still wanted him to come.

But I am tired of waiting to be found when no one is looking.

"Seems for the best now that Maggie's Revenge is finally open." I ignore the swoop in my stomach. "I shall set out tonight. I don't want Cecil's man to spot me again and ask you questions."

Even with setting up Inigo's bakery, I still possess a fair amount of the coin James stashed in the saddlebags. I use it to procure my supplies that afternoon and search my soul for the spark of joy or excitement that should accompany me setting off to find my family, but instead all I've got is a rootless anxiety that tangles my innards like a bad meal. This is what I have wanted for years, is it not? My time in London was always temporary. Things are as they should be now.

Except the hollow feeling only grows vaster.

Ares is saddled and packed as the sun begins to kiss the horizon. Inigo gives me a cloth-wrapped parcel for dinner. "Zounds, I can't believe you're finally leaving."

I smile wistfully. "Remember when I said I'd only stay with you a fortnight?"

Inigo laughs. "I knew it was a lie as soon as you said it."

"Then why'd you let me stay?"

His eyes skitter away from mine. "I liked having you around."

Which implies I've since worn out my welcome. Not for the first time, I wonder how much he knew about Maggie's machinations and whether Inigo is partly to blame for what happened to me and James. He refuses to speak of it, which is, perhaps, all the answer I need.

"If I ever return to London, you'll be the first person I find—all right?"

"You had better." Inigo steps forward and embraces me. I hug him back and marvel at how easily goodbyes come to me. Perhaps it is my true calling—walking away and moving on. At this depressing thought, the hollow feeling yawns so wide, I fear it'll devour me whole. I straighten and swallow back the part of me that wants to say, *Wait, not now. Not yet.*

Inigo steps back and dabs at his eyes with the hem of his apron. "And, Elias?"

"Yes?"

"If he comes, I shall tell him where you have gone." There is no judgment on Inigo's face—only devastating kindness.

I cannot bear to witness it. My eyes drop to my boots. "Thank you. You were a true friend."

"Still am. I'm not dead yet."

We share a wry grin. "No, I suppose not."

At one point, leaving London felt like an impossible task. Something others could do, but not me. But that evening, as I pass through the city walls, leaving is the easiest thing in the world. Only one step forward, and another, until the city vanishes into the rolling green countryside as if it were never there at all.

# CHAPTER FORTY

THE AIR IS so sharp with salt, it hurts to draw breath.

My horse, Ares, picks his way down a pebbled trail along a ridge overlooking the sea. The grass grows lush in the fields, and weathered cottages with yellow thatched roofs dot the hills.

Every time I see one, my heart lodges in my throat. *It could be them.* I cannot remember quite how my family cottage differed from the other farmers'. All my memories are scraps too small to stitch together. My brother's sleepy, warm breath in the dark; a red ribbon tied in my sister's hair; my mother's singing voice rolling like the hills around us; my father's musky sweat as he returned from a long day in the fields.

I'm almost home.

Home, a place I can barely remember.

While traveling, I spent freely of my money and made my journey as a gentleman and not a beggar. But now that I'm in Devonshire again, I remember the winters: how the rain lashed against the shutters, and the wind was filled with a cold so deep, the ache did not unthaw until well into April. I thumb the leather satchel at my belt and wonder: Is this enough? Have I enough coin to satisfy this hungry landscape and spare my family from the toil and poverty which forced me from them years ago?

There, tucked into a lee against the coastal wind, I finally spot our cottage.

'Tis the blackberry bramble that gives it away, wild and twisting. The memory returns to me with the suddenness of a forgotten dream—sticky palms and pricked fingers.

Beyond the cottage, brown sheep graze. A young woman has her back to me, tending the creatures. Her red hair glints golden in a long braid.

My heart stills. Then stops.

My sister is exactly how I have been imagining her for ten years.

I dismount from Ares and tie his reins to the saddle pommel with shaking fingers.

We would assail the blackberry bramble each summer, our hands and mouths purple for days, lying to our younger brother about where the fruit had all gone. I can all but taste the burst of flavor on my tongue, sweet as a promise.

I reach the edge of the fence when my legs are shaking too much to go farther. "Margaret?" My voice falters. "'Tis . . . me, Elias."

She jerks up. And begins to scream.

Oh no, dear God. This girl is not my sister at all.

I lurch toward her. "Wait, I have questions! I mean you no harm!" The girl sprints past me farther into the pasture, screaming all the way. My words only make her run faster.

The door of the cottage bangs open. "What d'you want

with my daughter?" An older woman stands there with a kitchen knife trembling in one hand and her arm around a small child sucking his thumb.

Too late I remember that I am dressed fashionably and look the very part of a rakehell from head to foot. "Nothing, I swear. I'm looking for someone."

Her eyes narrow, and I realize that *looking for someone* is ominously vague, and a man who does possess the appearance of my station would not be out here for innocent reasons.

I hold up both hands very slowly. "My family used to live in this cottage. Do you know the people who were here before?"

The woman considers me for a long, hard moment before lowering the knife. "No. 'Twas abandoned when we came here two years hence."

I swallow back the acid which churns in my throat. "Do you know where the family who lived here might have gone? Do your neighbors? Can I come in and have a look around?" There's a desperate edge to my voice. I wonder if the dried poppies Mother placed under the eaves are still there. I wonder if I can find the spot where my brother and I scratched our names into the stone.

The woman edges closer to the door. "Sir, you ought to leave."

I follow her. "No, please—"

The door slams in my face.

Scraping sounds from within, as though someone is barricading the door. I stare at the weathered wood, disbelieving.

My family is missing.

Gone.

The promise my mother made me—*we will never leave here*—broken.

All at once the loneliness of it wallops me in the gut, harder than a blow. Did they leave? Are they dead? A fresh horror fills me. The queen spoke my siblings' names and knew this town. Did she send her soldiers here to butcher the people I love beneath a Tudor rose flag? Is this why no one from the court bothered to find me in London? Because they had already devised a punishment far crueler than death for me?

No. The farmer's wife said the cottage was abandoned two years ago. Well before the queen set eyes upon me. *They left because it took you years to return,* a wicked voice whispers. *If you had done better—if you had tried harder to return—it wouldn't have ended like this.*

Numb, I mount Ares and let the horse carry me wherever he pleases.

The sun's fingers stretch long and golden over the glorious fields. Night is falling, and I am lost in every possible sense of the word. Out here where no one can hear, I let great shuddering sobs tear through me. *Too late. I'm too late. I'm always too late.* The sky is the color of a bruised plum before exhaustion settles over my body heavy as a winter cloak.

Did my family leave because they were forced to?

Or did they leave because they wanted to?

What would make my mother break her promise to me? I move to touch the cross in my inner pocket, but—there's nothing. I gave it to *him*. The hollow ache opens in me again.

The dismal thoughts circle like vultures, plucking at the last dregs of my resolve. I cannot be false to myself. A part of me—a large part of me—wants to lie down. To give up. I've already struggled so much. I had a secret hope that this final leg of my journey would be easy. That a happy ending would be waiting for me.

Except . . . did I truly wander this far to give up so easily?

I scrape my sleeve under my eye and sit straighter in the saddle, grabbing the reins once more. The queen of England fears me. I've survived pirates and assassins and worse. I can't give up yet. There's a thousand reasons for my family to not be here, and I shouldn't give up until I've explored them all.

There's exactly one inn, with two rooms, in the quaint seaside town of Hope Cove. I book one for a fortnight up front and continue my search. Even though I lived just beyond the fishing village as a child, my memories of that time are worn thin and faded. I forgot that Devonshire can be lovely. The green is overwhelming after a near lifetime of London gray. Chartreuse fields, velvet-thick moss clinging to the crags that overlook the beaches with their rainbow pebbles and the turquoise tides. In the water bob the fishermen's boats like children's toys, noisy specks of seagulls always in their wakes like flocks of courtiers attending to their sovereign. Clouds thick as butter skim overhead, casting deep emerald shadows over the cottages and ripe gardens and fleecy pastures I visit deep in the countryside, asking everyone and anyone if they know of the Wildes. I'm met with shaking heads and apologetic shrugs. I start describing

them by their looks instead. Perhaps they changed their surname, just as I had to in London, to distance themselves from
their connection to being on the losing side of a brutal, treasonous rebellion that cost them all but their lives. Descriptions
earn me a few nods and thoughtfully stroked chins. *Yes, there
was a family who looked like that. Aye, a boy a bit younger
than you used to help us with the harvest. Haven't seen him for
a few seasons. There was a girl, too, yes; she made the loveliest
seagrass baskets!*

I tuck each borrowed memory and insight away, like trea-
sures found by the barefoot children who comb the beaches
and dredge the sea for its secrets, hoping each day this time
they'll find gold from the shipwrecks in the Channel just
beyond the sheltered bay.

My family *was* here recently, I think. Under a different
name from the one we came here with. But they're here no
longer, and no one knows the why or the how of it. To be this
close, to step where they stepped and see what they saw and
still not see *them*, is nearly more painful than all the time I
spent yearning in faraway London.

Each day I go out, the church perched on a hill above the
village watches me like an eagle. When I return as the sun sets,
the shadows of the crosses in its graveyard stretch long and
sharp over the village buildings tucked under its wing. They
reach through the windows of the inn where I dine, and I try
to ignore them. The church is the only place I truly remember
from my childhood. The cold dampness sinking into my body
at services that lasted an eternity in a child's mind. We did not

go often because it was far away, but I remember the vicar—a venerable old man—who sometimes shared iridescent shells with the children after the sermon. If there's a place in all of Hope Cove that has the answers I seek, it's the church and its graveyard of names and the old vicar's book that tracks all the births, marriages, and deaths for the parishioners. I should have gone there first, but I chose not to. If I don't find answers in the church, it means my search in Hope Cove is at its end, and I've learned nothing. And if I should find my answers there . . . I've a feeling they're not the sort of answers I'd want to find.

But after days of getting nowhere and learning nothing, I've no choice. 'Tis time to visit the church and confront whatever is waiting for me.

"Not taking your horse today?" the innkeeper asks that morning. She's an older woman with a suspicious, scrunched face who has not bought my lies about being a distant cousin of the people I search for. Enough men travel through the town that she knows Ares is of good stock, and more than once I catch her eyes running over my fine clothes and boots, and I know she knows I am not telling my whole story.

I murmur some excuse she won't believe and give her extra coin with which to feed Ares for the day. She counts it and pockets it with shrewd fingers. I still feel her gaze on me as I hike up the too-green hill to the church spire above, wondering who I am and how I'm able to pay her so freely. Could she know I'm a wanted man in London? A cold finger of unease races down my spine. She shouldn't know that—not far out here, where Queen Elizabeth's court feels more myth than flesh and blood—but I know Cecil is spiteful. I know he knows this is where my family fled, even if they're no longer here.

I know he knows there's a chance I'm here too.

My time here is running out, and I'm no closer to finding my family.

The church sits like a sentinel on the hill. Most of the white stone walls are covered with verdant moss which also creeps over the crumbling rock wall around the graveyard. Grave markers, some crosses, some simple stones, rise from the plush vegetation. The oldest of them are completely velveted in green, listing away from the sea from years of weathering its storms. Others are near pristine with their freshness. My throat grows tight. I make my way over to the newer grave markers and start to read.

The sun ascends to its midday throne in a cloudless blue sky. My doublet is long discarded in a patch of violets. The back of my neck itches with sunburn, and my skin is sticky with sweat. I lick my too-dry lips and squat lower, brushing the dew-damp grass away from another gravestone, squinting at the name and date. Every time I see one of my family members' names in the stone, my pulse lunges like a startled hare, but the dates are always wrong. Or the last name is a name from a foreign land. The work whittles away my composure, leaving my heart raw and bruised.

Well after midday a calm shadow cuts over me. "You've been here for hours. Is there something I can help with?"

The church vicar. Likely he's been poring over his sermons and books inside all morning, watching a strange boy slowly unravel in his parish's yard, perhaps touching a shell on his desk, wondering why something about me seems peculiarly familiar. As in most small villages, the church is the only place of record keeping for its parishioners. I dread knowing that if there's one person who would have the answers I seek, it's the kindly old vicar who's presided over the good people of Hope Cove for ages.

Except—my heart plunges into my boots as I turn around—this vicar is young, only a few years older than me. He's not the old man from my childhood.

"How long have you been at this parish?" I demand brusquely.

The vicar blinks, unsure if he should take offense or not at my rudeness. He has the same round, kindly face of the seals out in the bay. "I have been here a year this spring."

My shoulders sag. A year. There's no possible way this man crossed paths with my vanished family. But I'm here, and I've got to ask, even if every new dead end is a blister of hurt. "I'm looking for a family. The Wildes. They lived out in the country and might've used a different name here. Perhaps Smith, or Taylor?"

To my surprise the vicar brightens. "Why, yes! My predecessor told me about them. He feared for their souls because they rarely came to services. Does that sound right to you?"

I reach for my mother's cross in my inner pocket even though it's no longer there. "Aye, that might've been." Something that feels an awful lot like hope builds in my chest.

The vicar nods slowly. "A family of four, yes?"

"'Tis a family of five," I whisper desperately, the hope swelling stronger, near painful.

He gives me a long, measured look. He has heard rumors of me—who hasn't here, when a rich, desperate stranger tears up the countryside for missing persons—and I have just admitted to him I am a missing son finally returned home and not the distant cousin I claimed to be. Behind him the seabirds scream and dive into the surf. My hope teeters on a cliff's edge, a hairsbreadth from plummeting.

"That's all I know of them. But if you want to come inside and check parish registers, you're welcome to," the vicar says with a kindly smile.

I ignore the swoop in my gut and follow him. The inside of the church is quiet and somber as a tomb. Wooden pews face a modest pulpit, their dark seats weathered and worn with years of use. I trail my fingers over the wood, remembering how my brother kicked his feet against the pew in front of us, how the people seated there would glare, and my siblings and I would giggle. A sad smile tugs at my mouth.

The vicar pulls his books and leaves me to read in the nave. In here, the thick stone walls muffle the crash of the sea to a murmur, soft as a heartbeat. I think of James, how he always read with one finger beneath the words, and I do the same. There's dozens of births and marriages and deaths here. Far more than I expected from such a quaint place at the edge of the earth.

My finger stops and hovers under a single scrawled name. *Born 1585 Elias W—*

A smudge drowns out the surname, making it impossible to read. My heartbeat crescendos. I turn the book every which way in the light, urging the sun to get the ink to spill its secrets. The year is the year after I left, the name my own. An inchoate feeling tears at the walls of my chest, chokes the air from my lungs.

They wouldn't.

Or would they?

Could my parents have had another child and given him the name of the boy they'd already lost? Replaced me as easily as an axle in a wagon? I press a fist under my throat, holding back the frenzied gulps that threaten to split me in pieces. I always believed—with the ardentness of an orphaned child convinced they're the hidden heir to a secret kingdom—that my family thought of me returning to them as much as I thought of returning to them.

But maybe I was wrong.

Perhaps they knew, when they bade me farewell, that it was the end. I've spent my entire life chasing an empty dream, a false promise.

*There is not enough goodness in you worth loving.*

The hollow feeling that's plagued me since London opens into a howling void, sucking me down inside.

The book slams to the floor. I'm rushing into the vicar's private rooms, fists clenched, body quivering like a bowstring. "Did they leave anything with the church? A note, some guidance, a letter?!"

The vicar jerks up, his expression shocked as he looks from me to the thrown book in the nave beyond.

*"Answer me!"* My shout shakes the very rafters.

The vicar stands slowly. I expect him to shout back, to throw me out of his church, as would be his right. Instead there's nothing in his face save an endless patience and a kindness so deep and smothering, it drowns me.

I already know what he's going to say.

"I checked for you. They left nothing. I'm sorry."

# CHAPTER FORTY-ONE

I STAY IN THE church until the sky purples beyond the windows. When it's black as a mortal wound, when I can no longer even pretend to still be reading the registers without asking the vicar to light the candles, my legs straighten and take me to the imposing double doors. I feel like one of the resurrected dead upon Judgment Day, my body here but a vital part of me gone. No, a part of me cut out and cast into flames, gone to ashes.

Leaving the church means acknowledging that my family is gone and left nothing for me. Leaving means they left me behind and never wondered how I'd find them again. It means accepting that they gave up on me years before I gave up on them.

I push the doors open.

The walk down from the hill's crest to the town below feels like a funeral procession, each step heavier than the last. Despite the late hour, the tiny town center bustles with activity. Folks flit in and out of neighbors' homes, faces lit with the sort of excitement reserved for feast days and holidays. I catch a few words here and there. "Fire." "Plymouth." "Sunken ships." A gaggle of children shriek like excited goblins as they run around me—the same children who comb the beaches each day searching for washed-ashore plunder.

After hours of silence, the noise is startling. If I didn't know better, I'd say there's some sort of celebration underway. A knife of unease slices through my grief, pricking my instinct of survival. What's going on?

The innkeeper is waiting outside the inn. She frowns when she spots me. "Nothing strange has happened here for years until the likes of you came along."

I stop short, certain I've misunderstood her implication. "Are you . . . blaming me for something?"

She shrugs, neither confirming nor denying a thing. "All I'm saying is that it's not every day an entire fleet of ships goes up in flames at Plymouth. A few ships a year sinking off the coast is one thing, but an entire fleet? That's unheard of."

Plymouth. That's the largest city in Devonshire, the place where Lord Hughes pretended to hail from.

"What sails from the port?" I ask, an uneasy feeling building in me.

"Why, everything. The port's almost as big as London's. Her Majesty's navies. The ships to the New World."

I suck in a sharp breath. My body tenses as a horrendous paranoia courses through me.

It cannot be Middlemore's fleet.

It's got nothing to do with James. He's wedded and coursing across the sea already. I saw it happen.

*You saw the wedding,* I remind myself.

I never sought out when he was leaving for the New World.

I couldn't bear it, not after seeing him and his new bride in their wedding finery, his smile, the rotting roses all around me.

The innkeeper watches me sort through all this, a sinister smirk spreading across her face. Like she knows something I don't. Heat rushes through me—anger and exhaustion all tangling at once, making me reckless. "Are you implying that I set this fire, madam? When I have been in the church all day? When you were the one looking after my bloody horse and know I rode nowhere?"

She laughs darkly at my rudeness and pulls something from her apron pocket. "The flames were not set today. Today's just the first we learned of it here. And I ain't saying anything about you setting that fire. You're the one who's bringing up *that*." Her smirk grows triumphant, like she's caught me in a dirty lie. "Here, this came for you when you were gone." She slaps a battered folded piece of parchment into my chest. The unmarked wax seal is broken. I stare at it like it's the dragon slain by St. George come back to life and frolicking in the sea.

"Did you read my mail?" I ask, dumbfounded.

The woman squints like *Is this really the most important thing here?* and she's right, so I read the message with unsteady hands.

*It is done. Anne.*

There's only one Anne I know. Lady Anne Middlemore, now Bloomsbury. But . . . 'tis impossible. How would she know I'm here? How would anyone know I'm here, except for Inigo?

And Lady Anne doesn't know Inigo exists. A gruesome, familiar feeling creeps over me, noosing about my throat. Dread.

"Who delivered this?" I ask in a shaky voice.

"Some soldier. Didn't get his name. He was in a mad rush off to Plymouth to see what could be done about the fire."

Cold lodges in my chest and spreads like hoarfrost. Soldiers. Here, in Hope Cove, where they shouldn't be. "Well, what was his insignia? Was he one of the queen's soldiers or—"

The innkeeper throws up her hands. "You'd know better than me, boy! Why, that letter's addressed to you, and I don't like the look of what it says. Seems mighty suspicious to me, with you coming here and asking questions and then this fire happening and that note. If you were planning on staying here longer than a fortnight, you can forget about it! I want you gone tomorrow. I don't let my rooms to unsavory sorts, you understand?"

And with a final glare she turns away and walks inside, the door slamming behind her.

I stare after her, Lady Anne's letter crumpled in my hand, a sick feeling settling in my bones. Perhaps she's right. Bad things follow me like shadows. Maybe I am the reason for all the strangeness in this town.

*It is done.* What does Lady Anne's note mean? I thought we had parted friends, but I could be wrong. She did tell Queen Elizabeth about me and James, locking the fetters which bound him to her, which dragged him away from me. Perhaps that was not enough for her. Maybe she needed more from him. Maybe the queen charged Lady Anne with getting rid of me once and for all, giving her a chance to prove her loyalty for overlooking her new husband's suspicious activities.

Maybe.

The paranoid thoughts race through me all evening as I ready my things and pack my bags. The smell of smoke fills the town and casts a hazy, strange twilight over everything. Galloping and men's shouts tear through the town. People on their way to see what they can gain from the fire in Plymouth. One person's fall is always another's rise.

One thing is clear: I've got to leave. Between the strange happenings in Plymouth and the town's ongoing suspicions about me, my welcome in the village is well worn out. I'll—I'll do something, go somewhere. Perhaps Plymouth is a place that would have more answers for me. After all, it is a larger town. It could be a place where a family with a new name could go to forge a new life, a life among people who knew nothing of their past. Why, they could've—

A hideous, cold thought stops me at once. Upends my world.

Perhaps my family doesn't want me to find them.

After years of thinking of them, working for them, living my entire life with nothing but that star on my horizon, guiding my every action, the impulse to follow it is instinctual. But if there's one thing I learned here, it's that my family didn't think of me when they left. Which could mean . . .

They never wanted to be found.

The realization sends the broken part of me shuddering, threatens to split me open again. I shake my head crossly, gritting my teeth. I don't have to think of this now. I *can't* think of this now. Not when the town is crawling with strangers and any one of them might recognize me as the wanted man on the posters in London. I can't fall apart here, not yet.

I abandon packing and head downstairs for dinner.

And freeze.

Because for the first time in nearly two weeks, I'm not dining alone.

There, at the only other table in the dining hall, is a group of soldiers in the queen's livery. Fear spikes through me, the animal urge to run as every awful memory from the past year slams into me. A waking nightmare. No one has noticed my approach yet; the room is thick with smoke from the kitchen, where another abominable fish stew boils, and the smoke drifting in beneath the shutters outside.

"You eating or not?" the innkeeper snaps as she passes with stew bowls.

I see how she watches me watching the soldiers, remembering her keen stare when I read Lady Anne's note and demanded to know who had left it. She's onto me. Zounds, she already thinks I have something to do with the fire. And I know she'll not hesitate to turn me in as a traitor to these men if it means she gains something.

Swallowing, I take my usual chair, haunted by a memory of being forced to take another seat in another tavern, another group of men beside me and hungry for blood.

Is there nowhere in this godforsaken kingdom where I can go to find peace? Will I be running forever, no matter how far I stray to the edges of the earth?

For once I don't taste the fish stew as it goes down. But the blessing is tainted by the men roaring with laughter and playing dice beside me, by the way the smoke-smell fills up my lungs and crawls under my skin, begging me to flee before their mirth turns to violence.

An uncanny scream rips through the noise. Ares, out back. The soldiers all look up.

I jolt to my feet and leave without facing them.

Outside, there's more smoke than ever. It hangs low in the humidity and sticks to my skin. I prowl through the fog to the modest stable behind the inn. My stallion's head pokes over his stall, ears alert and nostrils flaring. He's excited about something. But what? I stroke his long nose and peer into his dark eyes.

"What's out here?" I whisper. But of course he doesn't answer. All he does is press harder against the door, yearning to be let loose into the garden just beyond.

My attention slides to the garden gate, observes how it wobbles. Like someone just shut it. I pull my bottom lip betwixt my teeth.

Were there four or five soldiers when I walked into the dining hall?

How many were there when I left?

A copper taste fills my mouth. I make sure the ropes are tied tight on my horse's stall. Without Ares, I've got no means of escape, and I've got an inkling I'll be needing to leave very soon and very quickly.

Then I go to the docks.

Out here, the moon has turned the smoke and water all

into a violet haze. The sea is scaled with silver, the ripples undulating softly out to the endless horizon, where they're swallowed by the deeper darkness. The glow of the sea nettles glints green underwater as the music of some night bird layers over the rolling of the waves. The briny air mingles with the smoke. If I close my eyes and breathe deeply, it smells of some distant feast.

It would seem like a dream, were it not for the second set of footsteps shadowing mine.

I more feel than hear them, a silent padding along the dock timed with each groan and swell of the wood in the waves. The hairs on my arms prickle. 'Tis not something I would have noticed before, if it weren't for the year and then some I've had to watch my back like a fox in the field, forever straining his ears for the baying of the distant hounds.

A minute passes.

Then another.

My hand drifts to the dagger belted at my hip. He's almost exactly where I want him.

A muffled creak.

It could be the dock.

But I know better.

I explode into a spin, knife in hand.

A gash opens the front of his soldier's uniform. My stalker falls with a surprised cry.

I straddle his chest, pinning his arms to the dock with my knees. I seize a fistful of his collar and press my blade to his neck.

"What are you truly after? Me or my horse?" I snarl.

His body rumbles beneath me. My thighs tighten, preparing to counter his movement. But after a wild, confused moment, I realize he's not trying to buck me away.

He's *laughing*.

And then, before I can make sense of anything, there's a voice I never thought I'd hear again.

"I must confess, when I imagined our reunion, there was a lot less stabbing involved."

Every inch of me freezes.

No. Zounds, it can't be.

I know this voice.

'Tis *his* voice. Which is utterly impossible, because this is no dream.

Brilliant points of light and color flash before me. I feel light-headed, sick, numb. He's married. He's across the seas; he's burnt in Plymouth. He's anywhere but here. I shake my head, but none of the feelings go away. There's lavender in my nose. Something that feels like a sob shudders through me.

I must've fallen. I must've hit my head and gone under. Perhaps I am already drowned, and this is the last gasp of my brain, a final glimpse of the thing I love most before 'tis all fire and brimstone for eternity.

The man pushes himself up. Beneath the slashed uniform he's all broad shoulders and eyes turned burnt umber in the darkness and that barely-there smile I know too well. His hair is cropped short.

I rub a quivering palm over the short bristles.

I never dreamt of him with short hair before. Which means—

*James.* My dagger slips and splashes into the water.

His brow furrows. I realize belatedly he's been speaking, and not a word has reached me.

He touches my body gently, reverently, searching for any injury. "Are you all right?"

He *feels* very real. He *sounds* very real.

His face swims over mine, blocking out the moonlight. "Elias. Please answer."

I reach up a shaky hand and cup his chin. My thumb brushes over a scar on his jawline—a mark that I kissed over and over during the night we spent together. "You're real."

He tilts his chin, nestling his face into my palm. "Of course I am."

My eyes begin to burn. "You're *here*."

"I am. And your family?" His voice lifts hopefully, like it's utterly normal we're out here together, like he never once doubted we'd be together again like I had. "Are they here too?"

The hollow ache rips open in me again. I'm at the church reading my name for a boy who's not me. I'm watching a stranger slam my family's cottage door in my face, and I'm sobbing. I cling to James like he's a raft in an ocean of hurt, the only thing keeping me from drowning. I say the words I couldn't say out loud, not even to myself. "They're gone, even though they promised they'd stay. I'm all alone!"

He shakes his head, brushing away my tears. "No, never alone. You have me. You'll always have me."

His words are a tourniquet, the rightness of them stopping up all the secret holes and leaks in my heart. I close my eyes and settle into him. He draws me closer as the ocean and sky roar and whisper around us. As I regain control over myself, a thousand questions bubble up, all demanding urgent answers.

"How did you find me? Zounds, I almost stabbed you! You shouldn't sneak up on people like that—'tis dangerous."

He touches the gash on his uniform. "I thought you'd be expecting me. Anne told me she sent you a note."

I snort and pull out the note. "Oh, you mean this helpful thing?"

James snatches the parchment from my hand. He reads it and frowns. The furrows on his brow are the deepest I've ever witnessed. Giddiness kicks through me, followed by an unhinged laugh. I thought he was gone, and here he is, frowning like usual! I've never been happier to see him look like an ancient old man.

"*It is done?* Why, Anne was telling you our plan worked."

"How was I supposed to know that? I wasn't in on any plan of hers. Anne *hates* me. She's always sniffed at me like I'm a foul smell."

"It's not that she didn't like you. It's that you were in her way. Elias, Anne's one of us."

"What do you mean 'one of us'?"

He grips my shoulders tightly, pulling us together until we're nose to nose. "She prefers women to men. Just how you prefer men to women, and I like either."

His meaning sinks in slowly, then snicks into place, the missing final piece of the puzzle. I remember my last conversation with Anne, her knowing smirk. *I can assure you, marrying a man would not be my preferred way out of this conundrum.* Of course. She told me directly, but I was too grief-stricken and battered to hear what she really meant.

"I understand that part." I gesture to him, short-haired and dressed in a torn soldier's uniform. "But it doesn't explain why you're here now and she's not. She's you're wife, James. I saw you *marry* her!"

James lifts his arms and throws his head back to the sky. "I did marry her. But you see, Anne is a widow now."

I poke him roughly, biting back frustration. There's a buzzing in my ears, a pressure building inside me. If he's appeared in my life only to vanish again, I could not bear it. "You don't seem very dead to me. God Almighty, if you don't explain straightaway and tell me why you're here—"

He presses a soft, shushing finger to my lips, wild grin fading. As if he's finally understanding the shocking effect his appearance is having on me, how he lost some measure of my trust these endless past months while I waited and hoped for him to come, and he never appeared. "You're right. You deserve answers. Let me go back and explain everything."

And so he does. How before their marriage Lady Anne came to James and told him she had a plan for them to both get what they wanted. For him, a life away from his family with me, his beloved, and for Lady Anne, enough money and power to never need another man in her life again. How James agreed and they put on a performance that even the

Rose Theatre would sigh with envy over. How they played the happy couple in newly wedded bliss for months to convince both their families their affections for each other were genuine. How James convinced Anne's odious father, Lord Middlemore, that James should take out an insurance policy on his New World fleet of ships under Bloomsbury's name. How an accidental fire claimed the fleet of ships with James lost to the sea when he dove into the flames to save the boats.

"So you see, now that I'm dead, the insurance policy will pay out to Lady Anne and not her father, because she was my wife, and now she will have her money and her power from my noble title." His hands hold mine so tightly, his tendons creak. "And as for me, I had to die because Queen Elizabeth threatened to behead me if I so much as sneezed in her royal presence again."

My own hands tremble, overcome with what he's telling me, what impossible things he and Lady Anne made possible while I was in London assuming he didn't care enough to find me.

"But now that you're dead, there's nothing they can do to us anymore," I say softly.

"Not unless we fancy going back to London and showing them all I've returned from the grave." He traces my cheekbone, tucking a strand of hair behind my ear. "I apologize for not finding you in London. I knew you were there. I felt it in my soul. Every day I wanted to seek you out, but I knew our best chance of being together was if I avoided you while all of court had their eyes on me and Lady Anne."

The keen pain of his absence these past months haunts me

again, the lonely ache a burden I could not carry. "I saw you get married. You were smiling."

"I was only smiling because I had to. It was you I wanted at my side that day. Elias." He cups my face in his hands. His expression is the most serious I've ever seen it. "I *always* want you at my side."

A soft feeling tugs at me, almost too tender to bear. "And I you." We embrace, the shape of him exactly as I remember, and an incredulous, unsteady laugh escapes me. "Did you and your lady wife truly commit arson and fake your death?"

He moves to drag his hand through his hair, but there's nothing there. "It seemed an effective enough method for you at Dover Castle."

I wrestle back a smile. "Zounds, you've become quite the player, haven't you?"

He stands and offers me his hand. "I learned from the best."

Things could still go awry. There's plenty of opportunities for that. The queen could find out we tricked her. Or—worse— we could tire of each other and the life we must painstakingly salvage from all we've lost.

But a house made of splintered boards and scavenged nails is still a home.

I take his hand and pull myself up. He smiles at me, almost shyly, and it feels like the first glimpse of a foreign shore.

I can no longer fight the grin spreading across my face. "And now that you're presumed dead by everyone in England, what shall you do now?"

He shrugs elegantly. "I suppose I shall have to forge a new

life for myself. Do you need a hand finding your family? I'm certain there's more to be learned from this church's books. We both know you're rubbish at research."

I thread my fingers through his. The moonlight refracts into a thousand silver shards in the violet night, on the velvet water. "You have truly cast aside your duty to country, queen, and God, haven't you?"

He laughs again and presses his lips to my temple. "To hell with duties to country, queen, and God."

Something soft and delicate lights in my chest. "I'd drink to that." I lift my head and kiss him. A wild, fierce feeling kindles in my soul, borne of this sea-swept land and the man before me. When I pull back, I catch the fire in his eyes and know that he feels it too.

Anything is possible now. Forever lies ahead of us like a great uncharted land, and if we step carefully, if we stay true to each other and all else that is good, perhaps we can find a safe place for ourselves and this bright, new love which burns me up from the inside like a star through the sky.

It won't be the life I imagined for myself. 'Tis even better.

It's the one I chose.

# ACKNOWLEDGMENTS

This book's journey spanned five years, and this final version owes its existence to many generous, talented people. First and foremost, thank you to my agent, Hilary Harwell. Hilary, your patience and enthusiasm keep me energized and excited. Thank you for being curious instead of alarmed when I told you in a pool in Arizona that I was thinking about switching from contemporary to historical for my next book. You are the best champion for my career, and I'm so glad we've been working together for all these years. You are an author whisperer!

The biggest thank-you goes to my editor, Nicole Ellul. Nicole, you understood this story immediately. I still can't believe I found someone else who thought an epic murder thriller smashed together with a sweeping romance set in the 1500s seemed like a fun idea. You saw exactly what I was trying to do and helped me make the heart of this story beat even stronger. Sometimes it feels like I wished you into existence!

A huge thank-you goes to everyone else on my team as well. At KT Literary, I would like to thank Kelly Van Sant and Kate Testerman. At Simon & Schuster Books for Young Readers, I would like to thank Sara Berko, Amanda Brenner, Justin Chanda, Kendra Levin, Alyza Liu, Brian Luster, Emily Ritter, Mitch Thorpe, and Krista Vossen. A special thank-you goes to Mona Finden for creating an absolute dream of a cover and to Hilary Zarycky for creating such a stunning interior design.

It's entirely likely my career would not exist without Carlie Sorosiak. Carlie, thank you for being the first person to view my writing as more than a hobby, for reading so many drafts, and for the endless pep talks, the writing sprints, our conversations about pets, everything. There are not enough thank-yous for you and the mentorship and friendship you've given me over the years!

Thank you to Rachel Lynn Solomon for helping me navigate everything Simon & Schuster–related, welcoming me to Seattle, and being one of the best people in publishing. Your generosity and support of other authors are unparalleled.

Thank you to Amelia Diane Coombs, who stuck with me in the writing trenches when they took an especially dark turn. (Yep, that would be during the pandemic!) I'm so glad we got to be neighbors in Seattle, even though the pandemic tried its best to keep us apart.

Thank you to Jamie Pacton for answering all my flailing-new-author questions and for keeping me calm through the debut process. I am so grateful for your support!

Thank you to Mackenzi Lee, Krystal Marquis, Jamie Pacton, and Jenn Bennett for their wonderful blurbs.

While *By Any Other Name* might be my first published book, I also need to thank the many people who have taken time to read my work or share their wisdom with me throughout the years. There are so many of you, I was afraid to name names for fear of overlooking someone, so please know that if you've ever taken the time to share your thoughts with me, I remember, and I'm so appreciative!

I would also like to thank the Pitch Wars class of 2017, who showed me that the act of writing does not have to be so solitary. It has been an absolute joy to celebrate your successes these past six years! Special thanks are owed to Gwen Flaskamp and Rachel Simon as well for being supportive and wonderful people.

I would also like to thank the Pitch Wars class of 2017, who showed me that the act of writing does not have to be so solitary. It has been an absolute joy to celebrate your successes these past six years! Special thanks are owed to Gwen Flaskamp and Rachel Simon as well for being supportive and wonderful people.

Thank you to the innumerable friends who cheered me on as I wrote and revised this book: Courtney Bertrand, Justin Bertrand, Jeff Boruszak, Sarah Brandt, Mike Capone, Dilara Cirit, Kyle Cocina, Jody Cook, Christine Coughlin, Jason Durbin, Reid Echols, Jesi Egan, Hannah Harrison, Emily King, Claire Lines-Mattei, Pat Lines-Mattei, Elliot Lopez-Finn, Courtney Massie, Sarah Mathis, Alyssa Morris, Jessica Piette, Joel Rapaport, Kaitlyn Farrell Rodriguez, Nick Rodriguez, Kate Schoonhoven, Skye Simpson, Megan Snell, Kate Stevenson, Anne Stewart, and Elliott Turley.

I would like to especially thank Meredith Durbin and Amanda Snell for wanting to read this book when I felt like it was time for me to give up and turn to a new project. Thank you for keeping this story alive!

Thanks also go to the rest of the miscreants in the UT Austin incoming English graduate cohort of 2012 and its associated members. This isn't the book we all thought I'd write, but I think this one's a lot more fun.

Thank you to Dr. Barbara Bono, whose early modern drama classes planted the seed of this story many years ago.

Though they will never read this, thank you to all the animals I have been lucky enough to share my home with over the years, especially Hermione, Tybalt, and Fiona. Fiona, you would've loved the boxes the author copies came in.

Thank you to my parents, Joyoa and Mark, and my brother, Kyle, who put up with my spending all day in a book and all night on the family desktop writing my own stories. Thank you to my extended family as well for always believing in and supporting my ambitions.

Loren Cressler, thank you for consulting on historical minutiae, helping with brainstorming, troubleshooting a myriad of technology disasters, and always gamely telling me whether the jokes were funny enough. I felt able to pursue my longest-held dream because of the life we've created together.

And, of course, thank you to you, reader, for picking up this book. None of this would be possible without you, and I'm forever grateful.